The Belfast Girl

CAROLINE DOHERTY DE NOVOA

Caroline Doherty de Novoa

First published by Papen Press, 2017

Caroline Doherty de Novoa has asserted her right under the Copyright, Designs and Patents Act 1988 to be identified as the author of this work.

Copyright © 2017 by Caroline Doherty de Novoa

All rights reserved. No part of this book may be reproduced or transmitted in any form or by any means, electronic or mechanical, including photocopying, recording or by any information storage and retrieval system, without written permission from the author, except for the inclusion of brief quotations in a review.

This book is a work of fiction and any resemblance to actual persons, living or dead, is purely coincidental.

ISBN-13:
978-1539834885
ISBN-10:
1539834883

This book is dedicated to Geraldine Mullen of Strabane,
Northern Ireland and in loving memory of Mary Gardner
of Long Island, New York.

*"I said nothing for a time,
just ran my fingertips along the edge
of the human-shaped emptiness
that had been left inside me."*

- Haruki Murakami

ACKNOWLEDGMENTS

It takes a village to make a writer, they say, or in my case, a small town.

Firstly, thanks to everyone who helped me with my first novel, *Dancing with Statues*—to all the readers and anyone else who championed the book (and to Tigre for believing it could be something else!). Your enthusiasm helped me believe I could climb the mountain again.

To Wendy Crossland, thanks for your careful copy-editing.

To Jacqui Lofthouse, thanks for creating a community of writers and letting me be a part of it, you are always an inspiration.

To Hannah Matthews, Lorena Waserman and Camille Mansell, who read drafts of the novel, thank you so much for your insights and your honesty, you made this book better.

To Carolina, Clara, Francisco, JuanMa, Monica, Peter, and Tony—aka the Bogotá Writers—and all our guests, especially the writing diplomat, Ian McKinley—thanks for battling *aguaceros* and *trancones* to share your stories and your passion with me.

To my fellow "struggling" writers—Vicki Kellaway and Richard McColl, thanks for the tea and biscuits, for continuing to ask my word count and for the fun times on Irish Gabo. I learned a lot from you kids.

To all my aunts and uncles and cousins, to the Novoa and Bustamante families, and all my good friends scattered across the world—thanks for your support, always.

To Erin, it doesn't matter if you are half a continent or an entire ocean away, it always feels like you are right there, thank you.

To my big sis, Laura, thanks for all those emails demanding the next chapter and for bringing four amazing new people into my life.

To my parents for absolutely everything. I love you, always.

And to my husband, Juan, love of my life. I wouldn't have finished this book if it weren't for you. I probably wouldn't have even started. No one else will fully know everything you do for me, but I know and I appreciate it all.

Finally, thanks to you dear reader, for taking a chance on this book. If you enjoy it, please help others to find it by spreading the word in real life and on social media or by reviewing it on Amazon or Goodreads.

CHAPTER ONE
JANET—BELFAST
DECEMBER 1993

Janet wondered what it was like for other women when they held their child for the first time. She had always imagined a smiling nurse. Joy rolling through her exhausted body. Tom in scrubs, sweaty and beaming at her side. The two of them staring at the small bundle in her arms. A tiny hand in hers.

But Tom wasn't even looking at her or the baby. He was 10 feet away, standing with a skin-headed man in a leather jacket, counting out bills.

And the baby wasn't swaddled in blankets, gazing in silent awe at her new world. She was screeching and flailing around in Janet's arms. With her tiny fists, Kathleen pounded Janet's chest. With each punch, Janet felt the sting of her real message. If she could speak she would be saying: I reject you. You are an imposter. You are not my mother.

She rocked Kathleen from side to side and repeated quietly, 'It's ok. Shush. Everything is going to be ok.'

Kathleen simply screamed back at her fighting, with all her might, to escape. She wanted back to the girl who was standing a few feet away. The girl was perhaps half Janet's thirty-six years, maybe even younger, and she and the baby had the same oval green eyes, rimmed red with tears.

'Did you bring any of her favorite toys with you? Maybe that might help distract her,' Janet said.

'No, I didn't. Perhaps I should take her for a minute, just to calm her down.' The girl reached out for Kathleen, and Janet immediately stepped back, beyond the girl's reach.

'It's fine,' Janet said.

The girl's arms fell at her sides. Janet turned away, humiliated by her own selfishness. A better person would have let her comfort the baby. But Janet could not allow the girl to hold her daughter again. She could not risk the girl changing her mind.

The girl cast her eyes around the room. 'Didn't you bring a buggy?'

'A what?'

'A stroller,' Tom said, looking up from the count.

'No…we do have a car seat…but I thought I'd just carry her from here to the car.'

'Oh, it's just she likes to be rocked back and forth in her buggy.'

Janet should have known that. All kids love their strollers. She should never have let Tom convince her to wait until they got home to New York before buying one. "What's the point?" he'd said. "We'll be in the car and then on the plane, soon as. We'll have no time for strolling around Belfast anyway. The faster we're out of there the better."

The girl reached out and stroked Kathleen's chubby little arm. 'It's ok. There's no need to be frightened.'

Behind the girl, the father stood biting his fingernails. Slim, pale, and red-haired, he was the picture of Ireland. He kept glancing at the door and then at his watch. Janet wondered if he was waiting for someone to burst in or if he was just desperate to leave. She studied the young couple, in their jeans and sweaters, the boy with teenage acne splattered across his chin, his hands in his pockets shifting nervously from one foot to the next, the girl holding a screwed up tissue in her hand, her face contorted, trying to fight back her tears. They were just kids. Why did they have to sell their daughter? How desperate were they? Didn't they have parents of their own to help them?

'What will you tell your families?' Janet blurted out. Tom looked over and scowled. He had warned her to let him do all the talking.

'We'll tell them she's been adopted by a good family. She is going to a good family, isn't she?' the girl said.

'You have nothing to worry about. She will never want for anything.'

'I just want her to have parents that love her.'

'Ouch,' Janet winced as Kathleen tugged angrily on her earring.

The girl stared at Janet, examining her, and Janet immediately averted her gaze. She didn't want to see herself reflected in the girl's eyes. She knew what she looked like—an incompetent fool who had no idea how to soothe a baby—a woman so inadequate she couldn't do the one thing women had done since the dawn of time—a complete failure of a woman.

Then Tom announced it was time to go. Ever the businessman, he paused to shake hands with the skin-headed guy on the successful conclusion of the transaction. He lifted the car seat and made for the door.

'C'mon, we should be leaving,' he said.

The girl suddenly started to hyperventilate, a red rash raced across her forehead, and tears started to roll down her face, fast and thick. It was as if she had just realized what all this had been leading up to. The boy put his hand on the girl's shoulder in an awkward attempt to comfort her.

Tom, already at the door, motioned for Janet to follow. But she hesitated, staring in shock at the strange swirl of emotions held within the girl's eyes—fear, torment, and just a hint of relief. She looked to Tom for guidance.

'Love, the car's waiting downstairs,' he said.

'Just go,' the girl spluttered between tears.

Janet's shoulder muscles loosened, ever so slightly. They were really doing this. This young couple was really giving them this beautiful, healthy child to bring up as their own. Janet almost giggled in relief, catching the inappropriate laughter before it could escape.

She had never fully believed this moment would come.

When they had started IVF last winter, after nearly two years of disappointments, Janet had thought it was a step forward. IVF had a certainty about it. The moment of conception would be planned, with scientific precision, taking place in the controlled environment of a laboratory and not within the messy accident of her body. That's the story Janet had told herself as she had endured the invasive scans, with a big camera pushed up inside her and moved forcefully around, and the daily injections, the bloating, the headaches, the nausea, the mood swings, and the painful harvesting of her eggs. Throughout that first painful cycle, Janet accepted all the indignities with grace and joy, for each one brought her closer to a child of her own. Not once did she imagine she could put herself through so much and not even have an embryo to implant at the end of it. But that's what happened on the first cycle, and the second and the third. "Poor quality and incompetent embryos," they said. "Another baby lost," Janet heard.

When their fourth cycle finally produced so-called "quality embryos," Janet had felt hopeful once again. But it had been short-lived. Even with a healthy embryo inside her, Janet had failed to get pregnant. And she failed again next time round too.

The turning point had come in the pressure-cooker of

the doctor's office after that fifth disappointment. With a mass of miracle babies staring down at her, their photos tagged to the wall with notes of gratitude from their joyful parents, Janet had pressed the doctor: 'I don't understand, you keep saying I'm fine. So why didn't I get pregnant when we, finally, implanted fertilized eggs?'

The doctor had shrugged. 'We cannot always explain everything,' she had said in her heavy Polish accent.

'But you said the problem was Tom's sperm swim too slowly. We got the sperm into the eggs and we're still not pregnant. I don't understand.'

'Yours is what we call unexplained infertility,' the doctor had said, as if that were an explanation. 'There are no guarantees. I am afraid we simply must keep trying.'

Janet had stared at her in disbelief, and the truth of the matter had suddenly hit her. It was all just luck. Even the best fertility doctors in the world were mere children tinkering with a complex technology they could barely understand. With all their jargon and protocols, with words like: "controlled ovarian stimulation", "FSH levels", "luteinizing hormone surge", and "hCG triggers" they tried to give the illusion of knowledge and control, while, at the same time, they kept their fingers crossed behind their backs, hoping their dabbling would bear fruit.

A week later, Janet had called the adoption agencies during her lunch hour to request some brochures. And afterwards, she had cried, locked in the toilets at work, for over an hour. She needed to grieve. Again. To accept that she would never share a genetic connection with a child of her own and to sacrifice the part of her which still hoped for that reality.

But when those first brochures had arrived in the mail, with pictures of smiling families on the front and detailed terms and conditions at the back, Janet could never have imagined this: a suitcase full of cash; a transatlantic flight; a dingy motel room in Belfast; a teenage girl in tears; Janet with a boisterous ten-month-old in her arms, about to walk away with her.

'Thank you, thank you so much,' Janet now whispered to the girl. The girl turned away, towards the boy, as a strangled howl exploded from deep within her. At this, Kathleen started to wail even louder and tried to fling herself out of Janet's arms. Shell-shocked, Janet almost dropped the child. So she tightened her grip, squeezing Kathleen to her chest, encircling her with her arms as if they were a ring of steel. The boy pulled the girl further into him and murmured soft words of comfort in her ear. He didn't even glance at Kathleen.

Janet stayed rooted to the spot, watching them. Fascinated. Unsure what to do next.

'C'mon, we don't have time for this.' Tom's bark shook Janet to life. 'Let's go. Now.'

Janet took one final look at the young couple and then turned and fled.

Kathleen screeched and beat Janet as she carried her along the narrow hallway. The elevator took an age to come. Finally the doors opened, and Janet and Tom stepped inside with Kathleen. For the first time ever, the three of them were alone together. Janet was shaking. Tom was jabbing the elevator buttons, cursing how slow it was. Kathleen looked terrified. This was not how the first moments with their daughter were supposed to be.

Inside the car, the clock on the dashboard said 4pm. They had been in the motel only half an hour but, in that time, the white afternoon sky had turned a dark grey. Outside, the streets of Belfast rushed by in a blur, and Janet prayed they would get out of Northern Ireland safely.

Like a common thief making a getaway, she kept glancing behind, searching for the police. Wild visions of sirens, hand-cuffs, interview rooms, prison, and, worst of all, some uniformed policewoman tearing Kathleen from her arms flooded Janet's mind. It was an irrational thought. She knew that. The police wouldn't come after them. After all, the man driving the car was an off-duty officer—one of the dirty cops on Geary's payroll, apparently.

When they pulled up outside their hotel, Tom turned around from the front passenger seat. 'Me and you can go get the bags, Trevor here will keep the car running and watch the baby.'

'No,' Janet replied. 'You and Trevor go. Everything is already packed. You don't need me. I want to stay here with her.' After all this time waiting, there was no way Janet could step out of the car and leave Kathleen behind.

'Fine.'

Tom snapped at Trevor to pull over into a parking spot and ordered him out to help with the luggage. Doors opened and a blast of cold air rushed into the car.

On the radio, the newscaster announced that, after another year of bloodshed, there was some optimism in Belfast today. He said yesterday's date of December 15th, 1993 would go down in history as the day the British and Irish Governments finally recognized the right of the people of Northern Ireland to self-determination. A commentator was saying self-determination meant the people had 'free choice over their own actions without external compulsion.' It sounded completely unrealistic. No one has complete freedom to decide the shape of their lives. Everyone is at the mercy of some external force, Janet thought.

She looked at Kathleen who was still screaming with her entire body. Janet felt the world shrink around her. What was happening outside no longer mattered. Janet's only concern, now, was for her family's safety. She had never before thought of her and Tom like that, as a family. However, their two had just become a three. Finally, people would look at them and see a family, rather than a childless couple approaching their forties, with hope of ever being parents fading fast.

She turned her full attention to Kathleen, filtering out the excited discussions of the radio presenters and all talk of the Downing Street Declaration. She had no idea, nor did she care, what this famous document meant for this place of Tom's birth. She only cared about what it meant for their escape to the airport where a private plane was waiting to take them to Manchester. Following this supposedly historic announcement, security in the city was tighter than usual. Thankfully, she didn't have to worry about passport control tonight. Even though they would cross a sea from one island to another, they would still be in the same jurisdiction. That would not change anytime soon, no matter how many petrol bombs were thrown in Belfast tonight.

It would be tomorrow, at the airport in Manchester, when they would have to use their fake passports. That morning, Janet had quizzed Tom about it. Was he sure it would work? Would the forgeries stand up to scrutiny? What would they say if they were questioned? He had lost his temper and told her if he was capable of buying a baby, he was capable of buying that baby a passport.

'Let's just say, the man I used forges papers for people who have gone on the run, and they've run far and wide. They've sauntered right past border control officers that should be looking for them. No one will be looking for us.' His voice became softer. 'We'll be ok. We are not criminals. OK, this isn't exactly a conventional adoption, but that young couple wants to give up the child as soon as possible. If we'd gone through an adoption agency, there would have been red tape. I assure you, when we go through immigration, no one will bat an eyelid.'

In the car, Janet stroked a scalding tear from Kathleen's cheek.

'Too-Ra-Loo-Ra-Loo-Ral,' she sang in an attempt to quiet the baby. Her mother always said she had an Irish voice, just like her grandmother's. Janet was one quarter Irish. The rest of her family was a mix of Swedish, German and Italian. With auburn hair and grey eyes, Janet had always thought she looked like Greta Garbo, but without the dainty bone structure. Kathleen stared up at her suspiciously, the green in her eyes standing strong against her dark mop of black hair. She looked nothing like Janet. But maybe, just maybe, people would think she took after Tom's dark-haired side of the family.

'Too-Ra-Loo-Ra-Loo-Ral,' Janet sang over Kathleen's screams. 'Too-Ra-Loo-Ra-Loo-Ral.'

Kathleen suddenly paused for breath and let her taut face unfurl. Confused. Still teetering on the edge of tears. Then she scrunched up her nose once more. Janet braced herself for another angry onslaught. Kathleen opened her mouth into an O and this time...this time she giggled. As she did so, she reached over and grasped Janet's thumb possessively. And with that tiny gesture, the full weight of the motherly love that Janet had been storing up for years came falling down at Kathleen's feet. *I have spread my dreams under your feet; Tread softly because you tread on my dreams.*

At Belfast airport, Kathleen clung on tight and nuzzled her head into Janet's shoulder as she allowed herself to be lifted from her car seat. Janet glanced over towards Tom. His eyes were misty and his smile was full of surprise and relief.

Together, the three of them walked directly from the car to their private plane, without having to enter the Terminal. Inside the aircraft, Tom fussed putting away the luggage, and Janet sat down with Kathleen and took out a plastic Tupperware of fruit. She held out a piece of apple. Kathleen took it and shoved it into her mouth. Before she was even done chewing the first slice, she lifted her hand up demanding another. Janet offered her a second piece, which Kathleen immediately grabbed. 'You must have been hungry,' Janet whispered.

If it were not for this simple act of handing her fruit, Kathleen would have starved. She was now wholly dependent on Janet and Tom to fulfill even her most basic needs. Janet shifted in her seat feeling the shape of her body stretch to accommodate this new reality. It was a strange, delightful and overwhelming feeling to be so important, to be needed so.

The doors closed, the engines came alive, and the plane started to move. Effortlessly, they rose up into the night air. Janet felt a swell of excitement surge from somewhere deep within. She and her family were heading home, together. Tom came over and stroked Kathleen's forehead and kissed Janet.

'She's a beautiful wee thing, isn't she?' he said.

Throughout the short flight, Kathleen clung to Janet, as if she was the only one she trusted in this strange new world. By the time they got to the hotel at Manchester airport, Kathleen was dozing in her arms. In the room, she drowsily took a bottle and then fell back asleep.

All night, Janet and Tom lay wide awake, side by side, not speaking, listening to Kathleen in the hotel cot. Even though the sounds of her gentle breaths filled the room, Tom still got up four times to check on her. He smiled over at Janet in the half-light and whispered, 'She's perfect.'

The next morning Janet and Tom got up early. They were both keen to get to the airport and start their journey home to America. Tom turned on the television to the news.

'I want to let her sleep as long as she can, please switch that off,' Janet said.

Tom put the TV on mute and went back to getting dressed while Janet made a bottle for Kathleen. She carefully measured out the formula, trying to remember how long it should take for the milk to be cool enough for Kathleen to drink. Over the past few years Janet had read every fertility book on the market. She always promised herself she would read the parenting books when she got pregnant. She hadn't wanted to jinx things by reading them before. She had thought nine months would be enough time to learn the basics. As it turned out, she'd had six weeks from first finding out about Kathleen until now. Despite the years of waiting, in the end, her gestation as a mother wasn't nearly long enough. She lifted the bottle and shook some milk on to her arm. It was still scalding.

'Fuck!' Tom suddenly cried out.

'What?'

'Where's the remote?' He leapt on to the bed, searching for the remote control under the blankets.

'What's wrong?'

'Nothing, just…' he jumped up and rushed towards the TV socket. But Janet saw it before he got to pull the plug.

On screen was a young man with jet-black hair and blue eyes, probably no older than twenty. He was pale and hollowed out looking. At the bottom of the screen the ticker read: "Father implores child's kidnappers to return her safely".

'No,' Janet said. 'It can't be.'

There, next to him, tissue in hand, sat a young woman dabbing her eyes. They were the same oval green eyes that were staring up at Janet from the crib. The same eyes that had stared into Janet's yesterday afternoon. On the TV, the girl had her arm around the father in support.

'I'm going to fucking kill Geary,' Tom shouted.

'Did you know about this?'

'No, of course not. I would never have let him convince me if I didn't think both parents wanted it.'

'But who was that boy yesterday? She said he was the father.'

'I don't fucking know.'

Janet caught sight of the remote control on the bedside table. She grabbed it, frantically looking for the mute button. Tom yanked it away from her.

'No.'

'Turn it up Tom, I want to hear.'

'No. We are not doing this. We have a plane to catch. I'm not having you sitting here watching this, getting yourself all wound up.'

'But she sold us their baby and didn't tell him! The police are looking for this child.'

'They'll be looking in Belfast, not here. If we get out of England today, we'll be ok.'

'But we can't just fly out as if nothing's happened. This changes everything.'

'What, so you want us to give her back? And how do you suppose we do that without getting caught? What would we tell the police? Here, sorry officer, we were going to buy this baby, but now we've seen her Daddy crying his fucking eyes out on TV, we've had a change of heart. So here she is, and we'll just be on our way. Oh, and would you mind asking that psycho mother for our money back? No way, darling. If we take her anywhere near Ireland they'll be consequences for us.' His voice was low. When he was angry, he reverted back to the menacing Belfast accent of his youth, stripped of all the mid-Atlantic charm he had worked so hard, over twenty years, to cultivate.

Kathleen started to whimper and stretched up towards them. Janet lifted her out of the cot.

'Really, what do you want us to do? I don't see a way out of this. But, please, enlighten me if you do,' Tom said.

Janet looked at Kathleen, smiling in her arms, with the tears of a moment ago still rolling down her face. She glanced at the boy on TV. It was now clear from where Kathleen's jet-black hair had come.

'But he must be going wild with worry,' Janet said. Tom did not respond.

Janet saw the three of them reflected in the mirror. Even Kathleen was still. They looked like actors frozen in position at the end of an act. In those seconds, all possible avenues for where their story might go were open. But a tableau lasts for only a moment before someone shifts and the action begins again.

Kathleen reached up and grabbed Janet's nose.

'What are you doing?' Tom cooed, approaching the two of them. 'Are you trying to steal mommy's nose?'

Kathleen looked at him and started to giggle, and then

she reached up for Janet's nose again, a look of sheer delight on her lovely face. Instinctively, Janet smiled. But then, out of the corner of her eye, she caught a glimpse of the boy on TV—his despair an unwelcome foil to their happiness.

'Tom, give me that remote.'

'No, love. Don't do this to yourself. You don't need to hear this.'

'You don't get it do you?' Janet walked over to the TV and turned it off. 'We have packing to do. We can't be late for our flight. We don't have time to be watching the television,' she said.

They quickly gathered up their belongings in silence. Janet put away their toiletries. She wrestled with the tiny buttons of the romper suit, so alien in her large hands, as she dressed Kathleen. She checked she had enough diapers in the change bag. She checked again.

Just before they left the hotel room, Tom hugged her.

'This child is ours,' he said 'and we are going to take her with us to America today. What's done is done, and we need to go home now and start our new life as a family.'

They were a family now. They were no longer a childless couple. Childless—a word with so many connotations. For years, Janet had thought of her and Tom that way. But now, thinking about that boy on television, she realized he was childless in a way they never were. He was without a real baby that he had loved for months, not just the promise of a child. She looked at Kathleen snug in the car seat, clutching a plastic sheep Tom had bought her yesterday, studying its shape. It was too late. There was only one thing to do. For Janet was already in love with her too.

CHAPTER TWO
EMMA—BELFAST
DECEMBER 1993

Seven hours after she'd sold Kathleen to the Americans, Emma took up her place on the landing just outside the nursery. She rested her hand on the nursery door, as if she'd just closed it, and she waited. She waited for nearly an hour. Still and silent in the darkness. The dead air trapped in her lungs. And finally he came.

There was a quiet shuffling sound as he opened the front door. Followed by a loud thud. He must have knocked the coat stand into the wall as he passed it. Wordlessly, Emma urged him to go into the living room and put on the TV. But instead he appeared at the foot of the stairs, looking up at her, swaying.

She moved towards him. With a deep exhale, she straightened her back and fixed a quivering smile onto her face. She was ready to give the performance of her seventeen-year-old life.

'How's the baby?' Aiden asked.

'She's fine.' Emma walked to the top of the stairs. 'I

only just got her down and settled. Don't be waking her.'

'I'll be quiet. I just want to give her a wee kiss,' he advanced towards her. His movements were slow and heavy. The effect of the pills, Emma hoped.

She stepped further down the stairs, meeting him halfway. She kept one trembling hand in her pocket and clenched the banister with the other. 'No,' she stood firmly in his way. 'Let her sleep. I need to go to work soon. And I don't want you setting her off and making me late.'

'Just let me have a wee peek in at her,' he pleaded, giving Emma a smile.

'Fine,' she turned and walked up the stairs. He followed right behind her. The drums of her heart echoed through her rib cage. 'Leave the hall light off. If she sees us she'll start crying again.'

Emma opened the nursery door a fraction, enough for Aiden to see the corner of the cot and the baby sleeping bag stuffed to make it look like there was a child inside. The big teddy bear was strategically placed next to the bars blocking the line of sight to where Kathleen's head should be.

'Awww, my wee dote,' Aiden said. He went to take a step forward.

Emma yanked the door closed on him—perhaps a little too forcefully than she should have. But she couldn't let him go into the nursery. It was too early. He couldn't find out Kathleen wasn't there. Not yet.

'I have half an hour before I need to leave for work,' Emma whispered. 'C'mon down to the kitchen with me. I'll make you a sandwich.'

He gave her a glassy-eyed look that she couldn't read.

'Aye, alright,' he said and turned to make his way back downstairs.

A cold cocktail of relief and fear snaked through Emma's capillaries. She'd passed the first hurdle, but she was still far from safe.

In the kitchen, Aiden sat down at the table and played

lazily with the saltshaker as Emma moved around the kitchen.

'What did I miss today then?' he asked.

'What's that?'

'Did she do anything special?'

'Nothing new.'

Aiden was always doing this, probing her to find out what Kathleen did when he wasn't around. She was a baby. Most days were pretty much the same as the day before. But Aiden didn't seem to understand that. He was always marveling at even the tiniest advancement in Kathleen's development.

'Well, did she pull herself up against the sofa again today?'

'Aye she did,' Emma lied.

'It's amazing that she's already standing, isn't it?'

'It is,' Emma responded distractedly as she buttered the bread. Aiden's voice sounded far too animated. Shouldn't he be getting drowsy? Shouldn't his speech be starting to slur?

'I might just go up to the bathroom to wash my hands.' He stood up.

Emma spun around wielding the butter knife like a weapon. A pretty ineffectual one, she imagined, if it came to that. 'You will not. Since when have you cared about hygiene? You're just sneaking up to see Kathleen. It was hard enough getting her down the first time. Let her sleep, would ye.'

Obediently, Aiden folded himself into the chair again. Emma turned her back on him and started cutting the cheese. The knife felt chilly next to her sweaty palms. God, when would the drugs take effect? She couldn't distract him all night. She really did need to get to work. That was a critical element of the plan. The only reason she'd taken that stupid part-time job nearly two months ago was so, when tonight came, she'd have an alibi.

Usually she only worked Friday and Saturday night as

she had school during the week, but she occasionally worked other nights and then skipped school the next day. The teachers always cut her some slack, given the circumstances.

Aiden had been away on a job with Geary that afternoon, and the official story was Emma had spent the afternoon in the house with Kathleen. What she had really been doing was handing her over to the Americans. After their job, Geary had taken Aiden to the pub. The plan was for him to drop Aiden back home around eleven, nice and drunk, and with a few sleeping pills in him for good measure.

But what if Geary hadn't been able to drug him? Maybe Aiden had been watching him the entire time. Maybe Geary never got an opportunity to slip the pills into Aiden's beer. What if Aiden didn't fall asleep before she had to leave for her nightshift at the care home? What excuse would she give him for not going? She couldn't leave him awake and alone in the house. The risk of him going into Kathleen's room before he went to bed was too great. Had he really looked drugged when he'd come in? Or had she imagined that?

'Was she crabbit the night then?' Aiden asked, still sounding very much awake.

'What's that?' She didn't turn around. The less eye contact they had the better.

'I said, was Kathleen not at herself tonight?'

'No, she's fine.'

'But you said you had trouble getting her down.'

'Do you want mayonnaise on this?'

'Aye, please…Listen, thanks for doing this. I know you need to get off to work soon.'

'That's ok,' Emma turned and forced a smile across her face. "Act normal," Geary had advised. "He can't suspect you."

She went to the fridge for the mayo and finished making the sandwich. Then she filled up the kettle and took out two cups.

'Are you having tea with this?' she asked.

He didn't respond. She turned to examine him. His head was on the table lying on top of his folded arms.

'Aiden?'

No response.

She edged towards him and poked him lightly.

'Aiden,' she said, more sharply than before.

Still nothing.

She lent down right next to his waxy ear and shouted, 'Aiden!'

He didn't flinch.

She glanced at the clock on the wall. 11:20pm. Should she wait five minutes before giving Geary the signal? Just to make sure he was really asleep? No, they didn't have five minutes. She needed to get to work on time. It had to look like a regular evening.

She tiptoed towards the back door, opened it a creak, and stuck her head out into the winter air. Aiden snorted loudly. She jumped and turned around. He was still folded over the table, still asleep.

She opened the door wider. Down the back alley the red glow of a cigarette bobbed around in the darkness. She waved, and the smoker started walking towards her.

'He doesn't suspect anything?' Geary asked as Emma closed the door behind him.

'No.'

'Good work.' He went to the corner cupboard and took out a bottle of whisky.

'What are you doing?'

'What does it look like?' Geary didn't even bother to drop his voice to a whisper.

'Is that a good idea? You're not supposed to be here, remember?'

'Don't worry. I know how to clean up after myself.' Geary grabbed a glass from the drying rack and poured himself a large shot. 'And besides, my prints are all over this place. Wasn't I here this afternoon picking up Aiden? Am I not here all the time?'

'Fine. But make sure you wash that glass afterwards and put everything away exactly where you found it.'

'Shouldn't you be leaving for work already?'

A couple of months ago, when they'd come up with this plan, Geary had got Emma a part-time job at a care home for the elderly that his sister-in-law managed. During the nightshift, her job mainly consisted of accompanying the residents to and from the toilet or changing the soiled bed sheets of those who didn't call her in time. The whole place stank of peas and bleach and death. She absolutely hated it. But it was the best way to ensure she had an ironclad alibi between the hours of midnight and 7am, which is what she needed.

She ran upstairs to the nursery and removed the T-shirts that she'd stuffed into the tiny sleeping bag a few hours ago. The desolate cot was so grey and bleak in the darkness.

'Don't cry,' she said to herself. 'Remember, this is what you wanted.' She slapped a tear from her face. She needed to arrive at work looking normal. She lifted the teddy bear from the cot and held it to her, letting its softness caress her cheeks. Then she dropped the bear to the floor and fled.

Back in the kitchen, Geary was resting against the counter sipping at his whisky and smoking a fresh cigarette. Relaxed as the summer days are long. He really had a constitution made for crime.

'Did Jonny give you your cut of the money this afternoon?'

'He did.'

'Tidy sum. What are you going to do with it?'

She shrugged. 'Maybe I'll use it to get out of this shithole.'

'Well, remember what I said, our work is only beginning. You need to be on form tomorrow. People need to believe the kidnapping story. You're going to get a lot of heat over the next few months, and we can't have you raising suspicions by swanning off on some fancy holiday.'

'I'm not an idiot. I know I need to wait a year or so. Don't worry. Now, do you need help carrying him upstairs?'

They planned to leave Aiden in bed and then stage a break-in downstairs so he'd think someone had come in and snatched Kathleen while he lay passed out, apparently too drunk to notice. Aiden would have no clue that he'd conked out from the sleeping pill rather than the booze.

'No. You go. You can't be late. This wee lad doesn't weigh much. I can handle him.'

Emma made her way towards the door and then glanced back at Aiden slouched over the table. This time tomorrow, she thought, they'd be back in this kitchen, and Aiden would be sitting on the same chair, in the same crumpled position. But he'd be awake, and he'd be sobbing. Emma imagined she and Aiden would be exhausted after spending all day at the police station. They probably would have appeared on every TV channel begging Kathleen's kidnappers to return her. And perhaps, by tomorrow night, Aiden might start to realize he'd really lost Kathleen. The child he doted on and adored with all his being. Looking at him now, fast asleep, unaware of the torment she had unleashed upon him, Emma almost felt sorry for him. Almost.

CHAPTER THREE
JANET—LONG ISLAND
MEMORIAL DAY WEEKEND 1994

It was three, perhaps four in the morning, and Janet was pacing the hall with Kathleen. She screamed when Janet put her down. She squirmed when Janet held her. She refused the pacifier. She wasn't hungry. She didn't have a dirty diaper. But, still, she cried and complained and combated sleep with everything she had, and there was nothing Janet could do about it.

Tom opened their bedroom door. The orange light from the bedside lamp spilled into the hallway but it didn't touch Janet. She was too far away, at the end of the long corridor, folded into the darkness.

'Love, c'mon back in here would ye?' he said in a loud whisper. 'No point disturbing everybody else.'

Janet rolled her eyes. They rented this house every year for the Memorial Day weekend with three other couples, all friends of Tom's from before he had met Janet. Over the past five years, Janet had spent countless nights, awake in bed, listening to their friends' kids crying down the hall and the sound of people padding around, preparing bottles, in the kitchen below. They could hardly dare complain now it was finally her turn.

A memory came to her from last summer: her and the other women sitting on the lawn, a child on each of the other's laps, hers completely empty, the sky an unbroken swatch of brightest blue, not a single cloud, nothing to soften the sun's scorching gaze. For two hours, Janet had barely spoken as the others had chatted about their kids—they had eight between the three of them. Eight. They had compared how old they were when they had first started to grasp and crawl and speak. They had talked about their kids' favorite foods and books and TV shows. They had spent forty long minutes talking about a Mr. Bump and Go, how all the kids had all gone through a phase of refusing to go to sleep without him and the frantic, epic searches to find him come bedtime—this much loved toy Janet had never even heard of

Finally, Janet had asked: 'And when did they start eating solids?'

'Four months,' each woman had replied, practically in unison.

'That's interesting,' Janet had muttered. The others shared a vernacular—a special language they all spoke fluently, and Janet had been just a tourist, awkwardly throwing out stock phrases she had picked up along the way. Solids—a word only mothers and dentists used, and she was neither.

'Has anyone read any good books lately?' she'd then asked in an attempt to revert to another language, one she used to know well before infertility took over her world. But all three of them had looked at her absolutely incredulous, and Connie had even laughed out loud.

'Don't worry,' Cynthia had said, 'wait until you join the club, then you'll realize how rare it is to finish a magazine article, never mind a whole book. I'm lucky if I get even a few minutes to go to the bathroom.'

The others had nodded in agreement, and the three of them had started swapping stories of showers cut short by screaming babies and days that whooshed by without time for lunch, and Janet had returned to her silent state under the sun's unrelenting glare.

Afterwards, she had watched them walk ahead of her to the house, the toddlers stumbling, like drunkards, their tiny hands reaching up for the steadying support of their moms who walked lopsided next to them. These women were the sun, the moon, the earth, and the stars for the little people who tottered alongside them. Janet had looked down at the empty space next to her. There had been no small hand grasping for hers. No anchor to hold her in place.

Now, in the darkness of the hallway, Janet felt Kathleen's weight in every muscle in her tired body. She kissed Kathleen's cheek and wiped the sweat from her brow. As she did so, she caught a glimpse of herself in the hallway mirror. To the untrained eye, she perhaps now appeared just as knowledgeable as any of the others. She looked like any other member of "the club." And she had learned a lot in the past five months. She could hold Kathleen with one arm and make up a bottle with the other. She could soothe a bump with an imaginary bandage and a kiss. She could change a diaper in a matter of seconds. She knew at least twenty-five nursery rhymes and the moves to go with them. She knew the soundtrack to *Disney's* Aladdin backwards. "A whole new world, a new fantastic point of view." She knew how to clean any fluid, including bodily fluids, off the wall, the carpet, the ceiling—and off her clothes, her skin, her hair. She'd done it. She'd done it all in the past five months. But, as she now clutched Kathleen to her, incapable of getting her to sleep, Janet worried she didn't have the right instincts, that sixth sense the others seemed to have, the reason people said: "mother knows." Janet didn't know. Just as she'd never carried a child inside her, she couldn't feel the instinct within telling her the right thing to do.

Janet approached Tom. 'Does she feel hot to you?'

He rested his hand on Kathleen's forehead. 'Not really love.'

'Should I wake Cynthia or Connie? They'll have a thermometer. I forgot to pack one.'

'She doesn't have a fever.'

'How can you be so sure?'

'I ah…'

'Cynthia will know.'

'She's just unsettled with the drive up here today, that's all.'

Kathleen shifted in Janet's arms and let out another sleepy, frustrated moan.

'Maybe we should call Dr. Rudman.'

Tom rolled his eyes. 'Fine, wake Cynthia if you want.'

Cynthia opened her bedroom door on the second knock, as if she'd been primed and ready to pounce when the call for help came.

'I'm sorry,' said Janet.

'Don't worry, is everything ok?'

'I can't get Kathleen to settle. She keeps crying and thrashing around half awake. She's never usually this bad.'

'She might be teething. We had an awful few weeks with Jacob when he was about fourteen months old too.'

'Do you have a thermometer? I think she's got a fever.'

Cynthia went back into the bedroom and reappeared a moment later. When Janet tried to place the thermometer in Kathleen's mouth, her little body stiffened angrily and she thumped Janet in the chest, with a sting that went right to the heart.

'Like this,' Cynthia whispered. She took the thermometer from Janet, held Kathleen's chin between her fingers, and managed to ease it into Kathleen's mouth. Janet studied the angle of the thermometer and the way Cynthia touched Kathleen. How was that different from what she had just tried to do? 'All normal,' Cynthia said looking at the temperature.

'But why does she feel so hot?'

'It's a warm night. Take her clothes off and lay her down on top of the covers. If that doesn't work, come back. I have some infant Tylenol in my bag.'

Janet thanked Cynthia and made her way back along the hall to Tom.

'Should I try her on the bed between the two of us?'

'That's what I suggested an hour ago,' he said.

She put Kathleen down in the middle of the bed on top of the covers next to Tom. Kathleen wriggled and moaned but she didn't scream like before. Janet stood up. She pulled off her shirt and unhooked her bra. Three peas fell to the floor and rolled away into the darkness. They must have been from Kathleen's dinner. She'd have to find them in the morning, if she didn't step on them first. She got into bed on the other side of Kathleen and propped herself up on a pillow, so she could look down on her daughter.

'If she still hasn't settled by the morning, we should take her to see Dr. Rudman,' Janet said.

'We're not driving the length of the Island just because Kathleen's had a bad night's sleep.'

'She might be sick.'

'Well if she's sick we should take her to a local doctor. There's bound to be one on call in town.'

'No. I don't trust anyone else.'

Tom let out a long sigh: 'For God's sake, not this again. The emergency doctor will hardly ask for a full medical history.'

'You don't know that,' Janet said.

'Well, if they do, Rudman can fax over the records he made. Isn't that what we're paying him for?'

'Will you lower your voice?'

'Anyway, she's not sick. It's probably just the new surroundings.' Tom lay down and closed his eyes.

'I don't trust anyone else,' Janet said again.

Tom let out a long, exasperated sigh. 'Fine. If she's no better in the morning we'll phone Rudman.' He reached over and gave Janet's hand a squeeze. 'Now try to get some sleep love.'

Janet stared ahead at the gray shadows on the wall, thinking about that awful day when she'd gone to register Kathleen with a pediatrician, someone a neighbor had recommended not long after they had returned from Belfast. Janet had told the doctor's receptionist the same story they told everyone: a Texan adoption agency, reams of paperwork, an excruciating wait and then, thank the Lord, a Christian girl who had gotten herself in trouble, a rat of a boy who had disappeared, a few difficult months as she'd tried to go it alone and, finally, the sad realization she couldn't bring a child up by herself. A closed adoption. Better for all in the long run. No, they weren't planning on telling Kathleen she was adopted. Perhaps when she's an adult, but not before. Or maybe they'd never tell her. They hadn't decided. They'd warned their friends they must never mention it to their kids. Not ever. They didn't want someone blurting it out by accident. And they expected the doctor not to say anything either. Not ever.

The receptionist had stared at Janet, waiting for her to shut-up.

'OK, you'll need to fill out these forms and we'll need the child's medical records.'

'But she's not registered with any physicians yet. Like I said, we just adopted her.'

'I know but we need her previous medical records.'

'What previous records? She's not even a year old.'

'The agency must have given you an anonymized report with all her medical information.'

'No, they didn't.'

'It's standard procedure.' The girl had eyed Janet with suspicion.

Janet had felt sweat spring to her pores. 'Oh, you mean the medical *report*, of course. I was getting confused. I thought you meant…'

'You do have it then?'

'Yes, of course.'

'So can I make a copy?'

Janet had felt all eyes in the waiting room staring at her, studying her reaction.

'No. I mean…I have the papers at home. I'll come back another time.'

'Fine. Do you want to take these forms with you to complete at home?' the receptionist had said, but Janet was already walking, nearly running, out the door.

'I'll fix it,' Tom had said when she'd called him, in tears, from the parking lot. 'I promise I'll fix it.'

That night, Janet had sat up all night on the chair in the nursery, somewhere between waking and nightmares, keeping a vigil over Kathleen. What would they do if the receptionist had seen through her, if uniformed officers arrived at their house in the morning? What would they do if Kathleen got sick? What if she had an allergy or a genetic condition they knew nothing about? What if there was an emergency? How could a doctor treat her without any information? How could they have been so selfish, so irresponsible to bring Kathleen into their lives like this? Why hadn't they thought this through properly? Why hadn't Tom planned this better? It was his fault. It was all his fault.

A week later, Tom had taken Janet and Kathleen to meet Dr. Rudman. One of Tom's Russian investors had recommended him. 'The man knows which questions to ask and which to leave well alone,' Tom had said. And Dr. Rudman had asked a lot of questions. He had wanted to know if Kathleen was eating well, sleeping through the night, and if she'd had any sniffles recently. But he never once asked about the adoption agency, or papers, or her history. With a deep nausea, Janet watched Tom cradle a screaming Kathleen while Dr. Rudman took several blood samples from her arm and then from her foot. 'I'm sorry little one,' he'd said, 'so many tests to do.' At the end, he'd congratulated them on their healthy, bouncing baby and assured them he had all the information he needed to reconstruct her "lost" medical records. As he was walking them to the door, he had given Janet his pager so she could get in touch with him any time she wanted.

'Don't worry, Mrs. O'Connell,' he'd said, 'all my patients are guaranteed the utmost confidentiality.'

In bed in Montauk, Janet now moved Kathleen's black hair away from her sticky forehead. She seemed to be fast asleep now. Finally. She was snoring, almost in time with Tom, snuggled into the nook under his arm. Janet smiled. She eased herself down into the small sliver of bed Kathleen and Tom had left for her.

Whatever trouble had been haunting Kathleen was now gone. It had probably been the heat, or her teeth, or over-exhaustion from the long drive up here today. She was probably fine. But Janet couldn't help worry if something else had been disturbing her, causing her to fight her sleep like that.

Did she dream of them, Janet wondered, the green-eyed girl who sold her and the black-haired boy who was probably still searching? Janet had only seen him for a moment, on television, that morning in Manchester. In the first weeks at home with Kathleen, she had not watched the news. She had not read the papers. Not that it had made the headlines in the US, Tom had assured her. Even so, she had shut herself off from the world. For the past six months, she had devoted herself to Kathleen. She hadn't wanted to know any more about that sad waif of a boy. Forget he even existed.

Janet shifted in bed, curling herself protectively around her daughter, and she let out a long breath, ready for sleep. But when she closed her eyes, there he was, pleading for his daughter's safe return. She could see him. She could hear him. It seemed like she could even touch him, he felt so close. It felt like he was always there. Only, during the day, there was so much to distract her. There were lists to write, errands to run, and a fifteen-month-old to attend to. During the day, she could ignore him. The nights, however, were a different matter entirely.

CHAPTER FOUR
EMMA—BELFAST & NEW YORK
JUNE 1994 TO SEPTEMBER 1994

On the weekends, the bar could get lively, busy with people full of the *craic*. But tonight was Tuesday. Only the professional drinkers came in on a Tuesday. In front of her sat a disheveled row of men supping pints in silence. Melancholy hung thick in the air, as it always did.

All of her friends were over in the University Quarter right now celebrating the end of their A-level exams. Emma didn't belong there. She had hardly been to school since Kathleen's "kidnapping". Most of her old classmates were hoping to get into Queens. Except for her best friend Victoria. She had her sights set on art school in Manchester. But Emma's sights reached only as far as tomorrow's plane journey and no further.

She stood in a corner, drying glasses, staring at the drinkers along the bar. They reminded her of her long-dead father. They were lonely, isolated men, incapable of holding down work. Many of them lived off subsidies shelled out by the very Government they fought against. At one time, they had been able to give off a certain kind of quiet menace, which had probably made them feel powerful. But they were mere pawns. They would never admit it, but they had been scammed. While these men had been busy creating a distraction in the name of the "cause" their commanders, men like Geary and Aiden's uncles, had been growing rich on the profits of unchecked organized crime.

The men drank heavily, so much so that they'd often fall off their chairs and slur their speech. But they never lost control, they never said anything they shouldn't, their facial expression always remained fixed. Emma could only imagine the secret shames they kept stored up inside. You could make an educated guess, but you'd never find a chink in their armor big enough to expose the fleshy mess they hid inside. She studied them, knowing she needed to be more like them.

As the evening passed, the customers filed out one by one, until it reached closing time, and only Jim remained at the bar. Jim was probably in his late forties. He wore the same unkempt wooly jumper every day and sported wildly outdated seventies style side-burns. Night after night, he came and sat at the bar alone, for hours, usually only speaking to order a drink. He was almost always the last customer of the night.

He handed his empty glass to Emma and started pulling on his jacket, which was frayed and torn in several places.

'Did I hear right? Are you off to America?'

'That's right.'

'Well, good luck girl,' he said. 'Here, buy yourself a drink when you get to New York, will you?' He shoved a five-pound note across the counter towards her. This was a man that sometimes counted out his beer money in pennies and often had to ask for credit until his benefit check came in on a Thursday.

'Jim, you're very kind, but I can't accept that.'

'Take it,' he said, staring at a spot to the right of her temple, not meeting her eye.

'Thank you.'

'Have a nice life, isn't that what they say? Well I mean it.'

'No need to get so dramatic,' Emma smiled. 'Sure I'll see you when I'm back in September. You can only stay a few months as a tourist.'

'No offense, but I hope I never see you in here again. You're far better off in America. Get as far away from this hell-hole as fast as possible and don't look back.'

For three months now, Emma had served this man night after night, and yet she knew practically nothing about him. Not anything real. This was the longest conversation they had ever had.

'Can I ask you something?' Emma said, emboldened. 'Why don't you ever look me in the eye?'

The whole time they'd been talking he'd looked in her direction, but he never met her gaze.

He stood back, with his hands in his pockets, looking incredibly uncomfortable, his eyes darting around the bar. Perhaps she should have kept her mouth shut.

'It's what I've been trained to do,' he eventually said. 'Words are easy. You can choose what you want to say and how you want to say it. But you've no such control over your eyes. They can betray you. They can show you up for who you really are. So we all learned never to look anyone in the eye. I didn't even know I still did that, I suppose I'm too institutionalized to change.'

'Sorry, I didn't mean to pry...'

Jim zipped up his jacket. 'Go have yourself a great life girl. Of all people, you deserve it.' And out he walked, leaving Emma alone in the grimy bar.

The next morning, Emma sat at her kitchen table going through the contents of her handbag again to make sure she had everything she might need for the flight, the first of her life. Victoria was hovering around, shivering and hugging a cup of coffee, with last night's mascara still thick on her lashes. Emma's mother sat opposite her at the table drinking tea and smoking, dressed in her nightie and flimsy pink dressing gown.

'I don't know how I'll cope, you so far away and me here by myself. My whole family gone,' her mother grumbled. Emma rolled her eyes at Victoria.

Victoria gave Emma's mother a sympathetic look. 'Sure it's only three months Mrs. McCourt. She'll be back in no time.'

'After all that's happened this year, I can't believe you're just taking off for a summer holiday. What if there's a break in the investigation? Don't you want to be here for that?'

'If there's any news, I'll change my flight and come back earlier. Of course I will.' In the six months since Kathleen's disappearance, the police hadn't made a single meaningful breakthrough. Geary's man on the inside was making sure of it. If there were a true break in the investigation, Belfast was the last place Emma wanted to be. 'Now, I gave you Patrick's phone number didn't I?' she said to her mother. Emma had arranged to spend the summer with Patrick Doyle. He was the twenty-one-year-old friend of her cousin. Emma didn't really know Patrick well, but she'd hung about with him around the Falls Road, with her cousins, when they were younger. A few phone calls from her cousin and Patrick had offered to let her crash with him for the summer.

Emma stood up. 'I need to get going,'

'You can't wait to get away from me, can you?'

'Mommy, that's not true. We've been over this.' Outside a car horn beeped. 'That'll be my taxi. Are you going to give me a hug goodbye or what?'

Her mother got up, cigarette still in hand. Emma reached tentatively out, wrapping her arms around her mother in something that just about passed for an embrace. Under her polyester nightdress her mother's fragile collection of bones stayed stiff and straight.

As Emma gathered up her belongings, her mother cleared away the teacups and started washing them. Victoria grabbed Emma's suitcase and dragged it out the front door, leaving Emma alone with her mother.

'I'll see you soon,' said Emma.

'Aye, look after yourself,' her mother said without turning around.

***

Emerging bleary eyed out of the Terminal, not really knowing how she had survived the crowded arrivals hall or the daunting business of going through immigration, Emma looked around for Patrick. She quickly found him leaning up against a construction van in the drop off area, the sun lighting his smiling face.

'Welcome to the Big Apple,' he said.

In the van, Emma clung to her backpack and stared out the window. Patrick drove far above the speed limit, skirting between the traffic as if they were in a Hollywood high-speed car chase. Trucks and people carriers lurched at them from all directions. She'd never seen cars so big.

'So we've got this apartment on a third floor walk-up just on the border between Woodside and Astoria,' said Patrick.

'On the border of where and where?'

'It's in Queens. Don't worry it's not too rough. It's no Park Avenue either, but compared to the shithole we grew up in it's not bad at all. And if you like Greek food, well it's the place for you.' Emma suppressed an anguished yelp as they narrowly made it back into their lane before an oncoming truck plowed into them. 'So it's a three bedroom place and, including you, there's ten of us living there. Do you know Jo and Niall Fitzpatrick?' Emma shook her head. 'They're good lads. I was going to put you into their room. Theirs is the only room with a spare bed. It's either that or the living room floor. The sofa's taken.

Hope that's ok.'

'I don't mind sharing a room. I'm used to it,' Emma said.

'Aye.' Patrick averted his eyes. 'Right, so…' He trailed off.

Emma tugged at a piece of loose skin on her thumb, ripping it off and leaving a raw pink line all along the nail. 'Umm, just one question, are any of the lads friends with Aiden Kennedy?'

'Nah. They're not that kind,' Patrick said and then quickly added. 'Sorry, I didn't mean anything by that. No offense.'

'None taken.'

'I just meant, they are the kind of lads that wanted to get away from all that sectarian shite. That's why they're here. They wanted to get away from people like the Kennedys constantly trying to recruit them. I don't know Aiden personally. I'm sure he's a good lad.'

'That's fine, I was just curious.'

'Listen, I didn't mean to speak out of turn. The Kennedys must be like family to you, after all you and Aiden have been through.'

'There's no need to explain yourself to me. Aiden and I are still friends, of course. But since Kathleen disappeared, he's gone off the rails. So I try to keep my involvement with him to a minimum these days. That's why I wanted to come away for the summer. To leave all that behind me.'

'I've told the lads not to be asking you about, you know, what happened. I'm sure you've come here for a clean slate, just like the rest of us.'

'Thanks Patrick,' Emma smiled at him, just as he swerved into another lane. But this time she didn't flinch.

When they got to the apartment, Patrick lugged her suitcase up the narrow stairs and kicked the apartment door, which was lying open.

Inside were six guys dotted around smoking and drinking tins of beer.

'Right, Emma, let me introduce you. That's John, James, Charlie, Connor.' Patrick pointed to each one and they gave her a wave and a smile in turn. 'And those two on the sofa are Jo and Niall who you'll be sharing with.'

Two big strapping lads with tattooed arms stood up and said hello in strong West Belfast accents. Emma shook their hands and forced a smile on her face.

'Don't worry. They look like degenerates but they're both big pussy cats,' Patrick assured her. 'I wanted to ask ye, are ye looking for work?'

'Yes, definitely.'

'There's a pub down the street called *Durty Nellys* that we frequent from time to time.'

'Try every bloody night,' Jo cut in.

'Anyway, the manager's looking for help over the summer. I told him about you. You used to work in Brennan's on the Falls didn't you?'

Emma nodded.

'Well, as we're such loyal customers, he said the job's yours if you want it. It's cash in hand, and the rent here is practically nothing, so you should be able to save a bit.'

'Patrick, it's so good of you to arrange that for me,' Emma said.

'Sure it's no bother. We look after our own here. Now sit yourself down and I'll get you a beer.'

Joe and Niall moved to make space on the sofa and Emma sat down, sandwiched comfortably between the two.

***

With tips, and not paying any tax, the money at the bar was more than Emma needed to live on. The lads all worked construction. They got up early and grafted on sites across the city all day, leaving Emma alone in the flat. But she couldn't stand those long days by herself with nothing to distract her. So when someone mentioned that another Irish girl, Johanna, had gotten a working visa and social security number, Emma borrowed it and headed off to Manhattan in search of work.

She found a job in a discount shoe store a few blocks from Washington Square. Becoming someone else was surprisingly easy. It took Emma only a day or so to get used to answering when someone called for Johanna.

She usually went to Washington Square for lunch. Lounging on the concrete, munching on falafel bought from a nearby street vendor, with the Empire State building far off in the background, she'd watch kids playing in the fountain, chess players scamming happy tourists out of a few dollars, a cappella singers busking, and students lazing on towels with their text books lying untouched next to them.

As the summer days went by, Emma felt more and more like she belonged in this crazy milieu, like she had found her place in the world here amongst the construction workers, the Italians, the homeless people, the artists, the Vietnamese, the tourists, the Lebanese, the students, the bankers, the Pakistanis, the musicians, the models and the Mexicans.

And then, all too soon, September came, and it was time for her to go home.

The cheapest way to get to Newark airport was to catch a coach from China Town. Usually, they only took people from the Chinese community, but Patrick and his crew had done renovation work on a restaurant there, and Patrick, ever the charmer, had made friends with the waiters who had hooked Emma up with a spot on the coach.

Patrick drove her to the meeting place just outside the Catholic Church on Mott Street. He parked the van and took her suitcase out of the back.

'I'll wait with you until the bus comes.'

'Patrick it's fine. You have things to do.'

'We're going to miss your Ulster Fry ups on Saturday mornings. Nothing cures a raging hangover quite like one of your breakfasts.'

'Patrick, seriously, you don't have to wait with me.'

Emma was feeling bad enough about having to go back to Belfast, the last thing she needed was some teary goodbye with Patrick on the sidewalk when the bus came. Over the summer, she'd learned the lads, despite their tattoos, shaven heads and borderline alcoholism, were all big softies inside, and Patrick was the worst of all. 'I don't know how to thank you for all you did for me this summer.'

Patrick dug his hands into his pockets and kicked an imaginary stone. 'You know, McCourt, you're a lot nicer than people give you credit for back home.'

'What's that supposed to mean?'

'You have a reputation for being, how shall I put this, a bit feisty? But you're all right. It's been good sharing with you this summer.' His eyes looked like they were misting over.

'Jesus Patrick, you have to go now.' Emma pushed him into the van.

She watched him drive off, his arm waving like crazy as the van disappeared around the corner. Around her were colorful shop-fronts, with all sorts of plastic tat for sale. All the signs were in Chinese, and there were buckets lined up along the sidewalk piled high with crabs. There were bakeries with trays of dumplings and buns displayed in the window, butchers with sticky, whole, marinated pigs swinging above the counter, and old ladies weaving in and out of the crowds, dragging canvas shopping bags behind them. How strange that this place, with its indecipherable language and unusual smells, should feel more like home to her than Belfast. That she should feel more herself here than she had ever felt before.

The coach arrived and people started putting their luggage into the hold. Emma hung back trying to breathe in as much of the city's magic as possible. The sun was a ball of butter in the sky, and the street was hot and noisy.

'Hey, Irish lady, put your case here,' the driver motioned to her as the rest of the passengers started filing into the coach.

Still she hesitated, thinking about the scene waiting for her at home. Her mother, drawn and depressed, the darkness of the Falls Road with its boarded-up shop fronts, tribal graffiti, and soldiers in combat gear and rifles stopping cars. She thought about Aiden coming round her house whenever he felt like it, usually drunk, sometimes high, with that photo album he carried everywhere of "his girls." The one that was now grubby from him pawing over it so much. She thought about the bar and what Jim had said about hoping she never came back. She thought about the lies she had to tell and the sympathy she had to endure in Ireland. In Belfast, people looked at her like a half person. People defined her not by who she was, but by what she was missing. Emma had a hole the shape of herself carved into her soul and, back home, it was all people could see when they looked at her.

'Irish lady, we have to go now. People must catch flights.'

'Ok,' she said, picking up her case.

Patrick just laughed when she showed up at the apartment in Queens. He handed her the bottle of *Budweiser* he'd been drinking, and she took a giant mouthful and smiled.

'Boys,' he shouted as he lifted her suitcase and carried it in to the apartment. 'Looks like we'll be harboring an illegal from now on.'

Illegal. A law-breaker. That's exactly what she was, and she would just have to get used to it.

CHAPTER FIVE
EMMA—NEW YORK
MARCH 1995

Emma heard Larry before she saw him.

'It's not my fault you have Sasquatch feet honey.'

'What's a "Sast Watch" Daddy?'

'A big monster that lives in the woods.'

'I do not have monster feet!'

'I'm not saying that, but for such a small girl your feet are exceptionally large.'

'Daddy, I want these ones.'

'But, I told you, those ones don't fit you.'

The man sounded like he was about to give up all hope. Emma went to see how she could assist. In the midst of a sea of pink, was a bright-eyed, raven-haired little girl, sitting on a bench swinging her white-socked feet. She looked to be about five or six years old. Another little girl, who looked like a carbon copy of the first save that she was a few years younger, sat in a stroller chewing on a shocking pink sneaker from the display. Between the two, a middle-aged man was crumpled on the ground looking utterly defeated.

'Can I help?' Emma asked.

He looked up at her. 'You couldn't get me a stiff drink, could you?'

'No, I'm afraid I drank the last of the liquor this morning. It is Monday, after all. But perhaps I can help you with these sizes?' She sat down on the floor next to him and turned to the little girl. 'Now, which pair of shoes do I need to find in a dainty princess size for you?'

Relief and gratitude washed over the man's face.

'Thank you for this. I bet my ex-wife knew there was going to be a break in the weather today so she orchestrated this whole thing to mess with me. I should be on the golf course right now.'

'What do you mean?' Emma asked.

'Last night, as I was dropping off the girls, she just happened to mention that she'd read about a discount store near Washington Square that was having a sale on Kitty Kit shoes for girls. But it was ending soon, so I'd better bring them today. Of course, she made sure to say all this in front of Meg here, who was just thrilled with the prospect of a shopping trip into the city with Daddy to buy lots of pink crap. Isn't that right, honey?'

'It's not crap Daddy, they are beautiful,' Meg said with adult seriousness.

Emma smiled. 'That's right sweetheart, you tell him.'

Twenty minutes later, Emma was ringing Larry up as the girls ran around the handbag section nearby.

'Thank you so much,' he said. 'You saved my life today. Or you saved Meg's life and spared me a life-sentence for murder.'

Emma laughed. 'That'll be two hundred dollars.'

He handed her his credit card.

'Are you sure you don't have a shot of whiskey for me Johanna?' he said, looking at Emma's name badge. 'I think I need it to face the streets of New York with these two. We live all the way out in Jersey City. I'm sure my ex-wife is sitting at home like some Bond villain, stroking a white cat in glee, thinking of me suffering in the city with these two.'

'But Jersey City's not that far is it?'

'Oh, it's only eight minutes into downtown they'll tell you. Maybe for normal people, but it's a not a journey you should be making with two annoying, unreasonable, little humans clinging to you. Like Charlotte, the youngest, she's just plain lazy. She can walk, but she insisted I bring her in the stroller, which wouldn't be so bad, except Meg walks at the slowest pace known to man. So there I am, with one hand I'm shoving this stroller in front of me along a crowded street, and my other arm is stretched about three feet behind me holding Meg's hand as she dawdles along chatting to herself. Or maybe she's talking to me. I don't know. I don't care at this point. I mean, she's six, there's absolutely nothing she's going to tell me that will change my life, is there? All she'll be saying is totally pointless shit like, "Daddy, taxis are yellow."'

Emma laughed again, imagining this.

'Here's your receipt, there's no money back on sale items but we will exchange any unworn shoes. So, if you get home and the girls decide they don't like what they bought, you can always come back and do the whole thing again.'

'Jesus Christ Johanna, is that a threat?'

'It's not a threat.' Emma paused, letting a tiny subversive smile cross her face. 'It's an invitation.'

Larry blushed a little, and Emma wondered why she was flirting with this man. He wasn't repulsive, but there was certainly nothing handsome about him. He had dark red hair with a pinch of grey around the temples, a high forehead, honey-brown eyes and pale skin. He was about six feet tall and looked like he needed to lose a bit of weight. But, most importantly, he was probably twice her age.

'Thank you for all your help today,' Larry lifted the

bags, barely meeting her eye. He probably wasn't used to young women teasing him like she'd just done.

Emma watched Larry as he gathered up his raucous daughters and maneuvered his way through the shop, knocking down high heels and boots from the carefully arranged displays as he went. As her eyes followed him all the way out the door, a strange melancholy settled into her chest.

The next morning, when Emma arrived for work fifteen minutes before opening, she found Larry loitering on the sidewalk outside the store.

'Was there a problem with the shoes?' she asked, noticing his hands were empty, save for a paper cup.

'No.' Larry looked down as he traced a circle around the lid of his coffee.

'Do you want to buy some more? We're not open yet, but I'm sure the manager wouldn't mind if you came in now to browse.'

'No, that's ok.' He looked her in the eye. 'I couldn't sleep last night.'

'Ok,' she said slowly.

'I sat up all night trying to figure out a way of asking you out that didn't sound creepy.'

'And what did you come up with?'

'That was it.'

'Oh.'

'Shit, did it sound creepy? Of course it did. I mean, no matter how I ask you it's going to be wrong, I'm forty-three and you're…. how old are you?'

'Nineteen.'

Larry's mouth fell into a downturned O. 'I was kind of hoping you were older and just really knew how to take care of yourself. Never mind, forget I came here.' He went to leave.

Watching his back, lumbering away from her, Emma suddenly felt a sense of panic.

'Just for the record,' she called, 'my answer was yes.'

'Yes it's creepy?' He turned back towards her.

'No, yes I will go out with you.'

'Really?'

'I finish work at six today, if you want to grab dinner together.' It was her night off from *Durty Nellys*.

'Definitely.'

'Good, meet me back here later then.' Emma walked into the store, leaving him standing in the middle of the sidewalk with a huge grin on his face. It was just dinner. She didn't have anything else to do this evening anyway. Plus, it felt good being able to bestow joy on another human being, for a change.

***

As Emma followed the waiter through the French bistro in Soho, she started to think maybe it had been a mistake saying yes to this date. This place looked really fancy. It had large mirrors, a high ceiling, and art deco lighting, and the wait staff were all dressed in black ties and long white aprons. She hoped Larry wasn't expecting them to go Dutch. Not that she minded paying her own half. It was better that way. But she hadn't realized he'd take her somewhere so expensive.

'So what do you recommend?' she asked studying the menu.

'For starters, the lobster salad is good and so is the duck foie gras terrine, and, for the main, the steaks here are amazing.'

Emma glanced down at the prices. 'I might not have a starter. I'm not that hungry,' she lied.

'I'll feel like a big fatty if I get a starter and you don't, are you sure you won't join me? And, by the way, this is my treat, to say thanks for your help at the store yesterday with the girls. You were really good with them.'

Emma closed the menu. 'Everything looks delicious. Why don't you order for the both of us?'

After Larry had ordered, and the waiter had brought them their drinks, Emma said, 'So the girls were happy with their shoes?'

'Yeah, they were ecstatic. Too happy in fact. Halfway home, Meg decided she had to put hers on. She couldn't wait. So there I am unpacking them in the middle of a crowded train full of commuters. There are boxes and shoes and fucking pink tissue paper strewn all over the place, and people are stepping over us like we're trash. But Meg wouldn't take no for an answer. She's very strong willed, or maybe I'm just weak. When you first become a parent you read all these books, as if successful parenting is an exam you can study for, and you think, if I follow all the rules, my kids will be different. I won't be one of those parents who can't control their screaming kid in a restaurant. Those people are idiots, you think. But then the kid arrives, and suddenly your whole notion of good parenting changes. Now, if I just make it to the end of the day and the girls are still alive and I'm still reasonably sane, well, that's a fucking victory right there.'

'Perhaps that's why they say that being a parent is the hardest job in the world.'

'It's definitely the most stressful job. Before Meg was born, I made the mistake of reading up on Freud's stages of development. To this day, Freud's ideas still fucking haunt me. The first stage is called the oral stage. Sounds like it should be fun, right? But it's terrifying.'

'Why?'

'The oral stage is from birth to one year. Freud says a child can become fixated at any point, which can make them become stuck at that stage. So, if they become fixated in the oral stage, they'll probably become over-dependent on oral-stimulation like smoking, drinking or eating. And I dread to think what other kind of oral-stimulation they could become addicted to. That's no thought for a father to be having about his daughter, worrying that she grows up to be the girl who blows the entire football team just because I didn't wean her off the bottle properly. But, thanks to Freud, this is the kind of shit I now think about.'

Emma stared into her wine. She hoped Larry was wrong, she hoped, no matter what a child experienced in their first year, they could still course-correct. She had to believe that.

'Did you know that Freud thinks that personality is basically fixed by the time you're five? I still have a shot with Charlotte, but Meg? I dread to think what living with me and her mother for the first five years of her life did to her.'

'Did you fight a lot?'

'No, I'd worry less if Meg had seen us at each other's throats in a good honest argument. But Lisa's far too passive aggressive for that. Instead, it's the thousands of small humiliations and put downs that Meg was witness to that worries me.'

Tiny criticisms were hardly the worst thing a couple could do to each other, Emma thought.

'How often do you get to see them?' she asked.

'About eight days a month, I have them every other weekend and then, during the weeks I haven't had them for the weekend, I have them on Monday and Tuesday.'

'It must be hard saying goodbye to them when you leave them back at their mom's. Do you miss them when they're not with you?'

Larry thought for a moment. 'I'm supposed to say yes, aren't I?' he said with a small smile.

'No, you can be honest. I won't judge you.' *Who am I to pass judgment on anyone?* she thought.

'I do miss them. Of course I do. But this part-time father thing isn't so bad. So many of my friends whine about their kids for hours but then they'll suddenly do this paranoid turnaround thing and say something like, "oh, but little Jimmy is so wonderful, I just couldn't imagine my life without him." Which is such BS. When I was still married, I spent half my time fantasizing about what I'd do if I didn't have kids, and now I kinda get to live out that life for two thirds of the month.'

'And how's that working out for you?'

'Well it's a Tuesday night, and I'm drinking wine in a nice French restaurant with a beautiful young woman, so I'd say, right now, it's pretty fucking great.'

Emma looked at Larry's wide grin and couldn't help but smile too.

After their appetizers, they had steaks with bordelaise sauce and fries, red wine, and, finally, a huge cheese plate with port, deep in conversation and laughing the whole time.

At some point, much later, Emma became aware that the place had cleared out while she'd been lost in conversation with Larry. The staff were now all lined up along the bar staring at them with a murderous look in their eyes.

'I guess I should ask for the check,' Larry glanced at the mob of waiters. 'Or we might get lynched if we keep these guys here any longer.'

Emma looked at her watch. It was after 11pm. Door to door, it would take her at least an hour to get back home to Astoria. She could just picture the scene waiting for her. The lads would all be drunk, and there would be dirty plates, beer cans, and empty pizza boxes strewn everywhere.

She wondered what Larry's apartment was like. He'd spent 200 dollars on shoes for his kids the other day, and this restaurant wasn't cheap, so he must live in a reasonably nice place. At least somewhere with a proper sofa to curl up on that wasn't occupied by a group of guys chain-smoking in their dirty work clothes.

'Do you know if they have a pay phone here?' Emma asked.

'Why? Is everything ok?'

'Yeah, everything is fine. I just need to make a quick call.'

'It's back there by the restrooms.'

Emma excused herself.

'Please don't pick up. Please don't pick up,' Emma whispered as the phone rang.

'Hullo?'

'Patrick?' She had been hoping the lads were out so she could just leave a message on the answering machine.

'Emma? Is everything ok? Are you still out with the old bloke?'

'Yeah. Listen, I was just calling to let you know that I won't be home tonight.'

'Why? Where are you staying?'

'At Larry's place.' He hadn't yet asked her back to his apartment, but why wouldn't he? He was obviously attracted to her, why else had he asked her out to dinner?

'Is that such a good idea? You hardly know the man.'

'Patrick.'

'Emma you can't just go home with a random man on your first date. It's irresponsible.'

'Seriously? You're lecturing me about responsibility? You, the man who sometimes gets behind the wheel of a car after downing ten pints and who regularly misses a whole week of work because you've been on a five-day bender.'

'There's no need to get defensive Em, I'm just looking out for you.'

'I know you are Patrick,' she said. 'But there's nothing to worry about. I can take care of myself.'

'I'm just saying, we're not in Belfast anymore. You need to be careful.'

Like Belfast is so bloody safe.

'I promise, I will be, and I'll see you tomorrow evening.' She went to put down the phone.

'Hi,' Patrick's voice called out. She lifted the receiver to her ear once more. 'You have my beeper number, don't you?'

'Yes.'

'Well, if you want to come home, I don't care what

time it is or where you are in the tri-state area, just contact me and I'll come get you. And let the old bloke know that if he gives you any funny business, you have a small army of Irish lads at your disposal, so he better be on his best behavior. I will personally kick the shit out of him for you if he does anything you don't want him to.'

'Yes, big bro,' Emma put down the phone. She sometimes wondered what her life might have been like if Patrick Doyle really were her big brother, if things would have turned out differently if he'd been there watching out for her in Belfast.

She sat back down at the table, just as the waiter was handing Larry the credit card slip.

'Thank you,' she said. 'I had a lot of fun tonight.'

Larry folded the check and put it into his pocket, and then he spread his hands on the table, looking like he was unsure where to place them.

'I guess I should get the *maître d* to call two cabs for us.'

'Two cabs?'

'I'm not letting you go off to Queens on the subway by yourself at this time of night. But don't worry, I'll pay.'

'Oh, it's just,' Emma bit her lip unsure if she should go on. What the hell, she might as well just come out with it. 'I thought we'd both be getting the one cab.'

'What? New Jersey via Queens? That doesn't make much sense,'

'That's not what I meant,' she looked him squarely in the eye.

A reddish tone raced across Larry's face. 'Or you could come to my place for a nightcap. Only if you want to. No obligation.'

'Yeah, a nightcap, I'd like that.'

He studied her.

'What's that look?' she asked.

'You really don't have a very good sense of self-preservation, do you? It must be the innocence of youth, you've not yet become hardened by the realities of life.'

'Oh, my self-preservation instincts are excellent. Believe you me.'

'I doubt that. You barely know me, I'm twice your size, and yet you're still happy to come home with me.'

'I'm five seven, and you're what, six foot?'

'Six two.'

'Still, that doesn't make you twice my size.'

'But I'm easily double your weight.'

He did have a middle-aged paunch. But somehow that didn't put Emma off. She imagined his weight on top of her, crushing her in a reassuring kind of way. She could picture his face above hers, those deep brown eyes looking down at her, those big hands running all over her, his touch just the right balance between strength and softness.

'Are you trying to put me off going home with you?'

Larry put his head in his hands. 'I'm an idiot, aren't I? I'm just always impressed by how courageous women are, taking a chance on us men, when, statistically, we're like the biggest threat to women-kind,' and then he added hurriedly, 'but, just to clarify, I'm no threat. I'm a teddy bear.'

'I can see that,' she smiled. 'Perhaps you're trying to sabotage this because it's you that's worried about getting hurt. But don't worry Larry, I don't bite…' Emma paused and drank down the last of her whisky. 'Well…only when provoked.'

CHAPTER SIX
VICTORIA—BELFAST
FEBRUARY 1998

'Don't be staying on that phone all night.'

'It's just a wee call to wish her happy birthday.' Victoria tugged the cord, stretching the phone as far up the stairs and away from her mother as possible.

'And tell her to ring her Ma,' her mother shouted from the sitting room. 'The poor woman.'

Victoria dialed the number scrawled across the back of the postcard. Emma had sent it three years ago announcing her marriage. Since then, they had spoken maybe five times. Transatlantic phone calls were expensive.

The last time they'd spoken was last summer, just after Victoria had got home from Manchester with her degree in fine art stuffed in her bag. A 2:2, second-class honors, lower division. Not a great result, not the worst either. Victoria sometimes wished they'd failed her. At least then she could tell herself she wasn't mediocre. That she was a misunderstood artistic genius, someone who defied classification.

Eight months back in Belfast. Eight months back in her childhood bedroom. Eight months of rejections from advertising agencies. Not one single offer. Not even for an unpaid internship. Eight months listening to her mother go on and on about how her daughter was wasting her time waitressing—when you'd think, with her University education, she'd be able to get an office job, even if her degree was only in drawing.

It's temporary, she'd tell her mother. She planned to move to London as soon as she got a job. It's temporary, she'd tell herself every morning when she arrived at Penny Lane's, the café on the Lisburn Road where she worked, or "bistro" as her boss insisted on calling it. The sign outside said "Modern European Cuisine." The specials menu inside said: "Chili with rice and chips. Lasagna with garlic bread and chips. Mozzarella panini with chips. Chicken ciabatta with chips. Garlic chips 50p extra." And on Fridays they served nachos, that staple of the modern European kitchen. Rachel, the manager, insisted every beverage was served with a twist of lime. Bottles of beer, gin and tonic, even tea came with a big green wedge. Victoria was sick of telling her it was supposed to be lemon with tea, not that anyone in Belfast drank their tea that way anyway. Lime green was now Victoria's least favorite color. Thousands of hours chopping limes into perfect wedges had ruined it for her. It represented her failure, in Technicolor. She'd never be able to paint with it again, if she ever got back to painting. It had been months since she'd picked up a brush. Living in her squashed single bedroom at her parents' wasn't exactly conducive to creating any masterpieces.

'Hello,' a man answered the phone. Emma's husband—a concept Victoria still couldn't get her head around. Emma McCourt married. Of all of them, she'd always seemed the girl least likely.

'Hi, is Emma there?'

'Sure, who's calling?'

'It's Victoria, from Belfast.'

'Victoria! She'll be so pleased to hear from you. Let me go get her.'

As Victoria waited, crouched on the stairs, she flicked through the small pile of postcards from Emma she kept stuffed in the back of her address book. All of them with the Statue of Liberty on one side and short message on the back.

September 1994—"Just to let you know I'm fine. Couldn't face going back. So I didn't."

October 1994—"Halloween here is MENTAL!"

January 1995—"FUCK! Finally know what sub-zero means! Am now the owner of actual snow boots. Look like I'm heading to the slopes every time I leave the apartment!"

May 1995—"Guess who is getting a green card! Oh, and a husband…New phone is 001 201 435 5511"

June 1996—"Shit day. Never stop thinking what she'd be doing right now. Miss you. Got my high school diploma by the way."

September 1996—"Watch out NYU! Here she comes!"

February 1997—"21. How the fuck did that happen?'

June 1998—"Congratulations on graduating. So proud of you. Don't forget me when you're a famous artist. Remember, I know all your embarrassing secrets…"

Four years and the news from Emma had barely been enough to fill a side of paper.

Victoria heard shuffling at the other end of the line.

'V?' Emma said.

'Happy birthday.'

'God, it's so good to hear from you.'

'How are you? Are you having a good day?' Victoria asked.

'Any word from the agencies?' Emma replied.

'Not yet.'

'I'm sure they'll be in touch soon. You're really talented.'

'I don't know about that,' Victoria muttered. 'But what about you? How's Uni going?'

'College? It's grand.'

'And are you doing anything nice to celebrate your birthday?'

'God no, I fucking hate today.'

'It's still your birthday. You have a right to celebrate.'

'Celebrate what?' Emma said. Then she dropped her voice to a near whisper, 'another year without her, that's all it means.'

Victoria wished she could reach through the phone to hug her friend. A great big bear hug to show her how much she loved her. But words were all they had, and neither of them was very good at those.

'I know,' Victoria said quietly.

In the background Victoria heard children laughing.

'Fuck,' Emma sighed. 'Larry's kids just got here. I told him to change his days this week but his ex insisted she couldn't change.'

'Do you need to go?'

'In a minute.'

'How old are they again?'

'Meg is eight, and Charlotte just turned five.'

Victoria quickly did the math—Kathleen would also be turning five this month, wherever she was, if she was even still alive.

'Do you get on ok with them?'

'Yeah, they're nice kids, and it's only a few days a month. I just wanted a quiet day that was all.'

Victoria's mother appeared at the foot of the stairs. 'Are you still on that phone?' she said.

Victoria put her hand over the receiver. 'I won't be long,' she hissed at her mother.

'Did you tell her about Aiden?' her mother said.

'Go away,' Victoria mouthed, hoping Emma hadn't heard her mother.

'What about Aiden?' Emma said. Victoria glared at her mother. She still didn't move. 'What about Aiden?' Emma repeated.

'He was lifted the other night,' Victoria said.

'What for?'

'Shoplifting I think, booze from the off license down the road.'

'Idiot,' Emma said.

'Poor lad,' her mother said. 'The police are always picking on him.'

'He'll get off,' Emma said. 'The Kennedys will make sure of it. They always do.'

Victoria covered the phone again and whispered loudly, 'Mommy, would you please leave me alone?'

'It's costing a fortune,' her mother said before returning to the sitting room.

'Do you need to go?' Emma asked.

'No, it's fine.'

'I must run anyway, I promised the girls I'd watch Jurassic Park with them, again.'

'Jurassic Park? Are they not a bit wee for that?'

'Charlotte's going through a dinosaur phase. So we watch the beginning and then turn it off before all hell breaks loose. And then she makes us rewind it and watch the beginning again. I can't even tell you how many times I've seen that first half hour.'

'Well I hope you have a nice day with them.'

'Thanks for calling V. It's really good to hear from you. Let me know if you get any news on the job front. If you move to London, I'll come visit.

'You could come see me in Belfast.'

'I can't face going back there.' Suddenly there was the sound of a door flying open behind Emma and two little girls singing happy birthday, and the sound of Emma's husband shouting at them to get out and leave her alone. 'I must run. I'll call you soon, ok?' Emma said.

'Yes, talk soon,' Victoria said putting down the phone. She sat with the phone on her lap, crouched on the stairs for another minute. She remembered sitting in the McCourt's living room, speechless, hand in hand with Emma, who looked like she'd been torn in half, wondering what she could do to help her friend—fearing there was nothing anyone could ever do bring Emma back to life, after all she'd lost.

But there was Emma now, five years later, off living this entirely unexpected life in America, with a husband and step-kids, going to NYU. And it was Victoria who was stuck, still in Belfast, still being shouted at by her mother for being on the phone too long, still waiting for her life to begin.

Victoria felt a flash of annoyance, anger even, at how things had turned out. But she stopped the thought before it had a chance to take hold. She couldn't explain how Emma had done it, how she'd turned her life around. But what did it matter if it was luck or perseverance or something else? Victoria couldn't begrudge Emma her new life. For after all she'd been through, sure Emma deserved to be happy, didn't she?

CHAPTER SEVEN
JANET—MANHATTAN
AUGUST 1998

Kathleen ran away from Janet, straight into the arms of a T-Rex.

'I'll see you in an hour,' Janet called. Kathleen, enthralled by the puppets, didn't turn around. There was a time when the sight of a six-foot dinosaur would have sent Kathleen clambering up Janet's body in tears, her tiny fingernails clawing into Janet's skin. But not anymore. Not now she was "a very big girl of five and a half," as she loved to say.

Next to Janet, another woman was trying to peel a red-faced little boy off her leg. It was both amazing and terrifying how kids could pout and stare and scream and hold their breath almost simultaneously. Kathleen had been just the same on her first day at pre-school last year.

'I not go to pre-school tomorrow,' she'd announced one bedtime, a few weeks before the start of term, as she settled down with Teddy for a nighttime story.

'Not tomorrow, or the next day, but in fourteen sleeps' time.' Janet had held up her hands to show Kathleen. Two hands first, ten fingers, and then a single hand, with four outstretched fingers. 'Ten plus four equals fourteen.'

'No, I not go. I stay here with you.'

'And how are you going to make new friends if you don't go to pre-school?'

'I make friends in the park,' Kathleen had shrugged, as if the answer was so obvious it went without saying. Then her eyes had lit up with another idea. 'That's better because you can come to the park with me, and you can make new friends too.'

'Maybe. But I thought you wanted to be a big girl. Big girls have to go to school.'

'No, to be big I have to eat lots and lots of vegetables. Remember?'

Janet had allowed herself to feel a hint of pride at these quick retorts. She'd read to Kathleen almost every night from the very beginning, she'd taken her to all kinds of stimulation classes, and she tried to explain absolutely everything to her like she were an adult—even if it meant explaining where rain came from a thousand, exhausting times. 'Just tell her it's God crying,' Tom used to say as Janet launched into another long explanation about evaporation and precipitation. But it was these things that really mattered. These were the things a real parent gave their child, not hair and eye color.

Janet had even looked forward to this nighttime negotiating, in the weeks before pre-school, eager to see what arguments her four-year-old daughter would come up with next. It had seemed like a bit of a game, until the first day of pre-school actually arrived, and the game turned into war.

For the first month, Kathleen would fight Janet as she tried to dress her. She'd hide behind the sofa. She'd throw her shoes down the toilet. She'd kick and scream as Janet lifted her into the car. When Janet finally got her to pre-school, Kathleen would sit down on the steps at the entrance and wail, begging Janet not to leave her. They'd sit like that for half an hour, or more, with Janet trying to coax Kathleen into the school building, with all sorts of promises and threats, as the other parents stepped over them on their way in and out. Finally, the teaching assistant would come and intervene. 'You're not helping, Mrs. O'Connell. Go home, I can take it from here.' And the teaching assistant would forcefully restrain Kathleen and shoo Janet away with a look that said, "I know better than you."

Afterwards, alone at home, shell-shocked from the morning's assault, Janet would crouch on the floor and pull out the box of books she kept hidden under the bed. Books with names like "A parent's guide to adoption," or "Labor of the heart: a support guide for adopters," or "The healing parent: helping wounded children form attachments." Books she knew she would burn, soon, before Kathleen started to read. "Love, alone, cannot always heal the hurt," one of them said. "The harm may be irreparable," another warned. "Adopted children may suffer from poor self-esteem all their lives," the third one pronounced. But Janet had refused to accept it. Against Tom's wishes, and behind his back, she'd spoken to several counselors, experts in therapeutic parenting. On their advice, she'd created a morning-time routine and stuck to it religiously. Over breakfast, she'd tell Kathleen she loved her and she was always thinking about her, even when they weren't in the same place. In the car, she'd play "Hakuna Matata" from *The Lion King* and she'd sing along with forced frivolity, even as Kathleen cried from the backseat. At the steps, before handing her over to the teaching assistant, she would look Kathleen in the eye and calmly promise to return for her later, using the exact same words each day.

Over time, Kathleen's daily histrionics had lost their intensity and she'd even started to join in the singing in the car and now, as Janet watched her daughter confidently shake the paw of a huge green dinosaur puppet, she wondered where that clingy little girl had gone. Had it really been "just a phase" as Tom had insisted it was?

'C'mon Janet, this Dino-show only lasts an hour,' Debra's voice came from behind her. 'We're wasting valuable time. Momma needs a cocktail.'

Janet turned and smiled at her old college roommate. 'It's not even midday.'

'I'll have a Bloody Mary then.'

***

'Well, Museum of Natural History you have let me down. Imagine not even serving wine,' said Debra as they searched, each with a huge cappuccino in hand, for a free table in the café on the floor below the Dino-show. The place was absolutely heaving with families and groups of tourists chattering noisily.

Janet nodded to two free seats on the corner of a large table by the window.

'Do you mind if we sit here?' she asked the man who was already there.

'Go ahead, we'll be leaving soon...I hope.' Next to him sat two dark-haired little girls wearing dinosaur hats. The sandwiches in front of them lay barely touched, just the smallest of bites taken out of each corner. 'Aren't you done already?' he said to the girls.

'No,' they both replied.

As they sat down, Janet glanced at her watch. Only ten minutes had passed since she'd dropped Kathleen off at the show. Fifty more to go.

'You know why all the dinosaurs died, don't you? Because they didn't eat their food fast enough. So all the other animals took it instead, and the dinosaurs starved to death,' said the dad. He reached over and stole a sandwich from each of the girls' plates and stuffed them into his mouth. 'See,' he said, with his mouth still full, 'you better eat up fast or you'll suffer the same fate as old T-Rexy.' He moved towards their plates again and the girls leapt for their food.

Janet and Debra exchanged a glance.

'Ok, time to go,' the man lifted the smaller of the two girls to her feet and nudged the older one.

'Do we have to?' the older one said.

'Yes, she'll be waiting.'

'I want to go back to the show.'

'Well you can't.'

'But please.'

The man sighed. 'Move your tush. If you hurry, we might buy you something else at the gift store.'

'Really?' said the little girls.

'Fine. You can choose one thing each. Just one. Now scoot.'

Janet and Debra watched the man and his kids leave. The two girls rushed on ahead, weaving between the crowds, but the man was a big unit and couldn't maneuver quite so easily between the tables. 'Wait,' his voiced boomed over the din. 'Wait.'

'Poor guy,' Debra said. 'You forget how much easier it was when they're babies and can't run away from you.' She scooped up some cappuccino froth with her fingers and licked it. 'With Emily starting pre-school soon, I sometimes wonder if we might be ready for another baby. One more before we shut up shop.'

'Really?' Janet asked. Debra and Dave had an eleven year old, a nine-year old and a four-year-old. And now she was planning a fourth.

'We've talked about it.'

'But isn't it dangerous to get pregnant at our age?'

'There are plenty of women who have kids at forty.'

'I don't think the doctors recommend it though. It's risky.'

'Actually,' Debra shifted in her chair and hugged her cup as if to steady herself, 'we're thinking of adopting this time. That's why I wanted to speak to you today.' Janet felt the nerves pulse in her veins, just like they always did when anyone brought up the subject of adoption. 'Could you send me the details of the agency in Texas you used? They seemed to do a really good job for you guys. It was all so fast.'

'They closed down a couple of years ago,' Janet lied. 'We got a letter about records and things. I'm sorry. I wish I could be more help.'

'What about the others? You were dealing with a few at the beginning weren't you? Would you recommend any of them?'

'It's a really tough process Debs. Why put yourself through it if you don't have to?'

'But it must be worth it, knowing you've given this child a better life than they otherwise would have had.'

'It is, of course, but don't over-romanticize it. Remember what you said to me that first year when I was struggling to cope with Kathleen's teething?'

'No, what?'

'You said taking care of a baby is sometimes a really shitty job, and I shouldn't expect it to be any more gratifying just because I'd waited so long and been through so much to get her. I think your exact words were "adopted spit-up smells just as foul as home-grown spit-up."'

Debra laughed. 'That does sound like me.' Then her face became serious again. 'Listen, I know it hasn't been a walk in the park for you but I think you're doing an amazing job with her.'

'I try my best,' Janet said.

'Have you ever thought about adopting another kid?'

'No,' she said. 'OK, sometimes. But we're happy as we are.' We have to be, Janet thought. She looked at her watch, hoping the hour was up and she could go collect Kathleen and put an end to this conversation. 'We have half hour before we need to pick up the girls, shall we check out the gift store?'

'Excellent plan.' Debra stood and gathered up her things. 'And you'll send me the names of any other agencies you'd recommend? Just in case we decide to go for it.' Janet made a non-committal sound and stood up to leave.

As she walked ahead of Debra, towards the door, Janet recalled the night, five years ago, when she and Tom had sat down at the dining room table to look over the forms from the various adoption agencies.

***

Tom's face clouded over when he saw the information they needed to provide.

'How come so many drunken cheerleaders can get pregnant and have children, no questions asked, and we have to jump through all these bloody hoops?'

'I know it seems like a lot, but they just need some financial information and details of our family histories.'

Tom picked up one of the pamphlets and started scanning through it. Then he tossed it to one side and started leafing through the forms. The more he read, the more agitated he seemed.

'I don't see why you're getting so stressed,' Janet said. 'The company is doing well. You pay your taxes, you're a good citizen, right?' Janet shuffled the papers in front of her. 'Ok, let's go through some of the basic paperwork first. Can you get copies of our tax returns?' Tom nodded, and Janet made a note in her green notebook, the same one she'd been using to keep track of her menstrual cycle in the ridiculous hope of identifying her supposedly "fertile" days. Amongst the numbers and dates were a few draft poems she'd scratched down from time to time. None of them were finished. 'Next up, criminal check acknowledgement,' she thumbed through the file to find the correct piece of paper. 'We just have to sign this to say we consent to them running various background checks on us.'

'And if we don't consent?'

'Then they won't proceed with the application. But why wouldn't we…?' Her voice trailed off as Tom got up and went to the fridge for a beer. 'Tom, speak to me. Why wouldn't we consent to a criminal check?' He didn't respond, couldn't even look at her. 'Tom, tell me what is going on.' He shuffled from one foot to the next and gulped down some more beer trying hard not to meet her eye. 'Tom, please.'

'You know I was a bit of a lad in my twenties. I told you that when we met.'

'I know you cheated on your first wife, and you used to party too much, but what of it? This is about us and our marriage, they won't care that you're divorced.' He stared out the window as if lost in another time and place. 'Tom,' Janet shouted. She stood up and threw a pen at him, hitting him on the shoulder.

He turned suddenly and she expected him to be angry, but instead he had a sad, pleading look in his eye. 'Just sit down and listen will ye? And don't say anything until I'm done.'

Janet sat back down into her chair feeling cold and heavy. And she stayed there for the next half hour, as Tom paced the kitchen, gulping down beer after beer, confessing his sins.

At twenty-one, he had been in rehab for drugs and again when he was twenty-five and twenty-seven. The rehab had been state ordered after he'd been involved in various fights and public disturbances. Luckily for Tom, he had been married to his first wife at the time, an American citizen; otherwise he could well have been deported.

He had crashed a car once while drunk, and he had to be taken to the hospital with broken ribs. The police had been called, but he had gotten away with it because the crash had happened on private land and no one else had been hurt. After another car crash, this time on the highway, he had spent three months in jail.

He had also been present at an illegal poker game at a

five star hotel in New York when the police had busted it. He had been taken down to the station, but had been released the next day and ended up paying a fine. Tom's buddies, the Russians who had set up the gambling ring, had been imprisoned for nearly a year.

'I have spent a lot of time and money rehabilitating my reputation. But, if these people are looking for an excuse not to give us a baby, it won't take them long to find one,' he said.

Janet stared at him in disbelief. It felt like they were in the last chance saloon, and Tom had just torched the place, burning it to the ground, with Janet still trapped inside.

'How could you do this to me?'

'These are things I did before I met you. If I could change the past, I would.'

Janet looked at the documents in front of her, demanding that boxes be ticked, consents be signed and information be divulged. It had all been a waste of time. She swiped her arm across the table sending the papers flying to the floor.

'Love please, calm down.'

'Why? Why did I have to fall in love with someone like you? Why couldn't I have married someone else? Someone good. Someone decent,' she shouted. He approached her and she ran upstairs, stumbling as she did so, dragging herself up and away from Tom as fast as she could, into the spare bedroom. She locked the door behind her and then fell on the bed sobbing so hard her chest felt like it was going to collapse in on itself. She cried and cried and wept until her body could no longer withstand the physical strain and sleep overtook her.

The next morning, Janet woke with a thumping headache, her eyes still bulging and raw. She unlocked the door and stepped into the quiet hallway. Downstairs, there was no sign of Tom, but the papers had been picked up from the floor and stacked neatly on the table.

Some of the papers had colored post-it notes sticking out from the sides. On the top of the pile Janet noticed a handwritten note from Tom: *"Gone to the bakery. I was up all night filling out forms and getting the paperwork together. Let's just be honest with them and see what happens. I still want to do this. If you do, too, then sign the papers in the places that I've marked."*

By the time Tom got home with Janet's favorite *pain au chocolat*, she had signed all the documents. With each signature, she said a little prayer to the God she now barely believed in.

That summer was filled with tense home inspections and follow-up paperwork, and then, in late September, the letters from the various adoption agencies started to arrive.

Each and every one rejected them.

Throughout October, Janet barely left the house. She didn't want to be anywhere she might see children. Tom said they could still go back to the hospital and continue with IVF. After all, unlike other couples, money was no object for them. But Janet refused. She was an empty shell; no baby would want to grow within her anyway. She took unpaid leave from work, claiming she was suffering from stress, and spent her days on the sofa watching meaningless TV and her nights staring at the ceiling trying to ignore the weight pressing down on her chest.

Halloween was excruciating. All evening, she watched through a small gap in the curtains as groups of children paraded up her driveway in excitement, looking for treats, and then wandered away, disappointed, after the door went unopened.

On November 1st, Janet didn't even bother to get out of bed. She lay drowning under the duvet as the sun moved across the room and then abandoned her, leaving her in darkness once more. She heard Tom come home sometime around 8pm. He called to her, but she didn't call back. He moved quickly through the house, a panic clip to his step. And, eventually, his shape appeared in their bedroom door.

'What are you doing in bed?'

'I was asleep.'

He flicked on the light, sat down next to her, and handed her a photo of a baby girl, maybe seven or eight months old, with sparkling green eyes.

'You want a daughter? Is that what you need to be happy? Well I can get her for you.'

'I don't understand,' Janet said.

'She can be with us before Christmas, but you must promise to do exactly as I say, no questions asked.'

No questions asked. No one ever used that phrase when they were planning to do something legitimate. She looked at Tom, her mind overrun. Who was this child? Who was going to give her to them? Why? What did they want in return? Was this legal? No, of course it wasn't legal. People didn't give babies away without proper paperwork. There were rules, procedures. What was Tom thinking? This was madness.

'But... Tom...I don't know what's going on...but...' The whole thing was wrong, it was very wrong. 'I...ah...' Janet paused grappling for the words. She looked down again at the photo, into the baby's green eyes, entranced. 'I promise,' Janet suddenly heard herself say, her voice barely louder than a whisper.

'What's that love?'

'I promise. I'll do whatever it takes...No questions asked.'

***

Janet had never told anyone that story. Not even Debra, her best friend of twenty years. Debra who had married her college sweetheart at twenty-five, who had got pregnant the first month she and Dave had started trying, who was vice-president at a multi-national and had three kids at home. It was no wonder Debra believed she could just fill out a few forms and someone would give her another child. And they probably would, too. Even at forty, Debra still saw more babies in her future whereas

Janet knew that time, for her, was over.

Janet and Debra were at the entrance to the gift shop now. Inside, weary adults trudged along after overzealous little kids, as the kids gasped and grabbed at the merchandise, releasing all the pent-up energy from a morning spent looking at exciting displays from the other side of thick protective glass.

Debra nudged Janet. 'Our friend from lunch,' she nodded to the man at the cash register. In front of him, he had at least twenty different kinds of dinosaur toys. 'How much do you think they took him for?'

'Three hundred, maybe four hundred dollars?' Janet calculated.

'Poor guy, and he said they were getting only one each. Where are his kids anyway?'

Janet looked around. They weren't in the store. She spotted them in the rotunda outside. There were three now: the two little girls she'd seen in the café and an older one, who looked like a college student. The au pair, maybe? No, that didn't seem right. They looked like family. Perhaps she was an older sister, or a half sister from the Dad's first marriage. Janet couldn't get a good enough look to check for family resemblances. They were standing in a row, with their backs to the store, staring up at the fifty feet Barosaurus, who was rearing up to protect its young from attack.

The older girl was in the middle with the other two standing on either side of her clutching her hand. Janet thought about her own sisters: Jill in Miami and Judy in Chicago. They used to come to the museum once a year when they were kids growing up in Connecticut. But that was decades ago now. Her sisters had left the North East for college and never returned, so they hadn't lived close by one another in nearly twenty years. Yet, Jill was the only person on Earth who could make Janet laugh so hard she'd cry tears the size of grapes. And it had been Judy's counsel, and hers alone, Janet had sought a couple of years ago when she'd started to worry she and Tom were drifting apart—their marriage straining to near breaking point under the stress of parenting a difficult preschooler. For her entire life, or for as much of it as she could remember, Jill and Judy had been there. And they had been so many things to her: protectors and tormentors, confidants and tattletales, sources of envy and objects of pride. She didn't love her sisters because of their shared DNA, but because of the friendship formed while growing up, knocking against one another, conflicting and contrasting, sharing a life together. In many ways, her sisters had made her. Taught her about life in the way no one else could. Kathleen would never have that. She'd never share that kind of bond with anyone. And it was their fault. Janet and Tom couldn't give her a sibling, not even an adopted one.

Suddenly, someone or something jabbed the back of Janet's thigh. She stumbled slightly and turned. It was the man from the café. He was carrying five or six bags in one hand, with the horns of a plastic triceratops poking out from one of them, which must have been what hit Janet.

'Sorry,' he said. 'I'm a klutz.'

Janet gave him a forgiving smile and moved out of the way, letting him pass. She watched him as he walked towards the three girls, who still had their backs to the store. You could tell he was moving slowly, quietly, trying to sneak up on them. He moved towards the oldest daughter. He reached out his arm towards her. She didn't see him behind her. None of his daughters did. Then his hand swung low and he pinched the oldest girl in the butt. She screamed and swung round, red-faced, mouth in an O, eyes narrowed.

Janet suddenly leapt involuntarily. Something cold and scaly was wrapping itself around her neck. She grabbed it and turned to find Debra at the other end of the toy snake, laughing.

'Debs, what are you doing?'

'I was calling you to come check something out and you weren't paying attention, so then I saw this…Oh my God, the look on your face is just priceless.'

Janet's face softened. 'You're a mother of three Debs, you need to start acting your age,' she said with mock severity.

'I couldn't resist. Anyway, what the hell were you staring at?'

'The guy from lunch.' Janet felt a creeping distaste slide down her throat, as she remembered the girl turning, laughing, and immediately kissing him on the mouth. Janet's insides were almost shaking with revulsion. 'He was kissing a girl who was barely half his age.'

'What do you mean a girl?'

'Not a child, a young woman. I didn't get a proper look at her, she was maybe twenty or twenty-one.'

'So, what's the big deal?'

'Well…' Janet turned to the rotunda and looked for them again in the crowd, but they were nowhere to be found. They must have left. Janet didn't know what to say. Her insides still felt like they were crawling with cockroaches, and she couldn't explain why.

CHAPTER EIGHT
EMMA
NEW JERSEY & MANHATTAN
AUGUST 1999

'They were so young, so beautiful; they had their whole lives ahead of them,' said Margaret. 'What a tragedy. That family is cursed, mark my words.' She pointed one of her cerise pink talons at no one in particular. Emma, Larry and Bob remained silent, focusing on their cards.

It was the first Friday of the month, which meant yet another poker night at Bob and Margaret's. It had been a regular event in Emma's calendar since her marriage to Larry four years ago. Listening to them talk about interest rates, mortgages, 401k packages, or which dot-com they had heard was a good investment, it used to feel like she was conducting an anthropological study. "The American middle classes at play." But it had become like a movie she'd watched too many times. She knew their dull script by heart. At least John F Kennedy junior's recent death had provided a new topic, which Margaret had been chewing on for an hour at least.

'Did you see that Armstrong guy won the Tour?' Bob interjected, obviously tired of Margaret's diatribe about the end of Camelot.

'What a comeback,' Larry said. 'Two years ago, they told the guy he had just a 40% chance of living and now look at him. You have to give it to him, that's quite a transformation. It just shows that it's possible to come back from the brink, no matter what.'

Emma smiled at Larry. He gave her a wink in return.

'I don't know, if I beat cancer, the last thing I'd want to do is start a crazy training schedule just to win a race. I'd want to spend more time with Margaret and the kids.'

'Will you listen to him? My sweetheart.' Margaret reached over and tousled Bob's thin hair. 'I agree, I think cycling is so boring. It goes on for days on end.'

Emma was about to respond that that was the very reason she loved the Tour. She admired their stamina. The strength the cyclists needed, both mental and physical, to face those hills, day after day. But before she could speak Margaret said, 'C'mon honey, let's go make some sandwiches before we start the next round. Give these men a chance to talk about sports.'

Margaret was always breaking off their conversations and running to the kitchen the second the chip bowl or someone's glass was empty. It was as if she feared the hostessing Gods might smite her down if she left her guests without snacks for longer than thirty seconds. Emma got up and followed her.

'Can you believe this heat we're having?' Margaret moved around getting out the bread and cold meats. 'They said July was the hottest month on record since the summer of Sam.'

For over a month, the Tri-state area had been suffering unrelenting heat and paralyzing power outages. New York was at breaking point. So was Emma. She hadn't slept in weeks.

'The summer of who?'

'It was 1977. There was a serial killer going round the city killing women, he called himself the Son of Sam. You're probably too young to remember that. Were you even born then?'

'Yeah,' Emma said, and then added, 'I was one.'

'God, I sometimes forget how young you are.' Margaret pinched one of Emma's cheeks.

So do I, Emma thought. She started spreading margarine, mayo and mustard on the bread at the counter, and Margaret took up a position alongside her cutting cheese and cold meats.

'It's so sad what happened to John Junior, don't you think?' She was off again on her pet subject. 'I read in a magazine that he wasn't qualified to fly with just his instruments, but he took off anyway, even though the visibility was bad. That's men for you. They're more impulsive. They're bigger risk takers. It's in their DNA, they can't help it.'

'Is this enough?' Emma asked.

'No, honey, a few more slices please. I think that's why it's far worse when a woman cheats than when a man does.'

'Excuse me?' Emma dropped the butter knife and stared at Margaret. Could Margaret have somehow found out about the drunken one-night-stand she'd had with the Argentinean guy in her class after their final exam? Or their three not so drunken hook-ups since?

'That's why I could never forgive Lisa for cheating on Larry.' Emma let out a small, barely audible gasp of relief. Margaret was talking about Larry's ex-wife. 'Everyone else at the country club welcomed her back with open arms. They all believed the whole story about how she and Don had fallen in love, and there was nothing she could do to stop it. But I never bought it. She knew exactly what she was doing, Don less so. Men are dumb. They're impulsive. They can sleep with a woman without even realizing how they got there because their minds work different. But women aren't like that. Her cheating was pre-meditated and that makes it far worse in my book.'

'You can't honestly believe that when a man cheats it's fine because men are stupid and don't know what they're doing. Of course they know. They don't just shove it into another woman by accident.'

'I'm not saying it's fine. I'm simply saying when a woman cheats it's a far worse crime because the way we think is so different. Men act on impulse. We put thought and emotion into everything we do.'

Emma rolled her eyes and turned back to making the sandwiches. There had been no emotion involved when she had first slept with Ricardo, only lust and a lot of vodka.

'Why don't you take in the sandwiches, and I'll carry the drinks,' said Margaret.

When they resumed play, the first round of cards Emma received was woeful. The sensible thing would be to fold and save her money for the next round. But she didn't feel like doing the sensible thing.

'I'm going all in,' Emma said, shoving all her chips into the center of the table.

'Oh, someone must be confident,' said Margaret, her eyes wide, as if Emma had just announced that she wanted to be the second person to tightrope across the Twin Towers, rather than just having bet the equivalent of fifteen dollars.

'Are you sure you want to do that?' Bob asked with his usual concern.

'Yes,' Emma snapped. Bob would grab any opportunity to lecture her on the rules and what strategy she should be adopting—like he thought she was a moron who couldn't even remember the basics of poker.

'I fold,' Bob said. 'I'm not going up against this little one. I'd feel bad taking all your chips from you if you make a mistake thinking you have a full house when you have nothing at all.'

'This round is far too rich for me.' Margaret threw her cards on the table.

'So, what'll it be?' Emma said to Larry. 'Do you have the guts to take me on?'

Larry studied her face. 'You got nothing. I'll see your bet and call you. Show me what you got.'

Emma laid her cards on the table. All she had was a pair of eights.

Larry smiled as he turned over his cards. A pair of Queens. He scooped up his winnings.

'I knew you were bluffing. You forget, when I see you, I see me. I know what you're up to.' He looked so smug. It was all bullshit. He didn't know her. Not really. Even after four years together he had no idea who she was or what she was capable of.

'I'm going to get a glass of water,' Emma stood up and stalked off into the kitchen.

***

In bed that night, Larry radiated heat, making the air even more suffocating. Emma twisted one way and then the other. She felt like she was being mummified alive. The sheet stuck to her sweaty limbs, sucking the oxygen by osmosis straight from her veins. She shifted again and kicked her legs out of the bed in desperation.

Larry rolled over. 'Can you please try to get some sleep, or at least stop fidgeting?'

'I can't help it, it's too hot.'

'I told you, put on the air conditioning.'

'No, that's worse. I hate the noise of that thing, and then I get too cold.'

'You're too cold or you're too hot. You're never happy, are you?' He flopped around again, so he had his back to her.

Emma stared at the ceiling. There was something rising in her veins. Was it annoyance, frustration, panic? She had no idea. All she knew was she wanted to scream her lungs out, right then and there. Instead, she just sighed loudly, like a bulldog.

She glanced over at the clock. It was only eleven thirty. She wondered what her college friends were doing. Most of them had left New York and gone home for the summer to save up money for grad school or to live rent-free with their folks as they looked for grown-up jobs. Of the handful that had stayed, a few had internships at big banks and others had taken bar jobs for the summer. Either way, they would all be at work right now. They would probably meet at 3am at some late night joint to party, as she lay staring at the ceiling in New Jersey, listening to Larry snoring. She let out another long loud sigh.

'Goddamn it,' Larry slammed his hand on his nightstand and switched on the lamp. 'Do you want to watch a movie? Have a cold shower? Go out for ice cream? Have sex? What will it take to satisfy you? Tell me and we'll do it.' His hair was wiry and standing upright. His eyes were almost black. He looked as exhausted and strung out as she felt.

Emma shrugged. 'I guess we could talk.'

'Ok fine.' Larry plumped his pillows and sat up. 'What shall we talk about?'

'I don't know,' Emma said, and then smiled. 'Maybe John Junior's death?'

Larry laughed. 'What an absolute tragedy,' he said, mocking Margaret's nasal tones.

Emma giggled. 'I thought she was never going to shut up. You would think it was a member of her own family that had died the way she was going on.'

Larry nodded, and with mock sincerity said, 'He was America's son.'

'Why are you friends with them?' Emma asked, without thinking.

'I've told you, they're good people. Plus, they were the only ones that stood by me after Lisa and I split. Beggars can't be choosers.'

'But Lisa was the one that was in the wrong. Why did everyone else take her side?'

'I wasn't exactly a gracious loser.'

'What do you mean?'

'About a week after Lisa left me, I saw her at the club with Don. I'd known for months they had been seeing each other behind my back. But I'd kept my feelings pent up so I could plan, so I could move my money offshore, like I told you, make it look like the business had a few bad years so she couldn't get it in the divorce. Then, seeing them together for the first time, at the club, so brazen, it just set me off, and all that anger that I'd been storing up for months came exploding out.'

'How?'

'I threw a chair at them and called her a life-sucking, two faced, ugly whore.'

'No.'

'It's not something I'm proud of.'

'But still, couldn't your friends have cut you some slack? It's not that bad what you did.'

'Perhaps not, but it was a Saturday afternoon. The clubhouse was packed with families. Rebecca Landau asked me to leave because I was making a scene, and so I turned on her. I told her to get the fuck out of my business and called her a tight assed, busybody cunt. That didn't go down too well with the wives. A woman can fuck her husband's friend for the best part of a year and people will titter about it behind her back, but still welcome her with a smile plastered on their faces when she shows up for lunch at the country club. But a man uses the c-word in front of a few kids and you become a social pariah. Some of the guys tried to maintain contact. But their wives wouldn't have anything to do with me. Margaret was the only one who didn't ban Bob from having me over to the house.'

Emma snuggled up next to Larry. His bare chest was like hot coals next to her cheeks, yet she wanted to be close to him. Why was it that his failings were the most attractive thing about him?

'I'll try to cut Margaret and Bob some slack, even if they are incredibly boring' she murmured. 'But can we please do something fun tomorrow?'

'Sure,' Larry kissed her forehead. 'How about the Guggenheim?'

***

The Guggenheim was Emma's favorite building in all of New York. There was something so reassuringly orderly about its cylindrical shape and pristine white exterior. She usually loved making the pilgrimage up its ramp gallery, which extended from the ground level in a long, continuous spiral along the outer edges of the building, to the skylight at the top.

They stopped for a moment in front of a row of Kandinskys. Emma had always thought of his work as so playful, but today it looked like a disorganized mess, like the product of a crazed, mixed-up mind. There was no uniformity across any of the pictures. Some were painted in pastels, others in strong primary colors, and a few were almost monochrome. Also, the way he mixed the spirals with the geometric shapes seemed random and ill conceived. The black diagonal lines that cut across so many of the paintings looked like daggers, tearing them up, pointing threateningly out at the viewer. It was as if Kandinsky couldn't decide what kind of painter he wanted to be.

'Whimsical, aren't they?' Larry said.

'You think?' Emma shrugged unimpressed.

'Now even Kandinsky can't make you happy? We are in trouble.'

'What's that supposed to mean?'

'Nothing. It was a joke. You keep walking. I need to go to the restroom. I'll catch up with you.'

Emma sauntered up the spiral corridor, past a Japanese tour group and their annoyingly sunny guide. Further up, where it was quieter, she paused to wait for Larry in front of a painting by an Italian woman.

The picture was a swirling matrix of blue lines and shapes, with vaguely bodily forms that generated loose concentric circles, like bloodless figures drowning in a whirlpool. In the center there was a pale space. It looked like a stain of flesh-colored paint had been thrown onto the canvas from a great height. Emma stared at the void in the center of the painting. The image of a woman kept appearing and disappearing. Like she was shifting shape, struggling to find her form. As if the blue surrounding her kept swallowing her up. As if the limbs of the drowning bodies were clawing at her, dragging her down.

The air in Emma's lungs hardened to stone. Her ribs became heavy and sunk deep into her chest making it impossible to breathe. A smile crept onto Emma's face as she let the fantasy take her over. Something or someone was pulling at her, squeezing the life from her. She was falling into a large, dark body of water from which there was no return.

From the edge of her consciousness an arm reached out. A lifeline. But she didn't want to grab it. She wanted to fall further and further into the abyss. She raised her arm and, with all her strength, she shoved her savior away.

'What the fuck?' Larry cried out, stumbling backwards, winded by the blow of Emma's elbow striking his chest.

'Larry, I'm sorry. I didn't realize it was you.'

'Who the hell did you think it was?'

'I don't know. I was lost in my thoughts. You startled me. You shouldn't have been sneaking up on me like that.'

'Sneaking up on you? It's called being affectionate. Jesus Christ.'

Emma folded her arms in front of her. 'There's no need to be making such a big deal of this.'

'What were you thinking about?'

'Huh?'

'You said you were lost in your thoughts. What had got

you so distracted that you mistook me for some attacker?'

'Nothing,' Emma shrugged.

Larry looked at her with deep skepticism. 'Nothing? That's really your answer?'

'I don't know what you expect me to say.'

Larry came towards her and took her by the hand. 'Let's have a seat.' He led her into one of the side galleries and to a bench in the corner. They sat down next to one another, hand in hand.

'You know I fucking love you,' Larry started.

Emma looked him in the eye and nodded. His expression was so serious. Somewhere, deep inside, she started to shake.

'I never want to end up throwing chairs at you and calling you a bitch, but I feel like that's where we're headed. I can see you're dissatisfied with life. I don't know why. I'm not even sure you know why. But we have to do something about this before it pollutes everything we have together.'

'I know. I'm sorry. I'm sure things will get better in the fall when I start law school. It's just, right now…I feel a bit bored. It's just a phase. It'll pass.'

'Are you sure?'

Emma nodded.

'Is this the life you want? Being married to me, living in New Jersey and having the girls every other weekend. Are you happy?'

'I love Meg and Charlotte,' Emma said.

'And they adore you,' said Larry. When the girls arrived at Larry's for their overnight stays they were always so excited to see their "Aunty Emma" as they called her. She both loved and despised those weekends.

Once, Emma had overheard Lisa snidely remark, "It's no wonder the girls like her so much, she's like a big sister to them. After all, she is young enough to be their sister."

That may have been true, but Emma was fully aware that she was also old enough to be their mother. These past few years, Emma had watched Charlotte grow from the chubby toddler in the stroller, chewing on anything she could get her hands on, to a little girl with opinions of her own. Watching Charlotte play, Emma thought often about Kathleen. She wondered how she was turning out and whether she liked the same toys, and TV shows, and food as Charlotte did.

'But is this the life that you want?' Larry pressed again.

Emma felt a strange metallic taste rise up in her mouth. 'I'm confused. I'm not sure what I want.'

'When we got married, everyone kept telling me, "she only married you for the Green Card, she'll leave you eventually, she's too young for you" and I knew they were right. I knew we had an expiration date. So I told myself to simply enjoy it while it lasted. I promised myself I wouldn't make it hard for you when the time came and you wanted to go.'

'Larry, I don't want to go anywhere. We're good together,' Emma's voice was high-pitched and panicked.

'Even good things stop working sometimes.'

'Well, if it's broke, we fix it. Don't we?' She looked at Larry for confirmation. 'Don't we?' she repeated. Larry returned her gaze. His brown eyes were wide and misty. 'No,' Emma threw her arms around him, pulling him close to her, clinging on to him for dear life.

'I don't want to give you a chance to get sick of me. You're twenty-three. You need time and space to figure out who you are. You know it's true.'

Emma buried her head further into Larry's chest, trying to get lost inside of him.

'I don't want to lose you.'

'You won't lose me. You'll always know where to find me. I'm not going anywhere.'

'I'm sorry,' Emma whispered.

Larry lifted her face to his. 'Sorry? Are you kidding me? Jesus, I'm nearly fifty. I've had a young, beautiful, smart wife for four years. That's every guy my age's fantasy. And

I had it. I'm the man! But I never expected it to last. I always knew, one day, the fantasy would end and I'd have to do what everyone else does—find myself a nice divorcee in her late forties, with some snotty teenage children who will, hopefully, disappear off to the other side of the country to college in a couple of years' time. You have nothing to be sorry for.'

'We don't need to decide anything right now, do we?' said Emma.

'No, we don't.'

'Shall we go home and eat ice cream and watch movies in bed?'

Larry kissed her hair. 'Sounds perfect. Let's go. I'm sick of this gallery anyway.'

Emma nodded in agreement. The building that had been conceived as a "monument of the human spirit" had become, for Emma, the mausoleum of her and Larry's lost love.

CHAPTER NINE
JANET
JANUARY 2006

'Please let me in.' Janet rested her head wearily on the cold hardwood of the door.

'Go away.' Kathleen's voice came from the other side. It sounded strange, raspy, probably from so much crying. Janet felt her daughter's despair like a knife in her stomach. She tried the handle again. It was still locked.

Down the hall, Tom emerged from the master bedroom carrying his case.

'How is she?'

Janet gave him a withering look. 'You should've never put that lock on her door.'

'Love, now's not the time.'

'Something else you didn't back me up on.'

'She's twelve, she wanted some privacy.'

'Well she's in there upset and I can't get to her, and it's your fault.'

'Cut me a break would ye? Today of all days.'

Janet turned towards Kathleen's bedroom door again.

'Your father's ready to go.'

There was an unlocking sound and Kathleen flung open the door. Her black hair was pulled back in a messy pony-tail and she looked even paler than usual, except for the red blotches from crying which burned brightly on her forehead and cheeks blending with her pre-teen acne.

It still sometimes astonished Janet seeing how the soft, warm child she used to cuddle and read stories to at night had stretched, taking on sharper edges, longer limbs, and adult teeth. She was still a child, but only just.

Janet reached out her hand to embrace her daughter but Kathleen stepped back and folded her arms. She looked beyond Janet to her father. As if Janet weren't even there.

'Please take me with you.'

'We've been over this,' Janet said. 'You're staying here with me. You have school and…'

'Daddy, please.' Kathleen interrupted. She gave her father a pleading look. 'It's not fair.'

'Sweetheart, I'll be busy. I won't have time to look after you. It'd be better if you stayed here and kept your mom company.'

Janet glared at him. That was not the official line. She couldn't miss school. It would upset her too much. That was what they had agreed to say to her, this morning, when they got the telephone call with the news.

'Why don't we all go then?'

'Because you can't miss class,' said Janet.

'You never liked her. That's the real reason you don't want to go. And you're using me as an excuse.'

Janet gave Tom a look. Feel free to jump in at any time, she thought. He looked away from her glare and down at his watch.

'I really do have to go,' he muttered. He inched towards Kathleen and she shoved her way past Janet and fell into him in a tearful embrace. He hugged her and kissed the top of her head. 'Be a good girl for your mother, promise me.'

Kathleen nodded and he hugged her once more and then extricated himself from her arms and made his way downstairs. As she watched him go, more tears sprung to Kathleen's eyes and she started to tremble. Janet placed a hand on her shoulder for comfort.

'Don't,' Kathleen said, shaking her off. 'I will never forgive you for this.'

She turned on her heel, slammed the door and, before Janet could get to the handle, there was a click and the door was locked shut once more. Janet was, again, on the outside unable to reach her girl.

Janet hurriedly descended the stairs, hoping to catch Tom before he snuck away. She found him on the porch putting on his coat.

'Thanks for the support up there.'

He sighed loudly. 'What have I done now?'

'She said I never liked your mother, you should've stepped in.'

'Come on now. My Ma was never your favorite person.'

'That's not fair. We had our moments, but I always liked her. It was her that didn't like me. She blamed me for us never taking Kathleen to Belfast.'

Janet had once overheard Tom's mother, Doris, on the phone telling someone she thought Janet was too snooty, had too many airs and graces. She thought Janet was ashamed of the wee council house Tom had grown up in, where Doris still lived. Janet was sure Doris had known she was listening. She'd spoken loudly enough to make sure she'd be overheard.

'Well, you didn't want to take her to Belfast.'

'It was a joint decision.'

Tom came closer and took Janet by the hand, stroking it softly as if trying to tame her. 'There's no need to feel guilty.'

Janet yanked her hand back from him. 'I don't.'

'I'm just saying, my Ma got to know Kathleen anyway. Yes, my Ma would have loved having the whole family together but it wasn't to be.'

'You should go. You'll miss your flight,' Janet said.

As she watched Tom load his luggage into the car, Janet recalled the day he told his mother they'd adopted a baby. By then, Kathleen had been with them for nearly four months.

Doris hadn't known about their fertility problems, or the IVF, or their failed attempts to adopt. Tom had never told her anything, even though he used to phone his mother every Sunday and Wednesday without fail. And, without fail, Doris would make some kind of reference to "the pitter patter of tiny feet" during each one of those conversations.

'Just tell her it's not as easy as she thinks. Tell her what the doctor said about your sperm count,' Janet would say when Tom would become gloomy and disconnected after speaking to his mother. What Janet had really meant was: tell her it's not my fault.

Tom would look at her like she was crazy. Like suggesting he confide in his own mother was worse than asking him to run naked through the streets, and he'd take himself off outside to tinker with one of his cars.

So, when Tom had called Doris to announce they'd adopted a fifteen-month-old baby girl, Janet had prepared herself for an onslaught of questions. She thought they'd have to explain why they'd suddenly adopted. Doris, she thought, would demand to know why they couldn't give her a grandchild of her own flesh and blood, just as all Tom's sisters had. But Doris had simply said, "When do I get to meet my new granddaughter?"

Tom had promised he'd take her to Belfast "soon." In the meantime, they'd tried to appease Doris with blurry photos of Kathleen outside with a hat on or taken from a distance at a strange angle. Over time Kathleen's face became longer, less rounded. As the contours of her face revealed themselves, she started to look less and less like the ten month old whose face had been on missing posters all over Belfast. But still Janet worried someone might recognize her if they took her back to Belfast, even for just a short trip.

'We're still adjusting, we don't want to travel with her yet,' they'd say. Or, 'We're remodeling the new house, we can't go anywhere until that's done.' Or, 'She's at the "terrible twos" stage, a long haul flight isn't a good idea. We'll bring her next year, we promise.'

Doris had eventually snapped shortly before Kathleen's third birthday.

'Is there something you aren't telling me son?'

'No Ma, not at all.'

'Is she Chinese or something?'

'No, she's from Texas.'

'I'm sure there are Chinese in Texas.'

'Ma, she's not Chinese, what's got into you?'

'Why won't you let me see her? All I have is a handful of photos you posted me, but they could be of anybody. I'm starting to think she doesn't exist.'

'I told you, things are really busy at work right now,' Tom had said.

'Listen, I don't give two hoots if the wean is black, brown, yellow or purple. She's your daughter now and so she's my granddaughter. I have a right to see her.'

'And you will.'

'Now, if Muhammad will not come to the mountain, then the mountain must go to Muhammad.'

'I think that's the wrong way round.'

'Don't interrupt me. I want you to buy me a ticket to visit you in America so I can meet my youngest grandchild and that's that.'

'I will Ma, after we have the house sorted.'

'No, you will do it today. Or I will pawn every last thing in this house, every piece of jewelry you have given me over the years, until I have enough money and I will buy my own ticket. Do you want me to do that?'

'No, Ma.'

'Then it's settled. I'm coming over.'

Tom had only told Janet about this conversation when his mother was already on the plane. She had thumped him, a hard whack on the chest, almost winding him. He'd reeled back, falling against the kitchen counter.

'How dare you put us in danger like this,' Janet said in a low voice so Kathleen, who was in the family room next door, would not hear.

'She won't recognize her. I promise,' Tom spluttered, still not quite able to breathe properly.

Janet had toyed with the idea of bundling Kathleen into the car, pretending she'd had some family emergency and taking her to Connecticut to her mom's house. But Tom convinced her that would make Doris even more suspicious. And so she'd agreed to stay, and she'd waited nine excruciatingly long hours until Doris walked through their front door with a huge teddy bear in her arms, with Tom following, carrying her case.

And now here was Tom, ready to drive to the airport again. This time it was him making the journey across the Atlantic to Belfast, to see his mother one final time. She'd passed away at a family party the night before, felled by a massive heart attack at the age of seventy-six, surrounded by most of her family, with a wee glass of whisky in her hand.

Janet looked back at the house. She should try to talk to Kathleen again. The poor thing hadn't stopped crying since they'd told her this morning. After that first visit, when Kathleen was nearly three, Doris had returned three, sometimes four, times a year. In the last ten years of her life, this woman who had barely left Ireland for six decades suddenly became a frequent flyer. That was the rejuvenating power of grandchildren, Janet supposed.

Janet waved Tom off and went back inside. In the

kitchen, she made a grilled cheese sandwich and put it on a plate with some potato chips and a couple of cookies. She poured some lemonade and climbed the stairs with the plate and glass in her hands.

'Kathleen, darling, I made you something to eat.'

'I'm not hungry,' Kathleen's voice came from inside the bedroom.

'You have to eat.'

'Go away.'

'You wouldn't have liked it. Remember what your dad said? They'll wake her in her house for three days. They'll keep her body in her bedroom and you'd have to sit next to it, day and night, for three days. That's not how you want to remember her is it, in a coffin?'

'Leave me alone.'

'Not until you come eat something,' Janet sighed.

'If I take the food, will you go away?'

'Yes.'

The door opened and Kathleen stepped out. Janet noticed Kathleen's desk lamp was on and she had her textbooks out.

'What are you doing?' she asked.

'Studying.'

'Darling, you don't have to do homework today. Your teachers will understand.'

'But I want to. From now on I'm going to study really hard and get good grades so I can get into a good college.'

'That's great,' Janet said, slightly bemused. 'Your grandma would be so proud.'

'I want to get a good job when I'm older so I can earn my own money and then I can go wherever I want and you won't be able to stop me. And I'm gonna go to Belfast first to see my cousins and my aunties, and there's nothing you'll be able to do about it.'

Kathleen grabbed the plate and glass from Janet and went back into her room kicking the door shut behind her. Janet stared at the door in shock realizing it was true. One day Kathleen would be old enough to go wherever she wanted, and Janet couldn't stop her, no matter how hard she tried.

CHAPTER TEN
VICTORIA—MANHATTAN
FEBRUARY 2006

Victoria sat in the corner of the lobby trying to estimate how big it was. You could easily fit four basketball courts in here. There was a sleek desk in the corner with five receptionists in black suits, high ponytails, and red lips, almost hidden behind six-foot tall exotic flower arrangements. The vast floor was covered in Italian marble. In the entire area, there was nothing more than a reception desk, a handful of armchairs, and a sculpture made of driftwood. What opulence to have so much empty space right here on Fifth Avenue. Victoria smiled to herself and wondered if Emma worked for Satan, like in the film *"The Devil's Advocate."*

Victoria turned at the sound of high heels coming across the lobby behind her. She recognized Emma immediately, despite the transformation. Gone was the teenage girl in Doc Martin boots and heavy eye make-up, with bitten down nails, that Victoria had said goodbye to twelve years ago. Instead, the woman coming towards her was wearing a tailored suit and bright red heels. Victoria stood up to greet her.

'Oh my God, I can't believe you're really here,' Emma put her hands to her face in delight.

'Me either.'

'I am so sorry I couldn't pick you up at the airport. I got stuck on a conference call. Did the driver find you ok?'

'Yes, you have no idea how important I felt seeing a man with a uniform and a cap holding a sign with my name on it when I came out at arrivals.' Victoria took in the sight of her old friend. 'You look fantastic. I know the polite thing to say after twelve years is that you haven't changed a bit. But, my God, you look so much better than you did the last time I saw you.'

Emma let out a peal of laughter. 'That's exactly the kind of thing you're supposed to say to a woman on the eve of her thirtieth birthday. This is why I needed you here with me, to stop me from wallowing.'

Back at Emma's Chelsea apartment, Victoria wandered around taking in the living room while Emma ordered Chinese food from the phone in the kitchen. Apart from the furniture and a pile of what looked like court documents stacked up on the table, there wasn't much else in the room. There were no photos dotted around, and there was just one painting on the wall, which couldn't possibly be Emma's.

When Emma returned, Victoria pointed at the picture. 'What's that?'

'Don't worry I haven't become a religious fanatic, although my mother is always warning me not to be watching any of those televangelists. She thinks I'll get brainwashed and give them all my money.'

'So what's with the picture?'

'That's Saint Adjutor,' Emma said.

'Who?'

'One day, I was walking past St. Patrick's cathedral and

this was in the gift shop window, along with a sign that said *"Patron Saint of the Drowned"* so…well…I suppose it called to me.'

A shadow fell across Emma's face. For a moment, she looked just like she had as a teenager when Victoria had said goodbye to her on the street all those years ago, sort of empty and somber.

'Will you have a wee glass of champagne? I have a bottle in the fridge,' Emma said, rearranging her features into a smile once again.

'Don't mind if I do,' Victoria followed Emma into the kitchen. She glanced at the phone on the wall. 'Shit,' she muttered. It was nearly midnight at home. Ruben was probably going crazy worrying about her. He'd asked her a hundred times to call him as soon as her flight landed, and that was hours ago. 'Can I make a quick call home? I'll pay for it.'

'Of course, phone away, and there's no need to pay for it. As long as you're here *mi casa* is your *casa*.'

Victoria lifted the receiver and then hung back, watching Emma open and pour the champagne.

'Here.' Emma handed Victoria a glass. 'I'll leave you to it.'

Victoria dialed Ruben's number and waited, biting her lip as the phone rang five then ten times.

'Yes,' Ruben answered, an annoyed clip in his voice.

'Hey, it's me. I'm just calling to let you know I got here ok.'

'Was your flight delayed?'

'No…Well, um, a little bit,' Victoria lied.

'It must have been very delayed. I was expecting your call hours ago. Where are you?'

'I'm at Emma's.' Victoria leaned back against the counter and took a gulp of champagne.

'So you couldn't be bothered to call me from the airport. You'd rather leave me waiting here, worrying about you.'

'I'm sorry. I didn't see a payphone at the airport and there was a driver waiting for me, so I didn't want to delay him by running around looking for a phone.'

'It's late here. I need to get some sleep.'

'I'll call you tomorrow,' Victoria said.

'Whatever, I won't hold my breath. Your promises obviously don't mean anything. Not the ones you make to me anyway.'

'Ruben, I'm sorry.'

'It's fine. I need to go.'

'I love…' Victoria started but, before she could finish, there was a click and he hung up. Victoria replaced the phone on the receiver, took another large gulp of champagne and tried to plaster a smile on her face before stepping into the living room.

Emma was slouched on the sofa reading emails on her blackberry. Victoria went and sat next to her.

'So is Ruben the sculptor you've been seeing?' Emma said, as she tapped out an email.

Victoria nodded.

'Was he in a bad mood or something? You were on the phone for thirty seconds and you must've apologized about ten times.'

'Don't exaggerate,' Victoria said, feeling her cheeks flush red. 'He was just tired.'

'So tell me about him. All you've said is that he teaches sculpture at Belfast Art School. Where's he from again?'

'Istanbul, originally. When he left home at eighteen to study art in Berlin, his parents moved to Israel. He's lived all over. Paris, London…'

'And now he's teaching in Belfast.'

'It's not easy to get full time teaching gigs in the arts. He still does his own sculptures, and his work has been exhibited in lots of different countries. He's actually got an exhibition coming up next month in Edinburgh.'

'And is he a good guy?'

'Yes.'

'Well, that's the main thing. As long as he makes you happy.'

'He does.' Instinctively, Victoria pulled her sleeve down further over her wrist.

'What about your work? Are you still painting?'

'No, not really.'

'Why? You were always brilliant at art.'

Victoria scrunched her nose. 'I got bored of it. By the time I left university, I was sick of all that pretentious art school stuff.'

'You were sick of art school bullshit, so you got a job in an art school? Something doesn't compute,' Emma said.

'It's an admin job. I might as well be working as a dentist's receptionist for all it has to do with art.' Victoria had been working in the admissions department of Belfast Art School for five years now. She spent her days surrounded by papers and forms, reading personal statements from high school students about their grand plans for themselves and all that they would do with their degree in fine arts. Poor things, they had no idea that most people, even art graduates, end up shuffling paper for a living.

'I think it's so sad you don't paint anymore. I always thought that was an integral part of who you were. Even when we were really small, I remember you drawing all the time.'

Victoria hadn't turned her back on art entirely. There were still emotions inside of her that she had to get out, and the only way she knew how to do that was with shape and color and paint. So she had kept creating, quietly, in the corner of her childhood bedroom late at night. Eight years on since graduating and she was still stuck at home with her parents. Recently, she had shown Ruben a series she had been working on. She had taken photos of flowers, trees and people's faces and then blown up a tiny section of the photo and recreated just that single, enlarged detail by layering enamel on aluminum.

'What's that?' Ruben had asked, pointing to one of the paintings.

'It's a stamen from a lily.'

'The male sex organ,' he had said. 'Powerful. So what are you saying with this?'

'Um, I just wanted to show that there's beauty everywhere in the details, but sometimes we miss it. So I wanted to enlarge them in vivid colors, so that people couldn't ignore them anymore.'

He had cast another glance over her work, sniffed and said, 'I suppose it has a certain feminine charm.'

She knew what he really meant. It was fine, pretty even, good enough for someone's living room wall, but not for a gallery. Victoria may have gone to art school, but she was no artist.

'I grew up and realized art wasn't for me,' Victoria now said to Emma. There was no point telling Emma about her home doodles. They were hardly worth mentioning.

Emma lifted her glass to make a toast.

'To old friends,' she said. 'To the girls we were, the women we've become, and the men we've yet to have.'

Victoria smiled. 'I'll drink to that.'

'I'm so glad you're here,' said Emma. 'I normally get really down around my birthday, but not this year. Tomorrow night, you and I are going to hit the bars of New York and have some fun. The men of Manhattan won't know what hit them.' Victoria smiled. It felt good being back together with her old friend. 'Now, tell me all the gossip from home. Do you still see many people from school?'

'Not really, a lot of people have moved away. I did see Aiden at the chip shop a few nights before I left,' Victoria said and then quickly added, 'I didn't tell him I was coming to see you.'

'How did he look?'

'Awful. He's seriously into the drugs these days. He has been for a few years now. The whole estate knows about it. I heard that his uncles locked him up in a farmhouse for a few weeks to force him to quit.'

'Those bastards,' Emma spat. 'They're probably the ones selling the stuff to everyone else, but when it's one of their own that's hooked, it's a different matter.'

Victoria bit her lip, unsure if she should go on with her story.

'And so did it work? Did he get off the drugs?' Emma asked.

'No, as soon as they let him go he was back on them. I see him on the street from time to time around the Falls. He always looks out of it, like a lost soul.'

'He's weak. He always has been.' Emma's face hardened.

'Not everybody is as strong as you. I don't know how you cope with it, with what happened to Kathleen.' Victoria paused, but Emma just stared ahead and didn't speak. So Victoria felt compelled to go on, to say something to fill the silence. 'It must be so hard not knowing where she is, who kidnapped her…'

'It is, of course it is.' Emma interrupted, her tone flat and devoid of feeling. Victoria supposed it was a coping mechanism. Emma must have learned to mute her emotions and reactions to things. What was the other option? Let the loss overwhelm her? Become a broken soul, like Aiden, using drugs as an escape?

Emma picked up her now empty glass. 'I'm going to pour myself another.' She stood up and went into the kitchen. 'So let's plan. Would you like to go to the Met tomorrow?' she called, signaling that all talk of Aiden and Kathleen and the past was finished, at least for now.

CHAPTER ELEVEN
VICTORIA—MANHATTAN
FEBRUARY 2006

The next morning, Victoria stepped out of the shower and reached for the towel Emma had hung on the opposite wall for her. As she ran her hands along its fluffy softness, the door swung open with a thud behind her. She screamed and pulled the towel off the rack, flinging it around her as fast as she could.

'Shit, I'm sorry,' Emma said, rushing back out again, her eyes downcast. 'I thought you were still sleeping.'

'It's my fault. I thought I'd locked the door but obviously not. Sorry. I'll be out soon,' Victoria called through the door.

'Take as long as you need. I'll be in the kitchen.'

Victoria dried and dressed, putting on jeans, a t-shirt and a long-sleeved sweater.

Victoria found Emma at the dining table, a red espresso cup in hand, reading some work papers.

'Do you want some coffee?' Emma said, getting up.

'Don't worry. I'll get it,' Victoria went into the kitchen.

Emma followed and stood in the doorway watching her.

'So what happened?'

'What's that?' Victoria turned around to face her friend.

'Your bruises. Is everything ok with you?'

'Yeah, I'm fine.' Victoria turned away, unable to look Emma in the eye. She opened the fridge and the cool air hit her flushed cheeks like a slap. 'I'm a bit clumsy is all.' Victoria poured the milk into her coffee with shaking hands, spilling some of it on the counter.

'Clumsy is bashing your big toe against the bed. Your body looks like you got into a fight with an octopus. What happened?'

'Nothing.'

'Nothing?'

Victoria concentrated on cleaning up the mess she'd made of the countertop. What could she say to explain the state of her body? She was covered in black, brown and yellow marks. Some were a few weeks' old, others just a few days. Victoria folded the cloth and placed it next to the sink, then turned to face her friend.

'I took up yoga recently, and I'm rubbish at it. I keep falling over, losing my balance trying postures that are too advanced for me. It's so embarrassing.'

'Seriously? You expect me to believe you got all those from yoga?'

'What a klutz right?' Victoria rolled her eyes and forced herself to laugh. Emma's expression didn't change.

'Where do you do yoga?'

'At a gym near work.'

'What kind of yoga is it?'

'I don't know. It's just general. It's Belfast, we only have one kind.'

'What's the name of your teacher?'

'Um,' Victoria grasped for a name but couldn't come up with one.

'C'mon, what's your teacher called?'

Victoria felt the beginnings of a tear form in her eye

and she blinked hard to suppress it.

'Emma, what does it matter?'

'I'm just curious who this teacher is who lets you fall down so much.'

'Well, I can't remember right now. So, are we going to the Met today?' Victoria picked up her coffee and made to leave the kitchen, gently pushing past Emma who was still rooted in the doorway. 'I wouldn't mind going to the Guggenheim, too.'

'I hate the Guggenheim,' Emma said.

'How come?'

'I just do. But why don't you go this morning and then I can meet you at the Met for lunch? They aren't far from one another, and I need to pop into the office this morning for a couple of hours anyway.'

'I thought you'd taken the week off?'

'Yeah, but something has come up. I'll see you at the café at the Met at midday, ok? That'll give you time to get round the Guggenheim.'

'Sure.'

'I'm going to jump in the shower.'

Victoria bit her lip. 'Do you mind if I use the phone again?'

'Go ahead,' Emma walked off down the hallway and, just as she was turning into the bathroom, she muttered to herself, but loud enough for Victoria to hear, 'You wouldn't want to annoy lover boy now would you?'

***

Victoria sat at a table in the middle of the crowded café trying to count all the languages being spoken around her. She had thought she'd heard a family wander past speaking Turkish. She smiled remembering the first time Ruben had taught her anything in Turkish. They had been in bed one Sunday morning when he started saying a phrase over and over again, asking her to repeat it. If she said it to his satisfaction, he'd kiss her. First on the neck, then the chest, then down on her tummy. If she said it incorrectly, he'd tickle her until she shrieked with laughter. The words, which started with an "s" and then ended with a rounded "m" sound, felt soft and sweet in her mouth.

'Are you going to tell me what I'm saying?' she had asked as he reached her panty line.

'You are saying I love you, I love you, I love you,' he had said, pausing after each one to kiss her on the belly.

It was a good memory, but an old one. The kind, tender Ruben she had first met had been buried, recently, under the pressure of his upcoming show. It was his first solo exhibition in over five years, his comeback to the art world, possibly his last shot at making a name for himself. It was no wonder he was so tightly wound these days. Things would return to normal between them as soon as it was over.

Victoria glanced up and saw Emma making her way through the crowd, straight backed and walking with such purpose that the sea of tourists parted ways at the mere sight of her. It didn't matter if it was one of the world's most famous art galleries, or a bleak Belfast housing estate, Emma McCourt always dominated her surroundings with ease. When they were kids, Emma used to lead them on expeditions to nearby parks and rivers, forging ahead as Victoria and the others had hung back worrying about whether they should be so far from home.

Emma sat down opposite Victoria, shaking off her coat.

'How was your morning?' she asked.

'I loved the Guggenheim,' said Victoria. 'I've never been to a museum quite like it. The building is a work of art in itself. I don't understand how you can't love it.'

Emma didn't respond. She was too busy fishing in her handbag for something.

'Here they are.' She threw a bunch of documents, forms and brochures on the table.

'What's all this?'

'I went to see an old law school friend this morning

who specializes in immigration law. He said you can get a student visa quite easily if you're accepted to a government approved school. Here's the New York list. I've highlighted in yellow all the ones that have art programs. I called around, and one of them has a diploma program that has open enrollment. So you could join that now, with a view to joining their master's program in September.'

'Emma, slow down, what are you talking about?'

'You see, once you finish your studies, if you've been here as a student, it's much easier for companies to hire you because you can convert your student visa to a working visa. One of my clients is the director of an ad agency. I spoke to him, too. He's happy to meet you. He might be able to offer you an internship whilst you're studying, so you can get some experience.'

'Are you mad? I can't just stay in America.'

'I know you only have a week's worth of clothes with you. But your mother can ship your stuff out to you and, in the meantime, you can borrow anything of mine.'

Victoria stared at Emma for a moment, the sound of the tourists' chatter around them now a faded background murmur. Emma couldn't possibly believe what she was saying, could she?

'Em, clothes are the last of my worries. I have a job…'

'That you hate.'

'I don't hate it. I'm just a bit bored.'

'That's reason enough.'

'It's not just work. I can't afford to study in New York.'

'Of course you can. We can turn the living room into a bedroom and you can live with me rent-free. And if you need help with living expenses or school fees, well I can take out a loan.'

'Em, that's very sweet. But it's not just the money. I have a life in Belfast. I have a boyfriend and…'

'A boyfriend that beats you up.'

Victoria dropped the papers in her hand.

'What?'

'V, you and I both know that you didn't get those bruises from yoga,' Emma said. 'You look like someone's punch bag, and Ruben is the obvious suspect. It's him isn't it? It's always the boyfriend.'

'It must look worse than it is.' Victoria tugged her sleeves down over her hands.

'V…'

'That's it! I'm definitely giving up the gym. What's the point of going to all that effort to try to tone up if you end up with ugly marks in the process?' Victoria shifted in her seat as Emma stared at her impassively. 'Shall I go order and you save the table?' Victoria said after a moment.

'Sure, but before you do, just tell me one thing.'

'What?'

Emma reached across the table for Victoria's arm, grabbing her tightly by the wrist.

'Hey,' Victoria tried to yank her arm free but Emma held on firm, using her other hand to push up Victoria's sleeve.

'What's that?' Emma pointed to the vertical row of small black bruises on Victoria's upper arm.

'Let me go,' Victoria pleaded trying not to raise her voice. People around them were starting to stare.

'Those marks are from someone's fingers. Someone obviously grabbed you so tight they hurt you.'

'You're hurting me.' Victoria yanked her hand back and Emma released her, the force of the movement sending Victoria flying back in her chair.

'I'm sorry,' Emma said. 'But you're only here for a week. I don't have time to be pussyfooting around. I need you to be honest with me. I can't help you if you won't even recognize that you have a problem.'

Victoria pulled down her sleeve and fussed around smoothing out her jumper. She didn't look up at Emma, but she could feel, nonetheless, Emma's cynical look.

'I know it looks bad,' Victoria started uncertainly, still not knowing how she was going to vocalize all that had gone on between her and Ruben recently. 'But it's not what you think. He doesn't beat me up.'

'He doesn't?'

'No. It's just…we get into these intense fights…we both get carried away.'

'So he's covered in bruises as well, is he?'

'No. Of course not. But just because I'm not punching him back doesn't mean that I'm blameless. I provoke him.'

'Nothing you might have said or done gives him the right to do that to you.'

'I know that. The thing is…he's got an artistic temperament, which is great…but…'

'You're an artistic person, too, but you don't go round hitting him.'

'He's a real artist.'

'So are you.'

'I mean he's very passionate, but also very insecure and vulnerable. I often forget just how much, and I say stupid things, or I neglect him, and so he lashes out. But he doesn't mean to. He knows he has to change, and I can help him do that.'

'Oh my God,' Emma put her head in her hands. 'Can you hear yourself? The last time I saw you, you were eighteen, you'd just been accepted to a prestigious art school, you had so much hope and ambition. What happened to that girl?'

'She grew up. She learned that everything isn't black and white, that human relationships are complicated.'

Emma let out a long sigh. 'It's actually very simple. He beats you up and that's wrong, and the longer you stay with him, the worse it will get. You're in danger, and I won't stand by and do nothing.'

'Em, don't be so melodramatic. It's just a few bruises. He's not a bad person. He doesn't hurt me on purpose. He's really stressed these days. Things will get better soon.'

Emma rolled her eyes in disgust.

How could Emma possibly understand? She didn't

even know Ruben. She didn't know the bullying he'd suffered as a child or the way his parents had rejected him when he told them he wanted to be an artist. In those first months of dating, he had really opened up to Victoria. He said he had told her things he had never told another living soul. He could be sullen and withdrawn, from time to time, but he could also be incredibly tender and loving. He was a brilliant, difficult man and, most of the time, she felt lucky to have him.

How could she make Emma understand that, over the past few years, there had been more good times than bad? His moods were sporadic. Their arguments were exceptional rather than everyday. He made her laugh more often than he made her cry. He still made her feel safe when walking home on dark nights from the bus stop, his arm wrapped around her. They still had long debates about art and still enjoyed discovering new corners of Northern Ireland together. She wasn't the fool Emma obviously thought she was.

Tears started to pinch Victoria's eyes. She hung her head low so the other diners wouldn't see her cry, so she wouldn't have to face Emma's cold stare.

'Emma, can we please drop it?'

'I promise to change the subject if you'll answer me one question.'

'What?'

'When you fell off your bike three or four months ago and broke your arm, is that really what happened? Or did he do that?'

'It was an accident.'

'A bike accident?'

Victoria shook her head.

'So Ruben broke your arm?'

'He didn't mean it. I was on the floor crying. We'd been arguing. He just meant to stomp the floor next to me, to get some of his rage out. He didn't mean to break my arm. It was an accident.' Victoria's voice was no louder than a whisper. This was the first time she had admitted to anyone, out loud, the truth of what had happened, and as the words tumbled haltingly from her mouth, a sickening cloud of shame engulfed her.

'Oh V, how can I make you see that this isn't right?'

'You said you'd drop it.' Victoria gave Emma a pleading look.

'You're right, I did. This is my final word. Imagine if you had a daughter and this was happening to her. What would you say to her? Wouldn't you do everything in your power to get her away from the guy? Just think about it.' Emma started to gather up the papers from the table. 'Here, put these in your handbag. You might change your mind.'

'I won't.'

'Just humor me, please?'

Victoria took the papers and shoved them into her handbag. Anything to move this awful, shameful conversation to a close.

***

The following Saturday, Victoria was standing in Emma's living room packing, as Emma prowled around, becoming more agitated with each item of clothing that Victoria folded into her suitcase.

'Please don't go,' Emma said for the hundredth time that day.

'We've been through this,' Victoria said with exhaustion. Despite everything, they had had a nice week together. But every day, without fail, Emma had spent at least an hour trying to persuade Victoria not to return to Belfast. She had tried every tactic: pleading, cajoling, rational arguing, plain old arguing, and emotional blackmail, sapping Victoria's energy and very nearly wearing her down more than once.

'You're kidding yourself if you think he's going to suddenly stop.'

'I love him. I have to give him the opportunity to

change. But this week with you has helped. I'm going to put my foot down more when I go back, let him know that getting physical is unacceptable.'

'No, confronting him won't change a thing,' Emma's eyes were wide with panic.

'I promise, if things haven't gotten better in six months' time, I'll walk away,' Victoria tried to reassure her.

'Six months? That's way too long. Do you know how much damage he could do to you in that time?'

'It's just a few bruises. I keep telling you, it's worse than it looks.'

'What if something awful happens? I could never forgive myself knowing I could have prevented it.'

Victoria straightened up to face Emma.

'First of all, something awful is not going to happen. And secondly, you should have no regrets. I know everything you've said and done this week was because you love me. You tried your best, but I have to go home. I want to go home.'

'I can't let you do this.'

'Well it isn't your decision.' Victoria pressed down hard on her suitcase and pulled the zipper shut. 'Can you call me a cab please? I'm already running late.'

'No.'

'Emma, I have a flight to catch.'

'I'm not letting you go.'

'What? You're going to kidnap me?'

'If I have to.'

'For God's sake,' Victoria lifted up her suitcase and started making her way towards the door. 'I'll flag a taxi on the street.' Emma pushed past Victoria and reached the door before her, taking up a position in front of it, blocking Victoria from leaving. 'This isn't funny. I need to get to the airport. I'm already running late.'

Emma folded her arms and didn't budge.

'Get out of my way.'

'No.'

Victoria dropped her suitcase and tried to reach around Emma to the door handle, but she stood firm, blocking the way.

The seconds ticked by as the two stood staring at each other in silence.

'You can't keep me here,' Victoria said.

'It's for your own good.'

'Stop messing around and let me go.' Emma didn't flinch. Victoria stared at her, trying to figure out the right words to break this impasse. Even if Emma did get out of the way, how long would it take to flag a cab? Victoria had no idea. She was so late. Panic started to rise up in her veins. 'Please move.'

Finally, Emma stepped out of the way. Victoria sighed and picked up her suitcase, ready to leave.

'I'm begging you, please don't go back there.'

'I'll be fine. I'll call you when I get to Belfast.' Victoria turned to go.

'Kathleen wasn't kidnapped,' Emma shouted after her.

Victoria froze in the doorway. She turned around to face her friend. 'What did you say?'

'Kathleen wasn't kidnapped. I sold her and made it look like a kidnapping.'

'What are you saying? That's crazy...I don't understand...how...why?'

'Geary helped me. He drugged Aiden and staged a break-in while Aiden was asleep and I was at work. They gave us thousands of pounds for her.'

'Who did?'

'An American couple. I don't know who they were.'

Victoria examined Emma's pale face and round, hollow eyes.

'Sit down for a minute, I'll tell you everything.' Emma went and sat on the sofa, her arms hugging her body, her eyes staring up at Victoria waiting for her next move.

Victoria looked at her watch. Was this some kind of sick trick? She looked at Emma, crumpled on the sofa. She looked as if she, too, were in shock by what she had just confessed. Then something inside of Victoria clicked. A memory. An unresolved doubt. A question that had only ever existed at a subconscious level, but had now been pulled to the surface. An image of Emma, in the days after Kathleen's disappearance, came to Victoria's mind. She had been so intensely silent. She had walked around with a tissue dabbing it at her eyes, but she hadn't really cried. Victoria had always thought it was because Emma had been shell-shocked, or because she had refused to give in to the grief—that she had been clinging to the belief that Kathleen would be found. But, perhaps, there had been another reason.

Victoria recalled the night a few months after the kidnapping when she and Emma had to carry Aiden home from the pub. He'd collapsed in the hallway at the sight of Kathleen's wee coat hanging next to his by the door. Victoria could still recall how Emma had stepped over him, like he was a piece of gum stuck to the ground. And she'd gone to pour herself a whisky rather than comfort him.

'You're serious,' Victoria whispered, dropping her suitcase to the floor. 'But your mother, Aiden, his parents, they were all destroyed by losing Kathleen. None of them have been the same since. How could you?'

'I had to.'

'Why?'

'Please just sit down. I've never told anyone this, but it's time, and you're the only person I trust.'

Victoria closed the apartment door, and Emma drew in a deep breath and began to talk.

It was another three hours before Victoria became aware of anything else in the world other than the sound of her friend's voice. By then, it was too late to catch her flight.

CHAPTER TWELVE
EMMA—NEW JERSEY
AUGUST 2008

Emma awoke with a start. She got out of bed, grabbed a t-shirt from the floor and pulled it over her naked body. It had been lying in the direct sunlight, and it felt warm against her skin.

Larry lay on his belly on top of the covers, naked in the afternoon sun, softly snoring.

She poked him, and he opened one eye. 'You're voracious girl. Let a man get some rest.'

'Larry, wake up, we need to talk.'

He rolled around onto his back and propped himself up on the pillows.

'What if I don't want to talk?'

'Then just listen.'

'Really? Do I have to? I have a horrible feeling I'm not going to like what I'm about to hear.' He stretched his hand out towards her. 'C'mon, let's just sleep. Whatever it is, it can wait.'

Sitting on the edge of the bed, she turned her back to him so as not to see the look in his eye when she told him. 'It can't wait. I'm getting married.'

'So Golden Boy finally popped the question?'

'Yesterday,' Emma said without emotion, looking towards the window.

'Did he get you a ring?'

'It's in my handbag.'

'When's the wedding?'

'We haven't set a date yet.'

'Are you happy?'

'Yes, of course.'

'Then I'm happy for you.'

She twisted round to look at him. 'Are you? Are you really?'

'No, of course not. But what else am I supposed to say?'

Emma turned away again and stared glumly ahead of her. On the wall, there was a picture of Larry and Meg at Meg's High School Graduation. Emma hadn't seen the girls since she and Larry had separated nine years ago. They had been just children, back then. But Meg was now the same age Emma had been when she had married Larry.

Emma thought back to herself at that age. Living in the US illegally, working two jobs and sharing a crowded, dirty flat with a bunch of borderline alcoholic Irish lads. And yet back then, Emma would have punched anyone who had dared suggest she was a damsel in distress. At nineteen, her youthful pride would never have allowed her to accept a savior. Which may have been why fate had sent her a knight, not in shining armor, but, like a reverse Trojan horse, hidden inside a forty-something divorcee with a potbelly and a receding hairline.

'Can I ask a question?' Larry said.

'Sure.'

'If you're so blissfully happy about getting engaged, then why do I feel like I should run around the house and hide all the sharp objects?'

The reality of the situation suddenly slammed into Emma.

'Because this is the last time I'm ever going to see you.'

'What?' Larry jumped out of bed and pulled on his boxers. He came and hunkered on the floor in front of her. 'Just because you're getting married doesn't mean we can't be friends.'

Emma let her forehead fall to meet his. 'Larry, you and I can't ever be *just* friends. Look what lunch led to.'

'I know, my sheer animal magnetism is too much for you. But couldn't you try to control yourself?' He gave her a weak smile. Emma extracted herself from his grip and sat back on the bed, hugging a pillow in front of her.

'This isn't a joke. I love Daniel, I do.'

Victoria's voice came into Emma's head. "I know you only see Larry a few times a year but every time you do you wind up in bed together. How can you be 100% in your marriage if you always have Larry there distracting you?"

Emma knew Victoria was right. She had always been wise—even when they were kids growing up in Belfast, Victoria had been the voice of reason cautioning Emma about the risks of playing truant or smoking in the school toilets. Emma knew what she had to say next. She and Victoria had practiced this speech together all morning. Yet, despite all the rehearsing, the words still trembled, unconvincingly, as they left her lips. 'Now that Daniel and I are engaged, you and I can't do this anymore.'

Emma stared at Larry, silently willing him to fight, to say something, anything, to convince her she was wrong, that they could still be friends, that she didn't need to cut him out of her life. But he simply sat where he was, hunkered on the ground, letting a resigned sadness fill the space between them. Inside she screamed at him. But on the outside she remained straight-faced as she pushed her way past him and started to gather up her clothes from the floor and get dressed.

Half an hour later at the front door, Larry pulled Emma into a tight embrace, and she allowed herself to melt into his familiar softness one last time.

'I feel worse today than I did nine years ago when I watched you walk out that door with your suitcase and boxes,' he said. 'And that time you took the *George Foreman* grill, which was the only thing I knew how to use in the kitchen.'

Emma smiled. 'What are you complaining about? I left you the toaster.'

'God how I missed you when you left. This place was never the same after you moved out. There were no dirty teacups dotted around the floor, no chocolate stains on the bed clothes, no crazy girl talking to herself in the bathroom. Do you still do that? Have entire conversations with yourself?'

Emma shrugged. 'I try not to. I never realized you were eavesdropping.'

'I wasn't. I always went to the kitchen so I couldn't listen in. I knew it wasn't any of my business.'

Emma dropped her forehead to his chest.

'Do you remember the song I played for you the day you left?' he asked.

Emma looked up at him again. 'Dolly Parton's "*I will always love you*"—how could I forget?'

'And what did I say?'

'You said you'd put that song on to remind me of how bad your taste in music was, so I'd have no regrets about leaving.'

'Well nothing has changed. I still have woeful taste in music.' Larry stepped back slightly, he raised his hands so that they were cupping her face and lifted it up, so she had no option but to meet his gaze. 'Tell me, in all these years that we've been divorced, was there a moment I was supposed to have seized?'

Emma wondered if this was their moment. But she did

not say anything. Instead, she kissed Larry on the cheek and looked, for one final time, into his kind, honey-colored eyes, trying to commit to memory each fleck of light in his irises and every laughter line around them. She would leave here today and she would become the kind of woman Daniel deserved as a wife—someone kind and organized and honest and good. Someone new. Someone without ghosts. Someone who wasn't tainted by the past. It was possible. She had to believe it was possible. And so she turned and, using every single shred of her strength, walked out the door and away from Larry.

CHAPTER THIRTEEN
CAITLIN—MANHATTAN
MAY 2012

Caitlin surveyed the crowd of drinkers in office attire splayed out on squishy armchairs and sofas all around the bar. The thirty or so agency paralegals that had also just joined the firm were gathered in groups of three or four chatting with the lawyers working on the case. Caitlin was next to the drinks table talking to one of the senior lawyers, the Irish one, when she heard a man come up behind her.

'Ugh what is this female obsession with white wine? Get me a bottle of red, a whole bottle.'

'Caitlin, let me apologize for Michael. He has no manners at all,' the female lawyer said. 'You're giving us Irish a bad name. What are you doing here anyway?'

'I'm on your case now. Steve called me into his office earlier and gave me a big spiel about how he needed a junior partner on the case and what a great favor he was doing choosing me. Kathy said you were taking the troops out for happy hour so I thought I'd come join.'

'That's fantastic. I've been saying for ages that we needed a bigger team.'

'It's not great for me. He just wants a junior partner to deal with the bills and document production. He'll take all the glory when it comes to the hearing. What you associates fail to realize is that it doesn't get any easier when you make partner, you still get shit upon.'

'Yes, but the reward at the end of the month is worth it.'

'Oh shut up, it's not like we're paying you a pittance. Who is that dress? Ralph Lauren?'

'Who are you wearing? I like it. If the law doesn't work out you have a career in hard-hitting journalism on E-News,' the female lawyer said with a smile.

Caitlin stood by sipping her wine and watching them spar. It was almost as if they had forgotten she was there. She started to wonder if the etiquette in these situations was to excuse yourself and let the "grown-ups" talk. She was about to say she was going to the bathroom when Michael turned to her.

'So are you one of the new junior associates that has just joined us?'

The other lawyer pounced in before Caitlin could respond. 'No. She's one of the temporary paralegals we hired for the document review. Be nice, it's her first time working at a law firm.'

'Now I feel bad. I've probably put you off a lifelong dream of becoming an attorney. Don't listen to us. We're old and jaded. Well, she is anyway.'

'Hey.' The female lawyer thumped him on the arm.

'No, don't worry, you haven't put me off,' Caitlin said. 'I have no aspirations of becoming a lawyer. I'm just temping for the money.'

Caitlin was just finishing her freshman year at NYU. She had taken this temp job to save up for a trip later in the summer. She still didn't have a clear plan of what she was going to do. She felt like she should maybe learn a new language or volunteer—perhaps work in an orphanage or clean up the rain forest. But, deep down, all she really wanted to do was go to Europe, to Italy or France, and wander around beautiful plazas, drinking wine in the sun, and talking literature and philosophy with handsome European men, like in a Woody Allen movie. And most of all, she wanted to visit Ireland, again. That would be her last stop on the trip and the best of all.

'Listen, I should mingle with the team,' the female lawyer picked up the wine and topped up Caitlin's glass before she went. 'Don't let him bully you!' she said with a smile before wandering off.

'So what are you studying?' Michael asked.

'Political Science.'

'And what do you plan to do with that?'

'Something in international relations maybe.'

'When I was your age, I wanted to work in public international law. I even did a summer interning at The Hague.'

'Really? What did you do there?'

Caitlin tried to look serious and attentive as he talked about the International Criminal Tribunal for Rwanda. His voice was strong and masculine, but it also had a disarming softness to it. The way he spoke was both measured and melodic. Inside, she rolled her eyes at the cliché of it all…American girl swoons over man with an Irish accent.

'Would ye take a look at that,' Michael said, suddenly changing the subject. Caitlin followed his eyes to the door. A young woman was stumbling out on to the street, accompanied by a more sober male colleague. 'Sure it'd be like playing pool with a piece of rope.'

'Does that kind of thing happen often at happy hour?'

'That? God no. She's from our London office, just over on a short secondment.' Michael leaned in closer, as if he was telling her a secret. 'You see, over there, it's frowned upon if you don't drink heavily at office events. The English oscillate between extreme intimacy whilst inebriated and then over the top formality the rest of the time. On Friday nights, they are all confessional and hugging each other, but, if you mention anything personal during office hours, there's a risk they'll jump out a tenth floor window just to avoid having to respond. Here, it's the opposite; people are all about displaying the family photos on the office wall and asking how the kids are. But, if you order a glass of wine over a business lunch, they think you're an alcoholic.'

'And what are the Irish like?' Caitlin asked.

'Us? Sure we're dry as a bone. Isn't that what we're known for? Our sobriety?' He downed the rest of his drink in one swoop and then looked at her, his face breaking into a smile. 'Another?'

As he filled up her glass, Caitlin noticed a wedding ring on his left hand. Strangely, her good mood fell, just a notch, at the sight of it.

'And is your wife Irish or did you meet here?'

He looked at her, momentarily silent.

'My wife? What makes you think I have a wife?'

Caitlin's stomach sank. He could be a widower for all she knew.

'I just thought...'

'This?' He lifted up his hand. 'What makes you think this is a wedding ring? Maybe I just like jewelry.'

'It looks a lot like a wedding ring.'

'Maybe here, but in my country the men wear the rings on this hand to show they're available, and then when they get married, they swap it over.'

'I've never heard of that tradition.'

'You haven't?'

'No, and I've been to Ireland.'

'Well, you obviously didn't pay much attention when you were there. Look it up. It's an Irish custom, I'm serious.' He was probably kidding, but Caitlin couldn't be one hundred percent sure, and she didn't want to sound like some idiot who knew nothing about other cultures.

'You know I read a paper recently on bias in the International Court of Justice,' she said.

'Did you now?'

'Yes, it said judges tend to favor the states that appoint them, and they also favor states whose wealth level is close to that of their own. Was that your experience?' That should show him she was no dummy.

'Impartiality is a concern,' he said, and he started talking about proposals being considered when he worked at the Court to change the nomination process for the Justices. Within a couple of minutes, two of the junior associates joined them, obviously eager to schmooze with a partner, and they sort of edged her out of the conversation, so she mumbled her excuses and headed out.

***

A few days later, Michael emailed asking her to run a search on the database for a specific category of documents. And when he came to her desk to collect them, he asked her to go with him to meet a professor at the Rockefeller University. The professor was acting as an expert witness on the case. Michael said he needed someone who was familiar with the documents to help fish them out of the files while he interviewed the professor.

In the town car on the way to the University, Michael kept his head buried in his notes and only spoke to Caitlin to check if they had certain documents with them.

At the meeting, Caitlin tried her best to follow the discussion. It was something about biomedical software, and whether the other side had given the client clear enough requirements to know what kind of computer system to build. Most of the time, it seemed like the professor was speaking in another language, and Caitlin was astonished Michael was able to keep up. Indeed, any observer would think, from the way Michael so confidently threw the technical language around, that he was one of the professor's colleagues. It was hard to believe he'd been cramming for the interview, just an hour ago, during the drive across town.

Afterwards, when they got back into the car, Michael looked far more relaxed than he had on the journey there.

'Jesus, that was a tough one,' he said.

'Why?' Caitlin asked.

'I couldn't follow half of what he was saying.'

'Really?' Caitlin was surprised. 'It didn't look that way.'

'It's called acting,' he said. 'It's the first thing they teach you at law school. None of us lawyers are as we first appear.'

Caitlin stole a glance at his profile as he stared out the window. He did have the face of an actor. Not the boyish sort from modern day cinema, but the kind from old Hollywood, chiseled, with just enough wrinkles carefully etched into it to give him the look of an experienced man.

'What time is it?' Michael asked.

'Nearly four.'

'Fancy playing hooky?'

Before she could respond, he leaned forward to the driver and told him to turn off at the next right.

'Won't Kathy expect me back?'

'No, I'll email my assistant and let her know we're taking longer with the professor than expected. She'll tell Kathy, don't worry.'

'Where are we going?' Caitlin asked, still unsure if she should be going along with this.

'The Pierre Hotel. It's not far from here, and the bartender there is amazing.'

At the hotel, Caitlin followed Michael through the lobby and into the dark art deco style lounge. He sat down on a stool by the bar and she joined him.

'What'll ye have?'

'A screwdriver?' It was the first cocktail that came to mind. Silently, she prayed for the bartender not to card her.

'I think we can do better than that.' Michael turned to the bartender. 'She'll have a Vieux Carré and I'll have an

Old Fashioned.'

'What's a View…' unsure how to pronounce it, her voice trailed off.

'It's whiskey, cognac, vermouth and Benedictine liqueur.'

'Sounds strong.'

'It might sound like a bit much, but the way this man makes it, it's perfection.'

Wordless, almost breathless, they watched the bartender perform—spinning golden liquids in front of their eyes, swirling ice, tossing things from one glass to the other. Until, eventually, they both had insanely fancy cocktails in front of them, and the bartender left them alone.

'Now,' Michael said, turning his stool towards her so his entire body was facing her. 'To what shall we toast?'

Caitlin picked up her glass gingerly, taking care not to spill her drink. She held it up to her face. Even just the smell of it was intoxicating.

'To new experiences?'

'To new experiences with new friends,' he said, and they clinked glasses and smiled at each other.

'So with a name like Caitlin, and being from Boston, I suppose you have some Irish in you.'

'That's right, my Dad's from Belfast.' There was actually something about Michael that reminded Caitlin of her father. She couldn't quite put her finger on what it was. It wasn't the accent. Michael's Cork brogue was far less intimidating than her father's Belfast bark. It was something else.

'You're Dad's Irish? I knew there was a reason you and I clicked. Have you ever been back to the old country?'

'Yes, a few years ago we went to Dublin and then we drove across to Galway and up to Sligo.'

'And what did you think of our Emerald Isle?'

Caitlin thought back to the trip. She had been nearly seventeen at the time, but her mother had refused to let her out of her sight. In fact, her mom had been on edge the entire vacation. Caitlin had pleaded with her parents to go to Belfast to visit her grand-mom's grave and see her cousins, but her mom kept insisting they couldn't squeeze it in. Even though there was plenty of time for tedious literary tours, which Caitlin had absolutely hated. To make it worse, every five minutes her mom would quote a line from some long dead Irish poet, which got to be really annoying. Caitlin hated poetry.

'I loved it,' she said. 'We spent a lot of time in Yeats country. It was amazing to see the poetry really come to life.'

'You like Yeats do you? You know he's the one who said "there are only two topics worth thinking about; sex and death" what do you think of that?' Caitlin shrugged, trying to look casual, and took a sip of her cocktail. 'I agree with half of it,' Michael went on. 'I've never understood this Irish obsession with death. I'd much rather dedicate all my time to thinking about sex, wouldn't you?'

Caitlin blushed. This was inappropriate. She should steer the conversation in a different direction, she thought.

'Have you had a chance to travel round the US much since you've been here?'

'Not since I've been living here, no. Work and family don't leave much time for fun,' he sighed. 'But I did go round the States one summer, when I was in my twenties, on a motorcycle. Those were fine times.' He stared into his glass with a faraway look. 'Come to think of it, that's over fifteen years ago now. How time flies.'

'Did you go to college here?'

'No, I went to Trinity in Dublin, and after that I worked for a couple of years in Japan as an English teacher. Then I did a 5,000-mile motorbike trip around Europe for a few months, ticking off countries on a daily basis, as you do. After that, I decided it was time to get myself a career, so I moved to London to do a postgraduate degree and train as a lawyer. In the summer between law school and starting work I traveled around the US on my bike. Since joining the firm, I've spent six-months in Amsterdam, and a couple of years in Dubai and Hong Kong, with stints in London in between, and then they sent me here. I think there's an element of gypsy in me. I enjoy bouncing around from place to place. What about you? Do you suffer from the same itchy feet as I do?'

'I suppose.'

'And have you managed to see much of the world?'

'I've traveled all over the US. I mean, it is basically an entire continent,' Caitlin said. She wasn't exactly being truthful. She had been on family holidays to Florida, San Francisco and Chicago. But most summers she had spent at the family beach house in Cape Cod. She was still missing forty something states. Michael nodded at her with a smug smile, and she realized he probably wouldn't be that impressed by her having just seen her own country, so she added quickly, 'I've been around the Caribbean Islands too,' remembering the cruise she'd taken with her high school boyfriend and his family.

'That's grand, and sure you have the whole of your twenties ahead of you to see the rest of the world. And the rest of the continent. America is more than just the US you know.'

'I'm aware of that.' Caitlin shot him an angry look and took a sip of her drink. He might be a bit better traveled than her, but he hadn't seen the whole world either. 'Where do you think you'll go next, after New York?'

Michael laughed and signaled to the barman to serve them two more drinks.

'I'm afraid my wandering days are over. I met my wife in London. She's a lawyer too, or she was. She gave it up when our daughter was born. She wants us to go back in a year or two, when Naomi's old enough to start school. She wants us to stay there, settle down, bring up our children in England, so that's that.'

'Children?' Caitlin had only seen one child in the photos in his office.

'She wants to try for a second baby soon. I personally don't see the point. Don't get me wrong. Being a parent is great. Naomi is the fucking love of my life. But I'm over the whole baby thing. Naomi is only just starting to sleep through the night. Even then, some nights are touch and go. Why would we want to put ourselves through another few years of night feeds and nappies and teething? My wife seems to miss having something completely dependent on her. Whereas I'm the opposite, I say enjoy the child we have and thank God those tough years are behind us.'

Caitlin didn't know what to say in response. It was kind of strange imagining Michael with a home life. She couldn't picture him padding around in the middle of the night in his pajamas, with his hair messed and a screaming baby in his arms. To Caitlin, Michael existed only in sharp suits within the office, a domain he dominated with ease.

'Here, are those from Ireland?' He reached up and moved her hair back to look at her *claddagh* earrings. She felt his hand linger, momentarily, on her neck before he dropped it back down again.

'Yes, I got them in Galway.'

'And how was Galway?'

'Good,' Caitlin squeaked. She was still reeling from the physical contact a moment ago. 'We, ugh, we were there for the arts festival.'

'See anything good?'

'Ummm, let me think...' she scrambled to recall what she'd seen in Galway. Her brain suddenly felt really watery. God, get a grip, she silently admonished herself. It was a tiny bit of contact. It was unintentional. It meant nothing. 'We saw this amazing dance troupe,' she started. Michael waited for her to go on, gazing at her as if she was the most enchanting thing he had ever seen in his life. 'Yeah, so they were like Irish dancers but modern, you know? Like they danced to rock.'

Over the next few hours, they chatted and drank and laughed. Michael had so many great stories, but he never dominated the conversation. He was always interested to hear what Caitlin had to say, and she told a surprising number of good stories of her own.

At around 8pm, Michael excused himself. He was gone about fifteen minutes. When he came back, he placed a room card on the bar in front of her. She gave him a questioning look.

'I can't be bothered to go all the way back to Brooklyn tonight, so I've got myself a room. Do you fancy joining me upstairs for a bite to eat? They have a great room service menu here.' There wasn't a trace of mischievousness in his expression.

'Sounds good. I'm starving,' she said, equally as casual. She stood up, picked up the key and smiled at him, unflinching.

As they went out of the bar and through the lobby to the elevator, she walked slightly ahead of him, sensing him follow close by behind her. She felt like both the doe and the lioness at the same time. She was the hunter who was about to be devoured by its prey.

CHAPTER FOURTEEN
EMMA—MANHATTAN
MAY 2012

As she watched the pink light sweep over Manhattan's skyline, Emma wondered how many sunsets and sunrises she'd seen from that window. Hundreds. Thousands probably. But, even after ten years at the firm, she had not tired of the view. She was still sometimes surprised when she lifted her head from her papers and realized that she, little Emma McCourt from the Falls Road in Belfast, had ended up here, working on the thirtieth floor of a shiny skyscraper on Fifth Avenue.

Right now though, it was the last thing she wanted to be looking at. In front of her, Steve sighed and turned the page, rolling his blue eyes as he did so. In his youth, that piercing blue had probably given him some of the allure of his namesake, Steve McQueen. But that would have been more than twenty years ago. Now, everything about him, his hair, his skin, and his thin lips, all blended with his grey suit. He had the look, Emma thought, of a once muscular college football player now gone to seed.

God, how long was this going to take? She glanced at the clock on the wall. 8pm. By now, she should have been arriving at the rooftop bar, kissing Daniel, and perusing the cocktail list. But, instead, she was here, watching ol' blue eyes shuffle through a fifty page brief she had sent him this morning.

'It's fine,' he finally said 'it's just not that compelling.'

'Compelling?'

'It doesn't convince me.'

She wanted to say that was probably because the client's case wasn't very convincing. There were numerous damaging emails that were bound to come out in time. So far, she'd managed to keep them out of the record by performing intellectual back-flips in front of the arbitrators. Unlike litigation, they were only obliged to hand over documents the other side had specifically requested and, because of poor drafting on the other side's part, she had been able to convince the arbitrators those emails did not respond to the request. Her client had joked afterwards that she was a "master of burying the truth." Little did he know.

That was the part of the job Emma enjoyed, the mental ping-pong with the other side's lawyers at the hearing or during negotiations. She liked less the part that required her to hang around the office watching Steve read something she'd sent him over twelve hours ago.

'Maybe I just need a break,' he said. 'I'm going to order in some dinner. You should do the same. Why don't you come back at 9pm, and we can go through it, again, together.'

Emma took a deep breath. He wasn't going to like what she had to say next.

'I can't. I need to go soon.'

He looked over the papers at her. 'Remind me, do you have children?'

'No,' she'd been working with him for over three years now; he knew she didn't have kids.

'Because I do understand that it's important for a mother to be home with her children.'

'I don't have to worry about that. But I do have a husband.'

'Well, husbands can fend for themselves.'

Emma had learned over the years how to deal with schoolyard bullies like Steve. The best approach was to meet their stubbornness with an equal measure of bullheadedness. If you showed any signs of weakness, they'd walk all over you. And, when in doubt, lie.

'It's my husband's birthday, and we're having some drinks at home with friends. I really can't miss it.' She hoped he wouldn't remember she'd used the same excuse six months ago on Daniel's actual birthday.

Steve shoved the brief at her. 'I can't really concentrate anyway, it's riddled with typos.' Emma drew in her breath and fought the urge to slap him. 'And the font's too small.' It was house-style, but she bit her lip and let him go on. 'Go away and fix it, and then I'll take another look later, while you're at home sipping cocktails with your husband.' He spat out this final word as if it were poison.

Emma rushed back to her office, fixed the four typos that the proofreader had missed, changed the font, and emailed the brief to Steve. There was no way she was going to make the mistake of taking it round to his office in hardcopy and risk him delaying her further.

Walking to the elevator, Emma counted how many of her colleagues were still hunched over their desks. It was well over half of the department. What kept them all here night after night? Only the paralegals got paid overtime.

She supposed, for some, work provided an escape from unhappy marriages or empty homes. Staying in the office, in a place where you felt needed and successful, was preferable to going home and facing failures in other aspects of your life.

Or, perhaps, it was the pleasure of the work that kept them late. The sheer joy they derived from solving legal puzzles, the satisfaction at being good at something.

Or, maybe, they were simply so attracted to the label of "corporate lawyer" that they accepted, without question, the long hours it demanded. Even if the work was grueling, it was a safe pigeonhole that conveyed status, intellect, and a degree of respectability. When Emma told new acquaintances she was a lawyer, they rarely asked any further questions. They didn't think they needed to. They had already decided what box to put her in. All they saw was a stereotypical professional in her mid-thirties, and none of them could imagine the journey that had brought her from the Belfast council estate of her youth to this office, with its artwork in the lobby and sweeping views across mid-town. And Emma was just fine with that.

Outside on the warm street, Emma jumped in a taxi and headed towards Soho. The cab crawled along at a pace that was far slower than the average pedestrian. Emma used the time to respond to emails.

As they waited at the traffic lights, she heard a man calling to people outside a store. 'Fucking tourists, wandering around, no idea what you're doing, why don't you get into my fucking store and buy some fucking products!'

Emma smiled. She could never tire of New York.

The landscape changed from high-rises and department stores to lofts, cast-iron buildings and boutiques, and finally she arrived. She had arranged to meet Daniel at Jimmy's, on the eighteenth floor of the James hotel. She found him at the bar, chatting to the bartender. Like a blonde Frank Sinatra, Daniel had a winning smile that charmed everyone he met. Not that he was using it right now. He looked at her and then at his watch.

'If I'd known you were going to be this late, I'd have gone straight home. I'm starving.'

'Well you should have had some peanuts or something.'

He gave her a withering look. Daniel liked to eliminate

all risk from his life. He still had no idea of the risk he'd taken marrying her three years ago.

'C'mon those things are full of germs, you know that.'

She popped one in her mouth. 'See, no harm done.'

'Ugh, do you know how many people have stuck their hands in that bowl before? And I bet not all of them wash after they've been to the bathroom. You should be more careful, especially now.'

She knew exactly to what he was referring. Since they'd supposedly started "trying for a baby" last year, he'd begun taking an unusual interest in everything impacting her body—what she ate, drank, how much she slept, what exercises she was doing.

'So let's get it over with, what's the excuse this time?'

'The Capote case.'

'But I thought you already handed in that brief? You were up all night.'

Emma ordered a glass of sauvignon blanc from the bartender. Daniel raised an eyebrow. 'Have you told Steve you need more help on that case? You can't go on like this, you'll burn out.'

'I'm fine.'

'You need to slow down. I'm not lecturing you, but the more you work, the more stressed you get, and the more you drink.'

'C'mon, it's one glass of wine! I hardly have time to be drinking. I'm in the office every night.'

'Yes, but the nights you get home early, like at nine or ten, you can easily finish off a bottle of wine by yourself before going to bed.'

'That's not fair.'

'It's been ten months without any success. There must be a reason.'

'Lots of couples take a year to get pregnant. Don't worry.' The bartender placed the glass of wine in front of her.

'I get that,' Daniel said. 'But I read that eighty percent

get pregnant within the first six months.'

'Please don't throw statistics at me.'

'It's a fact.'

'So we aren't like the majority. It'll happen, don't worry.'

'It still wouldn't hurt to get your priorities sorted. You should be slowing down, but it feels, this year, like you're speeding up.'

'Well it's what's expected of someone at my level.'

'All I'm saying is think about eating more greens, getting some rest, cutting down on alcohol, that sort of thing.'

Emma reached her hand up and stroked Daniel's cheek. 'You're right, I'm going to tell them I need more help on that case. The baby project is still my number one priority.' She looked him square in the eye as she spoke. From experience, she knew it was the most effective way to lie to someone.

'Ok, good,' Daniel said, placated.

'So how was your day?'

As Daniel started complaining about his new interior design client, Emma started thinking about the birth control pills lying in her desk drawer. The ones she'd been taking, secretly, at the office each day for the past ten months. She necked back a large gulp of wine and frantically tried to recall if she'd taken that day's pill.

CHAPTER FIFTEEN
CAITLIN—MANHATTAN
JUNE 2012

On the last Tuesday in June, Caitlin was in a hotel near the Lincoln Center. It was 11am, and the rest of New York was slogging through yet another day at work, as she and Michael lay stretched out on top of the ruffled sheets, their naked bodies entwined together, letting the gentle breeze from the ceiling fan cool them. Everyone at the office thought they were in another meeting with the expert.

Caitlin thought about what her roommates would be doing right now. They'd probably be out on the mid-morning coffee run or hunched over their desks doing some mind-numbingly boring work, the kind of work that was only invented to keep summer interns busy. Except Lacey, she only worked two days a week in the graphics team of an NGO and, the rest of the time, she blogged about fonts. Right now, she was probably passed out at the kitchen table having been up all night stressing about whether Helvetica or Gill Sans should be her font of the week. Poor thing.

Caitlin pictured the other paralegals in her team, sifting though terabytes of documents on the database, looking for the "smoking gun" that Michael assured her never existed in real life legal cases. And then, for some reason, Caitlin's mind left Manhattan and wandered across the East River to Michael's house in Brooklyn. What was his wife doing right now? What did someone do all day at home with a small child? Did she spend her days watching trashy TV, having coffee, and gossiping with the neighborhood moms?

'A penny for them,' Michael said. He was lying with his hands above his head and Caitlin had her head on his chest. She shifted around so she could look at him.

'What?'

'A penny for your thoughts.'

'I'm not thinking about anything.'

'You're a woman, you are always thinking about something.'

'No, it's nothing.'

'C'mon, spit it out. What was it?'

Caitlin bit her lip, unsure if she should go on. In the six weeks they had been seeing each other Michael hadn't spoken about his wife, not since that first night when they went for cocktails at the Pierre Hotel. It was sort of an unspoken rule that his home life was off limits. But it wasn't fair. Didn't she have a right to know something about this woman that he went home to night after night?

'Actually, I was wondering what your wife was doing right now.'

'Why were you thinking that?'

'It's not so strange for me to wonder who she is, what she's like, what she does all day.'

'Why do you care?'

'I don't…I just…I just think it's weird that you and I are so…intimate and yet there's a whole part of your life that I know practically nothing about.'

'There's nothing to know.' Michael shifted so that

Caitlin's head fell off his chest and onto the pillow.

'Are you still in love with her?' Caitlin asked, trying to sound disinterested and failing miserably.

'What kind of question is that?'

'It's normal for me to be curious.'

'Listen, she's a good mother and a caring wife. She's not a bad looking woman. I wouldn't have married her if she were. She's funny and intelligent. I don't have a bad word to say about her. Happy now?'

'If she's so wonderful, then why are you here with me?'

Michael rolled his eyes. 'Is this the bit where I'm supposed to say, "oh poor me, my wife doesn't understand me" or "I feel trapped," is that how this goes?'

'I don't know how this goes,' Caitlin snapped. 'It's not like I've done this before.'

'And neither have I.'

'Really?'

Michael turned on to his side to face her. 'Obviously if I were still madly in love with my wife and one hundred percent happy, then I wouldn't be here with you,' his tone was matter of fact. 'But I'm not going to go around bad mouthing Carol. If I've created a life for myself that is lacking in something, then I've only got myself to blame.'

'So, do I provide something that she doesn't?' said Caitlin, grasping at the tiny thread he'd just thrown her.

Michael thought for a moment. 'I suppose you do. You make my life exciting again.'

'Exciting?' Caitlin sat up, clutching the sheet to her chest. 'So it's just because our relationship is secret, illicit. It's not about me in particular. It's just because you're having an affair. It could be with anyone. It just so happens to be with me.'

'Jesus, this is why I didn't want to talk about it in the first place.' Michael shoved her to one side and jumped out of bed. He started pulling on his boxer shorts. 'I'm afraid I don't have a neat, logical explanation for why I'm doing this. All I know is that you excite me. I feel alive again when I'm with you, and I feel like a fucking corpse the rest of the week.'

He was already getting dressed. Caitlin didn't want them to leave it like this. She got out of bed, went up to him, and started kissing his chest. 'You don't have to go just yet do you?'

'I actually do.' He kept his hands at his sides, willfully ignoring her advances.

Caitlin smiled. She knew how to make him stay. She got down on her knees in front of him. 'What if I promised not to bring it up ever again?' She moved her hand up inside his boxer shorts and stroked his thigh. 'What if I promise to be good and do as I'm told in the future?'

At this, he smiled down at her and stroked her face. 'I'm sure you can figure out a way to make it up to me,' he said. Caitlin smiled and started to remove his boxer shorts.

They checked out of the hotel an hour later and Michael suggested they take a walk through Central Park, as he didn't need to be back in the office until after lunch.

'I'm definitely a dedicated downtowner,' Caitlin said as they crossed the Bow Bridge and walked along the lake. 'But there's no denying it. Downtown, we just don't have any space that can compete with this.'

'So you've already decided that you're a "downtowner" have you? How long have you been living in New York?'

'Almost a year. But what has that got to do with anything? I do live downtown.'

'I don't really see New York as a city that's divided into downtown and uptown. It's more like a series of interconnected villages, each one with their own unique character. Real New Yorkers don't call themselves downtowners or uptowners. They define themselves by where they do their dry cleaning, or which gym they use or their nearest sushi joint, wouldn't you say?'

'What do you know? You live in Brooklyn with all the boring Wall Street types. The ones who work in finance but delude themselves into thinking they're hip—so they refuse to move to Connecticut where they belong.'

'Touché,' Michael said with a smile.

Looking at the sun filter through the branches, Caitlin remembered a word she'd seen in Lacey's book of illustrated words from other languages.

'Doesn't this remind you of that Japanese word, *Komorebi*?'

'And what does that mean?' He looked like he was testing her.

'It's that dappled effect that happens when the sun escapes through the trees. Like that,' she pointed at the scattered pattern of light and shadows on the ground in front of them.

'I'm impressed. Have I inspired you to learn Japanese? Don't tell me you're going to run off to Japan and leave me.'

'No, I'm not going anywhere.'

'But didn't you have plans to travel this summer?'

'I did think about it, but I've decided to save up some more and take a big trip in the fall or next spring.' Caitlin's original plan had been to work through June and July and then travel in August with Lacey. They needed to book the trip soon. But the flights to Europe were ridiculously expensive and Caitlin still didn't have enough money saved. "I don't know why you don't just ask your parents," Lacey had said. She didn't understand. If Caitlin asked her parents to fund her trip, her mom would insist on overseeing everything. She'd take over the itinerary, and a trip to Ireland would be completely off the cards. So Caitlin preferred to wait and pay for it all herself.

'I have to say, I am jealous of all the traveling you've got ahead of you,' Michael said. 'Use your long summers during college wisely, you'll regret it when you're working 60 hour weeks for fifteen days' vacation a year.'

'I'll probably go somewhere and volunteer next summer. I feel like it's my responsibility. I mean, my generation just knows so much more about the world than previous ones. We can't ignore the world's problems like people did in the past.'

'Your generation? Jesus, I'm not that old.'

'You're nineteen years older than me. Technically, you could be my Dad, if you'd had me as a teenager. So that makes the difference between us generational.'

'There's nothing exceptional about your generation, believe me. You may have the Internet and smart phones but, deep down, you kids are not that different to how we were.'

'We "kids" are creating social networks, which are starting revolutions and taking down dictators. You have to admit that's pretty remarkable. I mean, how many billionaire twenty-year-olds were there of your generation?'

'Please, every generation thinks they're special. Every generation thinks the world is changing in a completely unprecedented way. Everyone thinks they are living in interesting times, just like in the Chinese curse.' A light had gone on inside of him. He obviously loved sparring like this. It was what made him such a good lawyer and such a challenging dinner companion. But Caitlin wasn't intimidated by his intellect.

'So what? You're saying that even in ancient China they thought they were living in interesting times and so what I'm talking about is bullshit?'

'Actually, it was Kennedy, or one of his speechwriters, that made up that Chinese curse. I thought you were a politics student?'

Caitlin grappled for a smart riposte.

'C'mon let's sit down,' he said, before she could speak. 'My old feet are sore, but I don't want to go back to the office just yet.'

They sat down on a nearby bench, and he put his arm around her. Caitlin wriggled out of his embrace.

'Don't you ever worry about us getting caught?'

'You'd like that wouldn't you?'

'I don't want you for myself, if that's what you think. I'm perfectly happy with our arrangement.'

'Arrangement? Is that all I am to you?'

'You know what I mean, and you didn't answer my question.'

'No, I don't worry about us getting caught. Right now, everyone I know is either tied to a desk in mid-town or on Wall Street, or pushing a stroller around Brooklyn. If they are hanging out in Central Park at midday on a Tuesday, it's probably because they're doing something they shouldn't. So there's no need to worry about them ratting me out.'

'But what about when we go out for dinner in Soho or the Village?'

'All my friends are old farts. You'd never catch them out in those areas on weeknights. They're too busy working or running home to read to the kids. Don't worry. We won't get caught. You won't have to deal with me showing up on your doorstep with my suitcase, the wife having thrown me out.'

'That's a relief.'

Caitlin didn't care that he never planned to leave his wife. She had no illusions about them building a life together. The only thing they were creating together was memories, secret memories that she would never share with anyone. Well, except her roommates, Nicole and Lacey, who already knew all about Michael. And, perhaps, years from now, she would tell her granddaughter about the fling she had with an older Irish man, when she was young and living in New York city.

'Look at that,' Michael pointed at a group of senior citizens picking up trash at the other side of the lake. 'People always go on about how mean New Yorkers are, but in how many other places would you see that?'

'My grandmother was from Connecticut. I can't imagine her picking up trash in a public place.'

'Exactly. If you are losing faith in humanity, come to

New York.'

'But people say we are so aggressive,' Caitlin said.

'Not at all. In how many other cities do you find millions of people, from all corners of the world, living side by side in such a restricted place? If people come here and don't like it, it's because they don't understand the unwritten laws that New Yorkers have developed for successful living. The tourists complain that people here are always in a rush. Strangers to the city just see the person brushing past them on the sidewalk, without saying sorry. What they don't see is the bigger picture. There's just no time or space for millions of people to be engaging in social niceties. They've been dropped by consensus, so that we can live together in harmony. Rather than being a degradation of society, it shows an evolution. But that there, those people voluntarily cleaning up the rubbish, that shows the true face of the city. And it's a caring one. Even so, I bet every last one of them would mow you down with their walkers, if you dared to stop randomly on the street in front of them.'

Caitlin smiled at the idea of someone being run over by a senior in a wheelchair. She was sure it happened every day in the city.

'I guess you're right. My grandma was from a small town in Connecticut, where people wear their niceness on their sleeves. Everyone is all smiles at church, but that doesn't mean they are any more community minded. My grandma was dead two days before anyone found her. My mom couldn't get her on the phone, so she drove over to see her and found her collapsed in the kitchen. None of her neighbors noticed the newspapers and mail piling up on her porch. There were no organizations of volunteers visiting seniors like there are here in the city.'

'That's terrible,' Michael pulled Caitlin to him and kissed the edge of her temple. 'Were you close to her?'

'Not particularly. Although, I cried my eyes out at the funeral.' Caitlin gazed up at the light reflecting off the leaves above them. 'It was worse when my Dad's mom died though. I never got to say goodbye to her. I plan to visit her grave sometime. I want to lay some flowers down and tell her how much I loved her. One day, soon, I plan to go to Belfast to see the rest of my dad's family. And I'll tell my grandma that her dream came true, after all, that we were all together in her house, me and all my cousins.'

'May all your dreams come true, that's another Chinese curse,' Michael said with a knowing nod.

'How can having your dreams come true be a curse?'

'I think it means that, sometimes, we don't know what's good for us. It means that you should be careful what you wish for, because it may not be all it's cracked up to be.'

CHAPTER SIXTEEN
VICTORIA & EMMA
LONG ISLAND
JULY 7TH, 2012

'Hello?'

Victoria turned and jumped. Emma was at the bedroom door. 'You're here already? God, I'm so behind.' She paused for breath and took in the sight of Emma in a fitted white dress. 'You look gorgeous, by the way.'

'I thought I'd wear white to match my Goddaughter on her Christening. Shall I leave you to it?'

'No, stay, keep me company.' Victoria sat down in front of the dresser and started plastering herself with foundation. 'I'm sorry the place is such a mess.'

'God, V, it's grand.'

'I spent all morning tidying up downstairs but I didn't have time to do the bedrooms.'

Emma wandered over to the window. 'There are some seriously big houses on this street. Long Island is just a different world, isn't it?'

'I know. Our house looks like a shack in comparison.'

'That's not what I meant.'

This was the first time Emma was seeing the house since she'd helped Victoria and Eddie move to Long Island a month ago. Victoria glanced up at the faded wallpaper put up by the previous tenants, years before. She wished they'd had time to redecorate. Make the place look like them. Eddie was a graphic designer at an NGO and she was an account manager at an advertising agency in the city. Surely their home shouldn't look this banal.

Victoria couldn't remember the last time she had felt at ease. For months now, she'd been feeling like she was the wrong shape for her life. A square peg in a round hole. When Ava was born, Victoria had suddenly felt like she and Eddie were orphans, cast adrift in the midst of a great heaving city, ill-prepared for the responsibilities of adult life.

And New York hadn't made it any easier for them. It was as if the city resented them for having a child. A new love. After a couple of months battling to carry the stroller upstairs and tripping over baby paraphernalia, their cozy third floor walk-up in Alphabet City had started to lose its charm. Even strolling in Tomkins Square Park, her one time oasis, had started to annoy her. The place was overrun with costumed canines and their fawning, crazy owners. It was as if someone had been sending her a message—real New Yorkers have dogs, not children.

Victoria had thought a move to a house with a backyard would help. But she still felt like she was living in a bombsite. Picking through the debris of her former life. Trying to use those shattered pieces as the building blocks for a new one. And now here was her oldest friend, in her designer dress, inspecting the rubble with disdain.

'I noticed an easel in the spare room as I walked past,' Emma said.

Victoria felt Emma's eyes on her, waiting for a reaction.

'Yeah, we picked it up at a yard sale last week.'

'Are you going to start painting again?'

Victoria shrugged. 'I don't know…I've been trying to do a bit.' A huge smile spread across Emma's face. 'It's just a hobby,' Victoria went on. 'It's not easy to find the time. I have so much work these days. I'm knackered most evenings when I get home.'

'I think it's brilliant that you're back painting. It's who you are.'

'Don't get too excited. I'm just dabbling.' Every time Victoria picked up a paintbrush she felt guilty thinking of Ava, and she wondered where this feeling, this urge to paint, came from. Why was it gnawing at her, hollowing her out, just at the time in her life she should feel most complete? She had given birth to an incredible little girl. Shouldn't that be enough? With working full time she barely saw Ava as it was. Why was she so desperate for Ava to go to sleep so she could grab some time alone with her paints?

'Well, I can't wait to see your masterpieces,' Emma said.

'Don't hold your breath. I still don't know what to paint.'

'Ava must be an inspiration to you, right?'

'I guess so. Since becoming a mother, I do feel like I understand life a bit better. '

Victoria immediately cringed at what she'd just said. She sounded like one of those patronizing people who thought only parents knew the secrets of the Universe. Truth was, she did think those people who remained childless would never understand the full meaning of love, or the importance of the tiny moments, or what life was really all about. But she never wanted to be the type of person who said that kind of thing out loud, especially not around Emma.

'So you could use that.' Then Emma added snidely, 'Whatever that enlightened feeling is.'

Victoria turned to face her friend. 'I just meant, when you see a baby day in, day out, and how she develops.

How she learns to communicate, to express emotions, to discover taste and touch and music. It's just mind-blowing, and I'd like to express that in paint, if I could.'

'I know. I have been around a baby before.'

Victoria fell silent. There was no point going on. They'd just get into an argument. To live with what she had done, Emma had obviously asphyxiated a part of herself, which she'd buried and covered over with an enormous rock. Victoria now knew better than to push the issue. She had gotten injured before running up against that rock. It had been there too long. There was no moving it.

Suddenly Eddie barged in with his camera, clicking away.

'Eddie,' Victoria screamed. 'Delete that.'

'I was hoping to get a nice relaxed shot of the mom and Godmother getting ready for the ceremony.'

'I'm not even dressed yet.'

'I can see that. We should have left for the church already.'

'Fine, just give me five minutes.' Victoria turned back and started putting on blusher. 'Where's Ava?'

'She's down there with Daniel. To be honest, I think he's better with kids than I am. He's got Ava giggling her head off.'

'Aww isn't that sweet,' Victoria said. In the mirror, she caught Emma rolling her eyes behind her.

'He's a natural Em. So...any chance of you two having a little playmate for Ava anytime soon?' asked Eddie.

'Eddie,' Victoria hissed, slamming down her makeup brush.

'Emma's your oldest friend. You two have known each other since you were babies. She slept in our bath on her birthday a couple of years ago because she was too drunk to go home to Daniel.'

'Hey, you said you'd never bring that up again,' said Emma with a smile.

'My point is I think I know you well enough to make you feel uncomfortable if I want. So, will we hear the patter of tiny feet soon?'

'Who knows?'

'Does that mean you're trying?'

'Eddie, leave her alone.'

'It's ok,' Emma shrugged.

'I'm the first to admit that it's hard work, but being a parent is pretty good fun too,' said Eddie.

'But never underestimate the joy and love you can get from a dog,' Emma said.

'Em, are you comparing our child to a dog? Because, honestly, I think dogs are smarter.'

'Eddie, that really isn't funny.'

'Oh, lighten up Victoria.'

'Can you please leave us in peace? I'm never going to get ready with you standing there nattering.'

'Fine, but she's coming with me. Out. C'mon. You're not helping.' Eddie grabbed Emma by the elbow and frog-marched her down the stairs and into the kitchen-diner where Daniel was feeding Ava.

Looking at Daniel, smiling at Ava, making choo choo sounds as he brought a spoonful of orange mush to her mouth, Emma thought she must be a hard woman. The sight of her husband being so tender with a child was supposed to stir warm feelings within her, but she felt nothing.

She went over and opened the fridge. 'Look how much champagne there is in here,' she exclaimed with delight. 'Eddie, shall we open a bottle? Wet the baby's head?'

'It's not even midday,' Daniel shouted from the dining table, without turning his gaze away from Ava.

Emma gave Eddie a playful smile.

'Go on, but if we get in trouble I'm blaming you. That's supposed to be for the reception afterwards.'

Emma opened the champagne. She poured a glass for herself and one for Eddie, who was at the kitchen counter chopping.

'What are you doing?' Emma leant over him and grabbed a piece of carrot and popped it in her mouth.

'Making some kind of organic vegetable concoction for our young princess's dinner later today. Victoria doesn't believe in feeding her anything that's easy or convenient.'

Emma took a seat next to Daniel at the table. He gave her glass a disapproving look, so she took a big gulp from it in defiance.

'I keep telling her there's no need for everything to be perfect,' Eddie went on. 'The kid's only six months old and she's already got her playing saxophone and doing Pilates.'

Emma laughed. 'I think you mean baby yoga.'

'Yes, that's it. Her first word is going to be Om.'

'It's because your mom's a good mom, isn't she? Oh yes she is,' Daniel cooed at Ava.

'When we were kids, there were no parenting blogs, no baby stimulation classes, no organic vegetables. There was just a lot of screaming and a bit of love once in a while so they didn't look totally insane. And it worked didn't it?'

'I don't know Eddie. I look at you, and I think he looks like the kind of guy who was never taken to baby yoga as a kid, and it makes me sad for you Eddie, it really does.'

'Oh shut up,' Eddie fired a piece of carrot at Emma, missing her and hitting Daniel on the head instead. Daniel reached down and picked it up, placing it on the table, far out of Ava's reach.

'So what's with all the champagne? How many people are coming?' Emma asked.

'At the ceremony, it's just us, my college friend Rick and his girlfriend, and my Dad and his wife. They're going to the church direct from their hotel. Victoria's mother has been giving her grief for not doing it in Belfast, of course. We did offer to pay for her flight, but you know she's scared of flying, so she said no. Afterwards, a few of the neighbors are coming here for a party, and Victoria has invited a whole host of women from her mom and me meet-up.'

'Great, mommy friends, I can't wait to meet them,' Emma only caught the sarcasm in her voice once the words were already out.

'Do you want to hold it?' Daniel handed Ava the spoon, and Emma watched, horrified, as Ava started to shake it furiously sending orange mush in all directions, with the majority of it landing on Emma's white dress.

'Daniel' she screamed, jumping up and trying to wipe it off, which just made it worse.

At the sound of Emma shouting, Ava started to cry.

'Look what you've done,' Daniel said accusingly.

'Look what you've done,' Emma shouted back at him, pointing at the huge stains on her dress.

Victoria appeared in the doorway. 'What's going on?'

'I think Emma might need to borrow something to wear,' Eddie said, walking over to shove a pacifier in Ava's mouth.

'Sure. There's an Ann Tyler dress in the closet in the spare room. It's a bit too small for me. It should fit you perfectly.'

Emma scratched at the stains on her dress. It was a lost cause. 'Fine.' She ran upstairs to get changed as the rest of them fussed in the kitchen cleaning up Ava's Jackson Pollock from the wall. In the spare room, Emma stepped over the Christening gifts, kicking a few of them to one side to clear her path to the wardrobe.

She was too stressed about her outfit to care much about the gifts. So she didn't notice one of them was wrapped in the fancy branded paper of an expensive baby boutique. Nor did she notice the card stuck on the side. It said "*All the best on your daughter's Christening. From your neighbors Tom, Janet and Kathleen O' Connell.*" But even if Emma had seen it, she would not have paused. For those names meant nothing to her. Not now. Not yet.

CHAPTER SEVENTEEN
JANET—LONG ISLAND
JULY 7TH, 2012

'So you're not coming home this weekend either?' Janet sighed. It had been over a month since Kathleen had last been home.

'Mom, I need to work. We get paid double on the weekends.'

'You do not need to work.'

'I like making my own money. Most parents would be happy I'm learning to stand on my own two feet. Sometimes, I think you'd be happier if I stayed dependent on you and didn't grow up at all.'

'I'm not against you being independent, but there will be plenty of time after college for work. You won't get these years back. You should make the most of them,' Janet tried to sound conciliatory. Kathleen stayed silent at the other end of the line, so Janet tried a different tactic. 'If you insist on staying in the city instead of coming home, then why don't you take some summer classes? It's not too late to enroll. Your father and I will cover your expenses.

That would free up your weekends to come home to visit us.'

'You just don't understand, do you?'

'No Kathleen, I don't understand. Most kids would jump at that offer.'

'I have to go. I need to be in the office soon.'

'Well, what time do you finish work? Where's your office? What's the company called? Maybe one evening during the week I can come into the city and take you out to dinner.'

'Maybe. I'll let you know. Bye.'

'Kath?' She was already gone.

Janet slammed the phone down in frustration.

'You ok love?' Tom wandered into the bedroom.

'I don't understand that child.'

'She just needs her own space. That's all.'

'You know where she wants to go when she's saved up enough, don't you?'

'Love, we'll cross that bridge when we come to it.' He smiled. 'Hide her passport, maybe.'

She shot him a look. 'It's not funny Tom.' Janet let out a long sigh. 'She's not been home in weeks. I have no idea what's going on with her, what her plans are. Do you think there's a boy?' There had been several evenings recently when she'd called and Kathleen hadn't picked up.

'Could be, I don't really want to think about that. Those cretins she dated in high school were bad enough. I hate to think what college boys are like.'

'But if she's dating someone, why won't she tell us?'

'She's just at that age. Give it five years, she'll be here on weekends, borrowing your clothes and asking you for advice.'

'I hope so,' Janet said.

Tom moved about the room putting on his suit. 'Remember how she used to stalk you around the house? It used to drive you crazy and now look at you.'

'No it didn't.'

'C'mon, there were a few years when you couldn't even go for a piss without her trying to bash the bathroom door in to get to you.'

Janet smiled at the bittersweet memory. There had been days when Kathleen's persistence had bordered on the obsessive. What Janet would now give to have Kathleen adore her in the same way she had done when she was a toddler.

The tables had definitely turned. It was now Janet who wanted to stalk Kathleen. She could spend hours imagining what it must be like for her daughter living in New York City, sharing with four friends. She pictured them having impromptu parties in their bare apartment, drinking cheap wine and beer bought with fake IDs, eating potato chips from big bowls, and feeling so very grown up. She wondered if Kathleen still sometimes got up and went to the kitchen, ensconced in her duvet, to make herself a coffee, just like she used to do when she lived at home. She wondered if she still brushed her teeth in front of the television. Or if she still listened to the same song, on repeat, for hours at a time. It was this daily intimacy Janet missed the most—the ability simply to watch her daughter go about everyday activities.

Janet had realized, some time ago, that loss is woven into the fabric of motherhood. For most women, it starts with a physical separation, a cutting of the cord. That was something Janet had never experienced. But, with every milestone after that, from the first time Kathleen tied her shoe laces to the day she got her drivers' license, Janet's joy had always been muted by the realization that her child was growing, not only up, but also away.

During her teenage years, as Kathleen's journey into adulthood and away from Janet had accelerated, Janet had found comfort in those shared everyday moments. But now, even those were gone. She no longer wandered into the kitchen to find Kathleen in her pajamas munching cereal. Nor did she come across her reading in the sunroom anymore. Janet even missed seeing the light of the TV dancing under Kathleen's bedroom door late at night and the feeling of satisfaction it gave her, knowing her daughter was there with them, safe under the same roof.

She was bound to meet new people today at the neighbor's party, and someone would inevitably ask her "so, what do you do?" Janet still thought of herself as a stay at home mom, even if she no longer had a child to stay home for. But she'd tell them what she told everyone else; she ran a charitable foundation set up by her husband. They didn't need to know she only spent a couple of days a week on it.

'Which ones?' Tom interrupted Janet's thoughts. He was holding up two pairs of brown shoes, neither of which went with his black suit.

'Not those,' Janet went into his closet and pulled out his black dress shoes. 'Here,' she handed him the shoes.

'Where would I be without you?' he asked.

Out the window, Janet could see people already starting to gather on the neighbors' lawn. 'Right, I'm ready. How long will you be?' Tom said. Even in his fifties, he still cut a dashing figure when he put on a suit.

'I just need to put on some lipstick and figure out what shoes to wear with this dress.'

'Need any help?'

'No, I don't think I need style tips from you. Go on downstairs, I'll be down in five minutes.'

Tom left her alone, and Janet sat down by the dresser. As happened so often these days, she was taken aback by the sight of her own reflection. It was as if the mirror were magically distorted to show a picture of Janet ten years from now. But, in fact, it was Janet's own self image that was out of synch with reality. In her mind, she had far less wrinkles, a much tighter jaw-line and less droopy eyelids than the woman staring back at her. She was fifty-four. How old would she have to be before she could escape the tyranny of the mirror? When would she look in the mirror and not care what she looked like?

These days she often found herself sitting in front of the mirror wondering who the woman staring back at her was—and it wasn't just the effect of the wrinkles. It was more than skin deep.

She often wondered who she might be today if she'd married Ethan, the bespectacled boy with the dark, unkempt hair who sat opposite her in the Beat Generation class at Columbia. The one who had winked at her sympathetically that first class when she'd complained about Kerouac's depiction of women and the professor had cut her off with a sharp, "Who cares? The man is a genius." The one who'd caught up with her after class to tell her he, too, thought Kerouac was overrated and good for her for standing up to the professor.

When she and Ethan left Columbia in 1980 and moved downtown together, the only things they had in their studio apartment were a mattress on the floor, a handful of books, their two Masters in American Literature certificates, which hung side by side on the wall, and Ethan's records. But it hadn't mattered that their apartment had been small and empty. Their lives had been full to bursting with plans.

For four years they'd been happy in that little apartment, which was a quarter the size of her and Tom's current garage in Long Island. Janet had worked as an archivist at the New York Public Library and Ethan sold records at Connect Vinyl, and both of them wrote, as much as they could, and sent their work to magazines across the city. She used to picture them in their forties or fifties, as they hosted cocktail parties at their uptown apartment surrounded by academics and writers and theatre people. She used to imagine telling people about that little studio, their first home together. And they would laugh at how they had ripped the door off the oven and used the oven as a bookshelf and recall fondly her failed attempts to grow an herb garden on the inch-wide strip of natural light that came in from their single window. And they'd marvel at how they'd survived so many New York winters with a hole in their bathroom wall the size of a dime blasting cold air in from the alleyway outside.

As she now fixed her make-up for the neighbor's christening party in her six-bedroom Long Island home, Janet recalled the evening her life with Ethan came to an end, when the entire future she'd planned for them evaporated into thin air. It was April 6th 1984.

***

When Janet got home from work, she checked the mailbox in their graffiti covered lobby.

There was a bunch of junk mail. Nothing of interest, except one envelope with the return address of "*The Atlantic*" on the back. She'd open it later. It was too thin to be good news. When magazines accepted your work they usually called or they sent a thicker letter with the contract. Not that Janet knew this from personal experience. But that's what writer friends had told her.

Upstairs, the place was empty. Ethan wasn't home yet—he probably had a new shipment of records in from Europe at the store and had got carried away listening to them with some of his DJ friends.

Janet poured herself a glass of wine and took a seat at their fold-down table. She opened her journal and started reading through her most recent poems. She hated every single one. They were all insipid and lacking in substance.

She threw her journal to one side and picked up the newspaper she'd bought on the way home. "*Reagan calls for ban on chemical weapons*" read the headline on the front page. Inside, on the bottom corner of page two, was a picture of a young actress, probably no older than twenty-two. The article said she had come to New York less than a year ago from Minnesota to study theater. She had been raped and murdered by her landlord. It was the most typical of New York stories, worthy only of a couple of paragraphs on page two.

At around ten, Janet went downstairs to the payphone in the lobby to call Ethan at the store, but the phone had been vandalized, yet again, and wasn't working. A man lay passed out by the entrance to the building. She hurried back up the stairs two at a time and locked the apartment door behind her. Checking it twice.

Sometime later, she was woken suddenly by the sound of knocking on her door.

She padded over to the door. 'Ethan?'

A strange man's voice responded. 'Miss, can you please open the door?'

'Who is it? What do you want?'

'Miss, it's the NYPD, please open up.'

Janet put on the chain and slowly opened the door a fraction, taking care not to stand too close, so the person on the other side couldn't touch her.

In the hallway stood two policemen, both in their mid-twenties, just like Janet. One was tall, blond, Scandinavian looking, with red cheeks and clear blue eyes. The other was shorter, Latino looking.

'Miss, is this the residence of Ethan Green?' the tall one asked.

'Yes.'

'And can I ask who you are?'

'His girlfriend. What are you doing here? Where's Ethan?'

'Miss, we're sorry it took us so long to get Mr. Green's address. The Super let us into the building. May we come in?'

'Where's Ethan? Why are you looking for him?'

The officers exchanged a look, as if telepathically debating something between the two of them. The Latino looking one took a deep breath and spoke. 'Miss, Mr. Green was fatally wounded in a shooting this afternoon.'

'Fatally wounded?' Janet repeated the words as if they were a foreign language.

'There was an armed robbery at a store on Madison and 52nd. The owner pulled a gun on the robbers and a shoot-out ensued. Mr. Green was simply an innocent bystander.'

Janet shook her head. 'No, there's been some mistake. Ethan's store is on 23rd and 8th.'

'Miss, when you're ready.' The tall one stepped closer towards her. 'We'd like to ask you to come with us to identify Mr. Green's body.'

'No,' Janet said, her voice stronger than before. 'It can't be Ethan. He'd never be in Midtown during the day.'

'Miss, it's important that you come with us,' said the Latino one.

A cold, damp tingle crawled across Janet's skin, and her breathing became shallow and labored.

'No, please listen to me, it's not Ethan,' she said.

'Is there anyone you would like us to call?' the blond one asked.

Janet stepped back, away from them, clutching her nightgown to her body.

'There has to be some mistake.'

In the car, Janet barely spoke. Driving through the darkened city, she visualized, again and again, the moment when she would be taken to identify the body, the rush of relief she'd feel when she saw they had made a mistake, the way she would beat and hug Ethan in both rage and delight when she got home and found him passed out on their bed—exhausted, but alive, after a night of impromptu partying. She saw it all with such clarity that she believed, with every cell in her body, that the future would unfold just how she had pictured it.

Flanked by the two officers and a couple of people in white coats clutching clipboards, Janet stepped into the morgue. It looked like an operating theatre, cold and clean.

She recognized it the moment she walked in, the outline of Ethan's whip-thin body under the putrid green sheet.

'No,' she froze.

An older woman in her forties put her hand on Janet's elbow and edged her closer towards the table, murmuring that even though this was hard, it was important. Someone pulled back the sheet. Janet glanced at his face for no more than a second.

It was her Ethan, his fine cheekbones even more eye-catching beneath his sunken eyes and the waxy sheen of his lifeless skin.

'No.' Janet's howl was like a seismic wave, tearing up the earth beneath her feet. Her legs gave away, and a man's arms caught her before she hit the ground. The two officers reached for her and carried her out.

At around 3am, after the doctor had seen her and they had managed to calm her with some pills, the same two officers who had woken her up at the apartment just a few hours before drove Janet home.

As she was leaving the station, the Latino one handed her Ethan's belongings in a clear plastic bag—his keys, his wallet, a packet of gum, a piece of paper, and a small box.

Alone in their studio, with trembling hands, Janet opened up the box. There was a diamond ring inside. She collapsed on to the kitchen floor. She lay there, stripped red raw, disassembled, her head pressed against the cold tiles, sobbing, completely detached from the living Universe. Hours passed, and the only sound she could hear was that of her own wails. She wept violently, wantonly, crazily.

Eventually, her body could no longer withstand the pain, and it simply shut down—her voice incapable of making any sound, her eyes out of tears, her muscles paralyzed with exhaustion. She lay there, still, silent, alone, lost.

And she might have lain there forever if reality had not come scratching. But, somehow, the sounds of normality started to sneak into her consciousness: traffic, sirens, her neighbors shuffling around in their apartments, flushing their toilets, having showers, watching TV, and arguing with their partners. This mundane soundtrack reminded her that the world kept turning, and she continued to cling to its surface, even though she had no reason to keep holding on, and no anchor pinning her down.

And, so, Janet got up and looked around at her and Ethan's jumbled home. Ethan's half-full coffee cup from the day before was on the counter, cold now, his dirty socks lay at the foot of the bed, his spare glasses were on the bookshelf, and the ring he'd been buying for her when he was murdered lay in the corner, where Janet had thrown it, the blue morning light covering it in a melancholic haze. She could no longer stand to be there. She dragged herself up and climbed the fire escape to the roof.

The morning sun flooded the city below, like a tsunami. Forcing its way along narrow alleyways. Slivering, uninvited, through shutters and curtains, reminding New Yorkers that this day was going to happen, whether they liked it or not. The first day of Janet's life without Ethan had already begun, and there was nothing she could do to stop it from being so.

Three months and one day after Ethan's death, Janet woke up bruised and sore. She pulled the sheet up over her naked body and blinked a few times to moisten her dry eyes. She surveyed the room. Ethan's books and records were ordered alphabetically on the shelves, just as he had left them. There was an empty bottle of tequila on the fold-out table with two glasses. Her clothes lay scattered on the floor, and she was alone. The guy must have left already.

He was someone she'd seen a few times at *Danceteria*. He wasn't handsome, but he was muscular; a big, solid man who looked like he was up for a good time. She had approached him, she had danced close to him and whispered in his ear that he could come home with her and do whatever he wanted. He had been rough and forceful, and she felt she'd deserved it.

In the months since Ethan's death, she'd been going to the clubs almost every night, stalking them, searching for the euphoria she had once shared with Ethan, trying to replace her mental torment with some passing transactional physical pleasure. Everyone was saying the illness that had taken so many of Ethan's friends was no longer just the curse of the gay community. But Janet invited hazard into her bed night after night; she flirted openly with death and couldn't care less.

She threw off the bed-sheet and dragged herself up to a sitting position. She looked down. The guy's semen was still streaming out of her, and her inner thighs were starting to blacken.

Zombie-like, she got up and showered, scrubbing herself until her skin was scratched and raw, trying to remove the stranger's stench from her body.

Afterwards, wrapped in Ethan's enormous Ohio State University beach towel, she opened the wardrobe to pick out something to wear. She pulled on an old knee-length skirt and short-sleeved shirt. The skirt was too big for her and hung loosely on her hipbones, which jutted out like blades. She slammed the wardrobe door shut. She couldn't stand how it looked inside. There was now more than enough room for all her clothes. Last weekend, she had spent a harrowing couple of days packing up Ethan's belongings with Debra. Ethan's clothes now sat folded in boxes by the door waiting for David, Debra's fiancé, to come collect them in his car and take them to Goodwill.

Janet made herself a black coffee and set her cup down on the table with shaking hands, accidentally spilling coffee all over her poetry journal, which lay open on the table.

'Damn,' she muttered lifting up her soaked journal and wiping off the coffee. It was too late; half the pages were stained brown. Her latest poems were raw and desperate, probably exactly what all those damn magazines were looking for. She lifted the lid of the trashcan and tossed the book inside.

Outside on the street, Janet walked with her head down, letting the life of the city slide past her on the blurred edges of her vision. She hated this city now. Ethan's absence had become like a presence. No matter where Janet went, it was always there, following her around, pointing out street corners where they had kissed, their favorite diners and bars, and bookstores they had browsed through. It was as if she had a sadistic tour guide with her at all times, eagerly pointing out remnants from the golden past of a city that had now become a lonely, haunted place.

On the subway to work, Janet stared blankly at the newspaper the man standing next to her was reading, her thoughts filled with Ethan. But then something caught her attention. *"The New Home of Music"* it said in large lettering. It was an advertisement for a job at a cultural center in Long Island.

Before she could finish reading the whole thing, the man turned the page. But the words home and music still called to her. It was a message, a sign.

'Sir?' She touched the man's arm. 'There was a job advertisement on the previous page. Would you mind if I wrote down the details?'

'I'm getting off at the next stop,' he said, not unkindly.

'It will only take a moment.'

'Why don't I just give you the page? Where was it?' He started rifling back through the pages, and Janet pointed out the advertisement. The man carefully folded down the paper and tore out the page for her. *"The New Home of Music."* It was definitely a sign.

A few days later, Janet got the train out to Long Island for the interview. She was astonished at how orderly and clean the world could be just a short train ride away from Manhattan. This was what she needed, to be someplace boring, someplace that did not remind her of the life Ethan should still be living. The one they should have had together.

Three weeks later, in July 1984, Janet moved to a basement apartment in Glen Cove to work at the Tilles Center. Her job was to bring culture to the cozy classes of Long Island, so they wouldn't have to set foot in the ravaged city on their doorstep.

Over the following months, Janet spent her days organizing events and calling donors, using a mask of congeniality to cover up her shattered soul. Several evenings a week, she attended concerts at the center. There, listening in the darkness to the music, alone in the crowd, undisturbed, she spoke to Ethan, again and again. As time passed, Janet felt herself expanding. Like a Russian doll, she was adding to herself. On the outside, she looked the same. Yet with each layer she added on top, she appeared stronger and fuller. But it was just an illusion. The real Janet was still, and always would be, a tiny, hollowed-out shell hidden, deep down, underneath all the hard imitations.

Five years later, in 1989, Janet met Tom O'Connell at the Center's St. Patrick's Day Gala. His company was sponsoring the gala. O'Connell Construction billboards adorned half the building sites on Long Island and many in Manhattan. Janet was surprised to meet its owner and find he was in his early thirties, just like her. Attractive but not handsome, his small blue eyes stood out as the only thing of beauty in an otherwise ordinary face. He was tall, probably six-feet four, at least, and he looked like a man who had spent his life on construction sites, with slightly weathered skin, calloused hands, and strong shoulders.

As guest of honor, she seated him in the front row during the show, and he snored loudly throughout. At the reception afterwards, he took her aside.

'I'm sorry about falling asleep. I hope I didn't snore.'

'No, of course not,' she lied.

'This kind of thing isn't my cup of tea. I mean classical harp, it's all very well for a few minutes, but I can't listen to much more without falling asleep.'

Janet bristled. She had helped put the program together.

'She's a very well respected harpist, and we also had a soprano singing Danny Boy and other Irish classics, but you missed that.'

'I know, but it's not exactly the liveliest St. Patrick's celebration I've ever been to.'

'We're a cultural center, the program is designed to reflect Irish culture.'

'It's not the Ireland I know.'

'The harp is the symbol of Ireland,' she wanted to add "you idiot" but stopped short, reminding herself he was an important donor.

'I'm sorry, I've upset you.' He looked genuinely apologetic.

'No, I just wonder why you sponsored the event if this isn't your thing?'

'I suppose, I want the world to believe that I belong in posh concert halls like this. I fancy myself as a patron of the arts. But, to be honest, I couldn't spot a Mozart tune even if it came out of my own arse.'

'How could a Mozart tune come out of your…' she paused, unable to finish the sentence.

'My derrière does make some interesting noises at times, it can be quite musical.'

'Are you talking about Danny Boy, the Derry Air?' she said, wondering if he'd pick up on her play on words.

'You're right,' he said with a wide smile. 'My derrière does do a fine rendition of the Derry Air.'

'I'll remember that for when I'm putting together next year's St. Patrick's Day program.'

Tom laughed and Janet went to take her leave before the conversation spiraled into even more toilet humor, but he reached for her arm to stop her going.

'Listen, let me take you for dinner one evening next week to make it up to you, and I promise there'll be no snoring.' He gave her a lop-sided boyish smile. Even though she thought he was crass and rude and she was sure they'd have nothing to talk about over dinner, for some reason she would never be able to understand, she said yes.

On their first date, Janet asked Tom why he'd moved to America. He joked that a lying Leprechaun had told him the streets in America were paved with gold, and by the time he got here and found out that wasn't true sure he'd no money to fly home. So he decided he might as well get a job doing the only thing he knew how to do, building things with his hands, one brick at a time.

It was months later when Tom confessed he'd left Northern Ireland at eighteen, in 1974, because so many of his friends were joining the IRA and he was starting to feel pressure to do so as well. Tom told her he had as much sympathy for the cause as his friends, but he had bigger plans for himself than being a foot soldier in the IRA. He said he knew it was only a matter of time from joining until the day when a gun would be thrust into his hands, and he would be expected to use it. He wasn't sure he had the stomach for that. But what really convinced him to leave was that he knew, if he ever took someone else's life, he would destroy his own. He confessed he was prepared to take a life in Ireland's name, but he wasn't willing to lay down his own for her.

Janet knew if Tom had told her the real story on their first date, she would have walked away right then, horrified. But, by the time she learned the truth, Tom O'Connell was no longer just a one-dimensional acquaintance. It was much harder to judge him once she knew his full character, with all its complexities and contradictions. Tom was coarse and charismatic, stubborn and open-minded, argumentative and generous. For every element of him that gave her pause, there was another that drew her, helplessly, towards him.

Still, Tom O'Connell was not the kind of man a young

Janet Maurer would have imagined marrying as she lay on the quad in Columbia scratching out poems in her notebook. But by the time her thirty-something self met him, it did not matter that he was not the husband she'd planned for herself. For she was not the woman she'd planned to be either.

***

Twenty-two years later, Janet put the finishing touches to her make-up and pulled on her high heels and went downstairs to find her husband.

She found Tom waiting for her at the bottom of the stairs.

'Wow, you look stunning,' he said.

'You're very kind.'

'You know me, I'm many things, but kind is not one of them. You look beautiful.'

I'm as beautiful as a rotting pear, thought Janet. But she didn't say anything further to Tom because he was already out the door and charging across the lawn, enticed by the sound of champagne corks popping from the small house across the street.

Janet locked up their place and walked over towards the group gathered in front of the neighbors' house.

She found Tom on the neighbors' lawn with Eddie.

'Janet, so glad you both could make it,' Eddie kissed her on the cheek. He already seemed a little tipsy. Janet and Eddie had met for the first time on the street the previous week.

'Thank you for inviting us, we've been meaning to come over to properly welcome you both to the neighborhood.'

'You've got a fine day for it,' Tom said looking up at the cloudless blue sky.

It had been a day like this when they had held a similar party for Kathleen's fourth birthday, with balloons and a bouncing castle and even a clown. Not long after that party, they had rented out their house and moved away from this neighborhood. With Kathleen starting to mingle more with the neighborhood kids, they hadn't wanted the neighbors' kids hearing something from their parents about adoption that might be repeated to Kathleen. They had only moved back last September when Kathleen had started college.

'So how long have you lived in the US?' Eddie said to Tom.

'Oh I left Ireland many moons ago now.'

'I don't know if I mentioned, but Victoria, my wife, is also from Belfast.'

'Really? What part?' Tom said.

'The Falls.'

'You're joking. That's my old stomping ground. I can't wait to meet her. It's always good to see someone from back home.'

'Yes, she's really keen to meet you both.' Eddie turned, casting his eyes around the small crowd, looking for his wife. 'There she is, over there, with Ava's Godmother.' Eddie pointed to the other end of the garden where two thirty-something-year-old women stood chatting, both dressed in green. Janet squinted, trying to get a better look. She felt like perhaps she knew one of them, but she couldn't remember from where.

'Victoria,' Eddie called. 'Come and meet our neighbors.'

The two women glanced over towards their group. Squarely facing them now, Janet was able to get a good look at them. She did know one of them. She definitely did. Janet's throat suddenly closed in on her.

'Tom, we need to go,' Janet choked. She could barely speak. She could barely breathe. Her legs felt weak.

'What's that?'

She yanked the glass of champagne from Tom's hand and gave it to Eddie. 'I am so sorry. I forgot, we...uh...we have another commitment.'

'Love, what are you on about?'

'Tom, we have to go.' Janet looked over towards the women. They were on the move. They would he here at any moment. 'Right now.'

'All right, sorry about this,' Tom said to Eddie, his face ablaze with either embarrassment or anger. Janet didn't care which. The women were getting closer now. Janet turned away from the men and started striding back towards her house, hoping Tom was behind her, praying the girl hadn't seen them—the green-eyed girl who was now a woman.

CHAPTER EIGHTEEN
VICTORIA—LONG ISLAND
JULY 8TH, 2012

Wandering along the deserted street, with its well-tended shrubs and landscaped gardens, she felt like she was trapped in an architect's model. It didn't help that, after yesterday's party, her stomach was churning, and her head felt like there was a blue bottle buzzing around its dusty recesses.

It was 7:30am on the Sunday after the Christening. Every now and then, a car drove past, but otherwise there was no one around. That was probably for the best. While there was plenty of room for long driveways, huge lawns and swimming pools, there was no space for pedestrians. The sidewalk was non-existent, and Victoria wasn't exactly happy walking Ava along the road. But she'd had to get out of the house. She was starting to wonder if Eddie had been right all along, maybe they should never have moved to Long Island.

Large American flags hung outside most of the houses,

unmoving in the still air. They must have been put up for the July 4th celebrations earlier in the week. In Northern Ireland, flags were divisive symbols waved by the extremists. But here, waving the Stars and Stripes was one of the best ways to blend in. To show you belonged. It showed you knew who you were, with pride and all.

When she was pregnant with Ava, Victoria had read so much about the rush of love women were supposed to feel for their newborn child, and she'd been skeptical. More than skeptical, she'd been worried she was incapable of that kind of instinctive mother love. But there, in the hospital, in those glorious moments after the labor, she had felt it. First it was relief that Ava was healthy, and then came a shot of unadulterated love like she had never felt before.

In the hospital admissions form, Victoria had ticked "*Catholic*." Although, usually, when someone asked her about religion, she would respond: 'I was brought up Catholic, but I'm not really all that religious.' Then she'd quickly add, as if it were bad karma to deny a higher power that might be eavesdropping, 'But I am very spiritual.'

And it was true. She did think there was a higher power with a plan for all of us, one that we were supposed to follow. Although there had been times in her life when she had veered off its course, when she hadn't been able to hear the voice inside telling her what to do, or she had heard it and ignored it anyway. But that day in the hospital, with Eddie pale and bleary eyed in his green scrubs next to her, both of them staring down in wonder at their daughter, she had felt like this was what she had been put on earth to do. If someone had pulled out God's original plan for her from the celestial archives and drew a circle on it around the place where she was supposed to be at that very second, it would have turned out, despite all her missteps, she was slap bang in the middle of the circle, exactly where He had intended her to be all along.

She knew some people would say she had romanticized

the experience and those feelings were nothing more than post-partum hormones doing their job. Whatever it was, it was transcendental, life-defining, and fleeting. By the time she got home, the love remained, but the self-assuredness had disappeared and the fear set in.

Just a few short months later, and here they were strolling around their quiet suburban neighborhood, with the Stars and Stripes hanging from porches all around, one of which was the porch of the house she had bought with Eddie, and Victoria still had so many questions, most of which she could barely articulate. She wasn't unhappy. She loved Ava more than anything. She could not picture her life without her. So why did her life feel so unfinished? If someone asked her to paint a self-portrait right now, the image would be blurry, unclear, unfocused.

As she was reaching home, with Ava asleep in the stroller, Victoria noticed the neighbor opposite in his driveway. He was surrounded by tools and was tinkering with his car engine. He waved to her and came jogging over.

'Hi, I'm Tom,' he reached out his hand. Victoria noticed it was spotless. Neither his hands nor his clothes had a mark on them. He looked oddly clean for a man that was working on his car. 'I just wanted to apologize about us running off yesterday. We didn't even get a chance to say hello. Almost as soon as we arrived, my wife started to feel sick, and we had to go. I think she must've eaten something that didn't agree with her.'

'I'm sorry to hear that. I hope she's feeling better today.'

'Oh aye, she is. Did I hear you're from Belfast?'

'That's right,'

'Just like me. Your accent has flattened out a bit, but you can still hear the lilt. Is it West Belfast you're from?'

'That's right. I grew up on the Falls Road.'

'I'm a West Belfast lad myself. I'm sure if we put our heads together we'd probably have a whole list of people in common.'

'Maybe,' Victoria started to push the stroller back and forth, hoping Ava wouldn't wake up.

'And I think your husband mentioned that you had a friend here visiting from Belfast.' Victoria gave him a vacant look. 'I think he said she was the Godmother?'

'Oh Emma? Yes, she's an old friend from home. But she lives in New York too.'

'You know, I think I recognized her. What's her surname?'

'McCourt.'

'McCourt. That's it. I'm sure I know the family.'

Victoria searched his face for some trace of familiarity and came up blank. 'I grew up near Emma. I don't remember any O'Connells.'

'No, we didn't live close. But I think I worked with one of her uncles.'

Victoria cast her mind back to her teenage years. She knew for sure Emma's mum was one of three sisters. Emma's Dad had died when they were nine. A foot soldier in the IRA, he had blown himself up when the device he was supposed to plant at an army checkpoint had gone off too early. He had one brother. But Victoria was sure he had never worked a day in his life and had spent most of his time either in prison or on the run.

Victoria studied Tom's face. He must be mistaken. He seemed too relaxed to be lying.

'Anyway, I was hoping you could give me her phone number. I thought it would be nice to catch up, see how her family is doing.'

Victoria started to get the sense they were being watched. She cast her eyes towards her house expecting to see Eddie at the window. But all the curtains were still drawn.

'Actually, I can do better than that. She stayed over last night. I don't know if she'll be out of bed yet. But feel free to pop over later this morning. You can see her then.'

'No, I wouldn't want to impose. If you can just give me her number, I'll give her a ring sometime.'

'Well, I don't know it by heart, and I left my phone charging at home.'

'I'll come by during the week and get it.'

'Feel free to pop by today if you want.'

'Maybe…maybe…well, I must be getting back.'

Victoria watched him saunter away. Half way down his driveway, she noticed him glance up. She followed his gaze. Someone was looking down from one of his upstairs windows.

Ava was still fast asleep when they got home, so Victoria decided to leave her in the stroller rather than risk setting her off again. She found Emma and Eddie at the back of the house in the kitchen.

Victoria smiled. It was like stumbling upon two adolescents. Emma was sitting on the kitchen counter wearing a big t-shirt, her legs dangling beneath her. There was mascara smeared under both her eyes, and she was eating dry cereal straight from the box.

Eddie was at the dining table, crumpled, both of his hands clinging to his coffee mug. A piece of cold toast lay alone on a plate in front of him, with only a small bite taken out of it.

'Struggling are we?' Victoria asked.

'Ugh, not so loud,' Eddie whispered.

'V, I think you should know that we blame you for this,' Emma said. 'It was your responsibility, as the most sober one, to stop us from drinking so much.'

'Ha, like I could ever stop either of you from having a drink.'

She had given their guests way too much champagne and not enough canapés. So almost everyone had been quite tipsy when the Christening party finished in the early evening. Daniel had driven back to the city at around 6pm, leaving Emma to sleep over. He had said he needed to get up early for golf that morning and hadn't wanted to be driving late at night. After Daniel had left, Emma and Eddie had started in on the rum. They both now looked at Victoria with such vulnerability that she decided to go easy on them. 'Who wants eggs?'

'Oh yes please,' Emma said. 'I need some fat in me.'

'Yuck, how can you eat?' Eddie moaned. 'My digestive system is experiencing an existential crisis. It no longer knows what its purpose is. I think its trying to end it all.'

'Seriously, you'll feel better if you eat something.'

'Listen to her,' Victoria said. 'This is from a woman who has survived some epic hangovers in her life.'

Emma gave Victoria a fake scowl.

'I'm not sure I'll ever be able to eat anything again. I think I'm going to have to survive on coffee and vitamin tablets from here on out.' Eddie gave up on the pretense that he was sitting up and let his head drop the final inch. Victoria looked at him with his cheek squashed against the table, his eyes half closed. She went over and stroked his hair.

'This too shall pass, my love,' she told him.

'I could murder an Ulster Fry right now,' Emma said. At the mention of Ulster, Victoria remembered the conversation with their neighbor.

'Emma, the man across the street was asking about you.'

'You have an admirer,' Eddie muttered, without lifting his head.

'Tell him to come over and have a look at me now. There's not much to admire.'

'Actually, he said he knew you from Belfast. Eddie, what did you say his name was?'

'Tom O'Connell.'

'Doesn't ring a bell.'

Eddie sat upright again. His interest was obviously sufficiently piqued to justify making the supreme effort to balance his head on his neck. 'He's too old for you anyway. He must be well into his fifties. Victoria, I hope you told him Emma was married. Although, he's married too, so that may not put him off. Dirty bastard. I'll go talk to him just as soon as my internal organs find their rightful places again.'

'Is his wife from Belfast too?' Victoria asked.

'No, she's definitely American. From the North East I'd say,' said Eddie.

'Any ideas who they could be?' Victoria asked Emma.

'No.'

'The wife seems a bit strange if you ask me. A real tight-ass,' Eddie said.

'That's not fair, we barely know them,' Victoria said.

Eddie looked up at her with bloodshot eyes. 'She's weird, I tell you. They were barely here two minutes yesterday when she took off and dragged him with her. I bet she's a bit of a recluse. She was all "I want to be alone." Thinks she's Greta Garbo or something.'

Victoria noticed a flicker of recognition pass across Emma's face, and her already pale skin lost another couple of shades.

'Actually, I'm not hungry.' Emma jumped down from the counter. 'I'm going to have a shower.'

'But I thought you said it was better to eat something?' Victoria protested, but Emma was already out the door and running up the stairs.

'What got into her?' Eddie asked.

'No idea.'

Victoria busied herself making scrambled eggs for one, as Eddie sat at the table making odd grumbling noises that seemed to comfort him. In her mind, she started making a list of things she needed to do that day. She should write the thank you cards. She had checked their gift registry online this morning and almost everything had been bought. People had been so kind. Most of the neighbors had bought them gifts even though they barely knew them. She knew it had been a good idea to put the registry details on the invitation. Even the couple from across the street had dropped over something a few days ago. What were their names again? Janet and Tom O'Connell. And there had been another name on their message too. It must be their daughter. What was she called again? Kathleen, yes, that was it. Kathleen. Kathleen…

Victoria pulled the pan from the gas and rushed out of the kitchen.

'Where are you going?' Eddie called after her.

'I just need to give Emma a towel.'

'I already gave her one earlier. See, I'm not the terrible host you think I am.'

Victoria paused. 'You only gave her one? She needs one for her hair too,' she shouted, and then she continued climbing the stairs two at a time, trying to get to Emma as fast as she could.

CHAPTER NINETEEN
VICTORIA—LONG ISLAND
JULY 8TH, 2012

By the time Victoria got upstairs, Emma was already locked in the bathroom, and Victoria could hear the sound of the shower running.

'Emma, are you in the shower yet?'

Silence. Victoria knocked again.

'Are you ok?'

Still nothing. Maybe Emma had been telling the truth just now. Maybe she had no idea who this Tom O'Connell was. But there was something about the way Emma had fled the kitchen…She knocked a third time.

'Emma, do you think it's them?'

Victoria heard shuffling and the sound of the lock, and then Emma opened the door. She was still wearing the long t-shirt she'd borrowed from Eddie the night before. She had her phone in her hand.

'I just looked them up. There are some photos on the *Long Island Herald's* website. It's them.'

'Oh my God,' Victoria came into the bathroom and

locked the door behind her. 'Are you sure?'

'Yes. I've never forgotten their faces. It's definitely them.'

'Are there any photos of Kathleen?'

'No. I haven't found any yet. All I can find are pictures of them at black tie charity galas. When I search for Kathleen O'Connell I can't find anyone from Long Island that's the right age, but I'll keep looking.'

'It's strange. We've been living here nearly a month, and I haven't seen them with a daughter. How old would she be now?'

'Nineteen.'

Emma dropped on to the bathroom mat, crumpled, with her back against the bath. The bathroom was already filling up with white steam. It clouded up the mirror in a foggy haze. 'I really want to see her,' she said. 'You have no idea how often I try to picture her in my mind.'

Victoria sat down on the floor facing Emma. 'I know you do, honey.'

'I almost can't believe it. I've spent years wondering if I'd ever get a chance to see her again. I even phoned Geary once and begged him to tell me who they were. But he told me he couldn't give me that information. He said that wasn't the deal. I even offered to pay him back the money, but he just laughed at me.' Tears gathered at the edge of Emma's eyes and then tumbled onto her face, mixing with yesterday's mascara, falling down her cheek like a black watercolor.

'I'd given up. I've tried so hard to accept that I'd never see her again, and now this happens. What does it mean?'

'It must be fate bringing you two back together. I mean, of all the houses, in all the towns, in all the world, we buy *this* one?'

'What would I say to her? How could I ever explain? She can't know the truth.'

Emma was getting ahead of herself. 'Sweetie, they may not want you to see her.' Victoria watched as the realization that this was probably true passed across Emma's face. 'I just want you to be prepared.'

They sat in silence for a few minutes with the thunderous noise of the shower filling the room. Victoria tugged nervously at the mat. Emma stared emptily into the steam. Then, suddenly, Emma snapped to life and stood up.

'I want to talk to them. I at least want to know how she is and what she's like. I'm going to have a shower. I'm going to pull myself together and then go over and face them.'

'No. What if she's there? You have no idea what they've told her. I don't think that's a good idea.' Victoria stood up. 'Do you want me to invite them over here?'

'What about Eddie?'

'Don't worry about Eddie. I'll handle him. He doesn't know what happened. I've never told him, I promise you. But, he adores you. If we have to tell him something, he'll keep it a secret.'

'Are you sure?'

'Yes.' Victoria spoke with more confidence than she felt. She had no idea how Eddie would react, but what else could she say?

'Ok. That sounds like a plan. If we absolutely have to, we can tell Eddie…but Daniel can never, ever know.'

***

When Tom answered the front door, he had the same counterfeit casual demeanor as before.

'Hi, how are you? It's nice to…'

'I spoke to Emma,' Victoria interrupted him. She let her voice drop to a whisper. 'She told me about the affair you two had when she was young.' Emma and Victoria had decided that it was best if the O'Connells didn't know Victoria knew the truth. 'If you can get away from your wife, she'd like to see you. Can you come over to our place for coffee? Say in an hour?'

Tom glanced momentarily behind into the darkness

within. Then he turned to Victoria. 'I'll be there.'

Victoria walked back along their driveway. The air felt eerily still—there wasn't even a slight breeze. It felt like the moment of quiet, just after an explosion, when everything in the vicinity has been lifted, creating a split second of stillness on the ground, before the debris begins to fall.

An hour later, Victoria was standing in her hallway straining to hear what was happening in the living room. Eddie was next to her, rocking a sleeping Ava from side to side in his arms. Victoria tried, silently, to order him back to the kitchen. But he wasn't going to budge.

'I wanted to meet you to make sure we were all on the same page,' Tom said.

'What do you mean?'

Victoria listened for any signs of weakness in Emma's voice but there weren't any. She had put on her tough lawyer armor as soon as Tom had arrived.

'Before I answer you that, perhaps it's better if I ask you a question first. What are you doing here, in this neighborhood?'

'My best friend lives here.'

'And that's just a coincidence?'

'Of course. Up until this morning, I didn't know your names. I had no idea who had taken her.'

'Ok, I believe you. But, now that you know, we need to make sure that the original agreement stands. You were to have no contact with her. That's what we agreed then, and that's still the case. We need your assurance that you'll stay away from her.'

'God, he sounds like he's negotiating a contract,' Eddie whispered.

Victoria put her fingers to her lips to shush him and tuned her ears back to the conversation in the living room.

'Does she still live with you?'

Silence.

'Do you have a picture? Is she well? Can I see what she looks like now?'

'No. The less you know of her the better.'

'I'd like to know what she looks like. I have a right to know if she's well. I want some evidence of that.'

Victoria could hear Emma's voice start to crack, ever so slightly.

'You gave up that right some time ago.'

There was a long pause. Ava, still asleep in Eddie's arms, stretched her hand above her forehead. Victoria stroked her daughter's face and smiled briefly at her husband.

'I have one more question for you,' Tom said. 'Are you still in touch with the father?'

'No.'

'So we don't need to worry about you telling him about us then do we?'

'Not at all.'

'And I'm talking about the real father. Not that other boy you introduced us to. Because I know you lied to the real father and told him Kathleen had been kidnapped. You lied to everyone back then. So I need to be very sure that you are telling me the truth now.'

'Holy fuck,' Eddie hissed. 'What's this about a kidnapping?'

'Be quiet. I'm trying to listen,' Victoria whispered. All they had told Eddie was that Emma had given up a baby for adoption when she was a teenager and the O'Connells were the adoptive parents. Victoria had hoped that was all they would need to tell him. She hadn't expected him to come tip toe behind her to eavesdrop with babe in arms and all.

'Did you know about this? Does that make you an accessory?' Eddie whispered.

'I will tell you the full story later, I promise. Please know that Emma is our friend. She is a good person, and she had her reasons. Ok?'

Eddie nodded, still wide-eyed with shock.

Victoria got close to the door and started

eavesdropping again.

'If you need more money, we can give it to you. We thought we gave you enough at the time, but you can have more now if you need it.'

'I have money now,' Emma said.

'Money?' Eddie mouthed to Victoria.

'Later,' she murmured.

'I'm not asking you for anything. I just want to know if she's ok,' said Emma.

'Fine. I can tell you Kathleen is a happy young woman. She's beautiful and healthy. She has lots of friends.'

'Does she live with you?'

'She's off at college.'

'Where?'

'That's not your concern.'

Silence again.

Victoria stared at the living room door. She wanted to break through it. To go to her friend and comfort her.

'It would destroy her if she knew the truth,' Tom said after a moment.

'I would never do anything to hurt her.'

'Then you promise to stay away from us?'

'Isn't there another way? Couldn't we say I'm a family friend?'

'No,' Tom barked. 'It's too much of a risk. Fact is, I don't trust you and I don't want you anywhere near my daughter.'

'I would never tell her the truth.'

'You're never going to get the chance.'

'But…'

'Don't be selfish. You did a good thing giving her to us. She's had a far better life with us. And I'm not just talking financially. It was a brave thing you did, recognizing that. And if you have a shred of feeling left for her you'll stay away.'

'Fine…you're right…I know you're right,' Emma said.

'Good. I'm glad we're in agreement. I'm not the kind of

person you want as an enemy.'

'Was that a threat?'

'It's just a piece of advice.'

'I think we're done here. You can go now.'

'You've been warned,' Tom said.

At the sound of people standing up in the living room, Victoria and Eddie scuttled back to the kitchen.

'What's all this about money and a kidnapping? What kind of adoption was this?' Eddie said.

'Let's just say it wasn't conventional. I promise I'll explain everything later.'

'What happened to the money? Is that how she paid for college and law school? I remember she once told me her first husband paid for her college degree and was the guarantor on her loans for law school. But they'd already separated by the time she started law school. It never made any sense. Now I know why.'

'She didn't use the money for law school. She needed it for something else.'

'What?'

'Can we talk about this later?' Eddie wasn't going to calm down until she had told him everything, and, once he did know the truth, he was going to be even more agitated than he was right now. But the explanations would need to wait. For now, she needed to check on Emma.

As soon as she heard the front door close, Victoria rushed out into the hallway and threw her arms around her friend. At Victoria's touch, Emma's icy veneer melted and she started to tremble. Victoria held on to her tight.

'Eddie, put the kettle on,' she shouted, and then to Emma, 'What are you going to do?'

'I need to do what he says. He's right. I need to stay away. I just wish I could see her.'

'Well, she has to come visit them sometime. I could stake out the place. I'm sure Eddie has a long range camera lens I could use.'

Emma gave Victoria a weak smile and used her sleeve

to wipe the tears from her eyes. 'I can't go home and face Daniel looking like this.'

'Then stay here. Tell him Eddie and I are both sick and you've offered to spend the night looking after Ava.'

'V, what am I going to do?'

She pulled Emma into a tight embrace. 'We will work it out, don't worry.'

That night, Victoria and Emma sat up late getting drunk. The next morning, they got the train into Manhattan together for work. They gave each other a tight hug when they parted ways at Penn Station, and Emma promised Victoria she would be fine.

That evening, when Victoria returned from work, there was a "*For Sale*" sign in front of the O'Connell's house, and the place was in darkness.

'It's fine,' Emma said when Victoria called to tell her they had gone. 'I know their names now. A man like Tom O'Connell can't just disappear. I'll find them, when I'm ready.'

CHAPTER TWENTY
VICTORIA—LONG ISLAND
SEPTEMBER 2012

She felt like she was in a futuristic torture chamber. The kind of place where they might lock someone up and force them to listen to pan pipe music, on loop, to drive them insane. The floor was uncarpeted, and the furniture, the walls, the door, and the curtains were all a pristine white.

Most disturbingly, however, was the fact that the canvas in the corner was still completely colorless. Victoria wasn't sure how long she'd been staring at it, or how long her hand had been poised, ready to dip the brush into the blood-red paint. Nearly an hour, perhaps longer.

Just do something, anything, she told herself. Eddie will be back soon. I can't have nothing to show him.

From the laundry room, the washing machine started to beep, signaling that the cycle had finished. High-pitched and clear in the unusual silence, it called out to her, nagging her to go down and empty it. She knew if she just ignored it, the beeping would eventually stop. But she really shouldn't leave wet clothes lying in the machine.

They'd get moldy. It would only take ten minutes to hang them out. Plus, a quick break would do her good. Afterwards, she'd come straight back up and make a start.

Victoria threw down the paintbrush and fled, leaving the canvas untouched.

She was putting away the last plate, when Eddie got home. The kitchen was spotless, their clean laundry billowed in the back yard, and the washing machine hummed with another load.

'Finished your masterpiece already?' Eddie had a sleeping Ava in his arms, exhausted from the excitement of swim class.

'How was it? Did she like the water? She wasn't afraid of it, was she?' It had been Ava's first time in a pool, and Victoria was desperate to know how she had done. Victoria didn't want Ava to inherit her wariness of the water. It was vital that she become a strong swimmer, just like her Dad.

'She loved it. I'm just going to put her down for a nap.'

A few minutes later, Eddie came back downstairs. 'I see you're experimenting with minimalism.'

He had obviously seen the empty canvas.

Victoria tried to make a joke of it. 'I've always been a fan of Warhol's invisible sculpture. So I thought why not try an invisible painting? What do you think?'

'I'm thinking what have you been doing for the past two hours?'

Victoria motioned around the room. 'I didn't have the time. This place was a mess after breakfast, and the clothes needed to be hung out.'

'So?'

'So that's what I've been doing.'

Eddie opened the dishwasher and looked inside. 'Why did you empty the dishwasher? The nanny can do that on Monday. You didn't need to dry all the plates and put them away.'

'It wasn't just the dishes. I had to do a couple of loads

of laundry. The basket was nearly full.' Victoria couldn't believe Eddie had her defending herself for doing housework. Shouldn't it be her berating him for not having done any?

'Ava has enough clothes. She could wear a different outfit every day for a year. She didn't need clean clothes today. That's something else you could have left.'

Victoria grappled around for something else to say. 'There were crumbs all over the place from breakfast. We don't want to attract mice.'

Eddie came over and put his arms around her. 'You are right. I'm terrified of mice. So thank you for that. But how about next week, I promise to clean up the crumbs and put the plates in the dishwasher before I take Ava swimming, and you promise to resist the urge to run down here the minute my back is turned?'

The following Saturday morning, Victoria was once again back upstairs staring at the blank canvas, still not knowing where to begin. Outside, she heard someone shouting and she went to the window to take a look. There was a removals van outside the O' Connells' house. The new owners had arrived.

The neighborhood gossip had told Eddie they had sold the house for far below market value to get a quick sale. They'd apparently been on holiday since the weekend of the Christening. Of course no one, except Eddie and Victoria, knew why.

Victoria turned back to the canvas. She was wasting time. She lifted a brush and shoved it into the black paint, ready to attack the thirty-inch canvas. It loomed over her like an ice mountain. She paused and then let her hand drop to her side. Why had she thought she could do this again? Why had she ever thought she could do this?

Whatever she did would be average at best. She wasn't cut out to be an artist. Ok, she had the technical skill to put together a pleasant picture with paints. But, to be a true artist, she needed to have something to say, and right now she was mute. Victoria looked at the clock. She had already wasted half an hour. Eddie would be back soon and she had nothing to show for her free time. Downstairs, the washing machine started to beep.

CHAPTER TWENTY-ONE
EMMA—MANHATTAN
NOVEMBER 2012

'I can't believe you are going on another trip'

Emma could picture Daniel pacing around their monochrome living room. Their apartment was so pristine they might as well have been living inside a glossy interiors magazine. He'd have the phone in one hand and would be plumping cushions or lining up books on the shelf with the other. When she was angry, she drank. Daniel preferred to tidy. Emma thought her approach was the healthier of the two.

She swiveled round in her chair and looked down on to Fifth Avenue. It was 9pm, and the streets were packed with shoppers. Thanksgiving was still a couple of weeks away and yet the Christmas buying frenzy was already well under way.

'Can't they send someone else to Chicago? I've hardly seen you these past two weeks.'

'No, Daniel, they cannot send someone else. I'm the lead associate on this case. I'm the one that needs to meet the witness.'

'Fine, but does it have to be this week? Won't that be right in the middle of your cycle? Can't you go another time?'

'The witness statements are due on December 10th. If I don't go this week, we'll never make the deadline.'

Daniel maintained a seething silence at the other end of the line. Emma looked at the wedding photo sitting on her shelf next to the picture of Saint Adjutor. It looked like a reportage photo documenting a single fleeting moment— Daniel standing on the street offering his hand to Emma to help her out of a yellow taxi, their eyes locked in a spontaneous moment of shared joy.

It had taken nearly ten minutes to get that picture. The photographer had flagged a cab down outside the hotel and forced Emma to get in and out of the parked car, repeatedly reaching for Daniel's hand, with an "adoring bride" look plastered across her face. Emma had grumbled throughout about missing cocktail hour. Daniel, on the other hand, had been utterly compliant and patient with the photographer, happily striking whatever pose she asked him to.

'I'm sorry. I promise, once we get past this deadline, I'll slow down for a bit, and we can spend some quality time together.'

'It's not just this trip,' Daniel sounded dejected now. Emma preferred it when he was argumentative. 'For months, you've been consumed with work. On the odd occasions that you are home, it doesn't feel like you're here. It feels like your mind is always at the office.'

She knew she hadn't been herself in months. Not since the Christening. Meeting the O' Connells had stirred up old memories. Feelings, like weapons she had locked away, had been unleashed once more. And their capacity to hurt her had only increased with time. Daniel knew something was wrong but he had no idea what. He assumed it was work.

'I know, this case has been distracting me,' Emma said. 'I've been under a lot of pressure. But I have to go to Chicago. Once we get these statements out of the way, things will be better.'

'Ok,' he said, sounding placated. 'I love you.'

'I love you too,' she said mechanically.

She went to put the phone down, but Daniel called to her before she could hang up.

'Wait, before you go. Are you taking folic acid?'

'What?'

'Folic acid. Heather was telling me that you should be taking it if you're trying to get pregnant. Something about the health of the baby's spine.' Heather was one of the architects with whom Daniel often collaborated on his interior design jobs. They had obviously been talking about more than just soft furnishings and light fittings.

'No, I didn't know I was supposed to,' Emma lied.

'Didn't Victoria tell you? Maybe you should confide in her. She might be able to help.'

'I can't believe you've been talking to Heather about our private business.'

'I don't see what's wrong with confiding in our friends. You should learn to open up more.'

This was a favorite mantra of Daniel's—you should open up more—as if talking were ever the answer to anything.

'I don't see how talking to Victoria is supposed to help. Just because she had a child doesn't make her a fertility expert.'

'You're right; she's not a professional. Perhaps we need to think about going to see a doctor. Heather had the number of a guy. He's supposed to be one of the best.'

They didn't need the finest medic in the city to figure out why they hadn't gotten pregnant. With one blood test, it would be obvious Emma was still on birth control.

'I'll run to the pharmacy tomorrow and get some folic acid,' Emma said, completely ducking the issue of fertility tests. 'Listen, I really need to go, otherwise I'll never get out of here tonight.'

Emma swiveled back round to her desk and almost jumped out of her chair at the sight of Michael standing in the doorway leaning against the frame.

'You won't be too late will you?' Daniel said.

Emma glanced at the two large binders of documents that she had to read before the morning.

'I can't promise anything. Don't wait up for me.'

'I love you.'

'Ok, bye.' Emma put the phone down and looked up at Michael. 'How long have you been lurking there?'

'Just a few seconds. I'm after ordering a pizza. Do ye fancy some? We can bring it up to the cupola, enjoy dinner with a view.'

It was nearly 9:30pm and Emma still hadn't had dinner. The despair of low blood sugar was already engulfing her. A dose of carbohydrates was just what she needed.

'Pizza sounds good. But are you sure the cupola will be open at this time? I thought they locked it when there were no events on.'

The cupola was the meeting room at the top of the building. Perched on the roof, just above the forty-second floor, it was a large circular space with floor to ceiling windows on all sides and a high glass dome in the center. The firm used it for client entertaining.

'It is, but Cathal the security guard is going to open it for us. I'll ring you when it's here.'

When Emma met Michael by the elevator twenty minutes later, he had a large pizza box in one hand and his briefcase in the other.

'Don't tell me you're going to work through dinner,' Emma said.

'Not at all.'

'So what's with the briefcase?'

'Just wait and see. I've a wee surprise for you.'

CHAPTER TWENTY-TWO
EMMA
MANHATTAN & CHICAGO
NOVEMBER & DECEMBER 2012

The air inside the cupola was cool and still.

'Don't bother with the lights,' Michael said. 'Sure we can see well enough by the glow of the other skyscrapers.' He walked straight past the chairs and sat down on the floor by the windows looking out on Fifth Avenue. To the South, Emma could see One World Trade Center taking shape. It stood defiant and proud—unfinished but already a giant amongst New York's tallest buildings.

She plopped down next to Michael, feeling like a naughty kid at boarding school sneaking off for a midnight feast. He shook off his jacket, loosened his tie, and opened the top button of his shirt. Slim and strong, it was plain to see that he took care of himself. Not for him a bulging body inflated by too many client dinners and not enough time in the gym.

He opened his briefcase and produced a bottle of red wine and two plastic water cooler cups.

'You can't have pizza without wine now can you?'

Emma examined the bottle; it was a 2010 Californian Pinot Noir.

'Where did you get this?'

'I keep a few bottles locked in my filing cabinet for emergencies.'

'Is this an emergency?'

Michael took the bottle from her and started to work the corkscrew into it.

'I wasn't eavesdropping, but I did hear some of your conversation with your husband. I just assumed you could use a wee drink. I can put it away if you want.'

'No, don't do that.' Emma held her cup up to him.

'Can I say something?' Michael asked. 'It's a bit personal.'

Emma shrugged. 'Go ahead.'

'You know how it is in this place. It's like a lottery who makes partner and who doesn't. You shouldn't sacrifice having a family for some elusive partnership that may never materialize.'

That term "having a family" always slightly bemused Emma. Shouldn't she already have one? Wasn't that the whole idea of getting married? So Daniel would be her family? In a way, he was the only family she had. She spoke to her mother a few times a month, but she hadn't seen her in nearly two decades.

'You mistake me for someone with ambitious career goals,' Emma said.

'You're not?' He looked genuinely surprised. 'You certainly work at the pace of someone who wants to climb to the top.'

'Everyone here pulls long hours. It's just what's expected. It says more about the culture than it does about me.'

Michael gave her a sidelong glance. 'True, but you have

drive too. I can see it in you.'

Emma shrugged. 'I'm a grafter, I always have been.' She took a large gulp of wine from the plastic cup and savored the warm, familiar feeling as the alcohol rushed down her throat.

'It's not just that, you're a very talented lawyer.'

Emma smiled. 'Thanks. That's nice to hear.'

'So if it's not your career that's holding you back from having kids, then what is it?'

Emma picked up a slice of pizza, held it above her, and let half of it fold into her mouth. She gazed at the investment bankers in the building opposite as she chewed.

'I was once at a women's conference,' Emma began, 'it was full of senior managers, vice-presidents of banks and partners of law firms, and the main panel discussion wasn't about leadership, or how to win clients, or that kind of thing. It was on work-life balance. Isn't that funny? I can't imagine a men's conference talking about that.'

'That's because we don't have special male-only events. We'd get in trouble if we did.'

'I wouldn't complain if I were you, I've been to industry conferences where only five maybe ten percent of the speakers are women.'

'Fair enough.'

'Anyway, the only thing the panel seemed to be concerned with was how to balance career and kids. So I stick up my hand and say that I think work-life balance is about more than that. And the main speaker responds "of course, you single gals need to get out of the office too, otherwise how are you ever going to find a man to have children with?" and everyone else just nods along in agreement. I didn't say anything, as they'd moved the microphone on for the next question, but I wanted to shout "why does everyone assume parenthood is an inevitable step in human development?" Is it really? I mean, do men think that way?'

'I can't really speak for all men,' Michael responded.

Typical lawyerly response, always looking for the grey area. She wasn't letting him off that easily.

'Well, how did you end up deciding to have children?'

'If I'm honest, I can't say I ever really decided. The decision was sort of made for me. I mean it's not like Naomi was an accident. Carol and I had talked about it. I had told her I didn't think we were ready. But I was on thin ice with that one. We were both professionals in our thirties earning decent salaries, and she had good maternity cover. I held my ground for a few months, and she'd have the odd tantrum here and there. Then one day, she brought it up again, and I said I still wasn't sure, and she went absolutely mental at me. She was throwing things and crying, and so I stormed out. I took myself off for a walk, and I tried to come up with the perfect argument to dissuade her. But I struggled to think of practical reasons not to have a baby. So, when I got home, I said, "fine, let's go for it."'

'But readiness isn't just a practical question. If you weren't sure, it was wrong for her to force the issue.' Emma could never imagine behaving the way Michael's wife had.

'It's not like I was duped. She was upfront with me from the beginning. When we were dating, I knew she wanted kids, and I still asked her to marry me. And I'm glad she pushed the issue. I would have just drifted on until it was too late, and that would have been a damn tragedy because Naomi is the absolute love of my life. Anyway, I'm sorry for poking my nose in. If you don't like children, that's fine.'

'It's not that I don't like them. I love my friends' kids. I'm just not sure I want any of my own. My whole life I've felt this way. I was never one of those little girls playing house with a baby doll.'

'Well, that's fine then. Every kid needs a cool aunty to say yes when the parents say no.'

'Where are all the stars? I thought, this far up, we'd be able to see them,' Emma said.

They both leaned back on their elbows and looked up through the glass dome at the silvery blackness stretched out above them.

'Too much pollution,' Michael said. 'I grew up on a farm in County Cork, and I can tell you, for a fact, the night sky is not dark. We should be looking at an explosion of light right now, but it's hidden behind the pollution.'

'That's kind of sad. It's like our ability to fuck up has now reached as far as the stars,' Emma said.

'I was quite the astronomer when I was a kid. Although my parents rarely let me stay up much. In the country, when the stars come out you go to bed.'

'Maybe that's why they call New York the city that never sleeps, we've lost sight of the real sky. We've no idea when it's bedtime.'

'That's why I prefer cities,' Michael grinned. 'I kind of like the madness of breaking the natural cycles and seeing what happens.'

'Depends on the city, I'd take rural County Cork over Belfast any day.' Emma thought back to her childhood—to the squat council houses, the riots, the petrol bombs, and the concrete. If you asked her to describe Belfast's aesthetic, it would be "aggressively ugly."

'Cork was a fine place to be a young lad.' Michael lay down on his back, like he was laying in a meadow looking up at the clouds.

Emma pulled her knees up close to her chest and listened to him talk about his childhood. About how he was always getting in trouble for mucking around stealing apples from the orchard and climbing trees. And how he used to kiss girls behind the chapel during Saturday evening mass.

'Sure they were simpler, happier times,' Michael sighed. He sat up and poured them both some more wine. Even though she had a ton of work waiting downstairs, Emma didn't bother to stop him from filling up her cup.

'You're a bad influence,' she said.

'Sure ye have to have a wee bit of fun at work, otherwise what's the point?'

Emma examined him, sitting so relaxed and cool on the meeting room floor.

'There's something unusual about you,' she said.

'How do ye mean?'

'Even when we're up against a deadline, and the whole team is running around exhausted and anxious, you always have this knowing air of contentment. What's the secret?'

He laughed. 'Sure I've no idea what you're talking about.'

'Yes you do. C'mon spit it out.'

'Ok, you want to know the secret? I'll tell you.' He leaned closer to Emma, cupped his hand around his mouth and, in a fake whisper, said, '*Satori*.'

'What?'

'*Satori*. It's the first step towards Nirvana.'

'Ok, I'm going to need a bit more help than that.'

'It's a Japanese Buddhist term. It means the ability to understand one's true nature and the use of that self-awareness to inform everything you do in life.'

'That still doesn't answer my question,' Emma said.

'I'm happy being a lawyer. Maybe being a formula one driver or a master whisky distiller might be cooler, but that's not who I am. I'm good at arguing. I know myself. I also know I'm the kind of person that needs to have fun. So I don't beat myself up thinking about doing "the right thing." Of course I want to do well at work and be a good father and all that shite. But I don't try to be perfect at the expense of my own pleasure. My yardstick for everything is to ask whether I'm enjoying it or not, and, if I am, then I don't worry about anything else. That's my *satori*. I think you need to discover yours. And I use the word discover very deliberately. It's not something you can invent, you have to find it within.'

Emma burst out laughing.

'What's so funny?'

'It's just *satori*,' she started, before falling back into a fit of giggles.

'Here's me imparting my wisdom and this is how you react?'

'No, I'm sorry…but here we are in our designer suits, drinking expensive red wine and eating pizza. It's after ten at night, we're still in the bloody office, and we're talking about Buddhism? It's just such a ridiculous contrast, don't you think?'

'I'm sure the bloody Dalai Lama himself isn't as enlightened as I am. Now give me your cup, we might as well finish off this bottle, and I'll tell you my theory on the origins of the Universe next.'

***

The following evening, still hung-over and sleep-deprived, Emma flew out to Chicago. She spent the following day in meetings at the client's characterless offices. In the evening, she ate dinner alone in her hotel room and then drew herself a bath. She lay there, for hours, the water cooling around her, draining each of the tiny liquor bottles from the mini-bar, lining up the empties along the bath, staring upwards, her memories playing across the white ceiling like a sad movie.

She knew from Victoria that the O'Connells had fled after the Christening weekend and had sold their house not long afterwards. Emma wasn't worried about them having moved. She could still track them down, if she wanted.

But Emma now realized, for her own sake, she had to stop stalking the O'Connells on the Internet. It was useless. No matter how hard she searched, she could not find any trace online of a nineteen-year-old Kathleen O'Connell from Long Island. She had even scoured the websites of all the Long Island high schools, looking at photos of school plays and sports events, hoping to find Kathleen's face amongst them. But there was no trace of her. And all this fruitless searching was driving her mad and distracting her from work and from her life with Daniel.

When she handed Kathleen over, she had fractured her life, creating a fault line on which she had built a new one. Meeting the O'Connells had created huge tremors that threatened to send her world tumbling down around her. She couldn't let that happen. She would lock all those memories away again in a gun cabinet inside, where they couldn't hurt her or anyone else. It wasn't her *satori*, but it was her reality.

When the water got so cold she started to tremble, Emma climbed out and wrapped a towel around herself. In the mirror, through the steam, she could see a girl looking back at her. It wasn't a reflection of her thirty-six-year-old self, with her pronounced frown line, eye bags, and the very slight beginnings of crows' feet. No, this was a copy of her teenage self, fresh-faced, with rosy cheeks and questioning green eyes.

'I know what you're thinking, but I didn't have any other options. I couldn't have just left her with Aiden.'

The girl in the mirror didn't look convinced.

'I know he loved her. But what does that matter? I did the right thing for everyone.'

Emma stared at the girl, both of them unflinching.

'So if I'm so sure what I did was right, then what's changed since meeting the O'Connells? Is that what you want to know?'

Emma thought for a moment, grappling to explain why, since meeting Tom, she had become obsessed with seeing Kathleen again, to the point that she could barely focus on anything in her life apart from the mechanics of her work.

'Because…' Emma gulped down the stone stuck in her throat. 'Because…'

The girl's eyes reflected Emma's sadness back towards her, underlining the helplessness of the situation.

Emma stared at the girl for a moment longer in silence, fighting down her tears. Then she took a deep breath and wiped her hand across the mirror, removing the ghostly layer of steam, revealing the reality beneath—a drunk, thirty-six-year-old woman with black mascara running down her pale cheeks, standing, all alone, talking to herself in a soulless hotel bathroom.

'Enough now,' she whispered. 'It's over. What's done is done.' The past was an ugly, war-torn country. But she had no other. Like it or not, her life had been built upon those ruins. She grabbed the robe hanging on the back of the door and wrapped it around her, straightened up, and walked out of the bathroom—determined to bury her skeletons once more.

***

Over the next few weeks, Emma worked around the clock to get the witness statements filed by the December 10th deadline. Not that she could now relax. The expert reports were due in mid-January, and she was sure Michael hadn't done nearly as much as he claimed on the main expert report—despite all the afternoons he seemed to spend out of the office meeting the professor. But even so, Emma planned to take it easy for a week or so, just as she had promised Daniel. They needed some time to reconnect. And, somehow, she needed to figure out how to talk to him about kids. She wasn't ready to have a baby with him yet. She wasn't sure she'd ever be ready. He deserved to know. But, for now, she just wanted to have some fun. Honesty would have to wait.

On the Thursday after they filed the statements, she snuck away to meet Daniel for lunch at The Modern, the formal dining room at the Museum of Modern Art. They spent two hours chatting over rich Alsatian food and a bottle of white wine, and, at around 3pm, Emma floated back into the office, fully intending to spend the afternoon researching a sunny last-minute Christmas get-away for her and Daniel. When she arrived, she passed by her secretary's desk to ask if there had been any calls when she was out.

'Just one, I left the details on a post-it-note next to your computer,' Claire said.

'Thanks,' Emma went into her office, hung her coat up, and went over to her desk. She picked up the fluorescent yellow post-it note. In Claire's neat handwriting it said: "*Aiden Kennedy called. His number is 02890271475. It's a Belfast number. He asked if you could call him back as soon as possible.*"

CHAPTER TWENTY-THREE
EMMA—MANHATTAN
DECEMBER 2012

Emma moved through the streets of midtown without thinking about where she was going or what she would do when she got there. She walked aimlessly, on autopilot, her feet stepping mechanically one in front of the other, her mind divorced from her body.

Grubby steam seeped up from the underworld, lacing it's way around a roast chestnut vendor, giving the air a sickeningly sweet heaviness. Car horns blared, and a pneumatic drill screeched as it tore up the sidewalk. Millions of pixels danced deliriously across screens. And demonic beauties stared down from billboards so huge that they made Godzilla look like a pet lizard.

In all directions, people came hurtling towards her. Emma felt their eyes on her, scrutinizing her. It was like they could look inside her. They were on to her.

She noticed a sports bar up ahead. At first, she didn't understand why it had caught her attention. Then she remembered. It was the bar where she had first met Daniel. One of her co-workers had invited her to a joint birthday party he was having with his best friend at that bar. Daniel had been the other birthday boy.

She peered in the window. With the exception of the bartender, the place was empty. She pulled open the door and stepped inside.

It was mid-afternoon, and the winter sun was falling fast. The dark furniture, the redbrick walls, and the brown bar-top were barely visible in the low-level lighting. At the bar, Emma ordered a shot of tequila. The bartender placed it in front of her and then went back to polishing glasses in the corner.

It was as if she was in a mafia movie; the eerily empty bar, the barman leaning in the corner, a safe distance away, in well-rehearsed disinterest, twisting a cloth inside the same glass, again and again, until it squeaked, watching her out of the corner of his eye. Emma glanced around, half expecting someone to emerge from the back room and blow her brains out.

She threw the tequila into her. It was icy as it slipped down her throat and then a raw sensation enflamed her chest. She ordered a bottle of beer and went over to a high table in the corner to drink it. In front of her, a wall of TV screens replayed highlights from the night before.

Bloodied boxers with swollen eye sockets flung punches at each other, warrior-like NFL players charged out to battle, and hockey players tore through ice, whacking each other around the head. In the middle of all the carnage, handsome young men danced around the unnatural green of a soccer field, skillfully passing a ball between them, as if the object of the game were artful footwork rather than goals.

Emma took out the yellow post-it note. Her heartbeat pounded violently through every capillary of her body. She twisted around and asked the bartender to bring her over another shot of tequila. As soon as he put it in front of her, she thrust her head back and drank it down. It tasted tart and acidic, like rotten vegetables. It was the shot of adrenalin she needed to bring her back to consciousness. She needed her wits about her right now. She needed to focus.

She started to dial Aiden's number.

It couldn't have been too hard for Aiden to find her. It was common knowledge around the Falls Road that she was a lawyer in New York. A simple Internet search for "Emma McCourt, lawyer, New York" would have led him straight to her profile page on her firm's website.

The real question was not how he had found her, but why he had bothered to look for her at all, and why now? Emma took a deep breath. There was only one way to find out.

Don't jump to conclusions, she told herself as the sound of the phone trilled in her ear.

'Hullo?' She recognized his voice immediately.

'Aiden, hi, it's Emma McCourt. I got a message that you'd called?' she could hear a quiver in her voice. She tried to remember the calming techniques she'd learned in advocacy class at law school.

'Emma McCourt, how long's it been?'

'God, probably longer than a woman my age should admit. How are ye?' she said, feigning friendliness.

'I saw your picture on that fancy law firm's website. It looks like the years haven't touched you at all.' The firm hired a professional photographer to take identikit pictures of the associates for the website. Dressed in a black suit and set against a grey background, they were encouraged to smile, but not too much. They had to look approachable, yet serious. Most of them, Emma included, just ended up looking like depressed clowns, with their mouths turned up in a smile and their eyes dead.

'Whereas me,' Aiden went on, 'I have a face that would chase rats from a barn.'

'I doubt that's true.' Aiden was just twenty-one the last

time she had seen him. With hair so black it was almost blue and eyes the color of the Atlantic on a sunny day, he had always been popular with the girls. One of his legs was a bit longer than the other, so he limped slightly. But it had never made him look weak. On the contrary, the lop-sided swagger had given him a slight air of danger, as if he'd been in the wars, as if he'd been close to death and emerged victorious.

'The years haven't been as good to me as they have to you, Emma. The economy here is completely fucked. We were tricked. We were told, "make peace and prosperity will come." Aye, there was a whiff of wealth about Belfast for a few years there, but it was just an illusion. I got laid off last year. I'm living in a bedsit, which I can hardly afford. I'll probably have to move back in with my Ma soon.'

'How is you mother?' Emma took a swig of beer and tried to act as if she was at a cookout chatting to an old acquaintance.

'She's not a well woman,'

'I'm sorry to hear...'

'Sure she's never been the same since we lost Kathleen.'

From the screen in the corner, a wrestler leered out at Emma, deranged and looking for someone to tear apart.

'The day they took Kathleen, they might as well have taken my Ma too. The bastards.'

'It's been hard on both families.'

'But I was her Daddy, I was supposed to look after my girl. Some stranger walked in and took her right from under my nose, whilst I slept in the next room. Isn't that what happened Emma?'

For all his talk of his heart breaking, Aiden didn't sound like a man wild with grief. He spoke slowly, with purpose, the way a skilled advocate might cajole an opposing witness into revealing something they shouldn't.

'Don't blame yourself,' Emma said.

'Who should I blame then?'

Emma didn't say anything.

'She'll be twenty next February. Same age I was when she was born. Do you remember that day?' Aiden asked.

'Of course I do.' Emma's brain was swelling, pressing against her skull.

'She was such a red, wrinkly wee thing. I was so pleased because I thought she'd inherited my blue eyes. But then, one day, she must have been about six or seven months old, she was staring up at me from her cot and I realized she'd got the McCourt green. Ach, but it didn't matter, she was a beautiful wean wasn't she?'

Had she been worrying for nothing? On Sunday it would be nineteen years to the day since Kathleen's "disappearance." Perhaps, Aiden was just feeling emotional coming up to the anniversary. Perhaps, he just needed to speak to someone who understood, someone who'd been through that terrible time with him.

Emma used to have a script ready to deal with Aiden and his grief, but not anymore. She had no problem lying, but for the life of her she wasn't sure what someone in her position was supposed to say right now. It had been so long since she'd had to play that part.

'I miss her too. I find it really hard to talk about Kathleen. It's still too painful.' Emma sniffed, hoping it might sound like she was crying. 'It was nice to hear from you. Maybe I'll see you next time I'm in Belfast.'

'You haven't been back in years, have you? Sure what's there in Belfast to come back to? After Kathleen disappeared, there was nothing keeping you here, was there?'

'I just haven't had a chance to visit recently.'

'Your big job in New York must keep you busy.'

'That it does.'

'Who'd have thought young Emma McCourt would go so far and rise so high? You were always smarter than me, but maybe I underestimated just how smart you were.'

On one of the TVs, a Korean archer prepared to take a shot. His movements, so elegant and precise, stood out in stark contrast to the mass of limbs flailing around on the other screens.

'I wouldn't say I've done that well, but I do alright for myself.'

'Well, you'd want to be careful. You know what they say. The higher they rise, the harder they fall.'

'What?'

'Nothing. Just making conversation. I must let you get on. I imagine this call's costing you a small fortune…although I'm sure you can afford it.'

'Ok, well it was good to hear from you,' Emma croaked.

'Just one thing before you go, I was talking to Paul Magee the other night.'

On one screen, the archer released the bow, sending the arrow flying directly towards the bull's eye. On another, a boxer knocked his opponent cold to the ground.

'Paul Magee? God I haven't heard that name in years. How the hell is he?' Emma gulped down some beer.

'He's grand. He moved back to Belfast from Liverpool a few years ago. I thought you might have known that, especially given how close you two were.'

'Close?' Emma gripped the phone tighter to stop it falling from her sweaty palm.

'Mmm, "thick as thieves." Isn't that what they say?'

Fuck, he knows, she thought.

'So what did you and Paul talk about?'

'Let's just say he got me thinking.'

'About what?'

'When the police asked about the last time we saw Kathleen, what did we tell them?'

'I don't know Aiden, why don't you remind me.' Emma straightened her spine, making herself taller. When backed into a corner, Emma McCourt always came out fighting.

'We said that I'd looked in on her sleeping, after eleven. You were on the landing when I got home. Remember? You wouldn't let me turn on the hall light because it would wake her. But you opened the door and let me peek in. That's what we both told them, that I was the last one to see her. But something Paul said got me thinking. Did I see her? Or did I just see a lump in the cot in the darkness? You said she was in there, so I believed you. Why would you lie?'

'I wouldn't. Now, what exactly did Paul say to you?' There was only a handful of people who knew the truth, and Paul Magee was one of them. He had been with Emma in the hotel when she had handed over Kathleen to the O'Connells. He had pretended to be Kathleen's father.

'It's probably nothing. But I think any new information should be shared with the police.'

'What information?'

'That all those times you were sniffling next to me at the press conferences, clinging on to my arm, crying, saying you wanted Kathleen back, you were lying through your teeth.'

'That's rubbish. What half-baked story has Paul fed you?'

'If you were telling the truth, then I'm sure you have nothing to worry about.'

'I demand to know exactly what Paul told you.'

'You don't get to make demands Emma.'

In front of her, the TVs started to spin around like dirty clothes in a washing machine. The archer's arrow, the hockey sticks, the wrestlers' and football players' bodies all slammed into each other in one big, violent mess.

'I lost my daughter,' Aiden seethed. 'I'm a broken man. I could've been someone, but losing Kathleen ruined me. My life ended the day she was taken. I couldn't move on as easily as you did.' He paused, and then added, 'I've never been compensated for all the pain I suffered.'

Compensated. The legalistic word stood out from his

tirade of emotion.

Emma quickly tried to gather her thoughts as Aiden breathed heavily on the other end of the line. It was too dangerous to say any more on the phone. He could have someone else listening in. He could be recording the conversation. She needed to look him in the eye and find out what he knew and what he wanted.

'I'm actually coming home for a quick visit before Christmas. I fly out in a couple of days' time. Why don't we see each other on the weekend?' She chose her next words very carefully. 'I've no idea what Paul has been saying. But, whatever it is, I think it's in both our interests to sit down and talk this through.'

'Fine. I'll see you in Belfast on Sunday then.'

'And you won't go to the police?'

'I'll hear you out first,' he said.

'I'm sure it's all just a big misunder…'

The phone clicked and the line went dead.

CHAPTER TWENTY-FOUR
JANET—NEW YORK
DECEMBER 2012

Janet stared at the photo on the shelf of her, Tom and Kathleen. It was taken at Rosses Point in Sligo, or Yeats Country as they call it. They are standing on the cliff. The reeds below them are buckling under the force of the wind. Kathleen's hand is up at her head smoothing down her long black hair, which had been mussed by the sea breeze. They are all smiling. The sun shines behind them, lighting up the yellow sands of the beach below. But the waves are big, savage, and, in the distance, you can see the beginnings of a storm cloud rolling towards them.

'I told you. I don't know what he knows. But he definitely suspects something,' Emma said.

Janet was perched on the edge of the desk in Tom's home office as Tom paced around barking questions at Emma who was on speakerphone.

'Paul Magee said something to him, and all Aiden would say is that he knows I lied. But I don't think he knows the details.'

'Who's Paul Magee?' Tom asked.

'He's the boy who was with me that day, the one I said was Kathleen's father.'

The one you lied to us about, Janet thought.

'Did he mention us at all?' Tom said.

'No.'

'Or Geary?'

'No.'

'And this Paul, does he know who we are?'

'No. I didn't even know who you were until last summer.'

'And you said Aiden is threatening to go to the police?'

'Yes, but…'

'But what?'

'I think I can talk him out of it. I'm booked on a flight to London tomorrow night. I'll be in Belfast by Saturday afternoon.'

'That's two days away,' Janet spoke for the first time. Tom shot her a look that said, *let me deal with this*. Janet placed her finger on the mute button. 'He could have gone to the police by then,' she said.

Tom pushed her hand off the phone. 'What do you plan to say to him? Are you sure you going to Belfast is wise? How do you know he won't go to the police before then? They could be waiting to pick you up at the airport.'

A sharp pain pierced Janet's left hand. She glanced down and saw the imprint of her own nail dug deep into her palm. She hadn't even realized she'd been doing that.

It would be so easy for Emma to lead the police straight to them and straight to Kathleen. She had betrayed the father of her child. What was to stop her betraying them too?

'He said he wouldn't go to the police until he'd seen me, and I believe him. I said something about talking it through and coming to an arrangement, and he seemed to be willing to hear what I had to say,' Emma said.

'Do you think he'll take a pay off?' Tom asked.

'I don't know. I need to go there and find out what he knows and what he wants. He didn't ask outright, but he might want money. He talked about how bad things were for him financially. Then he made a point of saying how well I'd done for myself. He did mention something about compensation at the end...'

'So he's blackmailing you,' Tom said.

'No, not exactly. It wasn't clear what he meant. I can't tell you any more right now. I just thought you should know.'

'Fine, but I want to know the second you find out any more information. We can give you money if that's what he wants.'

Money. That was Tom's answer to everything. It didn't occur to him that Aiden might want something more. He might want to find his daughter. Just because they were able to buy Kathleen from Emma didn't mean that Aiden was for sale, Janet thought.

'And tell me more about this Paul Magee.' Tom stalked around the phone like an animal circling its prey. 'If he's talking to Aiden, what's to stop him talking to someone else, like the police?'

'I can't see Paul going to the police. He was an accessory. I couldn't have pulled it off without him. To be honest, I'm really surprised he's said anything.'

"Pulled it off." She talked as if selling Kathleen were a feat she was proud of.

'Well you obviously didn't choose your partner in crime very wisely,' Janet couldn't help saying.

Tom put up his hand to quiet her. 'I'm going to tell Geary,' he said. 'He needs to know if someone is going around blabbing.'

As soon as they got off the phone with Emma, Tom tried to get rid of Janet so he could call Geary in private.

But she refused to budge. As Tom dialed Geary's number, Janet looked, again, at the family photo on the shelf. Kathleen had thrown a tantrum shortly after they had taken that picture. She had said she was sick of the literary tour and had stormed off into the village in a huff.

Janet had been really enjoying sharing her knowledge of Irish poetry with Kathleen. She had assumed that her daughter would fall in love with those verses in the same way she had when she was a teenager. Standing in the lobby of their hotel, Janet fighting back the tears, watching Kathleen stalk away from them, Tom had tried to reassure her.

'She's just going through a phase. Teenagers are programmed to find their parents boring. Right now, no matter what we do with her on vacation, she'll hate it because we're her parents. I can guarantee you, when these horrible teenage years have passed and she's a bit more mature, she'll love this kind of thing,' he had said.

Kathleen's twentieth birthday was now just two months away. On the verge of adulthood, she was still railing against her mother, trying to figure out who she was by putting distance between them. This was the worst possible moment for her to find out the truth. She was not young enough to simply believe anything her parents told her, but nor was she mature enough to see their side of the story. No matter how they presented it, if Kathleen found out the truth right now, Janet and Tom would be the bad guys; the criminals who stole her away from her rightful family.

Tom slammed down the unanswered phone and scrolled through his cell looking for Geary's other numbers. Tears of panic sprang to Janet's eyes. Tom gave her a sympathetic look and then turned to look out the window.

'Geary, it's Tom O'Connell here. Something has happened. I need you to call me back as soon as possible. No matter what time of day it is. It's urgent.' He put down the phone and rubbed his eyes.

'You're just going to leave a message? Isn't there anything else you can do?' Janet said, her voice cracking.

'No. It's four in the morning there. He usually unplugs the house-phone and turns off his cell at night. We'll just have to wait.'

'But…' Janet trailed off, the emotion choking the words right out of her throat.

Tom got up and came round to her, wrapping his arms around her and pulling her close.

'I will take care of this, you have my word,' he whispered. 'It's late, let's get some sleep.'

'How can you even think of sleeping?'

'Love, there's nothing else I can do at this stage. But, rest assured, everything will be ok.'

'You can go to bed if you want. I won't be able to sleep. I'm going to make some tea.'

Downstairs, Janet stood for a long time, motionless, in the middle of the hallway at the bottom of the central staircase, just underneath the chandelier, looking at the moonlight shining in through the large windows. Everything looked so elegant and luxurious, just like the Titanic before it sank.

Their friends, many of whom had lost money in the financial crisis, had been hardly able to contain their jealously when Janet and Tom had bought this six-bedroom house in Westchester overlooking the water. To the outside world, it looked like they had left Long Island on a whim. Their friends probably thought of her as a fat house cat, spoiled and oblivious to the hardships of life. Little did they know.

Janet had not liked the wives of Tom's friends when she had first met them. But now, she was indistinguishable from those women, going to the same manicurist, driving the same S.U.V, and baking from the same recipe books. There was nothing exceptional about her. She had not changed the world or saved any lives. She had not contributed to the history of literature as she had planned to do when she was younger. She was just an ordinary suburban wife and mother. But she was a good person. She didn't deserve to have her daughter snatched from her. She didn't deserve to have the narrative of their lives tainted with words like blackmail, kidnapping, threats, and lies.

Old emotions engulfed her. Once more she was the twenty-something girl lying on a cold floor of her downtown studio, howling in pain at the loss of her first love. She was the woman staring numbly at yet another negative pregnancy test. She was back in the spare bedroom of their old house, crying uncontrollably all night, as Tom sat at the kitchen table below, pointlessly filling out adoption forms. How many times would life do this to her?

Every other time that she had been beaten and broken; she had eventually, somehow, chanced upon a new path. She had fled Manhattan, battered and bruised, for Long Island after Ethan's death. And it was there that she had met Tom. Then the torture of infertility had led them to Kathleen. The greatest joy she had ever known. Nothing in her life had gone as she had planned. None of it—the good or the bad—had been of her own making. But she couldn't just drift along anymore like she had in the past. It was time for her to take the helm. Steer right through the storm and out the other side.

Janet went into the kitchen and made herself a pot of coffee. She usually drank green tea, but she was hoping the caffeine would perform miracles, that it would ignite her synapses and show her the escape route. She grabbed her notebook from her handbag. It contained the odd line of poetry, here and there, but mostly it contained mundane lists—things like call the plumber for the downstairs bathroom, buy Christmas decorations for the garden, make an appointment for Tom's annual medical. She sat down at the dining table and placed the notebook in front of her, open at a blank page. Ready to write yet another list.

All the possible outcomes ricocheted around her mind. None of them good.

At 4am, after hours of scribbling, she stood up and went upstairs to wake Tom, the notebook still in her hands.

'What time is it?' Tom groaned and pulled the duvet up around him. Then, suddenly, he sat up wide-eyed. 'Did the phone ring?'

'No, but I need to speak to you before you talk to Geary.' Janet turned on the bedside lamp and sat down on the corner of the bed. She was still wearing her clothes from yesterday, and her face was grubby from exhaustion.

'You should try to get some sleep. I told you, I'll handle it.' He went to turn off the lamp.

'No. I want to talk about this now.'

Tom plumped up his pillows and sat up giving her a resigned look.

'I want to go through the list of people who know the truth. I want to see who we can trust.'

'Go on.'

Janet drew a deep breath and looked at her notes.

'First on my list is Geary. Are you sure…'

'The whole thing was his idea. He came to me, remember?'

'But are you sure he won't talk, no matter what? What if this Aiden makes him feel bad?' Tom tutted at this but Janet persevered. 'What if the police question him?'

'He knows how to handle the police. He's had his fair share of interrogations. Believe me, he won't suddenly have some crisis of conscience. He's done things far worse than this and got off scot free.'

Janet looked back down at the paper. She couldn't meet Tom's eye. How had she ended up married to a man whose best friend had "done far worse than this?"

'That boy who counted the money. The skin-headed one.'

'He was murdered a few months later.'

'Murdered?' Janet felt some bile rise up in her throat. 'What kind of stuff was he messed up in?'

'He was an innocent lad. He went to visit his granny for Easter in a wee village near Belfast. He was in the local pub when some paramilitaries came in with assault rifles and sprayed the place with bullets.'

'Why did they pick that bar? Who were they after?'

'They chose it because they knew there would be plenty of Catholics in there. They said it was retaliation for something the IRA had done. Northern Ireland was a different place back then. That lad, unfortunately, was in the wrong place at the wrong time.'

Janet sat for a moment in stunned silence thinking about the boy's mother. Every time a gunman went on a rampage, Janet would worry, for days afterwards, that Kathleen might be caught up in a similar random shooting. She used to think it was a fear unique to American mothers.

'Anyway, where's all this getting us?' Tom asked.

'So you don't think we need to worry about him having told anyone before he died?'

'I think if he'd told anyone we'd know by now. He's not a problem for us. God rest his soul.'

Janet ticked him off her list and moved on to the next name. 'What about our driver, Trevor?'

'He was a policeman, moonlighting for Geary. At the time, Geary had a few policemen on the payroll. He probably still does.'

Janet didn't understand what point Tom was making with this. 'Yes, but could he have told anyone?'

'Any of them *could* have talked,' Tom said impatiently. 'But I doubt they did. Why would they?'

'But is it worth Geary talking to Trevor? Just to be sure?'

'He'll need a psychic then.'

'Why?'

'I'm nearly sure Trevor keeled over on a golf course and died a few years back. Heart attack, I believe.'

As Janet ticked Trevor's name off the list, she tried to ignore the part of her that was relieved that half the witnesses were dead.

'What about those friends of hers, the ones she was staying with in Long Island? Do you think she told them?'

'No,' Tom sighed. 'She told them she and I had an affair, remember? What she did is so shameful I doubt she's told anyone.'

'That just leaves two other people who know the truth. This Paul Magee and Emma.'

'And I'll make sure Geary pays Paul a visit. Don't worry. Now, can we go to sleep?'

'But what about her?'

'What about her?'

'Do you trust her to speak to Aiden? What if she tells him about us?'

'Why would she do that?'

'He might threaten her. Or he might go to the police and she might crack under questioning. Or she might regret what she's done and want to find a way to undo it. She did say she wanted to see Kathleen again, remember?'

Tom looked at her confused. 'She won't talk, she'd only get herself in trouble if she did.'

He still doesn't get it, Janet thought. 'She was only sixteen or seventeen at the time. She could say we coerced her. She could say Geary or you physically threatened her. Who would you believe? The young girl or the ex-terrorist and the rich older couple who bought a baby and then snuck it out of the country using fake passports?'

Tom stared at her in the dim light, as if trying to read her thoughts. She knew what had to be said next, but she struggled to formulate the words.

'There are loose ends that need to be tied up.'

'What exactly are we talking about here?' Tom asked.

'I know you know people. I don't care how it happens,

but we can't live with this threat hanging over us,' Janet paused and then went on, softer now, but still resolute. 'She is a loose end…and she has to be dealt with.'

'What do you mean?'

'Don't make me say it out loud.' She held his gaze, wondering who he thought she was, wondering if she really knew herself.

'Like I said, I have this.'

'And you'll do what needs to be done?'

'I will, now get into bed.' Tom flicked off the light and rolled over, covering himself with the duvet.

Janet went into her *ensuite* bathroom and set about her nightly routine. First, she cleansed the grime of the previous day from her face. With special pads, she removed her makeup, staring with dead eyes at herself in the mirror. She flossed and cleaned her teeth and slathered on a thick layer of night cream, all the while breathing deeply, trying to stop her core from shaking. She threw her clothes into the laundry basket and put on her pajamas. Then she crawled into bed next to Tom and lay staring at the ceiling, trying, in vain, to quiet her thoughts.

Geary rang at around 5am. Tom got up and went to take the call in his study. This time Janet wasn't invited.

Later that morning, she overheard him on the phone with Emma.

'What flight will you be on?…Geary will pick you up at the airport…It's not safe for you to be wandering into Belfast on your own…Geary will take care of you…Good, I'll tell him. 4pm at Belfast City airport, coming in from London Heathrow.'

Tom came out into the hall where Janet had been listening.

'It's done. Geary will take care of her.'

CHAPTER TWENTY-FIVE
EMMA
MANHATTAN & BELFAST
DECEMBER 2012

'What flight will you be on?' Tom asked, ever so casually.

'Why?'

'Geary will pick you up at the airport.'

'That's really not necessary,' Emma said.

'It's not safe for you to be wandering into Belfast on your own.'

Emma was all too aware that going to Belfast was a risk. But she didn't have any other option. There was no way she could sort out this mess with Aiden from New York.

'Geary will take care of you,' Tom said.

Emma was about to tell him that Geary was the last person she needed taking care of her, but then she paused and thought better of it.

'I'm on the British Airways flight from Heathrow to

Belfast City. My flight gets in at four.'

'Good, I'll tell him. 4pm at Belfast City airport, coming in from London Heathrow.' He sounded so jovial, as if they were old friends making travel arrangements. But they weren't friends. Emma barely knew these people.

She put down the phone and thought back to what Patrick had said about Tom. After the Christening, she had called Patrick in Belfast pretending that she just wanted to catch up. Half way through the call, she had breezily mentioned that she had recently met the owner of O'Connell Construction at an event.

'Look at you rubbing shoulders with the great and the good of the New York Irish. I thought you hated that sort of thing,' Patrick had said.

Emma usually did everything she could to avoid networking within the Irish community. Michael had been urging her to join the Irish American Bar Association for months now, but Emma hated the idea of being defined by the place where she was born, the place she had spent her childhood and no more.

'I'm moving up in society, you know,' Emma had said to Patrick. 'Is he someone that's worth knowing?'

'I'd say so. They're a massive outfit.'

'But are they legitimate? I have a reputation to protect, you know. It's bad enough that I associate with degenerates like you,' Emma had said jokingly.

'They are fairly well known in the business. In the past twenty years, they've probably built half the office blocks from Boston to Washington.'

'And what's he like? I only spoke to him briefly.'

'I never had any dealings with the man himself. But…'

'But what?'

'You hear rumors don't you.'

'What kind of rumors?' Emma had asked.

'Let's just say, I don't think you get that far in the construction industry without ruffling some feathers and bending a few rules.'

'What kind of stuff did he do?'

'I don't remember anything specific now. All I know is that he's not the kind of man you want as an enemy. But listen, this is all just gossip. What's that term you lawyers use? It's just hearsay. It wouldn't stand up in court.'

Sitting in her office, thinking about her trip to Belfast, Patrick's words now rang loudly in Emma's ears.

Emma shook herself and tried to snap back into work mode. There was no point sitting around stressing about Tom right now, she had too much to organize. She looked down at the mess of papers on her desk trying to figure out where to begin.

'Are you ready for me?'

Emma glanced up. It was Jenny, the junior associate on the case, here for their 10am meeting.

'God, is it that time already? C'mon in, I'm not quite organized, but let's make a start anyway.'

'You look really pale. Are you sure you should even be here?' Jenny asked with concern.

To explain her sudden trip to Ireland, Emma had told work that her grandmother had died. When she had told Steve, her boss, he had squinted his face into a look of sympathy and had told her she should take as much time as she needed. With his next breath, he had asked her about the status of the expert reports and had reminded her that the deadline was less than a month away.

'Thanks. I'm fine,' Emma said to Jenny. 'I wanted to talk to you about the expert reports. I'm only going to be out of the office for a couple of days, but I'll need you to move them forward in my absence. You'll probably have to work the weekend.'

Jenny nodded, looking unsurprised. She worked most weekends anyway.

It was Friday. Emma was getting the red-eye out that night and was booked to come back on Tuesday. If everything went to plan, that would be long enough.

'Most of all, I need your help with the quantum report,'

Emma said. 'She's probably the most important expert we have.' They had hired a well-respected economist to study the other side's claim. Emma had already advised the client that they were likely to be found guilty of breaching the contract. Their main hope now lay with the economist. They hoped her evidence would prove that, even if there had been a breach, the other side had not suffered any financial loss. It would mean their client would technically lose, but they wouldn't have to pay anything to their opponent. It was a concept that Emma was familiar with—winning by losing.

'Can you get the draft of the professor's report from Michael, together with the supporting documents? The quantum expert makes some assumptions that are based on the professor's findings, so we need to make sure the two tie in together.'

'Ok,' Jenny said, scribbling down notes as Emma spoke.

'Can you get it today? I'll go through it with you this afternoon. It's probably easier if I show you what sections of the report I'm talking about.'

'The only thing is…Michael isn't in today.'

'What?'

'He said he had a dance recital for his daughter and then lunch with a client this afternoon.'

'Unbelievable.' Emma could barely hide her contempt. Emma was supposedly distraught from her grandmother's death, but she was still in the office working her ass off to make sure they didn't get behind. Michael, on the other hand, was off doing God knows what.

'His daughter's only two. How can she be dancing already? And why does lunch have to be a whole afternoon affair?'

'I don't know,' Jenny whispered, as if she had just been told off.

'Fine. Can you ask that paralegal that he's always taking to meetings? The one from Boston. I don't remember her name. She must know where the documents are.' There were now nearly twenty temps working in the sweatshop of the discovery room on the floor below. Michael and Kathy were managing that aspect of the case and Emma had little interaction with the paralegals, so she couldn't be bothered to learn any of their names.

'Caitlin? She's been off sick all week.'

'Typical,' Emma sighed. Michael had probably worked the poor girl so hard that she'd got run down. It was just a part-time job for the students after all. 'Looks like you'll just have to do what you can with the quantum report. I'll have a word with Michael about the professor's report when I'm back from Ireland next week.'

Jenny nodded and gathered up her notebook. 'Ok, I'll see you when you're back.'

Emma watched her young colleague walk out. 'That's if I make it back,' she muttered when Jenny was out of earshot.

***

Despite the holes punched through it by vandals, you could still make out what the sign said: "*Welcome to Northern Ireland*" and then underneath "*Speed Limits in miles per hour.*"

Emma stared out the window as the bus sped past. She was still groggy from the red wine and the pill she had taken to help her sleep on the flight from New York to Dublin.

Emma remembered seeing something on CNN about the uproar those signs had caused when they were introduced earlier in the year. It had not been reported on the main news, but rather on one of those curious news items from around the world type shows.

The Roads Service had said the signs were simply informative. They were to let drivers know that they were passing from one jurisdiction to another and, importantly, that speed limits were now in miles and not kilometers like they were in the Republic of Ireland. However, some nationalists had taken offense to the signs calling them "antagonistic." They said they were politically motivated to remind people of the partition of Ireland, which nationalists were against.

Even though she'd been brought up a nationalist, that wasn't why the sign had caught Emma's attention. For her, it was shocking that there wasn't more marking the frontier between the North and the South. Emma had left Northern Ireland as a teenager in 1994. Just months before the ceasefires, and years before the peace agreement. Back then, the border had been demarcated in a much more obvious and intimidating way with army checkpoints, barbed wire, and soldiers with rifles. She remembered, as a child, giggling with her sister at the strange English accents of the soldiers who stopped her family's car when they crossed the border on Sunday afternoon outings "down South." Things had certainly changed in the time she'd been away.

Just over an hour later, the coach pulled into the Europa bus station, and Emma flagged a taxi on the street outside to take her to the Hilton.

'We should be there in ten minutes tops,' the driver said. 'It's still early, so the roads are quiet. The protesters haven't come out yet.'

'Protesters?' Emma asked.

'Aye, flag protests. They've taken the Union Jack flag down from City Hall, and it's caused all sorts of trouble. They were out rioting last night. There have been peaceful demonstrations as well. But the police getting heavy handed with the protesters doesn't help matters.' Emma had forgotten how loquacious Belfast taxi drivers were. 'I heard some reporter describe it this morning as civil unrest,' he went on. 'That's such a nice word isn't it? I'd say it's more than just a bit of unrest, and it's anything but civil. We're living on a knife edge, and if we're not careful we'll end up stabbing ourselves with it.'

Emma sat back and took a deep breath. *Welcome home*, she thought.

The taxi rounded a corner and started driving alongside the River Lagan. The entire area smacked of corporate regeneration. Tidy trees stood at regular intervals along the sidewalk. Shiny office buildings still boasted a proud air of newness. Women walked past swinging luxury brand-name handbags. And most of the cars in sight were less than a couple of years old. The prosperity that Aiden claimed had eluded Belfast was everywhere she looked.

As she stepped out of the taxi, Emma tried to remember what this Waterfront area had looked like back when she was a teenager. But she couldn't conjure up the images. It was as if this whole section of the city simply had not existed back then.

Inside, the standard décor of the Hilton's lobby felt much more familiar. If she turned her back to the high windows and looked inwards, she could well have been in Dallas or Washington. That was partly why she'd chosen to stay at this chain hotel and not one of the more famous ones in town. She wanted to imagine she was anywhere but Belfast.

At the check-in desk, the receptionist asked Emma what the purpose of her trip was.

'Business,' she replied.

It was already 11am, and she had a lot to do. She showered quickly and headed out again. She checked her appearance in the elevator mirror. In her long-sleeve, figure hugging, woolen dress, high-heeled designer boots, simple make-up and expensive winter coat, she looked very different from the girl who had gone to see Geary all those years ago.

She could still picture herself standing on Geary's doorstep in leggings, Doc Martin boots and leather jacket, on the night he'd called her over to brief her on his plan. She had thought she looked powerful, like Linda Hamilton in the second *Terminator* movie, but without the guns. Back then, like today, Emma only had one weapon at her disposal. Information.

She opened her handbag to double check that the package was inside. There was something she needed to do before she could meet up with her old partner in crime.

CHAPTER TWENTY-SIX
EMMA—BELFAST
DECEMBER 2012

The lawyer wasn't very happy coming into work on a Saturday. He kept moaning about the rabble of Christmas shoppers and flag protesters that he'd had to fight through to get there. Emma didn't think he had much cause for complaint. She was paying him treble his usual rate and all he had to do was take the paperwork from her.

She had hired him before she left for New York nearly twenty years ago using the money the O'Connells had given her for Kathleen. He had said nothing when she showed up with his retainer in cash. He wasn't the kind of lawyer that bothered himself with his client's source of funds, which was just the kind of lawyer she needed.

After she left his office, she went back to the Waterfront. This time, she crossed the River Lagan and made her way to the Titanic Quarter.

The *Titanic Belfast* building stood out against the vast white sky. It was the centerpiece of a new complex that sat on the site of the old *Harland and Wolff* shipyard where the infamous liner had been built. To Emma, the building's glistening façade and sharp edges were disconcertingly reminiscent of the iceberg that had sunk the unsinkable ship and killed so many onboard. From maritime disaster to urban attraction. It was an ambitious, and not altogether convincing, shift in identity that mirrored Belfast's own aspirations.

Emma walked through the complex, taking in the strange newness of it all, looking for the name of his apartment building. With a quick check of the voting registry, she'd been able to find his address in a matter of minutes.

She buzzed his flat several times. There was no answer. She waited. Ten minutes later, someone came out of the building, and she snuck in. She took the elevator to the fifth floor and found his apartment. She rang the bell for thirty seconds straight. Still no one answered. She put her head against the door and listened. The TV was on and someone was moving around inside.

She thumped the door and shouted, 'Paul, it's Emma McCourt. I didn't fly all the way from New York just to stand outside. Let me in.'

The door opened just a crack. Paul's face appeared, very briefly, from the darkened hallway. He ushered her in without saying anything and quickly locked the door again.

She walked into the living room, and Paul followed her in.

'My God, it really is you,' he said, a slight slur to his voice.

As he walked into the light, Emma drew in her breath. His pale skin was covered in a patchwork of red, purple and brown, the result of repeated punches to the head. His bottom lip was split open, and the congealed blood on it had turned black. Where his eyes should be, there were just two slits, and the skin around them was dark and swollen.

'Who did this?' Emma asked, although she already knew the answer.

'Our old friend Geary, of course. Well, it was those henchmen of his. He doesn't like to get his hands dirty these days. Afraid my blood might leave a stain on his Armani suit.'

'Have you been to the hospital?'

'No time.' Paul eased himself onto the sofa, wincing with the pain. *Broken ribs*, Emma thought as she sat down next to him.

Items of clothing were strewn around the living room. A half packed suitcase lay open in the middle of the floor with shoes, clothes and a framed photo of two little girls stuffed haphazardly inside. The scene had all the telltale signs of a fugitive scrambling to flee.

'What's going on?' Emma said.

'I've 24 hours to get out of Belfast.'

'Will you go back to Liverpool? Your brother's still there isn't he?'

'No. For now, they want me well out of the way. I'm not to be any place where I might run into Belfast folk. He doesn't want Aiden finding me, or the police, if it comes to that.' Spittle gathered at the corners of Paul's mouth, and he spoke slowly, as if the effort of moving his facial muscles was almost too much to bear.

'So where are you going?'

'Poland. To some farm in the arse end of nowhere. Back in the day, Geary's crew used it as a safe-house for lads who were on the run.'

Banishment from Belfast to the bleak Polish countryside sounded like a cruel punishment, but at least he was still alive. Emma had worried that Geary might have already silenced Paul for good.

'And you're just going to go?' She knew as soon as the words were out of her mouth that it was a naïve thing to say.

'They have men with guns sitting outside my Da's and

my sister's house too. I can't put my nieces in danger.'

Twenty years after the ceasefires, Belfast was still flooded with guns. And there were still plenty of thugs with a talent for intimidation and people with money willing to pay them to use it.

'The only reason I'm still alive is that Geary did time with my Da when Geary was just a lad. I think my Da watched out for him in the Maze, so he feels like he owes him. But I know that won't stop him putting a bullet in my Da's head if I open my mouth again.'

'So it's true, you did speak. Paul what were you thinking? After all these years, why did you talk now?'

'I didn't talk. Not really.'

'Not really?'

'I was stupid, that's all.' Paul repositioned himself on the sofa, unable to get comfortable.

'Tell me everything. You need to tell me exactly what Aiden knows,' Emma demanded.

Information is power, she thought.

'I was in Glennon's Pub in town last Tuesday having a quiet drink with John Coyle. Do you remember him? He was captain of the Gaelic under twenty-ones, back when we were teenagers. He lives in Sydney now. He's a physiotherapist. He's doing very well for himself. Apparently he treats a lot of their cricketers. Anyway, he was home for a few weeks, so I went into town to meet him.'

Paul spoke slowly. His wounds were obviously tormenting him. But Emma didn't care. He had to tell her everything, pain or not.

'Anyway, so this TV show comes on. It's called "Thirty Years of Trouble." It's been on for months now. Each week they cover a year in the troubles from 1968 to 1998. They show archive footage and interview the main players, that sort of thing. Anyway, this night it was 1993. They mention the bombings in Warrington, and London, and on the Shankhill and the shootings across the country. You forget now how bad it was. Every other week there was some kind of massacre. At the time it just seemed normal didn't it?'

Emma nodded. Normality was a relative concept. In the early nineties, news of bloodshed on the streets of Northern Ireland was as everyday as the weatherman forecasting rain.

'I remember, but what has all this got to do with us?' Emma asked.

'So they get to the Downing Street Declaration in December. They say it was really historic, and that it laid the groundwork for the peace process.'

Emma hadn't paid much attention to that announcement at the time. She had been too busy putting the final touches of the plan together with Geary. She had handed Kathleen over to the O'Connells the day after the Declaration had been made. In it, both the British and Irish Governments had formally set out their commitment to finding a constitutional solution to the troubles. It was easy now, with the benefit of hindsight, to see that as the moment that Northern Ireland had set a course for peace. But, at the time, no one believed that either side of the conflict would be willing to put down their arms. For months afterwards, it had seemed like the Declaration was just another meaningless piece of paper. But then, after several more months of murders and mayhem, the first ceasefires had come in the summer of 1994. If only they had come a year earlier, Emma had often thought, then things could have been so very different.

Paul went on, 'And, just after the bit about the Declaration, they start talking about how Belfast became galvanized and united that week, for the first time in decades. They said it wasn't the Declaration that brought the communities together but the disappearance of a baby the following day. They showed footage of all the people out searching the area for clues. Remember how the Shankhill Football Club sent a group of volunteers to help? These kids that had grown up no more than ten minutes away were suddenly mixing with Catholics for the first time in their lives. And they talked about how the ladies from the Donegall Methodist and Presbyterian Churches had made tea and buns for the volunteers and helped put up flyers. It really was unheard of, wasn't it? The two communities helping each other out like that.'

Emma nodded remembering how kind everyone had been giving up their time to help search for Kathleen. Day after day, she had looked volunteers in the eye and thanked them for their efforts, and, every night, she had gone to bed praying that all their work would be in vain and the truth would remain hidden.

'So, towards the end of the piece, they say something like "Kathleen Kennedy was never found and no one was ever prosecuted in relation to her disappearance. What happened to her remains a mystery." And then you come on screen. You're all tearful making a statement to the press, and John Coyle says to me, "that poor girl, she looks torn up." And, I've no idea why, but I say, "Maybe she's just a good actress." And John says, "God you've a suspicious mind. Look at her. She's shivering. She's pale. She's clearly distraught."'

'And let me guess, you decided to correct him.'

Paul looked down at his hands, too embarrassed to meet Emma's eye.

'What did you say next Paul?'

'So I start sprouting off, trying to be clever in front of John. I'd had quite a few jars at this stage, and I was getting sick of all his stories about how brilliant his job was and all the famous sportsmen he'd met. So I start telling him about this Open University degree in psychology that I've been doing.'

'What the hell has that got to do with me?' Emma said, unable to hide her impatience.

'Last semester, one of the modules was about non-verbal communication. I suppose I was trying to impress

John, so I set about proving to him that you were lying by talking about your body language. Like when they asked you what you'd say to the person who had Kathleen you said "Please just let her go." But when you said it, your head was shaking. With your words you were asking whoever had her to release her. But with your gesture, you were saying the opposite. You were saying "No, don't let her go." It was a tiny gestural slip, but any body language expert worth his salt would have picked up on it.'

'Well, clearly, they didn't,' Emma said. The police had never shown any signs that they thought she'd been involved. In fact, most of their investigation had focused on Aiden.

'It wasn't just that,' Paul said. 'There were other things too.'

'Like?'

'Like that teddy bear you carried everywhere. I said to John, "that's really common in cases of missing children. The family clings on to some symbol of the child. But she looks like she's just carrying a prop. It's just something she thinks she's supposed to have with her." It was the way you held the bear that gave you away. As you were walking into the press conference, you had it up at your face. People probably thought you were upset. But, as I said to John, you weren't clinging to it for emotional support; you were using it to hide behind. I said maybe you were embarrassed by the attention, or you were afraid of all the scrutiny.'

After all the media interest and the search had died down, Emma had thrown that bear into a box under her bed, unable to look at it anymore. She wondered if it was still there, in her childhood bedroom, in her mother's house.

'So John is telling me that I'm a suspicious sort,' Paul continued. 'And I'm going on and on about the small behaviors that show someone is lying. Like the way your blinks were just a bit longer than normal. That's a clear indication that someone is thinking very carefully about what they're saying.'

'I was being careful about what I was saying.'

'And you stuck to your story brilliantly. In terms of the details, you didn't slip up once.'

Emma was getting tired of his armchair psychology bullshit.

'Paul, can you please just get to the fucking point. Did you need to prove how fucking smart you were by telling John Coyle the truth? Is that what happened? Did you drop us all in it just to prove a point to John fucking Coyle?'

'No! I've never told a single soul the truth. Why would I do that? I was an accessory. I was just talking theoretically. I was saying stuff like "that's an indication that someone's lying." I never once actually said that I knew for sure you were lying. I never mentioned anything about what we'd done, selling Kathleen to those Americans.'

'So where does Aiden fit into all this?'

Paul's blotchy face turned a darker shade of red.

'He was sitting in the next booth over listening to everything. I swear to God, I had no idea he was there. It's not like I was saying these things in a pub on the Falls Road. I was uptown. How was I to know he was there? But, suddenly, he appears at our table and starts questioning me about what I'd been saying.'

'And how did you respond?'

'I told him to pay no heed to me. I was just trying to be the smart man. I'm no expert. I just did one wee course on the matter. But he wouldn't buy it. He kept going on about how you and I were fairly tight. And maybe I knew more than I was letting on. I kept telling him that I was just talking shite. I said, of course, I didn't really think you had lied. "Why would she lie?" I said to him. But he wouldn't let it go. He starts causing a ruckus. He seemed drunk. He might even have been high. You should've seen the needle marks all over his arm. Disgusting. Eventually the pub landlord comes over and chucked him out. He made a real scene, he did. And, as he's leaving, he shouts at me. "This isn't the last of it. I'm going to get to the bottom of this." When he left, John Coyle turns to me and says, "Jaysus, you should have seen the look on your face when he appeared. I've never seen color drain from anybody so quick." I suppose my expression gave me away.' Paul looked down at his hands 'He knew, as soon as he saw me, that he was on to something.'

'Clearly they didn't teach you how to control your own body language on this course,' Emma said. 'When did this happen?'

'Tuesday night.'

'And then he phoned me on Thursday. All he had to do was mention your name to me and I reacted. Fuck. I might've been able to handle him better on the phone if I'd known you'd not told him anything specific. As it was, he took me completely off guard. Why couldn't you have warned me? Now me flying over here will have made him even more suspicious.'

'I'm sorry. For eighteen years, I've kept what happened a secret, and then I open my stupid mouth, just once, and he's listening.'

'And you're sure that's all that you said? Just all that stuff about the body language?'

'I promise. I wouldn't be sitting here if I'd said any more.' Paul's battered face twisted into a wry smile. 'If I'd told Aiden any specifics, Geary wouldn't have been so lenient with me.'

Emma believed him. Geary's men were excellent interrogators. If Paul had tried to lie to them, they would have known, and he wouldn't be sitting here talking to her now.

'Me and my big mouth. Emma, I am so very sorry.'

'Stop apologizing.' Emma's mind was already whirring, thinking about her next move. 'What will you tell your family?' she asked.

'Geary says I can phone them from the airport when I get to London and tell them I'm on my way to Thailand. I'm to tell them I've been saving up for a trip for a while, and I'll come back when the money runs out. I'll be allowed to call them once a month, but I'm not to tell them where I am or give them any contact details. I don't know where I'm supposed to have got the cash for this trip. Everything I had went into buying this place. I'm in negative equity as it is.'

Emma looked around the apartment. Despite the clothes flung around during the hurried packing, she could tell the place was well kept. Paul must have worked hard to afford a home in this new development. A few years ago, when the Belfast property bubble was at its height, this apartment would have been expensive, and now he just had to abandon it. He had to give up everything, his home, his job, and his family. He'd probably have to give up studying psychology, too, although perhaps that wouldn't be such a bad thing.

'Hopefully, you won't have to stay away too long. If I'm able to smooth things over with Aiden, and Geary calms down, then maybe you can come back in a few months' time.'

'Even if you can convince Aiden that it's all in his head, I'm not sure Geary will take the risk of letting me back into Belfast. There's only a handful of people that can link him to this, and I think he'd prefer we were kept well out of the way.'

'Don't I know it,' Emma sighed. She looked at her watch. It was 3:45pm. Geary's thugs would be getting to the airport now to pick her up from the 4:00pm flight from London. It was time for her to go.

CHAPTER TWENTY-SEVEN
EMMA—BELFAST
DECEMBER 2012

The taxi passed by gastropubs, fancy delis and designer boutiques. The street was buzzing with affluent students and professionals defiantly buying expensive clothes and sipping on cocktails, as trouble seethed a few streets away. The flag protests outside the Town Hall were bound to explode into a full-blown riot at any moment. But the people outside seemed determined to ignore them.

In Belfast, there were still plenty of people who clung to the old identities of Republican, Nationalist, Unionist and Loyalist. But Emma wasn't sure the well-heeled clientele of the Lisburn Road would describe themselves in those terms anymore. There were other tribes now carving up the city and claiming parts of it for their own kind. Today, the deepest division in Belfast seemed to be between the rich and the poor.

The car turned off the main road and through a tree-lined street of redbrick, Victorian villas. It then swung right on to the Malone Road.

The driver pulled up outside a grand white residence. 'Number 189, did you say?'

'Yes, this is the place.' The house was surrounded by a high wall and probably protected by a state of the art security system. A new BMW and a Range Rover sat in the driveway.

Back in the day, Geary would often give rousing speeches at the funerals of slain youngsters, foot soldiers who had fought and died for the "cause." Through a loud speaker, he would quote Marx and shout calls of repression and rebellion across the graveyard. Even though he had been quite well off, he had lived modestly in those days. Big houses and fancy cars hadn't gone with the image of the downtrodden Catholic that his party used to like to project. Times had clearly changed. Evidently, peace had been a profitable business for Geary.

With a plum job in Stormont and a foot still in the underworld, Geary had obviously cashed in on the financial stimulus Northern Ireland had received as a reward for peace.

Emma buzzed the intercom.

Geary's wife answered. 'Hello?'

'Hi, this is Emma McCourt.'

'We weren't expecting anyone. Are you sure you have the right house?' Geary's wife's ingrained suspicion of strangers rang loud in her voice. At one time, there must have been a long list of people who had wanted Geary dead, including the British Government, the Loyalists, and even some in his own party. It might have been years since Geary checked his car each morning for booby trap bombs, but the family still lived looking over their shoulder. Old habits die hard.

'Tell your husband. I'm sure he'll be expecting me.'

'Love, there's some woman here. Says her name is Emma McCourt,' Geary's wife called to him, leaving her hand on the speaker button.

'What?' Geary's panicked voice came through the intercom. Emma heard his footsteps as he rushed to his wife's side. She smiled into the camera and waved. There was a buzz and the electric gate opened.

Emma took a deep breath. *This is just a negotiation*, she told herself. At work, she had a full arsenal to deploy when negotiating: charm, intellect, logic, bargaining, threats, trading and walking out. But the most effective tactic was always to look for common ground. She would approach this discussion with Geary like it was just another day at work.

Geary opened the door and flashed her a wide smile. His gracious welcome was probably for the benefit of any neighbors who might be watching. Inside the hallway, Emma could see through to the back of the house where two girls were playing in the sunroom. They looked to be about eight and ten. Good Catholic that he was, Geary had a big family and must have continued to have children well into his mid-forties.

It was good that some of his kids were at home. With them in the house, he would be less likely to get violent.

'Emma, I wasn't expecting to see you until later. I sent a car to the airport to pick you up.'

'I got an earlier flight.'

'Well, you should have told me. I don't like surprises.' His smile was full of menace, just how she remembered it.

He ushered her into the main reception room and closed the door. Looking at the huge sofa, velvet curtains and thick carpet, "plush" was the first word that came to mind. This was not the setting Geary would have had in mind for this meeting. His men probably had instructions to take Emma to a farmhouse or the cellar of a quiet bar in some housing estate. Either way, Emma was sure Geary had ordered them to set up a solitary room with a wooden chair and plastic sheeting on the floor so they wouldn't have to mop up her blood.

'You're looking well, very well indeed.' He looked her

up and down. 'Please, have a seat.'

Emma sat on the buoyant sofa and Geary sat down on the armchair opposite.

'How long's it been?'

'Nineteen years.'

'Two decades. How time flies. There have been a lot of changes in that time.'

'When did you move out of the Falls?' Emma asked.

'About eight years ago. That terraced house was getting a bit cramped.'

'Nice place you've got here.'

'We like it. Have you been to see your mother yet?'

'No, she doesn't know I'm back.'

'It's probably best if you keep a low profile. When have you arranged to see Aiden?'

'Tomorrow afternoon.'

'That's good, we need to work out a plan. I've spoken to Paul.'

'I know you did. I saw him earlier.' Emma stared directly at Geary. He shrugged nonchalantly. There wasn't a glimpse of embarrassment or remorse on his face.

'We had to be sure he was telling the truth.'

'And is he?'

'I believe so.'

She didn't think Paul had been lying, but it was good to have it confirmed.

'So, as long as I stick to my story with Aiden, we have nothing to worry about. Aiden doesn't know anything at all,' Emma said.

Geary nodded, but it was clear that he wasn't really listening to her. His mind was somewhere else.

'Where's my manners? I haven't even offered you a drink. Let me get Brigit to put the kettle on.' He stood up.

'I'd rather a whisky.' There was a fine collection of whiskies on the sideboard together with some Waterford crystal glasses. Emma nodded towards them. 'I'll take a glass of that twenty-one-year-old Bushmills.'

'Right,' Geary took out the bottle and a glass. He turned towards the door. 'Let me just go get you some ice.'

'I'll have it neat.'

'Well, I think I'll join you, and I need some water with mine.'

He opened the door. Before he could walk out, Emma spoke. 'Are you sneaking out to phone your lads?'

He stopped short at the door. 'No, I wasn't. But you're right. I should call them. I sent them to the airport to pick you up. They'll be wondering what happened to you.'

'You can tell them to take the rest of the day off.'

He turned to her, his jaw set hard. 'I'll decide if I need my men or not.' Geary was a big man, both physically and in ego. He wasn't the kind of man who took lightly to being told what to do. He had particularly hated it when Emma had dared speak to him like that when she was just a teenager. He didn't seem to like it any better now that she was a woman in her thirties.

'I went to see the lawyer this morning. I updated the paperwork to include your involvement in Kathleen's disappearance. But, otherwise, their instructions remain the same.'

Geary closed the door. He walked back to the sideboard and poured two whiskies.

'I think I'll have mine neat after all.' He handed her a glass and then sat down again opposite her. 'You know I don't like touts,' he said.

'I told you before. As long as I live, I'll never be a tout.' Emma took a sip of whisky.

Geary's face broke out into a smile. 'I forgot what a fire-cracker you were. It's a shame you didn't want to come work for me. I could've used someone like you in the organization.'

He leaned forward in his chair, so that his hands were just inches from her knees. 'You're a smart girl, I'll give you that. But do you really think you can just have a wee chat with Aiden and he'll forget the whole thing? Even you're not that good.'

'So what if he doesn't believe me? As long as I stick to my story, what's he going to do? No one is going to talk. You've made Paul disappear. The other two people who knew what happened are both dead.'

'But what if Aiden goes to the police?'

'They have enough on their hands trying to solve thirty-year-old murders. Why would they listen to the rants of a drug addict?' Emma said.

'They're sick to their back teeth of investigating old sectarian shit. They can't win with those cases. If they don't prosecute, the families cause a stink. If they do, people call their actions politically motivated. Either way, it's a bad headline for them. They might like a good news story for a change. Missing child reunited with father after twenty years. Has a nice ring to it doesn't it?'

Emma didn't respond. She knew he was right. Geary thought he was correcting her, pointing out the flaws in her plan. But, in fact, he was talking his way towards the common ground. Exactly where Emma needed him to be. She stayed quiet and let him go on. 'If he does go to the police, they might just think it's worth having a wee chat with Paul to clear things up.'

'But won't they think it's odd that he's just up and left with no way for his family to contact him?' Emma said.

'Of course they're going to smell a rat when they discover Paul has disappeared.'

'Then why did you send him away?' She already knew the reason. But that was the first rule of cross-examination; never ask a question to which you don't know the answer.

'It was the lesser of two evils. If I let him stay, there's a risk the police will come knocking. I don't think Paul would stand up to police interrogation. And I can't imagine how quickly he'd squeal if Aiden's uncles got their hands on him. I admit it's not the most elegant solution. I know it will make Aiden more determined to get to the truth. If Aiden does go to the police, you'll be the next person on their list to speak to. You know as well as I do that we can't have that. So we have to sort something out.'

'I stood up to their questioning back then. What makes you think I couldn't do it now?'

'Because you had a watertight alibi back then, so they weren't suspicious of you. They didn't treat you like a suspect. In their eyes, you were a victim. You were questioned, but you weren't interrogated. They are two very different things. Believe me. And what if it's not the police? What if it's Aiden's uncles? That's why I sent my men to pick you up. I wanted to protect you. If Aiden's family gets a hold of you, God knows what could happen.'

Emma forced a smile on to her face. 'But you know me. I'm tough. I wouldn't crack. Why would I? I'd only be incriminating myself if I did. If I told Aiden's family or the police the truth, then that'd be the end of me, one way or another.'

'I don't have your confidence. What the Kennedys might do to you to extract the truth doesn't bear thinking about.'

Something similar to what your men were going to do to me, Emma thought with a shudder.

'That's good of you to worry. But there's no need. Really. I'm a survivor. I'm sure I could convince them that someone else was behind it. That would probably save me.' Geary flinched, and Emma went on. 'I could say you threatened me, that you threatened my whole family. You were doing your rich American friend a favor getting him a baby. And I was just a teenager. Do you think they'd really believe that I sold Kathleen voluntarily? Why would I have done that?'

Geary clenched his whisky glass so tight that Emma thought it might shatter right there in his hand. 'Don't you threaten me, girl.'

'I'm not a girl anymore.' Emma stood up and went to pour herself some more whisky. 'This is good stuff,' she said.

Geary's eyes darted about the room. He was probably looking for something to smash her head in with. Emma took a deep breath, remembering that his wife and daughters were at home. She was safe. For now at least.

'So you're in a bit of a Catch 22, aren't you?' Emma said. 'If you hurt me, the lawyers will release all the information I gave them. As I said, their instructions haven't changed from twenty years ago. But if you don't sort me out, there's a risk that the police or Aiden's family will get to me, and I'll lead them straight to you and your friend Tom O'Connell.'

Geary stared up at her, a look of utter hatred on his face.

'But there is a solution,' she said.

'What's that?'

'Kill Aiden.'

'I offered to do that years ago, and you wouldn't let me.'

'I had my reasons then.'

'I thought we were talking about not drawing the attention of his family or the police. Don't you think a bullet to the head might get them asking questions?' said Geary, looking at her with utter disgust.

'Why? I don't think he'll have told anyone about his suspicions. Not yet anyway. I think he wants to blackmail me. I know the Kennedys. They would never allow him to take money from me. They'd want to punish me. They care more about family and honor and all that crap than the Mafia. If he told them, they'd want to do things their way. I'm convinced he wants to speak to me first, to see if he can extract something from me before he goes to his uncles. After Kathleen disappeared, Aiden got heavily into drugs. He's an addict. His main priority these days is getting cash to feed his habit. That's the only thing he cares about now.'

'That's a big assumption.'

'What will he have said to them? He doesn't actually

know anything other than Paul said I looked strange on TV. It's such a crazy conspiracy theory that, even if he has spoken, I doubt anyone has paid much attention to him. He's such a druggie, he probably comes up with paranoid stories like that all the time. And I'm still convinced he wants to see what he can get from me first, before he involves his family.'

'Yes, but let me repeat myself,' Geary said. 'If he ends up with a bullet in his head, they might start to wonder what the fuck happened to him. Don't you think?'

'But what if he had an accident?'

Geary rolled his eyes. 'This isn't some murder mystery movie. Our methods here are a lot less subtle. It's not that easy to kill someone and make it look like an accident.'

Emma narrowed her eyes. 'I think it is possible.' Geary averted his gaze and didn't respond. 'And I think I know a way,' Emma said.

Geary looked up, studying her face. 'Go on, I'm listening.'

CHAPTER TWENTY-EIGHT
EMMA—BELFAST
DECEMBER 2012

Emma arranged for a late checkout and left the hotel after four in the afternoon. The streetlights of Belfast were already starting to come on. When the taxi pulled into the Falls Road, she immediately recognized the row of mundane terraced houses where she had grown up. There were cars lined up along both sides of the street. Emma smiled to herself. Word must have already got out.

The door to her childhood home opened slowly. Her mother was probably wondering who it could be calling, unannounced, on a Sunday afternoon.

'Holy Mary mother of God, is that really you?'

'Yes, the prodigal daughter returns.'

Her mother, so tiny and frail, put her hands up to her mouth in disbelief and simply stared. Not even sixty yet, the etchings of a hard life were scrawled all over her mother's face. She looked even older in the flesh than she did on the video screen. Emma resisted the urge to pull her mother into a bear hug. Her mother had never been the tactile kind and, after nearly two decades away, Emma didn't feel like she had the right to demand physical affection. Her mother would probably just make some crack about Emma having become too American, too "touchy feely."

'So are you going to let me in?' Emma asked, keeping her hands at her sides.

'Aye, I suppose you'd better come on in and explain yourself.' Her mother held the door open, and Emma lifted her case into the narrow hallway, past the family pictures, and out to the kitchen at the back.

'Why didn't you tell me you were coming? The house is a mess.'

Emma looked around. Her mother's lit cigarette burning in the ashtray was the only stain on an otherwise immaculate picture.

'I was in Paris for work, and my meetings tomorrow were cancelled last minute, so I thought I'd pop over to see you.'

Her mother moved around the kitchen putting on the kettle and getting out teacups. Why couldn't she just sit down? Emma thought. Why couldn't they pause to look at one another?

'It's been eighteen years love, and you just decide to pop in?'

'Am I not welcome? I can go stay at a hotel if you like.'

'Don't be an eejit. I'm just saying…I'm in shock. I hardly knew who it was when I opened the door.'

'Mommy, I send pictures all the time, and you see me on Skype.'

'But I haven't seen you in the flesh in years. It's not the same seeing you on the aul computer. I'd much rather have you in front of me.'

Emma took a deep breath.

'I did send you a ticket to come to my wedding.'

'I wasn't well then.'

'And I'm always telling you, I'll pay for you to visit me in New York. You just have to say the word.'

'I'm too old to be taking long flights like that.'

'You're not even sixty.'

'You're not even in my house five minutes, and you're attacking me,' her mother tutted. 'Now sit yourself down. Standing there like that, you're making me nervous that you're going to run away again.'

Emma sat down at the table. Her mother placed a cup of tea in front of her.

'Do you want a wee sandwich?'

'No, I'm ok. I ate on the plane.'

'Are you sure?'

'Yes, definitely.'

Her mother sat down at the opposite end of the table. She picked up her cigarette again, sucking in a long drag, without taking her eyes off Emma.

'The taxi could hardly get down the street. There are so many cars. Is there something going on?' Emma asked with a voice full of innocence.

'Aye. There's a wake on at the Kennedys'.'

'Did something happen to Mr. or Mrs. Kennedy?'

'No, it's Aiden. He was found in his bedsit this morning.'

'My God, what happened?'

'They still have to do a post-mortem, but everyone round here knows it was an overdose.'

Emma could picture Geary's men in Aiden's bedsit holding a gun to his head, forcing him to inject himself with toxic quantities of heroin. Once he was unconscious, they might have injected him with some more just to be sure. The previous night, Emma had warned Geary that his men needed to stay with Aiden until his body became so relaxed that it stopped breathing. Then, when they were sure he was dead, they needed to clean his flat of any traces of their presence.

'Poor Mrs. Kennedy swears he'd been clean for a few months now. They thought he'd really kicked it this time. But he must've slipped back into it, and his body just couldn't handle it like before. That's what they say. Someone was telling me if you get clean and then use again you are more likely to overdose, because the body can't take the dosage it used to.'

'That's terrible,' Emma tried to look shocked. Geary had phoned her this morning to say he'd been round at the Kennedys' house to pay his respects. He had spoken to Aiden's uncles. He was sure Aiden had not told anyone about what Paul had said. They were in the clear.

'He was never the same since they took Kathleen,' her mother said. 'At least he might have some peace now. I don't think he ever forgave himself for what happened. I mean, they just stole her right from under his nose, the bad bastards. Excuse my language.'

'Do you have any biscuits?' Emma asked.

'Aye in the top press there.'

Emma got up and fished a packet of *Penguin* biscuits out of the cupboard. She unwrapped one of the bright, shiny wrappers and took a bite of the cheap chocolate covered cookie. She smiled. It tasted like home.

'I think she's still out there,' her mother said when Emma sat back down again. 'I can feel it. She's my blood just as much as she is yours. Don't you sense that she's still alive?'

'Yes, I do. But I have no idea where. She could be in Australia for all we know.'

'Did you see there was that young American girl who was returned to her family after eleven years? Eleven years, can you imagine it? But they got her back. She'd had weans, too, when she was in captivity. I could be a great grandmother, and I'd have no idea. It makes me sick to my stomach thinking our Kathleen could be locked away somewhere all this time.'

'Remember the police had a theory it was a woman

who stole her? Someone who was desperate for a baby. I like to believe that's what happened. That whoever took her loved her and gave her a good life.' Emma looked into her mother's eyes hoping she might take comfort from this theory. But her mother had a far off look, as if she wasn't even listening.

'I think we could have done more,' she said eventually.

'Mommy, please don't do this to yourself.'

'The investigation never really had much momentum. We didn't keep the story in the news. It's up to the family to do that, and we didn't. I feel like I should've done more, but you went to America just six months later, and I was left alone. You and Aiden were just children at the time. I suppose it was up to me and Mr. and Mrs. Kennedy to keep up the search, but I'm not a sophisticated woman. I didn't know what I was supposed to do. I hadn't even heard of the Internet back then.'

'It's been nineteen years, and not a day has gone by that I haven't thought about her,' Emma said. 'But we shouldn't blame ourselves. We did what we could.'

'I was thinking maybe we could start one of those, what do you call them, social media campaigns? Maybe get one of those e-fit things, you know, of what she would look like today. If we put that on the Internet, she might recognize herself and come back to us.'

There was no danger of her mother starting a campaign to search for Kathleen alone. She would need someone to help her, and she had no one, except Emma.

'I'm tired. I've been traveling all day,' Emma said. 'Can we talk about this tomorrow? I just want to have a bath and go to sleep.'

'How long are you staying?'

'Just tonight. I'll stay in Dublin tomorrow. My flight leaves early on Tuesday.'

'One day, that's all I get? I must've been an evil witch in some past life to deserve everything I got in this one. Everyone I loved is either dead or snatched away from me.

You're all I have left, and even you can't stand to be around me.' Her mother reached for her cigarettes and lit another one, fighting to hold back the tears.

'I promise, I'll come back next year for a holiday. I swear.' Emma reached out and touched her mother's bony little hand.

Upstairs, in her old childhood bedroom, the posters on the wall had been taken down, but otherwise it looked the same as it had on the day Emma left. It was still painted yellow. The same blue and white curtains still hung from the window. Their bright color now faded. There were still two single beds neatly made up with white duvets. There were still teenage romance novels lined up on the bookshelf.

On one of the beds sat a small teddy bear. Emma recognized it. It was Kathleen's bear; the one Emma had clung on to during those first weeks after Kathleen's "disappearance." The one she had stuffed under the bed before she had left for America. Emma lay down and hugged the bear, staring at the empty bed across from her, and started to weep.

CHAPTER TWENTY-NINE
VICTORIA—LONG ISLAND
DECEMBER 2012

Ava would be awake in a couple of hours. Hopefully Eddie would get up with her. Victoria desperately needed a lie in. Her eyes were burning raw from lack of sleep. These days, exhaustion felt like her default state of being. Not that she could blame any of the usual things tonight. Ava wasn't sick or teething, Victoria wasn't working on a new painting, there was no work deadline to stress over. No, tonight's sleeplessness was all because of Emma.

Emma was already slurring her speech when she arrived, unannounced, at their door at 10pm.

'You're back,' Victoria said.

'How did you know I was away?' asked Emma, her bloodshot eyes like rubies against her pale skin.

'Daniel called on Sunday morning asking for your mother's number. He said he was worried because you weren't answering your cell. Is your mother ok? He said she was sick.'

'She's fine.' Emma teetered into the hallway, looking like she was concentrating hard on walking.

'I told him I didn't have her number. I wasn't sure you'd want him calling. So what happened? Why did you suddenly go back to Belfast?'

'Pour me a drink, and I'll tell you the whole story.'

Emma had drained that first glass of wine faster than a marathon runner might down an energy drink at the finish line, and then she had demanded another and another. By the time Victoria put Emma to bed in the wee hours of the morning, she knew everything. She knew why Emma had returned to Belfast and what had happened there. It was information that Victoria longed to un-know.

Victoria stayed close, as Emma tackled the stairs. Half clinging to, half hanging from the banister, Emma propelled herself upwards, looking like there was more strength in her arms than her legs.

Once upstairs, Victoria guided Emma along the narrow hallway trying, unsuccessfully, to stop her from slamming into the walls. When they reached the spare bedroom, Victoria momentarily let go of Emma, so she could turn on the light. As soon as Victoria loosened her grip, Emma fell forwards, sending the dresser lamp crashing to the floor, narrowly missing slamming her head against the corner of the bed, ending up on all fours on the ground. A thud reverberated through the nighttime silence, shaking the whole house.

'Sorry,' Emma whispered loudly.

Victoria reached down and pulled Emma up onto the bed and then started undoing the buckle on Emma's shoes. Emma lifted Victoria's face and looked into her eyes. 'I don't deserve you. You know that? You are such a good person. You shouldn't have someone like me in your life.'

'That's nonsense,' Victoria said.

She turned away to put Emma's shoes in the corner, so

she wouldn't slip on them if she got up in the dark. When she turned back, Emma was already curled up, fully clothed, in the fetal position on top of the covers. Victoria pulled the spare blanket from the wardrobe and placed it over her. Emma pulled it up over her shoulders, her eyes closed, and murmured, 'Aiden had it coming to him, didn't he?'

Victoria didn't know how to respond. She waited with baited breath and Emma's breathing soon settled into a sleepy rhythm.

Victoria turned off the lamp and tiptoed out into the quiet hallway. She let out a long sigh. Her work for the day was almost, finally, done—even if it were only for a few hours.

In the kitchen, Victoria placed the empty wine bottles in the recycling box. She looked out at her backyard. In the moonlight, she could make out Eddie's prized BBQ shining in the corner and one of Ava's teddy bears lying in the middle of the grass. The sound of Ava's light snores coming through the baby monitor filled the room. On the table, next to the glasses and plate of chips, was a pile of dirty napkins. She and Emma had both used them to wipe away their tears and blow their noses, but neither of them had shed a single tear for Aiden.

A wave of nausea passed through Victoria recalling how coolly Emma had spoken of her meeting with Geary and how they had plotted, together, to kill Aiden. Suddenly weak, Victoria lent over the sink, the bile thick in her throat. She gagged for a moment and then it came, an eruption of vomit from her mouth, burning her throat and covering the sink and everything in it with a dark red, textured liquid.

Victoria groaned and spat out her rank-tasting saliva and poured herself a glass of water. Then she set about cleaning up her vomit. She turned on the tap and rolled up her sleeves, revealing the long, ragged scar that ran from wrist to elbow. She still told people that she had broken her arm falling off her bike. The scar was a reminder of what her life once was, etched forever into her flesh with Ruben's unique signature. She could have had so many more scars if Emma had not stopped her getting on the plane that day.

Victoria swept around the sink, now cleaned of all her vomit, and put the wine glasses on the counter and climbed the stairs. She looked in on Ava and then on Emma. Both of them were fast asleep, as was Eddie. Her family was resting now. But it was after 4am and they would all be awake again very soon.

CHAPTER THIRTY
VICTORIA—MANHATTAN
FEBRUARY 2013

'Are you excited about tonight?'

'I think nervous is probably a better word.'

Victoria twirled a piece of lettuce on her fork and then let it drop back on to the plate. Even salad was making her nauseous.

She and Emma were having lunch in their usual spot. It was the same restaurant where they had eaten nine months ago on Victoria's first day back at the office, when she'd cried for almost an hour. They had given her a disused office to pump. Except for an old swivel chair, the place was dusty and bare, and the pump had made a horrible rasping sound that could be heard all the way down the corridor. Victoria had cried as she pumped, wishing she was back in her apartment, surrounded by Ava's toys, nursing her on the rocking chair next to her cot.

But she could now see that, if she hadn't gone back to work, tonight wouldn't have been happening. Not only because they couldn't have afforded to pay for it, but also because it would have taken Victoria much longer to learn that being a good mother didn't mean giving her whole life to her daughter.

Before having Ava, Victoria had known it was essential for her to continue working. They could never have survived on Eddie's NGO salary. She reminded herself of that when "working mom guilt" threatened to overcome her. But it was the other moments she stole from Ava she found the hardest to justify. These past few months, she had selfishly given so much of her energy to another love that wasn't her family. Victoria's stomach started to churn once more. Yet it could turn out to be a complete disaster. A spectacular waste of time.

'It's going to be brilliant,' Emma said, almost reading Victoria's mind.

'I'm terrified no one will show up.'

'Stop stressing. Besides, if no one comes, Eddie and I will take care of the booze. That won't go to waste. Plus, I'm bringing a friend, so there will at least be four of us.'

'A friend?' Victoria tried to read Emma's expression. 'Is it a male friend?'

'Yes, he's a colleague, an Irish guy.'

'A colleague, ok.' Victoria smiled.

'Wipe that grin off your face. It's not like that. He's married. Even if he wasn't, I'd never go for his type anyway.'

'Is he ugly?'

'No.' Emma paused for a moment. 'He's actually not bad looking. He's just a bit too smooth for my liking.'

'Ok, I believe you. Tonight's not a date. But do you think you will start dating again soon?'

Emma shook her head.

'Is it because you might get back together with Daniel?'

'How many times do I have to tell you? That's not going to happen. Even if I wanted to, there's no way he'd have me back anyway. After what I did, he only wants to talk via our lawyers now.'

You could hardly blame Daniel. It had been a horrible thing Emma had done, pretending she was trying for a baby, when she'd secretly been on the pill the whole time. When Emma got back from Belfast, Daniel had insisted she be honest with him about what had been distracting her for so many months. As Emma explained to Victoria at the time, she had felt she needed to tell him something, but she couldn't tell him about Kathleen or what had happened in Belfast. Instead, she had confessed that she didn't want children. 'That was the only truth that I could share with him,' was how Emma had put it.

'I'm sorry to hear things have got ugly,' Victoria said.

Emma shrugged and took a sip of water, her expression perfectly composed. Victoria hadn't seen Emma shed a single tear over the end of her marriage. Not since the night she'd shown up drunk at her house, and that night Emma's tears had more to do with what had happened twenty years ago than the fight she'd just had with Daniel.

'It's fine. I just want to focus on my work now. My case is coming up to trial in April,' Emma said.

'Don't take this the wrong way will you?' Victoria knew Emma would probably go down her throat over what she was about to say, but she had to say it anyway.

Emma sighed and put her fork down, giving Victoria her full attention.

'Don't wait too long will you?'

'Too long for what?' Emma's eyes narrowed.

'To, you know, move on. I mean, you're thirty-seven now and…well…' Victoria's resolve melted under the burn of Emma's stare.

'If I didn't want kids with Daniel, what makes you think I want them with someone else?'

'Is it because of your career? Maybe, when you make partner, you'll be able to take your foot off the gas and focus on having a family.'

'You talk like I'm some kind of workaholic with no perspective. Don't get me wrong. I love my job. But not wanting kids has nothing to do with my career. I don't see it as a choice between work and family. I know I can have both if I want, but I just don't have that yearning for children. I value my freedom too highly. I always have. I want to enjoy my life. I don't want to be tied down.'

After two failed marriages, Emma's attitude was understandable. She was probably terrified of how a baby could tie her fate to a man's, Victoria thought.

'You could use a sperm donor. I'm not saying being a single mother would be easy, but you're so strong. I'm sure you'd cope.'

'V, you're missing the point. I don't want kids at all. Not with Daniel. Not with anyone. And especially not on my own.'

People at nearby tables glanced over. For someone with so many secrets, Emma had no problem raising her voice in public.

'I just don't want you to have regrets later on.'

'I've never wanted kids. Even when we were teenagers, I always knew I didn't want them.' Emma's tone was softer this time.

'But we were so young then,' Victoria said.

'Oh for God's sake.' Emma slammed down her fork. 'This is going to sound harsh, and I don't mean it to be, because I love and respect you.' Emma looked Victoria directly in the eye. 'I don't want your life. I love spending time with Ava. I think she's brilliant. But I never leave your house thinking that's what I want. In fact, I think the opposite.'

'Maybe I'm not the ideal example of motherhood. I know I look stressed out and complain a lot, but I love being a mother. There's nothing else in the world like it.'

'V, don't take it so personally. It's not just you. I never look at any parents and think that's what I want. Remember, when you first got married, how you couldn't help looking at kids in the street, like all the time? Everywhere we went, you were cooing at some baby. Whereas I never even noticed them. Or if I did it was because I was thinking why would someone bring a two-year-old for brunch at a restaurant that's forty dollars a plate? You and I are just different. That's all.'

There had to be more to it than that. There had to be a logical explanation for why Emma didn't want kids. Victoria suspected that it had a lot to do with what happened when they were teenagers. Emma had lost so much, at such a young age. Perhaps, deep down, she was terrified of loving another person that strongly because she knew how much it would hurt to lose them.

'I just want you to be happy. I think you should, at least, start dating again,' said Victoria thinking, if she just met the right man, Emma would change her mind about kids.

'I appreciate your concern,' Emma said. 'Of course I want to meet a man, but not to have children. I want a partner in life, someone who makes me laugh, someone I enjoy being with. I want someone I can go to jazz bars with on a Tuesday night, or to the cinema, or to late-night gallery openings, or poker nights at friends' places. I want someone to stand in the kitchen with in our PJs, having coffee and toast, listening to *"Bohemian Rhapsody"* and chatting about how we slept and what we're going to do that day. I want the man, but not the family.'

'Fine, I get it.' Victoria still didn't believe Emma, but she knew her friend well enough not to push the matter.

The two fell silent and sat munching on their salads, each lost in their own thoughts. Eventually, Victoria said, 'Hey, thanks for coming tonight. I really appreciate your support.'

Emma smiled. 'I wouldn't miss it for the world.'

CHAPTER THIRTY-ONE
CAITLIN, EMMA & JANET
MANHATTAN
FEBRUARY 2013

As they walked through the door, Lacey whispered, 'You'll be glad I talked you into this. Wait and see.'

Caitlin looked around the gallery, blinking under the glare of the lights. Her eyes searched for the toilets. It was now almost an instinctual reaction when she entered somewhere new. Even though she hadn't been sick in over a week, and she was supposedly coming out of "that stage," she was still terrified about being overcome with nausea in strange places. She hadn't quite got over the shame of vomiting on the auditorium steps in the middle of a security studies lecture.

A man came walking towards them, probably in his late thirties. He was wearing skinny jeans, oversized plastic frame glasses, black sneakers, and a tight *Pink Floyd* t-shirt, which stretched over his paunch. It was basically the same uniform that the boys at college wore, except this guy was nearly twenty years older than them.

'Lacey, so glad you could make it.'

'Caitlin, this is Eddie, my boss at Action 4 Latin America. Eddie, this is my room-mate Caitlin.'

'Nice to meet you. Can I take your coats?' Eddie said.

Caitlin hesitated. Her coat was her armor. She didn't like the idea of taking it off. *Stop stressing*, she told herself. *No one here knows you. They'll just think you have a bit of Freshman belly.*

Eddie went off towards the cloakroom with their coats, and Lacey left in search of alcohol, leaving Caitlin alone to take in the artwork. One picture was obviously paying homage to Salvador Dalí. His clocks were instantly recognizable. Except, next to each one, there was a woman who was also melting or exploding, just like the clocks. Another was based on a famous silent movie image. In it a woman was dangling from a clock, clinging on to its hands, high on a skyscraper. Caitlin didn't know the film, but she was sure the original had featured a man. She scanned the room. All the images involved women and clocks.

Lacey rejoined her, a glass of wine in one hand and some sparkling water in the other for Caitlin.

'So what do you think of the paintings?' Lacey asked.

'I'm not sure yet.'

'Well, don't say anything bad. Here comes Eddie with his wife. She's the artist.' Lacey turned to greet the couple. 'I just adore your work Mrs. Riesman.'

'Thank you, and please, call me Victoria. It's quite nerve-wracking seeing it exposed on the walls like this.'

'I love your adaptation of Dalí's "*The Persistence of Memory.*" Did you want to say something specific about memory with your re-interpretation?'

Of course Lacey would know the name of the original painting, Caitlin thought.

'I wasn't really thinking about memory,' Victoria

responded. 'I was more thinking about time, as you can probably tell by looking around. One of the surreal things about Dalí's original is that the clocks still keep the right time, even though they're melting. I wanted to draw parallels with the modern woman, who somehow keeps functioning despite all the pressure she's under. When our daughter was born last year, I became obsessed with time because I suddenly had so little of it.'

'So when did you find the time to paint?' Caitlin asked. She had also become obsessed with time recently. She longed to upturn the hourglass and start again because the days were going in far too quickly, and she had some big decisions to make.

'Eddie helped me find the time. He's been really supportive.' Victoria smiled at her husband. 'Having a child is an eye-opening, intense experience. It can be kind of all consuming. I think painting was my way back to myself, and Eddie saw that too.'

'That's so sweet,' Lacey cooed. She looked around. 'Are there any paintings of your baby?'

Eddie and Victoria exchanged a look.

'No, I wasn't planning on including Ava in this exhibition. But it's funny, people look at a new mother and sometimes assume that the only thing she thinks or cares about is her child. Strangers see you with a baby and think they have you all figured out. When I phoned a gallery owner I know to say I'd started painting again after having Ava and to ask if she would be interested in seeing my work, she dismissed me out of hand without even reviewing the paintings. She said, "In my experience, new mothers only ever produce excessively dull baby art. I'm not interested in babies sitting in plant pots. I'm looking for someone with something serious to say." Can you believe it?'

'That's such rubbish. You don't have to be some tortured soul to be an artist. You're better off without her anyway,' Eddie said. 'These days, you don't need some gallery owner to sell your work.'

Caitlin noticed how tight Eddie was holding on to his wife's hand. It was a small gesture that represented years of love and support. She felt a pang of loneliness and, without thinking, put her hand to her belly.

'Will you excuse us?' Victoria said. 'My friend has just arrived.'

Caitlin watched as Eddie and Victoria walked, hand in hand, through the small crowd.

'Aren't they the cutest?' Lacey said. 'When I'm old, I want to be in a relationship just like that.'

Caitlin nodded in agreement, still watching the couple. At the door, they greeted a woman who had just arrived. Caitlin's chest tightened. It was the senior associate from the law firm she used to work at, and she wasn't alone.

'Hold this.' Caitlin thrust her glass into Lacey's hand.

'Are you ok? You look pale.'

'I need to go to the bathroom.'

A look of concern came over Lacey's face. 'Do you want me to come with...?'

'No.' Caitlin was already turning away from Lacey and away from the door, rushing towards the back corner of the gallery, looking for a place to hide, praying that he hadn't noticed her.

***

Emma moved through the San Remo Art Centre saying hi to friends and acquaintances. She and Eddie had been busy promoting the exhibition within their networks, and their hard work had paid off. The place was almost full. Hopefully, bodies through the door would translate into sales for Victoria.

Emma looked around for Michael. They had hardly been there two seconds when he had excused himself and headed in the direction of the toilet. That was ten minutes ago.

Finally, Emma noticed him emerge from the bathroom. She waved at him, but he ignored her. Instead, he walked straight out the door, immediately flagged a taxi, and drove off, without even glancing in Emma's direction.

Less than a minute later, the bathroom door opened, again, and a young woman stepped out. It was the paralegal that used to work with Michael, the one who had quit recently leaving them in the lurch. She looked like she'd been crying. She went to the cloakroom, grabbed her coat and then she, too, left in a rush.

Emma spotted a waiter in the corner. She sidled over to grab a glass of champagne.

Suddenly the panicked screech of tires shuddering to make an emergency stop echoed through the gallery. Emma ran to the windows to see what had happened, together with several other people. A taxi was stopped just a little down the street, and the driver got out.

'Caitlin,' shouted a young woman standing nearby. She shoved her way past Emma and ran outside. Emma followed, as did Eddie, Victoria and a couple of others.

'She just ran out in front of me,' the taxi driver was saying to no one in particular. 'It's not my fault, I swear.'

'Caitlin, are you ok?' The young woman kneeled down next to her friend, who was lying in the middle of the road.

'I'm fine.' Caitlin tried to get up, but struggled, and sat back down again. Emma noticed a deep, bloody scrape on Caitlin's hand and lower arm, where she'd obviously tried, unsuccessfully, to break her fall.

'No, don't move. It might be dangerous,' the friend was saying.

'Really, I'm ok. I just want to get up.'

Eddie rushed over and helped Caitlin to her feet.

'We should get you to the hospital. I'll drive you,' he said.

'No, I'm fine,' Caitlin insisted.

Emma stepped forward, 'Caitlin, remember me from *Sheldon, Brown and White*?'

Caitlin nodded. 'Seriously, please don't fuss.'

'Listen, you at least need to get that arm looked at.

Eddie and I can take you to the hospital.' Emma tried to sound both caring and firm at the same time.

'They're right,' Caitlin's friend said.

'Lacey, I don't need to go to the hospital.'

'Yes, you do. You need to get yourself checked out,' Lacey said and then added softly 'especially in your condition.'

'No.' Caitlin stared at Lacey.

'Enough of this nonsense. You have to look after yourself.' Lacey turned to Emma. 'We'd really appreciate a ride to the hospital. She needs to see a doctor.'

In the car, Lacey sat up front with Eddie chatting about work, and Caitlin and Emma sat in silence in the back. Emma glanced over at Caitlin, who was staring out the window, her hand resting on her belly. She looked so young. What a scary time this must be for her, Emma thought. She could just imagine how freaked out Michael had been when he'd seen her and realized she was pregnant. What an asshole. He was supposed to be the grown up in the relationship.

When they pulled up outside the hospital, Lacey jumped out and helped Caitlin out of the car.

'You two go on in. I'll follow in a sec,' said Emma. She watched the two young women walk into the hospital. Lacey tried to put her arm around Caitlin, but Caitlin shrugged her off.

'Eddie, can you tell Victoria I'm sorry for missing her big night. I just feel kind of responsible for this girl. I don't really know her that well, but she worked at our firm, and I think one of the partners was having an affair with her.'

Emma got out of the car. She paused at the entrance and took out her phone to call Michael. Then she thought better of it. She wasn't sure Caitlin would appreciate her telling Michael what had happened.

She found Lacey in the waiting room.

'How is she?'

'I don't know. The doctors are with her now,' Lacey

said. 'I texted her mom from the car. Caitlin will kill me, but I think she needs her mom, and she's too embarrassed to admit it. They're on their way here now.'

'From Boston?'

'No, they live in Westchester. But they were at an event a few blocks away. They should be here any minute.'

'I must have misunderstood. I thought Caitlin told me she was from Boston.'

'She grew up there, but her parents moved back to New York last year.'

'How far along is she?' Emma asked.

Lacey's face flushed red. 'What do you mean?'

'C'mon, it's obvious she's pregnant.'

'I really shouldn't say anything.' Lacey bit her lip and cast her eyes around looking for eavesdroppers, even though it was just the two of them in the waiting room. She leaned forward towards Emma. 'You work at that law firm don't you?' Emma nodded. 'So I guess you know Michael?'

'I wouldn't say anything to him, I promise.'

'I think she's coming on for four months. Apparently it was mid-November when it happened.'

'What happened?'

'The condom split on them,' said Lacey with a voice full of drama. 'He had assumed she was on the pill, but she wasn't. I had no idea she wasn't on birth control. Otherwise, I would have marched her down to the clinic myself.'

'Poor girl,' Emma said.

'It's crazy isn't it? One of my aunts could never get pregnant. They tried IVF and everything, but nothing. And the one time the condom splits poor Caitlin gets knocked up.'

'Does she know what she's going to do?'

'I don't know. I really shouldn't be talking about this.' Lacey sat back in her chair and pulled out her phone, indicating that the conversation was over. They sat in silence, Lacey scrolling through pictures on her phone and Emma checking her inbox. In the two hours since she'd left work, she'd received twenty emails. She tried to read one or two and then quickly gave up and picked up a magazine instead. She couldn't concentrate on that either, so she just stared out into the corridor.

In the distance, she saw a man and woman walking towards the visitors' room at an anxious clip. The man was wearing a tuxedo, with the tie undone, and the woman had her hair up and sprayed perfectly into position, revealing the white pearls at her neck. As they got closer, their faces came into focus. Emma knew those faces. She had been staring at them in the society pages of the *Long Island Herald's* website for months now.

'What's Caitlin's full name?' Emma demanded of Lacey.

'Caitlin O'Connell. Actually, her real name is Kathleen, but she likes to be called Caitlin, she thinks it sounds more Irish.' Lacey stood up and peeked through the blinds to the corridor outside. 'There are her parents coming now.'

***

Janet rushed down the hospital corridor silently cursing how restrictive her high heels and evening dress were.

'Slow down love,' Tom said. 'We're here now. There's no need to panic. Lacey said it was just a wee bump. I'm sure she's fine.'

Janet ignored him and charged on.

Kathleen was supposed to have brought an end to their pain. But, instead, the raw longing for a child had been replaced with a deeper kind of anguish. When Kathleen was small, terrifying images of her being hurt, or dying, or being taken away, would intrude on Janet's mind several times a day.

Over the years, the rhythm of those frightening thoughts had slowed, yet the anxiety had never fully disappeared. The only way Janet was able to cope was by telling herself that those fears were irrational, and yet here they were, in the E.R., searching for their injured daughter.

'Isn't that Lacey in the visitors' room?' Tom said.

Janet caught a glance of Kathleen's friend through the blinds. She quickened her step, flung open the door, and immediately froze.

No matter how often her nervous system had rehearsed it, her body was not ready for this moment.

Adrenaline overwhelmed her. Her heart thundered inside her rib cage. Her breath became trapped in her lungs, almost suffocating her. Her blood hissed in her ears.

She looked to Tom. All color was gone from his face.

'You must be Caitlin's parents. Hi. I'm Emma.' The woman stood up and reached out her hand. 'I worked with Caitlin at *Sheldon, Brown and White*.'

'What?' Janet asked, unable to process the words.

'The law firm,' Emma smiled, her arm still outstretched. She glanced towards Lacey. Still Janet stayed frozen in place, as did Tom next to her. 'It's nice to meet you,' Emma said very deliberately.

'What are you talking about? What law firm?' said Tom.

'It's the place she was temping at. She was working as a paralegal,' Lacey said.

'Are you telling me she had an accident at work?'

'No, she quit that job.'

'So what are you doing here?' Tom glared at Emma.

'Lacey works with my friend Eddie. His wife was having an art exhibition tonight, and Lacey brought Caitlin along. The accident happened right outside the gallery, and I came along to make sure she was ok.'

'I don't follow,' Janet muttered. Tom shot her a look.

'Tom, I didn't realize Caitlin was your daughter,' Emma said. 'I don't know if you remember me, we met at last year's Irish in New York Ball. We must have a catch-up sometime. There is a lot for us to talk about.'

'Where's Kathleen?' Janet said, unable to stand this confusing game any longer. She wanted to see Kathleen.

She needed to find out what Emma had said to her.

'She's with the doctors, Mrs. O'Connell,' Lacey said.

Janet felt Tom grip her shoulder. 'Listen love, why don't you and Lacey go find out where Kathleen is, and I'll see Emma out, ok?'

Janet nodded distractedly. Her mind was still overrun with all the different possibilities of what had happened tonight.

'C'mon Mrs. O'Connell, the nurses' station is down there, around the corner. They'll be able to give us an update.'

Janet let Lacey guide her out of the room and tried to arrange her features into something approaching normality.

Half way down the corridor, she glanced back and saw Tom and Emma in the visitors' room, standing close, deep in conversation. Over Tom's shoulder, she caught Emma's large oval green eyes staring back at her. And, for a second, Emma's face was replaced with Kathleen's.

Janet felt a chill course through her. The two looked so alike, but Janet loved one and despised the other.

CHAPTER THIRTY-TWO
EMMA—MANHATTAN
OCTOBER 2014

Emma flung open the door of her apartment, dropping her briefcase and soaking umbrella at her feet. The place was a tip. High heels littered the living room floor. There were bowls dotted around encrusted with days' old milk and cereal. Unread newspapers were piled high on the table. She had another trial coming up, so she was practically living in the office. In the past week, Emma had only been home each day to sleep between the hours of 3am and 8am. How she had managed to make such a mess in that time, she had no idea.

She ran around the living room picking up scarves, handbags, magazines, paperwork and shoes. She threw them into the bedroom and closed the door. Sometimes, she missed the order that Daniel used to bring to her life. Other times, like now, she was glad that he wasn't standing in the corner giving her one of his disapproving looks.

She didn't have time to clean the dishes, so she collected them up and shoved them into the cupboard where the food would be, if she ever did any grocery shopping. As she did so, the doorbell rang. Emma ran to the door and buzzed her visitor in.

Usually, they met for lunch on the first Monday of each month in a restaurant near Emma's office. They weren't due to see each other for another week. But something had come up, apparently. Something that was better said in person.

Emma hadn't been able to concentrate all morning. Not since she'd got the phone call. She had spent the past couple of hours prepping a witness, getting them ready for their cross-examination. Somehow, with the junior's help, she'd managed to get through the session. Even though she could barely think of a single question. Her mind was washed white with fear.

She heard the sound of the elevator doors opening outside. She took a deep breath and opened the door, forcing her facial muscles into a smile. In the eighteen months since they had struck their deal, she and Janet had developed a diplomatic modus operandi. It wasn't quite friendship, you needed trust and respect for that, but sometimes, to a disinterested bystander, it may well have looked like they were enjoying each other's company.

Janet always kept up her side of the bargain. Each time they met, she came with a phone full of photos and videos of Ben and Kathleen, as well as lots of stories about each of them. Emma now knew that Ben would make a face of disgust when he ate a slice of orange, but as soon as it was finished, he would demand another. She knew, in the summer, he had become obsessed with Janet's straw hat and would scream if they tried to make him leave the house without it, even though he could barely balance it on his small head.

Emma also knew that Kathleen had caught up on her studies and wouldn't need to skip a semester after all. Janet had even shown Emma photos of Jack, Kathleen's new boyfriend, a serious-looking twenty-six-year-old medical student. Michael, Janet reported, called Kathleen regularly from London and sent money every month. He was planning to come see Ben again, for the second time, in November. His divorce had just gone through, and he was already dating someone else, a Lebanese woman who was a professor at the London School of Economics. Kathleen said she didn't care about this new woman, but Janet thought she detected a tinge of jealousy in her tone when she spoke of her.

For her part, Emma kept her silence. She had left the hospital that night without saying a word to Kathleen. She had returned to the gallery and, after all the guests had left, had gotten drunk with Eddie and Victoria on the leftover booze from the opening. The following day, Janet had shown up, alone, at Emma's office—ready to beg. That day, they thrashed out their agreement. Emma would never speak to Kathleen again and, in return, Janet would keep her fully informed of everything that was happening in Kathleen's life.

A week later, Kathleen had called Emma. Emma asked her secretary to pretend she was in a meeting. Afterwards, Claire had passed her a handwritten message, which said, *"Caitlin called to say thanks for driving her to the hospital. She said to tell you she's fine now."* Emma still kept Claire's note in her desk drawer at work. She had not returned Kathleen's call. And she had not heard from Kathleen again.

Emma was taken aback by the sight of Janet as she stepped out of the elevator. Without its usual layer of make-up, her skin looked pale and pinched. Her frown line seemed to have deepened, like her face was tearing apart.

'Thanks for meeting me at such short notice,' Janet said

'It's no problem. Can I get you a drink?'

'No, I'm fine.'

'Have a seat.' Robotically, Janet walked to the sofa and sat down. She stared down at her nails, and Emma noticed the polish was chipped in several places.

'I won't be long. I know you are busy.'

'That's fine. You said it was important.'

'It is.'

'So? What's this all about?'

'I have some bad news…I'm afraid…Sorry,' Janet reached into her handbag and took out a handkerchief. 'I just need a minute.'

'What's going on?'

Janet rubbed at her eyes, soiling her handkerchief with a black mix of mascara and tears.

'Janet? What the fuck? Speak to me.' Emma loomed over her guest. 'Are Ben and Kathleen ok?' Janet shook her head. 'What's wrong? What's happened?'

'It's Ben…He's sick.'

'Sick? How sick?' Emma stared down at Janet whose cheeks were wet with tears. 'Janet, you're scaring me. What's wrong with him?'

'He has um… leukemia… acute… lymphoblastic leukemia.'

A shiver ran from the tip of Emma's head down through her entire body, freezing her blood as it went.

'You know how he's been walking for a few months now,' Janet said.

Emma remembered the video of Ben, just ten months old, half stumbling, half walking the six feet from Tom to Kathleen, a look of absolute glee on his face.

'Well, in the past few weeks, he started to go back to crawling…especially when he first woke up in the morning, and he'd be rubbing his legs as if they were sore…There were quite a few days when he had a temperature, or he'd take really long naps. At the beginning, we just thought he was lethargic because he had some teeth coming through. But he didn't seem to be getting better…Even on the mornings when he'd slept right through the night he looked pale and tired. So Kathleen took him to see the pediatrician, and she immediately admitted him to the hospital for tests.'

"Lethargic and pale" were not words that Emma could associate with Ben. He always looked like such a joyful little boy in the photos and videos, so full of mischief and energy.

'What have the doctors said? He's going to be ok, isn't he?'

'They say they're optimistic, but…'

'But what?'

'They keep warning us it's too soon to tell.'

Emma sunk down on to the sofa next to Janet. The two women stared at each other for a moment. Janet's eyes narrow and brimming with tears, Emma's wide and black with shock.

'How's Kathleen?'

'She's coping amazingly well. She has the strength of a woman twice her age.' Janet looked away. 'I suppose she gets that from you.'

'Is there anything I can do?'

'I don't know.'

'There must be something.'

'Ben's already had one blood transfusion, and the doctors are saying that he's likely to need a lot more. What blood type are you?'

'O negative.'

'Same as Ben and Kathleen. The doctors keep saying that the family members usually provide blood for the transfusions, if they can. But Kathleen's anemic, so she can't give blood, and, well…we haven't told her this yet, but Tom and I are both A positive.'

'I'll go to the hospital tomorrow. Just tell me where to go and who to speak to. Presumably I can donate anonymously, without the doctors having to give Kathleen my name.'

'Maybe, I'll ask the nurse.' Janet stood up and started pacing up and down behind the sofa.

'Ask them, and I'll do it.'

'I've been thinking,' Janet said. 'Perhaps we should tell Kathleen the truth.'

Emma spun around to face Janet. 'No. Are you crazy?'

'Isn't that what you wanted?'

'Maybe, at the beginning, when I first saw you again in Long Island. But I was in shock. I wasn't really thinking straight. I can't believe you, of all people, are suggesting this.'

'I think, on some level, she knows anyway.'

'Knows what? Does she know about me? What have…'

'Nothing,' Janet lifted her hands up to silence Emma. 'I haven't said anything…yet.'

'What do you mean "yet"? You aren't going to say anything at all.'

'Maybe it's time.'

'Janet, sit down will you? You're doing my head in pacing around like that.'

Janet came and sat back down on the edge of the sofa, her back as straight as a ballerina's.

'Ever since Ben was born, Kathleen has been asking about our family history. She keeps pouring over family albums. She keeps asking if Ben looks like my side of the family or Tom's. I told her Ben looks like Michael, but I get the sense she's not just looking for Ben in those old photos, she's looking for traces of herself. One day, she asked where all the photos of her as a newborn were. She said she was making an album and she wanted to put her baby photo next to Ben's. I had to tell her they'd gotten lost when her father and I moved to Boston.'

'So? That sounds like a reasonable explanation. Things get lost all the time.'

'She didn't believe me.'

'Why? What did she say?'

'She didn't outright accuse me of lying, but she did say how strange it was that I still had boxes of books and records belonging to my college boyfriend up in the attic but her baby photos had gotten lost. It's obvious that she knows something isn't right and, now that Ben is sick, I'm not sure how long I can go on lying to her.'

'What has Ben's illness got to do with anything?'

'The blood transfusions are one thing. That they can get from any donor. But Ben might need a bone marrow transplant. Kathleen wants Tom and me to get tested. She wants us to ask my family and Tom's as well. It's only a matter of time until she figures out for sure she's adopted. So I'd rather tell her first. It gives me a chance to control the message.'

'Tell her what you like, but leave me out of it.'

'But don't you want to help Ben?'

'Of course I do. I'll give blood, bone marrow, a kidney if he needs it, but it has to be anonymous.'

'I don't know why you are so opposed to this,' said Janet, annoyed. 'I thought you'd be delighted. This way, you get to have a relationship with her. Isn't that what you wanted?'

'What I want is irrelevant.' It was getting dark outside, and shadows were starting to fill the room. Emma got up and turned on the floor lamp in the corner, pausing briefly to look in the mirror. As always, the face staring back was both her own and someone else's. 'Why do you have to drag me into this? Can't you tell Kathleen that her real mother never wanted to see her and that's that?'

'No. She'll still ask to see the adoption papers. She'll want to know what agency we used. The more questions she asks, the harder it will be to maintain the lie. But if she meets you, if we tell her that you are her biological mother, it may just be enough.'

'Does Tom know about this?'

'No, not yet.'

'I didn't think so. He'd never agree to it. It's madness.' Emma stood in the middle of the room staring down at Janet. Despite her elegant way of speaking and confident air, this woman was an utter fool. 'Let me spell it out for you. If she meets me, that won't be the end of it. She'll want to know who her father was. She'll want to find out about her grandparents. What are we supposed to tell her then?'

Janet rolled her eyes. 'If we take control of the situation, it will be much better for everyone. We can make up a story. We could say you were raped.'

'No.'

'We could tell her it was a one night stand and you don't know who the father is.'

'No.' Emma sighed deeply. 'Anyway, the question of her father is just half the story. What if she wants to meet her grandmother, my mother? It could all unravel so easily.'

'But that's what I'm telling you, it might unravel anyway—even if we do nothing. I'd rather take the initiative. We have a better chance if we…'

'Yes, take control. I heard you the first time. But it's not happening. I won't go along with it.'

'So you never want her to know you are her biological mother?'

Emma didn't respond.

'Well?'

'No, I don't.'

'What kind of woman are you? I'm offering you a chance to have a connection with your daughter, and you're just throwing it back in my face.'

'It's not like that.'

'I understand you giving her up. You were young. You probably didn't have that much support. You did the right thing. She'll understand that too.'

'We're not telling her.'

'What's wrong with you?' Janet looked at Emma in disgust. 'Most women in your position would be desperate to see their child again. She's your daughter and if…'

'But that's just it. She's not my daughter.'

CHAPTER THIRTY-THREE
EMMA—BELFAST
JULY 1993

Emma twisted and re-adjusted her position. She sensed the crowd shift in their seats, leaning in to judge her. She swallowed hard, and the saliva rolled slowly down her throat—viscous and sour. The smell of artificial pine needles scratched at her nostrils. She stared at the ground, just ahead, in front of the witness box. The carpet was threadbare. The courthouse was a typical Belfast building, so cheaply done it must have looked out of date as soon as it was built.

'Miss. McCourt?' a man's voice came. Emma turned her head towards him. He had asked her something, just a second ago.

'Can you repeat the question please?' she said.

'In the written statement you provided to the police, you state that your sister could not swim. Can you please tell me why that is?'

Emma shuddered and felt the river's angry roar tear through her. Suddenly, she was back on the riverbank—screaming. She stared ahead in white shock, just as she had that day, and the terror overtook her once again.

'Miss. McCourt?' the coroner pressed. 'Why couldn't your sister swim?'

An image of Becky came to Emma. She was sitting on the bed in her good black velvet dress and patent shoes, her hair freshly brushed. They were nine years old again, and Emma was ransacking the closet for a matching dress. Their mother was making them wear the same stupid outfit, even though Emma hated doing that. But she hadn't fought her mother, not that day. It was the day of their Daddy's anniversary mass. Even Emma knew better than to play up on a day like that.

'Will you help me bury the time capsule in Granny McCourt's garden?' Becky asked.

'It's not a time capsule. It's a biscuit tin,' Emma mumbled as she yanked the clothes hangers, one by one, to the side of the closet.

'It will become a time capsule, in the future, if no one opens it for a hundred years. Will you help me with the digging?'

'No, it's stupid.' Emma was so sick of the time capsule. For weeks, Becky had been preparing it. She was obsessed with the idea of communicating with future generations. The night before, she'd lain in bed blabbering on about how someone, in a hundred years' time, would open the capsule and learn about their lives.

'I'll dig the hole myself then,' Becky said.

'Ha! There's no way you'll able to dig a hole big enough on your own.'

'Girls, are you ready yet?' their mother called from downstairs.

'Have you seen my black dress?' said Emma, crawling onto all fours and pulling scrunched up t-shirts from the back of the closet.

Becky opened the contents of the tin and laid them in a row next to her on the bed. 'I put a photo of us with Daddy in here, so people would know who we were, and last week's Belfast Telegraph, and some sweeties so they would know what we ate, and a letter. Do you want to hear what I wrote in the letter?'

'Girls,' their mother shouted again.

'I've no time for your stupid letter. I need to find my dress.'

'If I find it for you, will you help me bury the capsule?'

'Fine,' Emma sighed.

Becky hopped off the bed and went over to the chest of drawers. She opened the top drawer, moved back some cardigans and socks, and pulled the dress from the back corner. She handed it to Emma. 'So you'll dig the hole with me? Deal's a deal.'

A smile flickered across Emma's lips as she recalled Becky's satisfied grin. And then Emma felt a chill again. It had been that afternoon, after they'd finished digging the hole, that Becky had fallen, slipped on those shiny patent shoes their mother loved so much.

Emma lifted her eyes to the coroner. She'd forgotten he was still waiting for an answer.

'There's a river that runs past my grandparents' house out in Antrim. We were out there playing one winter afternoon when we were nine. It must've rained hard all week because the water was really high, and it was moving faster than I'd ever seen. We were messing about, playing. We shouldn't have been anywhere near the water. My mother had warned us to stay away from the riverbank. But I'd convinced Becky to come with me. I'd probably called her Miss Goody-Two-Shoes or something.'

'And what happened?'

'We were chasing each other around, laughing and giggling. She was behind me, racing to catch up. And then, suddenly, she screamed and there was a splash. I turned and she was nowhere to be seen. Then I heard this strangled cry, a good bit away, and I saw her downstream. She'd fallen in. She was trying so hard to keep her head out of the water, but she kept getting dragged down into it. I didn't know what to do. It was all so fast,' Emma's breath caught in her windpipe, and she gulped for air. 'The last I saw, the current was taking her around a corner…and then she was gone.'

The scene replayed itself again in Emma's mind—how Becky's face had emerged, momentarily, from the water. How their identical eyes had locked together for a split second—reflecting panic from one to the other. How Becky had disappeared again. Swallowed up just before the corner. How she'd run for help. How she'd lost valuable seconds when she'd stumbled on the grass. How she'd flown into her grandparents' kitchen, shrieking, causing her granny to drop the good Belleek teapot, which had crashed to the floor. This was a tale they'd told so often it felt like a fiction—a story removed from their reality by the passage of time. But it was no longer merely a memory. It was now part of the present and stitched forever into the future. It was the flap of a butterfly's wings that had caused a deadly hurricane thousands of miles away—and Emma was now trapped within the eye of the storm.

'And what happened to your sister?' asked the Coroner.

'I didn't see it myself, but, further downstream, she grabbed hold of a large branch that was lodged between some rocks, and she clung on to it, screaming for help. Some local farmers heard her and came to her rescue. They threw her a rope, and she dragged herself out.'

'What impact did that event have on her?'

'She became quite frightened of the water. We both did. Seeing her being swept away, it was as if I had drowned too. She and I never went to play by the river again, and when our class would go swimming at school, our mother always wrote us a note so we wouldn't have to go.' Emma looked down at the scrunched up tissue in her hands. 'We were never strong swimmers anyway. But, after that, we gave it up completely.'

'That was when you were both nine, you say.'

Emma nodded.

'So your sister had not been in a public pool or any kind of body of water for eight years. Is that correct?'

'That's right.' Emma looked up to the public gallery. Aiden was sitting on the front bench, like a scared little boy, between his parents. Behind them, in the shadows, Emma could make out the broken image of her mother, folded in on herself. She had her hands over her mouth trying, unsuccessfully, to contain her sobs. Emma knew what she was thinking. She'd said it often enough over the past month. 'Why didn't I insist? Why didn't I make you girls learn to swim?'

Why didn't you, mother? Emma thought. Why didn't you?

The coroner shuffled some papers and cleared his throat. 'I have reviewed the medical report from your sister's GP. He states he was treating her for post-natal depression. Did your sister ever discuss her diagnosis with you?'

'No. Never…'

'She said nothing of her condition?' The suspicion rang clear in his voice.

'I knew she was tired, very tired. But she had a small baby at home, so…' The coroner blinked, waiting for Emma to go on, but she had no more information for him. 'I should've seen the signs. I should've helped her with Kathleen. I should've gone round there more often.'

'So would you say you and your sister had drifted apart?'

'I don't know. Maybe. Becky moved into a council house with Aiden last December when she was seven months pregnant. Until then, we'd shared a bedroom our whole lives. We'd had the same friends…went to school together…did everything together. We'd been very different people but we'd had the same life. And then, all of a sudden, she had this completely different one…separate from mine. I used to think, we're seventeen, we should be out having fun, and you've abandoned me and gone off to play house with Aiden. I actually thought that. How selfish can you get? I guess she picked up on it and…well…I suppose we did drift apart… a bit…you could say that.'

The coroner nodded and wrote something down on his notepad. He studied Emma over the edge of his reading glasses. 'Did you tell your sister how you felt?'

'No,' Emma whispered. She had shut Becky out and, in return, Becky had done the same. Regret flooded through Emma's veins. It was a physical part of her now. Just like Becky had been.

'In Mr. Kennedy's statement, he says that Ms. McCourt was not eating properly and seemed disconnected from their child. Was that your experience?'

'No…not really.'

'What do you mean "not really"?'

Emma stared down at the glossy wooden railing that encircled the witness box. In it, her reflection was warped and strange.

'I mean…I know she didn't have an easy time of it. But I didn't think it was anything so serious.'

'Please, this is important,' said the coroner. 'Did you see a change in your sister after the baby was born?'

'Well, when Kathleen was three weeks old, Becky developed mastitis and had to be hospitalized. She gave up breastfeeding after that. The health visitor had tried to get her to start again, but Kathleen had refused to feed. She would only take the bottle. Becky did say a few times she felt Kathleen was rejecting her and she was a bad mother for giving up on the breastfeeding…But they were just passing comments, so I didn't take much notice. Maybe that's what he means by disconnected. I don't know.'

'Do you know Mr. Kennedy's older sister, Clodagh Kennedy?'

'Yes. Not very well. I'd see her at Becky and Aiden's house from time to time.'

'Her statement says the following, and I quote: "*One afternoon, I popped round out of the blue to say hello. Kathleen was in the living room, alone, screaming at the top of her lungs. I found Becky sitting on the kitchen floor with a knife in her hand. She said she had no idea how long she had been sitting there. I took the knife from her and made her a cup of tea. We talked it through, and Becky confessed she was having fantasies of killing herself. I urged her to get counseling, and she promised me she would go see her GP.*" The coroner put his paper to one side and turned to Emma. 'Did you witness any similar incidents? Or did your sister ever tell you that she was thinking about ending her life?'

A boiling tear dropped on to Emma's cheek. With an aggressive swipe, she rubbed it away. 'Never. If I'd known, I would have done something. I would have marched her to counseling myself.'

'Thank you, Miss McCourt. I appreciate that this is hard for you. Now, I want to move on to the day of your sister's death. As I understand it, you were the last family member to see her alive.'

'I believe so, yes.'

'Can you talk us through what happened?'

Emma drew in a deep breath. 'It was the first Friday in June. She had arranged to have my mother babysit for the night. It was about 5pm when she came by to drop Kathleen off, and my mother had just gone out to the shops, so I was at home alone. Becky had an enormous bag with her, with formula and nappies and spare clothes to last a week.'

'Did that seem strange to you?'

'No. Becky was always over-prepared for everything.'

'Did she wait for your mother to return before leaving?'

'No, she looked to be in a bit of a hurry. I asked her what she had planned. She said nothing. She said she needed a break and was going to spend the night relaxing at home.'

'Did she say anything else?'

Emma paused. From above, she could sense Aiden's presence shifting in his seat.

'Miss McCourt?'

Emma stared ahead, deliberately not looking up at the public gallery. 'She said she was happy because it looked like Aiden had finally agreed to move to Scotland. She asked me not to say anything to our mother because they hadn't made a final decision, yet. There were a few things to sort out, and she didn't want our family, or his, finding out before they had a chance to tell them.'

'What was your response?'

'I said I didn't want her moving. But she told me not to worry. She said we'd still see each other all the time. They planned to find a place near the coast. She said I could even go to Scotland and back in a day, on the boat, if I wanted to visit them.'

'Why did she want to move?' asked the coroner, searching his papers for something.

Emma glanced up towards Aiden and his family. Mr. Kennedy leaned forward with purpose, staring straight at her, his large hands resting menacingly on the railing in front of him. It was well known that Aiden did odd jobs for his dad and uncles. Things like driving cars with a boot full of guns across the border. But it was obvious that, soon enough, they'd expect him to do more with the guns than just move them around the country. That was why Becky had wanted to move to Scotland. She hadn't wanted Kathleen to lose her Daddy like they had. Taken from them when they were just eight years old. Blown up by his own bomb.

Becky had said, again and again, she wanted to get Aiden out of Belfast. As if the problem were geography. Becky couldn't see Aiden had been born into the IRA. He'd been signed up before he'd even left the womb, and that was that.

Emma chose her next words carefully. 'She just wanted to get out of Belfast, away from the troubles. She wanted a more peaceful life for her daughter. Our father died in an explosion when we were young, and she didn't want anything similar happening to Aiden.'

The coroner leaned forward in his chair and slid his glasses down his nose, giving Emma his full attention. 'Was she aware of some threat to Mr. Kennedy's life?'

Out of the corner of her eye, Emma could see Aiden's ragged mop of black hair hung low over his eyes. 'Miss McCourt?' the coroner pressed again. 'Was there a known threat to Mr. Kennedy's life?'

'No. But it's Belfast. Anything can happen.'

'And, on the night of her death, what time did your sister leave you?' the coroner asked, sitting back in his chair again.

'Shortly after five.'

'And how was she when she said goodbye? What would you say was her state of mind?'

'She kissed Kathleen and told me to remind our mother she'd be back for her early the following evening, and off she went.' Emma remembered the image of Becky walking down the garden path, waving back at her and Kathleen, a huge smile on her face. 'She seemed fine, happy even. It just doesn't make sense that she'd...' Emma's throat constricted, strangling down the words. Her body would not speak them.

The coroner nodded sympathetically. 'Now, when did you first find out that your sister was unaccounted for?'

'Aiden phoned our house at around two in the morning asking if Becky and Kathleen were there. I told him Kathleen was, but I thought Becky was at home. He said he'd been out with his uncles. When he got home, the house was empty. He said Becky never mentioned going anywhere.'

'And did this news alarm you?'

'Of course it did. As soon as I got off the phone with

Aiden, I called the police. They took down some details and said there was very little they could do because she hadn't been missing for very long. They said they would send some officers round later in the morning. They were too worried about their own safety to send a patrol car around to the Falls in the middle of the night. They didn't take it seriously enough.' Emma remembered the voice of the officer at the other end of the line—completely unconcerned. 'Young women stay out late all the time,' she'd said condescendingly.

'I am sure they have their protocols,' said the coroner.

'They should've done more. Write that down in your notes.'

The coroner stared at her impassively. 'So, after you'd gotten off the phone from the police, what did you do?'

'I called the hospital, but no one matching Becky's description had been admitted. So I rang Aiden back, and we decided to go out to look for her. About ten minutes later, Aiden and his uncle Connor arrived at my house. Connor drove us up and down the nearby streets, as Aiden and I kept a look out for any sign of her.'

'And what was Mr. Kennedy's emotional state during this time?'

'He looked awful, really upset. He seemed scared. We both were. "There has to be some reasonable explanation," I kept telling him. I really believed that, too. Becky is level-headed, sensible. She wouldn't just run off, I thought. We drove round until the sun came up, every now and then checking back at my house and their place to see if Becky had come home.'

'What did you think had happened to her?'

'I had no clue. I kept hoping that she'd gone to a friend's house or something and had fallen asleep. Not that it was like her to do stuff like that. At about half five, I woke up our friend Victoria.'

'Victoria?'

'Victoria Mullen. She's been our best friend for as long

as I can remember. Victoria hadn't heard from Becky either. So she and I went back to my house to start phoning around our other friends. But no one had heard from her.'

'As I understand it, the police pulled Ms. McCourt's body from the water at Belfast Ferry Port shortly before 7am And it didn't take them very long to link this to the disappearance of a young woman on the Falls that you had reported a few hours earlier. According to the police report, two officers arrived at your family home at 7:30am. I know this is very difficult for you, and this is the final point we have to cover, can you please tell me what happened when the officers arrived?'

'I ugh,' Emma took a deep breath and cleared her throat and tried to start again. 'I was with Victoria…we were in the living room, planning how we'd divide up the streets to look for Becky again and…ugh…I looked up and saw them through the window.' Emma tried desperately to suppress her tears. 'I saw the police car pull up, and two officers got out and…and…I don't remember anything else. I knew at that moment she was dead, and I blacked out.'

'How did you know she had died?'

'She was my twin sister. That's how I knew. I was nine years old again, back on that riverbank, calling out for her. But this time I felt it. This emptiness. This time, I knew she hadn't made it out of the water.'

The coroner smiled compassionately. 'Thank you Miss McCourt, that's all. You can go now. You have been very brave.' He addressed the courtroom. 'Right, I think it's time for lunch. Let's take a recess and reconvene at two.'

Emma rose slowly to her feet and walked out, barely noticing the activity around her as officials and public alike stood and stretched and chatted after a long morning of stillness and silence.

Outside, in the corridor, Victoria was the first person Emma saw. Her friend walked quickly towards her and put her arms around her.

'It's done now,' she whispered.

Emma stepped back and looked at her friend. 'V, why didn't I know what was going on with her? I could have helped.'

'It's not your fault. She never told me she felt that bad either. She was trying to be strong. How could we have known she was suffering so much?'

Over Victoria's shoulder, Emma saw Aiden coming along the corridor towards them. She pulled away from Victoria's embrace and stepped into his path.

'Why didn't you tell me that she was depressed? You should have told me you thought she was suicidal.'

'Emma, if I could go back and do things differently I would.' He scratched his head. His hair was matted and his face was gaunt and pale, like he hadn't slept in months.

'This is your fault, you should have made her get help.'

'Emma!' Victoria stepped between them.

'I'm sorry,' he croaked. Emma glared at him. His lip trembled, like he was about to cry. Victoria touched her arm. 'Em, he's hurting too,' she said quietly.

'I wish I knew what to say to you,' Aiden said, staring at the ground.

'After the funeral, I tore our old bedroom apart. I searched the bag she'd left with Kathleen, her drawers at home, everything, but I couldn't find it.'

'What?' Aiden's eyes opened wide.

'A suicide note,' said Emma. 'I know that's what the coroner was getting at in there. But Becky would, at least, have left us a note. Wouldn't she have told us why?'

Aiden's father slapped him on the shoulder. 'It's hard to say what she was thinking. Now, excuse us ladies, but I have to get this wee lad something to eat. It's been a hard morning for us all.'

Emma watched Aiden and his father walk away. Aiden was stooped over like a prisoner on death row shuffling along in chains.

'He's lost a lot of weight hasn't he?' Victoria said. Emma shrugged. 'He loved her too.'

Emma rolled her eyes. 'I know that.'

'Remember how he'd meet her every day after school at the gates with a bar of chocolate, or some other treat for her? Every single day.'

'It was so stupid the way those two carried on. All those love letters they wrote, even though they saw each other all the time, and the little presents, and the way they'd sit on the sofa, laughing at some private joke, as if they were the only two people in the room. I used to tell her it was just a dumb teenage infatuation and she'd outgrow him eventually. And she'd respond, "sometimes your first love really is your last."' Emma felt a deep swell of emotion within. Aiden had been the first, last, and only person Becky would ever love. That bag of bones was all her sister ever knew and ever would know. It simply wasn't fair.

Three days later, Emma was back in court, this time sitting on a bench in the public gallery. Victoria sat next to her, gripping Emma's hand, as they listened to the coroner's conclusions.

'The rules state that, without a suicide note, I cannot definitely conclude that Ms. McCourt took her own life because I need clear evidence of her intentions at the time of her death. We have heard from Ms. McCourt's doctor that she was suffering from severe post-natal depression. The evidence of her partner and members of his family would support the conclusion that her depression had taken a turn for the worse in the weeks before her death and she was having suicidal thoughts. Given this, and Ms. McCourt's inability to swim, I believe there is a strong possibility she jumped into the water at the Ferry Port with the intention of ending her own life. I have reviewed the results of the post-mortem examination and found no evidence of pre-death injury or signs of force on Ms. McCourt's body. I therefore conclude that the cause of death was drowning, most likely due to suicide.'

Emma hung her head low. There it was—in cold, measured reasoning, how her identical twin had left her.

CHAPTER THIRTY-FOUR
EMMA—BELFAST
JULY & AUGUST 1993

It would be so easy. She could get the last train out to the docks one night, find a quiet spot between two rusty old ships, walk to the edge, and step forward, letting herself fall towards the icy water. The run-down port was deserted at night. No one would hear her screams. She would be sure to die. Even if her survival instinct set in, she would be helpless to save herself. She couldn't swim. No matter how hard she fought, the sea was stronger. It could easily drag her down into its dark, murky depths. Her lungs would fill with water, and she would choke and splutter and howl in pain as the life was thrust out of her. And there would be nothing she could do to stop it. In the days and weeks and months following Becky's death, this fantasy was the only thing that gave Emma any pleasure.

People kept telling her there were stages she would go through, as if that would somehow help her make sense of it all. But she couldn't discern any pattern to her pain.

Some days, there was simply numbness. Other days rage. Others, a torment so great that she longed for the numbness once more. And then the rage would take her again. Today was one of the better days, Emma thought as she lay in bed staring at the ceiling. Today, she felt like she was brain-dead. She was just the physical remnants of the person she and Becky used to be—still breathing but barely alive, nothing more than the echo of a life that once was.

Emma turned in her single bed to face the wall, her back to Becky's bed. Behind her, there was a knock on the door. Emma ignored it. A second later, she heard the door swing open and she shut her eyes.

'Wake up,' you're not fooling anybody.' Emma felt her mother's hand jab at her shoulder. 'I need to run out to the supermarket so you're going to have to take care of your niece.'

'Can't you take her with you?' Emma grumbled into her pillow without turning round.

'No, I cannot.' Her mother leaned over her and plopped Kathleen down on the bed, just in Emma's line of sight.

'Mommy, I can't. I don't know how.' Emma turned just in time to catch sight of her mother's back leaving the room. 'Mommy…' Emma called. A few seconds later, the front door slammed shut.

Emma got out of bed and pulled on a pair of pajama bottoms and some socks that were lying in the pile of dirty clothes at the foot of the bed, and then, awkwardly, lifted Kathleen into her arms. She felt heavier than Emma remembered. Emma clung on tight to her niece as she descended the stairs. In the living room, she placed Kathleen on the mat and then sat down next to her.

She stared blankly down at the baby—unsure what to do next. With wide eyes, Kathleen watched Emma, studying her face. And Emma felt a strange, inexplicable fear rattling within her. 'Please don't cry,' Emma whispered. 'I don't think I'll cope if you do.'

Kathleen started moving her head from one side to the other, taking in her immediate surroundings. She caught sight of a toy giraffe lying on the floor, about a foot to her right, just beyond her reach. Emma was about to hand it to her when she noticed Kathleen start, ever so quietly, to rock herself from one side to the other. Eventually, she worked up enough momentum to flip herself over towards the right, on to her belly. Once there, she tried to grab the giraffe, but it was still too far. So she stretched her chubby little arm a bit more and made another grab at it, getting a hold of it this time. She pulled it close to her. Then she flipped herself on to her back again, a small, satisfied smile on her face. And there she lay, giraffe in hand, holding it up to her face, inspecting it.

Emma smiled for the first time in months. 'You're a determined wee thing aren't you?'

Kathleen was just like Becky: quiet, conscientious, secretly stubborn. Emma used to complain to people about how stubborn Becky was and they would always shake their heads in disbelief—because Becky was never the bull in a china shop type. She'd been so unassuming in the pursuit of her goals people had sometimes been fooled into thinking she was a pushover. But, just like Kathleen with the giraffe, as soon as Becky set her sights on something, she strove, consistently, to make it happen. Whether her goal was to get good grades, or to win a writing competition, or to bury a time capsule, or to build a happy family life with Aiden, Becky never quit. Ever.

Emma shuddered and hugged her knees to her chest. Once again, she was forced to question if she'd really known her sister at all. Because Becky had quit in the end. Instead of stubbornly forging ahead, she had given up on life, just when it was getting started.

Kathleen waved the giraffe in front of her and rubbed its fur against her cheek.

'What are you doing?' Emma asked.

Kathleen smiled up at Emma, then ran the toy along her cheek, again, and giggled. Instinctively, Emma smiled as a tear fell onto her cheek.

'You're so happy. You've no idea what you've lost, have you? Not yet anyway.' Emma lifted Kathleen into her arms. She stood up and looked at the image of the two of them in the mirror over the fireplace. Kathleen's round rosy cheeks and smiling eyes were the epitome of life itself. Emma was a grey shadow next to her.

Emma kissed Kathleen's forehead. 'I won't let you become like me,' she whispered. 'I promise.' Suddenly, the idea of continuing to live, of continuing to breathe in and out, of standing up straight and facing the world, didn't seem so overwhelming. In fact, it now felt like an absolute necessity.

After that day, Emma tried to help Aiden out with Kathleen as often as she could. Because when she was with Kathleen, she didn't feel the emptiness within her quite so much.

One evening towards the end of August, Emma was walking back from a friend's house when she decided to drop in on Aiden and Kathleen. The sky was still blue and filled with light. But it was after nine, so Kathleen would probably be in bed already. No matter, Emma thought, all she wanted was to glance in on her, just for a moment.

As she turned on to Aiden's street, Emma heard the sound of Kathleen's screams. She bolted towards the house and banged on the front door. No one answered. She ran down the street, along the alleyway at the backs of the houses, into Aiden's yard and through the unlocked kitchen door. She rushed through to the living room and found Clodagh, Aiden's sister, watching a film with the volume up full blast.

'Where's Aiden?'

Clodagh turned round with a start.

'Jesus, where did you come from?'

'Where is Aiden?'

'He's out.'

'Can you not hear that?' Emma grabbed the TV remote and muted the sound. 'Kathleen's crying.'

'I was watching that! How dare you come in here shouting at me.' Clodagh stood up to face Emma.

'It's a good thing I did. Are you going to go see what's wrong with her?'

Clodagh flopped back down on the sofa. 'She has to learn that people won't always come running. Don't worry, she'll settle down soon.'

Emma ran upstairs. She gagged as she entered the nursery. The room stank of dead cabbages. Kathleen was in her cot. Her face was bright red and soaking wet from crying. Her entire body shook with the force of her screeches. Emma lifted her up. There was a long brown stain all the way up the back of her sleep suit. She'd had diarrhea, and the shit had leaked out of her nappy and up her back. There was even some of it on the bed sheets. Emma quieted Kathleen as best she could, stroking her face, kissing her and making comforting noises. She laid her on the changing table, stripping her of the soiled clothes and sodden nappy. The shit on her clothes had started to dry. She must have been lying like that for at least an hour.

Emma cleaned Kathleen up, changed her bedding, got her settled back into bed, and then went downstairs. Clodagh was still watching her stupid romantic comedy.

'All ok then?' Clodagh asked, not even taking her eyes off the screen.

'What do you care?' Emma spat.

'I just thought she was looking for attention, was there something else?'

'She'd shit herself and was crying because you'd left her there, lying in her own filth.'

'My bad, I should have checked on her earlier,' Clodagh said and then added, 'don't tell Aiden, will you? She's fine now. There's no need to get him involved.'

'I think he should know who he's leaving her with.'

'C'mon Emma, it was a mistake. There's no need to make a big thing of it. She's fine.'

'Her bottom's red raw.'

Clodagh rolled her eyes. 'It's just a wee bit of nappy rash. It'll clear up in no time.'

'You better not leave her crying like that again.'

'Of course not.' Clodagh's tone was devoid of remorse. 'And you won't tell Aiden?' she asked again.

'Fine. I won't say anything, this time. But it better not happen again.'

That night, Emma lay awake until the wee hours going over what had happened. Since Becky's death, Aiden had taken to the drink in a big way. He couldn't cope with Kathleen by himself and was always leaving her with his mother or Clodagh. But Mrs. Kennedy wasn't a well woman. There was only so much she could do. And Clodagh, obviously, wasn't fit to look after a cactus, let alone a child. Aiden needed a kick up the arse. The next day, Emma called social services to make an anonymous report. It wouldn't hurt to have them pay Aiden a visit. It might just force him to get his shit together.

A few nights later, Aiden appeared at Emma's house. It was Wednesday, mid-week bingo night, and her mother was out. As soon as Emma opened the front door, Aiden charged into the hallway, snarling.

'It was you, wasn't it?'

'What are you talking about?'

'You called the fucking social services, didn't you?' He pointed at her face like he was getting ready to scratch her eyes out with his dirty fingernails.

Emma stepped back from him and folded her arms. 'So they paid you a visit. What did they say?'

'They said everything was fine, that Kathleen looks great. They apologized for bothering me and said they wished they knew what time-waster had phoned them. I fucking knew it was you.'

'Everything is fine? Are you sure about that? It didn't look so good when I was round there the other night.'

'Clodagh told me you'd come in screaming at her over nothing.'

'Over nothing? Clodagh had left the poor wee thing lying in a pool of shite for half the night.'

'You're exaggerating.'

'You better get yourself out of the pub and start taking responsibility for her, instead of leaving her with that moron of a sister of yours. If you don't, I'll go for custody.'

'Who would give you custody? Sure you're still a child yourself. And besides, you have no fucking right. She's my daughter.'

'You're a drunk. You don't deserve her. You might have fooled social services, this time, or maybe your uncles intimidated them, I don't know. But if you don't sort yourself out, I'll keep calling them, again and again, until they have to act.'

'How dare you.' Aiden came right up into Emma's face and shoved her. Her back hit the edge of the banister with a hard whack. Then he grabbed her, just under the chin, and looked her squarely in the eye. 'I won't lose her too. You hear me? Stay out of my business. Or else.'

'Don't you dare threaten me,' Emma said coldly, staring at him with contempt. 'I always told Becky you were a low life. A dirty useless thug. I hope she's looking down at you and can see you now for who you really are.' Aiden dropped his hand, a look of shame on his face, as if he'd suddenly woken up and had no idea how he'd ended up standing there, with his hands on Emma's throat. He started backing away from her towards the front door; so she pursued him. 'Think you're such a big man just because your uncles are provos? I'm not afraid of you or your family.'

'I'm warning you, stay out of my family business,' Aiden muttered, his gaze cast downwards.

'Your threats don't scare me. If you don't get your act together, I'll keep calling social services until they finally do take Kathleen away from you.'

'Believe me, you do not want to do that.' He opened the front door.

'I'll do whatever the fuck I like,' Emma said, coming up right behind him.

'Don't. You have no idea who you're dealing with,' he said quietly, sadly almost. And then he left, head down, hands in pockets, hunched over.

Emma slammed the door after him. 'Asshole,' she screamed and kicked the wall.

She went into the kitchen and opened the fridge. Her mother sometimes kept a wee quarter bottle of vodka in there. Emma could do with a shot right now. She rummaged through. There were a couple of packets of ham and corned beef, a few limp vegetables, and lots of glass jars—pickles, cranberry and mint sauces, things like that. Stuff they never ate. They'd probably been there for a couple of years. From before Kathleen was born. Probably from before Becky had even got messed up with Aiden. How were these stupid condiments still here and her sister wasn't? Emma slammed the fridge door shut. She opened the top cupboard. She remembered seeing a bottle of whisky stashed in there. She grabbed a chair and climbed up on it. On the top shelf there was just an old McVitie's biscuit tin stuffed with old utility bills. It was just like the one Becky and Emma had buried in their grandparents' back garden when they were nine. The "time capsule" Becky had called it. It had contained a letter. It was supposed to be her message to the world after she had gone, written in her neat, schoolgirl handwriting. At the time it was written, Emma had no interest in reading it. But now she longed to know what it said.

That weekend, Emma visited her grandparents. After lunch, she told them she was going for a walk, and she snuck behind the green house with a shovel. It was easy to know where to dig. The large rock they had left to mark the spot was still there. Emma pushed it to one side and dug and dug without pause until she found the tin. It was exactly where she and Becky had left it when they were nine-years-old.

Emma fell to her knees and started scraping out the dirt around the tin with her hands. She worked quickly, soil flying everywhere. Finally, she dislodged it and yanked it from the ground. She sat back, leaning against the green house, with the box on her knees, and wiped the lid, cleaning as much muck off it as she possibly could. She rubbed her hands against her jeans. Then she slid her nail under the lid and popped it open. The tin was stuffed full of papers and photos, and there was even a couple of cassettes.

'What the...?' Emma muttered. It was not at all what she had been expecting to find.

CHAPTER THIRTY-FIVE
EMMA—BELFAST
AUGUST TO DECEMBER, 1993

The tropical heat, the vibrant colors, the exotic plants stretching far up above her head, the tranquility—if it weren't for the feeling of dread in her stomach, Emma might almost have forgotten that she was in Northern Ireland.

She had chosen the location. The grand 19th century Palm House at the Botanic Gardens in the University Quarter. She found an isolated bench in the middle of the conservatory under the great dome—within sight of the crowds. It had to be a place like this. Somewhere far away from the prying eyes of the Falls, but public, full of families and school kids. A place with too many witnesses for him to harm her.

At three on the dot, he came striding in. The rows of

flowers shrunk away from him as he passed, and the perfume in the air became polluted with an acidic smell.

He sat down next to her and cast his eyes about, assessing the surroundings. 'So what's so important you have to drag me all the way to South Belfast?'

'Like I told you on the phone this morning, I know who was responsible for the bomb in London earlier this year, and I have the evidence to prove it.' Her voice was barely louder than a whisper.

'Do you? Why are you telling me and not the police?' The expression on his face remained set. If he was worried, he gave nothing away.

'Because the evidence I have is too valuable.'

'Valuable? Are you looking for money?'

'No,' Emma paused and wiped a small bead of sweat from her forehead. 'I want more than money…I want protection.'

'Why should I protect you?'

'Because if you protect me, you'll protect yourself.'

'How do I even know that you're telling the truth? Where the hell would a wee girl like you get evidence like that?'

Emma glanced behind to make sure no one was within earshot. 'I know you and the Kennedys planted the bomb.'

'That's quite an allegation. I wouldn't go round saying stuff like that if I were you.'

'I know you got the fertilizer from McCreary's Farm Supplies. I can tell you the date and how much you paid for it if you like.'

Geary tilted his head towards her and raised his eyebrow. She saw something change deep within his dead stare. A glimmer of suppressed surprise. Perhaps even a modicum of concern. Until that moment, Emma hadn't been sure if Geary had known what Becky had done. If he did, then he would almost certainly have had a hand in her murder. But Emma had guessed, rightly it now seemed, that the Kennedys had been too proud to tell Geary one of their own family members had spied on them.

'When you were planning the operation, you used my sister's and Aiden's house as a meeting place, didn't you?' Emma reached into her pocket and pulled out a cassette. 'My sister recorded all your conversations. That's a copy of one of the tapes. There are more. She also took photos of your documents. Like the maps of London you annotated to show where the truck would be parked. And your handwritten calculations of how many explosives you'd need. I even have your timelines of what would happen on the day of the bombing.'

His eyes narrowed just a fraction and the color receded from his cheeks. He kept his expression neutral. But Emma could tell he believed her, and he was worried. 'Why would she have done a thing like that?'

'She had her reasons.'

Becky had approached the gathering of the evidence like a school project, indexing it all, together with a list of dates of who attended the meetings at her house and when. She must have planned to use it to force Aiden to leave the IRA and move to Scotland. Perhaps she was threatening to turn his uncles in if he didn't do what she wanted. She must have believed he'd choose her and Kathleen over his family and his fucking cause.

Geary examined the cassette in silence for a moment, then he put it in his pocket and straightened up, turning his body towards her.

'I'll listen to this later. But let's assume I believe you, where is everything else?'

'I have it all hidden.'

'I'm sure my lads can convince you to give up whatever you have,' he said with a smug smile. He nodded towards the door to where two of his thugs were loitering.

Emma had rehearsed what she was about to say next a thousand times. She forced herself to meet Geary's stare. She had to be believable. This was her one shot to convince him it was in his interest to help her, rather than having his henchmen follow her home, bundle her into a car and torture the information out of her.

'I gave everything to a lawyer. Someone from the other side, someone you can't get to.' Her voice started to crack. She paused and tried to steady herself. 'If anything happens to me, or if I fail to check in with the lawyer any day, he has instructions to send the evidence to the police.'

Geary snorted. 'You're a clever girl, aren't you? I'll just have to wait it out then. There is no way a girl like you could afford to pay a lawyer for very long.'

'My mother had a life insurance policy out on Becky. She gave me all of the money. That's more than enough.'

It was all a lie. There was no life insurance. There was no lawyer. The box of evidence was still buried in her grandparents' garden, exactly where Becky had left it. Emma waited for Geary's response, the breath dying in her throat.

He rubbed his hands together. 'Fine, I'll play along for a minute. Let's talk business, see if we can work this out between the two of us. You agree to hand over the evidence and what is it that you want from me in return?'

'No. I agree not to take the evidence to the police and, in return, you get Kathleen away from Aiden. I want for her and me to disappear together.'

'Being on the run is tough enough without dragging a baby around. Are you prepared for that?'

Emma didn't respond.

'Will your Ma be going with you?'

She shook her head.

'If you disappear with Aiden's daughter, the Kennedys will go after your mother. Can you convince her to go with you?'

'No,' Emma whispered. She hadn't thought this part through very carefully.

'If you're happy to leave her behind for the Kennedys, God bless her, well, that's your choice.'

'No. We can't put my mother in danger. I want to get

Kathleen away from him and for no one in my family to get hurt. It's up to you to figure out how to make that happen.' Emma tried her hardest to sound authoritative. She didn't feel like she had the upper hand, but she had to act as if she did. If Geary didn't agree to help her, what else would she do? Despite her threats, going to the police wasn't really something she wanted to do. Yes, she had all the evidence she needed to put Aiden's uncles away, maybe not for her sister's murder, but definitely for the bombing. But it wasn't that simple. If she went to the police, she would be making powerful enemies in Geary and the Kennedys. There was no way the police could protect her or her mother, not with all the dirty cops Geary had on the payroll. She needed an ally that was more powerful than the police. She needed Geary.

'We could kill Aiden,' said Geary after a moment's reflection. 'I could make it look like the police or the army did it. I actually have a man inside the police who might be able to help. It would clean up your mess, and it's always good PR for the cause when the state executes a young Catholic man.'

In the humid, tropical air, the sweat on Emma's brow froze as she listened to Geary plot and strategize. The Kennedys were supposed to be his friends.

'You would do that?'

'Aye. Why not? It'd kill two birds with one stone. Just say the word.'

Emma thought about it for a moment, smiling as she imagined Aiden's father and uncles, hunched over with grief, carrying Aiden's coffin on their shoulders down the Falls Road.

'No,' she finally said. 'Killing Aiden doesn't solve my problem. When Kathleen was born, Becky and Aiden named his sister as Kathleen's guardian. If he dies, the Kennedys will still have her.'

Geary sighed.

'You're not making this easy for me are you?'

'There has to be a way.'

'What if I find a nice family to take her? I have a mate in America who was looking to adopt. They are good people. Rich too. We could do a bit of business with them.' He was nodding now, a plan obviously forming in his mind. 'No one can suspect you were involved. So we'd have to make the Kennedys believe that she was kidnapped by some stranger.'

Emma didn't say anything.

'That might just work,' Geary said looking pleased with himself.

'Who are these people? I can't just hand her over to complete strangers.'

'I wouldn't hand the wee thing over to just anybody. I'm not a monster. I can assure you, they'd look after her. He's a businessman. He makes a lot of money. The wife's very respectable. Used to do something in the arts. They'd give her everything a child could want.'

'But will they love her?'

'Of course they fucking will. They are desperate for a wean of their own, but they can't have one. They'd love her to bits. I'm sure of it.'

'And I'd still be able to see her, wouldn't I?'

Geary rolled his eyes. 'No. That's far too risky. If you want my help, you have to do things my way.'

Emma stared down at the grey floor.

'So?' Geary pressed.

'Can I have some time to think about it?'

'Fine. You know where to find me,' he stood up. 'In the meantime, I'll listen to this tape here. Make sure you aren't playing me.'

'Before you go…Can I ask you something?'

'Fire away.'

'Why did the Kennedy's kill my sister?'

'I thought she'd killed herself.'

'C'mon, you don't believe that.'

He turned the tape over in his hand. 'If this is what you

say it is, then I suppose it does seem like too much of a coincidence.'

'Why didn't they just make her give them the evidence and let her live?'

'I don't know. Maybe they did try to get her to give it up but she refused.'

'But they should have tried harder. They couldn't have pushed her that much. The coroner said there were no signs of force on Becky's body before she fell into the water. If they had tortured her, wouldn't there have been some kind of marks?'

'You'd think so.'

'Why didn't they do that instead? They should have really pushed her. She would have told them, eventually. And then they could have let her go.'

Geary looked down at her, his expression softening.

'I knew nothing about this, so I can't say for sure. But, the way I see it, the Kennedys had two options. Torture her until she cracked and then kill her and bury her body in a bog some place where no one would find it. Or not harm her physically and just kill her and make it look like a suicide. If they'd gone for the first option, questions would have been asked. Young women don't just disappear for no reason.'

'So they were worried about the police?'

'No. I'd say they were more worried about your Da's brother, Frankie.'

'He's in jail. We haven't seen Uncle Frankie in years.'

'That doesn't mean he wouldn't care. Family is still family. Frankie's got plenty of men that are loyal to him. Jail or no jail, there would be nothing stopping him ordering a hit on one of the Kennedys if he thought they made his niece disappear. And it wouldn't take a genius to work it out. It's always the boyfriend. Isn't that what they say when a woman dies?' Emma felt a rough lump rise within her throat. 'I reckon the Kennedys decided to make it look like a suicide so no eyebrows would be raised. They probably tried to make her give up the evidence before she died, with threats and the like, but they stopped short of anything physical because they knew that would ruin their suicide story. When she didn't crack, they probably decided to kill her anyway and keep their fingers crossed that she hadn't told anyone about the evidence. Fucking amateurs. I would never leave a loose end hanging like that. They were sloppy. And, if you want, you and I can make them pay for it. All you have to do is say the word.'

Emma swallowed hard, pushing down her emotions. 'Let's do it,' she said.

Geary slapped his hands together, like he was relishing the prospect of this new project. 'You're on. It might take a few months for me to organize things. In the meantime, you need to get close to him again. Whatever happens, he must think you are on his side. Do we have a deal?' Geary reached out his huge hand. Emma shook it, letting his fingers engulf hers. She felt her skin shrink back to the bone, recoiling at the thought of all the blood Geary had on his hands somehow intermingling with her own.

***

'She's going to look so cute in this,' Aiden said holding up a red velvet dress in Kathleen's size. They were in Aiden's kitchen wrapping Christmas gifts that he had bought for Kathleen. At their feet sat shopping bags full of touch and feel books, bathtub squirt toys, dolls, shape sorting cubes, a drum, a walker and so much more.

'Adorable,' Emma replied.

Aiden put down the dress and picked up a baby xylophone. 'I have a feeling she's going to love this. She really responds to music. Have you noticed? She gets that from my side. I'm thinking as soon as she turns three, I'll buy her a piano and start sending her to lessons.'

'You're such a good Dad,' Emma said.

'I want her to have the best life possible. I don't want her to ever want for anything.'

'Aiden, I have no doubt that Kathleen will have an

amazing life,' Emma smiled at him and he smiled back. The idiot was completely unaware of what she really meant.

Two days later, they were back in his kitchen, sitting at the same table, glasses of whisky in front of them, the wrapped Christmas presents now piled up in the corner. Aiden had his head in his hands. His cheeks were soaked. There was snot running out of his nose and a deep, inconsolable howl reverberated from his chest.

Emma placed a hand on his arm.

'Aiden, we'll find her. We have to.'

'I can't live without my baby.' He took a swig of whisky. 'You must really hate me,' he said, looking up at her.

'What?' she said, startled.

'What kind of father lies drunk in one room, whilst some stranger comes in and steals his daughter right from under his nose?'

'Don't blame yourself,' Emma forced herself to rub Aiden's back sympathetically. She could feel the outline of his spine and the sharp blades of his shoulder. He'd lost so much weight since Becky's death. In his oversized jumper, he looked like a small boy wearing his dad's clothes. 'You are a good father. I know you love Kathleen with all your heart.'

'I do, I really do.' Another enormous tear tipped down on to his soaking face. His skin was a dirty white, like the rain clouds that gather over Belfast each morning emitting a sad, powerless drizzle.

'Let me get you another drink,' Emma lifted Aiden's empty glass and took it to the counter.

Standing with her back to him, listening to him sniff, pouring the cheap whisky into his grubby glass, Emma couldn't help but smile. She hadn't felt this joyful since the day Kathleen had been born.

CHAPTER THIRTY-SIX
EMMA—MANHATTAN
DECEMBER 2014

Emma had been staring at the multi-colored boxes stacked high in front of her for over half an hour. She looked at her watch. She really should be back in the office by now.

She had taken a couple of hours off to go to the hospital to give blood and had then headed uptown to FAO Schwarz.

In her basket, she already had a toddler sized easel, paints and plastic golf clubs and balls for Ava, as well as a "*more than just a princess*" hoodie. She was sure Victoria would hate it. She'd probably think it was a dig because she had dressed Ava up as Cinderella for Halloween. Emma didn't care; she wasn't going to have her Goddaughter growing up with tiara syndrome.

Now there was just the question of what to buy Ben. She'd been staring at the 0 to 1 year section for ages. She was having a hard time choosing. She wanted to buy him everything.

'Aunt Emma?' a voice came from behind her.

Emma turned at the sound of her name. A young woman in her twenties was walking towards her. She looked so familiar, and yet she was a stranger.

'Hi,' Emma said, still trying to figure out who she was.

'You don't recognize me do you?' The young woman looked a bit embarrassed. 'But it is you, isn't it? Emma McCourt.'

'That's right.'

'I'm Meg, Larry's daughter.'

Emma hadn't seen Meg since she was nine years old. The skinny, raven-haired child of Emma's memories had grown into a beautiful young woman.

'Oh my God. Meg, I didn't recognize you. How long has it been?'

'Maybe fifteen years?'

Meg had her father's wide smile and hazel eyes. Larry's smile had been one of the things Emma had loved most about him.

'That long?' Emma said. 'How are you? What are you up to these days?'

'I finished law school earlier in the year. I'm going to take the bar exam in January.'

'Congratulations, I don't know if your Dad ever told you, but I work at *Sheldon, Brown and White*. When you start looking for a job, I'd be happy to pass on your résumé or help you out with applications to other firms.'

Meg smiled. 'Dad has mentioned a couple of times that I should get in touch with you. But I wasn't sure. I know you guys haven't spoken in years, and I haven't seen you since I was a little girl.'

'I'm more than happy to help.'

'Thanks. It would be great if you had time for a coffee one day.'

'We could grab a drink now if you like,' Emma said.

An hour later, Emma and Meg were settled in the lounge bar at the Pierre Hotel, laughing like old friends.

They had just ordered a third round of drinks—a Cosmopolitan for Meg and an Old Fashioned for Emma.

'I'm so glad I ran into you,' Meg said. 'Of all the women that our Dad has been with since he and my mom divorced…'

'And there's been many.'

Meg smiled. 'There's been a few, you're right. But, of everyone, you were our favorite.'

'How is your Dad?'

'He's fine. He's dating a lady called Gloria. She seems nice. Who knows how long it will last.'

'You probably don't remember the day I met your Dad, do you?'

Meg shook her head.

'I was working in a shoe store downtown. He came in with you and your sister. I found him in a corner looking really stressed. You know him, shopping for shoes is the last thing he'd ever want to be doing. You were running around trying on every hat and scarf in the store, and Charlotte was chewing on some high heels. Your poor Dad looked like he was about to have a breakdown. But he was so funny at the same time. I must've spent an hour with him picking out shoes for you guys and laughing at his jokes. I remember watching the three of you as you left the store. Your Dad was struggling with the bags and the stroller. He was trying to keep a hold of you, and Charlotte was screaming. It was so chaotic. But, even so, I had this strange urge to follow him. I didn't, of course.'

'So when did you two bump into each other again?'

'Your Dad was waiting for me on the sidewalk when I arrived for work the next morning.'

'What a stalker!' Meg laughed. 'What if you hadn't been interested?'

'That's one thing you can say about your father, he's not afraid to take risks. I'm glad he did come back that day. I know it only lasted a few years, but we were really happy, for a while at least.'

'I have such good memories of the weekends we used to spend at my Dad's when he was married to you. You never tried to act like our Mom, not like some of the others. You were just fun Aunt Emma. After you two split up, every time we got to my Dad's for the weekend, Charlotte would run around the apartment calling out "Aunty Emma, where are you?" I think she thought you were playing hide and seek. She couldn't believe you were gone.'

Emma looked down at her empty glass, unable to meet Meg's eye.

'I'm sorry I never saw you guys after your Dad and I separated. I did miss you, but I didn't think I had any right to see you. I mean, who was I? I was just your Dad's ex-wife. I don't know if Larry told you, he and I stayed in touch for a few years after we split. We used to meet up from time to time for dinner. But then I got married, again, and it just didn't feel right seeing your Dad.'

'I understand,' Meg said. 'What's your husband's name?'

'Daniel. He's my ex-husband now. We got divorced last year.'

'I'm sorry to hear that.'

'It was for the best. He was a good man, but we weren't right for each other. We never really had that much fun together.'

'I guess we can be friends now, if you'd like that? Unless you still think it's weird hanging out with your ex-husband's daughter.'

'No, it doesn't feel odd at all. I'd love it if we could be friends.'

Later, in the elevator of her apartment building, Emma checked her phone. There was a meeting request in her inbox from Steve to talk about her partnership nomination. He had told her last week he was putting her name forward next year. It would be a long process involving lots of schmoozing, drafting a business plan, several interviews and an assessment center. If she went for it, she would have a grueling twelve months ahead of her, and there was no guarantee she would be made partner at the end of it.

She was meeting Victoria later to talk it through. She already knew how Victoria would react. She would be worried about Emma working too much and not being able to find and keep a man. Emma was less concerned about that. To the outside world, it probably looked like her career had played a big part in the breakdown of her marriage to Daniel, but that wasn't the case. From the start, the foundations of their marriage had been shaky. What looked like a solid build had fallen easily.

Daniel had not known her. And never understood that he never would. He had seen the shadows she carried within and had tried to throw a light on them. He should have left it alone. The right man for her was not the one who opened up those dark places, but the one who simply accepted they were there.

There was also a message from Janet. They were now in almost daily contact. 'Test results good. Still long way to go. But doctors are positive.'

Janet had sent a picture of Ben too. He looked pale and there were dark circles under his eyes, but he was giggling and full of life. Emma felt her eyes fill up, and she blinked to stop the tears from falling.

If Ben continued to respond well to the treatment, he wouldn't need a bone marrow transplant after all. However, if it came to that, Janet and Emma had come up with a plan.

Emma was still in touch with Michael and he had told her about Ben's illness. If they did need a donor, Emma would tell Michael that she'd like to be tested. She would pretend she was doing it to help Michael. Kathleen didn't need to know the real reason she cared so much.

'I'll do anything for Ben,' Emma had told Janet. 'Absolutely anything.'

Once inside her apartment, Emma rushed around getting changed. She was now late for her dinner with Victoria. Her phone bleeped again. This time it was Meg. 'Charlotte is so excited to see you again. She was like, Aunt Emma? OMG!!!! Lunch this weekend?'

Emma tapped out a response. 'Lunch this Saturday sounds good.'

'Great. Will call you Sat morn to arrange where. Dad says thanks for helping me with law firms.'

Emma wandered into the living room. She stood for a few minutes in the middle of the room, staring at her phone. She started to type. 'Talk to you Sat.' She paused and then added, 'Tell your Dad I said hi.' She pressed send and waited, watching the screen, biting her lip. A minute later, a new message popped up from Meg.

'Ok. Can't wait! Dad says to tell you that nothing's changed, his number is still 435-5511, in case you ever need it.'

'Nothing's changed,' Emma whispered to herself with a smile.

She decided to walk the ten blocks to the restaurant. She walked to the brisk rhythm of the city, the freezing air barely touching her. The streets were filled with New Yorkers, all dressed in their winter armor, rushing from one place to another.

Standing at a crossing, Emma looked at the crowd around her. There was a young woman carrying a briefcase on her way home from the office; two teenage girls in leggings and furry boots, sharing headphones, their heads shaking in unison; an older woman wearing a floor-length, black puffa jacket and an orange and blue African headdress; a white haired woman wearing a mink scarf and walking an old bull dog; and two friends in their thirties, weighed down with shopping bags, debating where to have dinner. She wondered what paths had brought all these women to this crossroads. And where they would go from here. It was a fleeting thought, gone before it really had a chance to form.

The avenue stretched out in front of her, noisy and full of life. The lights changed and Emma stepped out onto the street with the crowd, charging ahead, focused on the lights of the restaurant up ahead where her friend was waiting for her.

ABOUT THE AUTHOR

Caroline Doherty de Novoa grew up in Northern Ireland. She has lived in Spain, England and Colombia. Home is wherever she and her husband Juan are together.

You can get in touch with Caroline via her website:
www.carolinedohertydenovoa.com

She is the author of the novel, *Dancing with Statues* and the editor and co-author of the non-fiction collection *Was Gabo an Irishman? Tales from Gabriel García Márquez's Colombia.*

BY THE SAME AUTHOR

Dancing with Statues
A story of love and conflict set in Ireland and Colombia.

When Laura was just a teenager, her mother killed herself. She has lived with the mystery of why for ten years. Miguel is a Colombian lawyer investigating a bombing that took place at the end of the Northern Irish Troubles, only days after her mother's death.

Miguel's appearance in Laura's life initially gives her hope for a brighter future. Yet when he starts asking questions about her mother and the circumstances surrounding her death, their relationship begins to unravel, forcing Laura to delve into her family's history in search of answers of her own.

Was Gabo an Irishman?
Tales from Gabriel García Márquez's Colombia.

This collection brings together 26 personal essays by writers from across the world, all of whom have lived in Gabriel García Márquez's homeland. With magical rain, young lovers, grumpy old men, ghosts, conflict, politics, heartache, music, madness and more, these non-fiction stories are at once both singularly Colombian and universal in theme.

Printed in Great Britain
by Amazon